This book is dedicated to my three children: Daquaria, Charles III and Chandler. Everything mommy do is for you! To my better half, my husband, Charles Jr. life wouldn't be the same without you Bae! To my mom, Terry and pops, Bryan, life for me would be nonexistent if it weren't for you two! Heartfelt love to my siblings, VA5: Veeasa, Vayama, Vulana and Angelo, from the womb to the tomb, baby! XOXO. My aunties and the entire Lewis Family for their unwavering support and a special shout out to VX4 especially my sister Voynara! And last but not least, this book is dedicated to my grandparents, (the late) Archie and Pauline Lewis...forever indebted!

This too is dedicated to the hopeful romantics of the world. Those who have found the other half of their soul and are happily connected, many blessings. To those of you still searching, be patient, the best is awaiting. Just remember, it's not only about finding the right partner but being the right one as well.

ACKNOWLEDGMENTS

I always have to acknowledge and give praise to God, the most high for blessing me with the gift to write. I would like to recognize my close friends. The women in my life who continue to be an integral part of my social circle and who continuously show their love and support for my personal and professional accomplishments, you know who you are, THANK YOU!! Special thanks to Shakyra, Amber "Chanel", Shay, Taleesha, Telia "Marshae."

I also want to salute my beta readers. Those of you who spent personal time reading my 600-page raw manuscript and gave your honest feedback to help me make this novel a better read. To all my loyal fans and readers of my first book, thanks so much for the love!!

"Like a bottle of fine wine…writing gets better with time" – Mrs. Lips

Then

Roxanne sat with her back against the padded headboard of her queen-sized bed as she read the paper she held:

> *Love is felt in different forms*
> *It's romantic, tender, passionate and warm*
> *It can be shown as an idiom, noun, or verb*
> *People express it through gestures, actions,*
> *and words*
> *Parents and lovers tend to keep it close*
> *While millions of others cherish it most*
> *It is exactly what God created it to be*
> *To eclipse hate and promote renowned peace*
> *It's never too far and always within*
> *There from the beginning of life, right to the end*
> *Some may ask, what is love...*
> *Love is bliss!*

"What are you reading that has you so captivated?" Chauncey asked his wife.

Roxanne gasped and placed her hand over her chest. "You startled me, honey. I didn't even hear you enter the room. It's a poem that Autumn wrote. I swear that girl is going to do great things in life. She's smart, driven, hardworking, and she's passionate. This poem is beautiful. I noticed she asks a lot of questions about how we met and when we fell in love, and all her poems have a lot to do with love. Sweetie, I think we birthed a hopeful romantic."

"I've always said she is wise beyond her years. Remember that time when the boy she was 'head over heels in love with' dumped her for another girl? I was so worried that her little heart would be broken, but the way she handled it even surprised me. I'll never forget how she looked into my eyes and said, 'Daddy, if he was good for me, he wouldn't have quit me.'"

Roxanne giggled. "I remember it like yesterday. She has such a strong mind that I wonder if she'll ever meet someone who is on her level."

"Well, even though she's only twelve, I hope I'm around long enough to make sure the one she picks for a husband is the right one for my Sunshine," Chauncey stated as he sat on the bed and leaned in to place a gentle kiss upon his wife's lips.

Summer and Autumn both ran into their parents' bedroom and dove onto the bed, wiggling themselves between their mom and dad.

"Did you read my poem, Mommy?" Autumn asked.

"Yes, sweetie, and it was very nice! I have a little poet on my hands."

"Autumn read it to me too. It was okay," Summer joked. She was known for her sarcasm and big sense of humor, even at the tender age of eight.

"Whatever, Summer," Autumn retorted.

"Now, now, don't you girls start. You two picked out all your clothes for your stay with Grammy?" Chauncey asked.

"Yeah, but why can't we go with you?" Autumn asked.

"Yeah," Summer added with a pout.

"Because, this trip is something from Grammy, just for me and your daddy. As husband and wife, it's not just important for us to make sure you two are well and taken care of, but we have to also be there for one another, and sometimes that means spending time away from our children. But you'll be in great hands. You have the best grandmother ever looking out for you. After all, she did a fine job raising me and my siblings," Roxanne boasted with a proud grin.

Chauncey changed the subject. "So Autumn, what's all this lovey dovey stuff you writing? You got another boy after you?"

"Yeah, she do," Summer bellowed.

"Shut up, Summer. No, I don't. But there is this boy in school who said he likes me. But Daddy, I see him talking to *all* the pretty girls, and I don't like that. I want to grow up and marry a man just like you!"

"Aww, that's right, baby. Never settle for less when you know you deserve more! And don't give any man your heart unless you feel he's worth it. You either, Summer. You two girls are Daddy's Sunshine and Blue Skies, and whatever men capture your hearts, make sure they know your worth." Chauncey always schooled his girls on the ins and outs of life, following his motto: "No one lives forever, and sometimes, words and advice are all you're left with."

"Come on, girls, let me walk you to bed. Daddy and I have an early flight, so you girls have to get your rest." Roxanne told them to kiss their father goodnight. They exchanged "I love yous," and then she turned to walk them to their room. She peeked back at her husband and winked. He had a thing for watching her walk away, and she'd turned just in time to catch him taking a glance down at her round backside. It made her giggle.

"What's so funny, Mommy?" Summer asked.

"Nothing, girl. Grown folk business. Come on."

That was the last night Autumn and Summer had spent with their parents. On their way back from the Dominican Republic, Roxanne and Chauncey's plane crashed, killing all 236 passengers and crew. After their parents' deaths, the girls stayed with their maternal grandmother. Grammy was up in age, but she still had wit and spunk. She always told the girls, "I can never replace your momma or be your daddy, but I promise that I will love you as much as they did and care for you the best I can." Grammy was keen to the fact that the girls had different personalities. Summer was more of an executive type. She was assertive, outspoken, and driven. Autumn, on the other hand, was a nurturer. She was more quiet and conscientious, placing the needs of others above hers. Autumn valued stability and welcomed tradition. Of the two of them, she would be the one to marry, have children, and take her roles as wife and mother seriously.

Because of the sisters' differences, Grammy would preach to them different sermons: "Summer, be careful pointing that finger. There's always three pointing back at you!" or "Autumn, you be careful of who you love, because you love hard. Marry a man who loves you just a little bit more than you love him. That'll be the one who places a ring on your finger faster than you can extend it!" Grammy's sermons, love, and affection helped the girls through.

Autumn and Summer were hurting from their parents' deaths, but they could tell how much their Grammy was hurting too. In fact, Mrs. Chandler was never the same after burying her last living child. When she left this earth, Roxanne took a big chunk of her mother's soul with her. She thought the girls were oblivious, but they heard her cries every night. They could see the residue from her tears that she'd quickly try to wipe away when she heard them entering a room. They never called her on it. They just gave her hugs and told her how much they loved her and were grateful to have her as their Grammy. If it wasn't for her, the girls would have been hauled off to some foster home. There were no other living relatives to take them in.

Roxy was the last of the Chandlers, so Mrs. Chandler continued to look after the girls and raise them the best she could. But she was only getting older, and she was living off of a fixed income. She had refused to accept help from her daughter and son-in-law, and she never allowed them to pay her for babysitting the girls while they worked. She would always say, "That's what grandmothers are for." In fact, she had paid for their trip to the Dominican Republic, using a big chunk of her savings. Deep inside, Mrs. Chandler felt responsible for the death of her only living child. But she knew she couldn't give up. She had two young girls who relied on her.

She taught Summer and Autumn life skills. "Now Autumn and Summer, y'all get in here and learn how to cook. Ya gotta eat. Old Grammy ain't gonna be here forever, and you can't rely on anyone but yourself, God, and each other." She made sure they knew how to do everything from cleaning to balancing a check book. She wanted her girls to be self-sufficient. One of her most famous "Grammyisms" was "The more you do and learn now, the less you got to do and learn later."

She reiterated that they were to always stick together and be all they could be. "Y'all make sure you get your education. As your Grandpa Henry would say, 'How is it that there's free schools and dumb niggas?' And he meant all people." Mrs. Chandler was big on education. She had never completed grammar school, but it was one of many requirements for her children. Either they earned a degree, got a job, or they got out. If they weren't working or in school, they were leeching, and society had no room for freeloaders.

The school year had just ended, and Autumn and Summer couldn't be happier. Autumn would be starting her senior year of high school in the fall, and Summer would be going into the ninth grade. They met outside of school before walking home and compared report cards. Both girls had done exceptionally well and couldn't wait to share the good news with their grandmother.

Summer was the first to barge into the house in search of Grammy. "Grammy! Grammy!" she called. Spotting her sitting on the couch, Summer ran over to tell her the good news. "Grammy, guess what. Me and Autumn got all A's this quarter. Grammy!" Summer called out again. She nudged her grandmother, trying to get her to wake up, but Mrs. Chandler never moved. "Oh my god! Autumn, come here. Something's wrong with Grammy!"

Autumn raced to the back of the house and could instantly tell that something was wrong. Their Grammy looked pale and bloated. She felt for a pulse but knew she wouldn't find one when she discovered how cold Grammy's skin was. "Summer, call nine-one-one!"

The ambulance arrived within five minutes. Autumn was astute enough to recognize the looks of hopelessness on the paramedics' faces. She held Summer closely while she cried loud and hard. At the hospital, the doctor pronounced Mrs. Chandler dead. The staff called child welfare services because both of the girls were underage and had no one to care for them. Not only were they the only living relatives on the Chandler side, but on their father's side of the family as well. Chauncey was an only child, and both his parents had died long ago. Once in state custody, they had to go back and forth to court to confirm placement. They ultimately had to deal with what they'd hoped would never happen—separation.

Autumn wasn't about to allow the system to separate her from the only family she had left. When they went to court and the judge denied her plea to be her sister's legal guardian, she helped Summer escape from her foster home. Together, they boarded a bus with everything they'd gathered from Grammy's and headed south. While on the bus, Autumn heard a woman talking on the phone about how she had attended Maya Angelou High School in Dallas. Maya Angelou was her and her mother's favorite poet. She took that as a sign from her family and headed to Texas. Dallas would be the place Autumn and Summer called home from there on out.

Although Autumn would have to do a lot of lying about her age and circumstances, she vowed to do whatever it took to keep her and her sister together. As she and Summer endured the long trip from New York to Texas, she silently wondered if their new home would be the place she'd find the kind of love she'd grown to admire between her parents.

Now

Chapter 1: Autumn

Autumn sat anxiously at a table, waiting for the speed-dating charades to begin. She hated that she had allowed her sister and best friend to talk her into it. She had tried this before, and it hadn't worked. She wondered why the heck Summer and Karashae were so convinced that *this* time would be different. As she looked around the room full of desperate singles, she was almost certain that none of the men in attendance were right for her. As soon as the thought crossed her mind, the first prospect to sit in front of her confirmed it.

"How you doing, beautiful? You sho is lovely. Since we only got a few minutes, I'd like to skip to the chase and go straight to the catch. I got five kids, three baby mamas, and I'm looking for a pretty, young thang like yaself to settle down with. Know what I'm saying?" When Autumn didn't reply, he kept talking.

When the bell chimed, signaling the time to switch "dates," Autumn didn't even bother exchanging information. In fact, when he offered her his contact card, she declined. One hour and ten men later, she left the facility and scampered to her car. She couldn't get away from that place fast enough. She was sick and tired of dating, sick of no-good, deadbeat men, asking her out with no promises of tomorrow. She was tired of opening her heart to men she thought were worth her while but turned out to be far less. Autumn wanted love, something promising and long term. She wanted what she had witnessed her parents share for the twelve years she was blessed enough to have them. She had received the love, attention, and affection she needed from her late parents and continued to receive it from her sister, but that special, one-of-a-kind love from a man was still unaccounted for. Autumn needed a happily-ever-after kind of guy because she was that kind of girl. She wanted someone with whom she could spend a few forevers, someone worth waiting for.

When Autumn was about to pull off, her cell rang. "Hey, frister!" That was what Autumn called Karashae, her best friend, who was more like a sister.

"So, how'd it go?"

"Horrible! I hate that I let you and Summer talk me into this crap again! There were a couple of cute guys, but none promising. One guy was really attractive, very educated, but the down side was that he was extremely narcissistic. He talked about himself for the whole ten minutes we had together. Not once did he ask about me, my goals, or future plans. Major turn off." Autumn sighed.

"Oh, Autumn, I'm sorry. I thought, for sure, this time would go better."

"It's okay. Story of my life, I guess. What's my handsome godson doing?"

"Girl, come get that boy. He is a mess. I heard water sloshing around in the bathroom, and when I went in there, he had the nerve to have on the rain boots his Uncle Tony bought him and the plunger in his hands, with just a damn Pullup on, talking about he was fixing the toilet. I went to the toilet, and there was a glob of toilet paper in there."

Autumn laughed. She knew just how mischievous Sebastian could be. "Did you spank him?" she asked.

"I started to. But no, I didn't. He looked at me with those big, round, bright eyes and threw on his sad face, and I melted inside. He has to be the cutest, baddest kid I ever met. I just called Stephon in the bathroom and let him deal with his lil' man. You know he's always jumping to his defense. That boy can do no wrong, and between the three of us, he is rotten, just plain rotten. Here he comes now."

Autumn could hear Stephon saying to Sebastian, "Go on, tell her." She then heard Sebastian say, "I sorry, Mommee, for making a mess. I was just trying to help." Autumn's heart melted. She loved Sebastian. When he was born, she thought he had the cutest face. His cheeks and lips were the juiciest she'd ever seen, hence her nickname for him: Juicy. In essence, he was the kind of kid she always hoped to have but she was terrified of not being as good a parent as the ones she'd had, so she just put all her love and money into her godson.

"It's okay, baby. Mommy don't want you playing in the bathroom. It's yucky in there. Lots of germs. Okay, baby?"

"Okay!" Sebastian said, sounding livelier. "Let me talk to him real quick, Shae." Karashae handed Sebastian the phone. "Hey, Juicy Pooh."

"Hi, Aunt Lully."

She loved when he called her that. Whenever they were out together, Sebastian would hear guys refer to how "lovely" she was, so Sebastian had started calling her the same, but couldn't quite pronounce it correctly. "Aunt Lovely's baby making a mess, huh? I miss you."

"I miss you, too. I want to come to your house."

"Oh Juicy, Aunt Lovely has to go somewhere tomorrow, but I promise, you can come next weekend, okay?"

"Okay! Mommy, Aunt Lully said I can go to her house."

"Okay, baby, we will hold her to that, too." Autumn and Karashae laughed.

Autumn's call waiting beeped and she ignored it. "I really can't do him right now!"

"Who?" Karashae asked.

"Jerrell. Shae, he calls me like fifty times a day to talk about nothing. I hate that we even started dating. I thought for sure once I told him I was celibate, he would run the opposite way, but nope! He swears I'm going to be his missus. And after what I experienced today, I just may die a single, old maid!"

"Well, give it some time, Aut. You two have only been kicking it for a couple of months. And I thought speed dating would give you some better prospects."

"Yeah, I know. It's okay. That's what bothers me about him. It's something about him, I'm telling you. He's sneaky, too evasive. I haven't even been to his home yet."

"Autumn, do you realize you say that about every man you date? I think it's you!" Karashae laughed.

Autumn snickered. Lately, she wondered if it really was her. It seemed like she always found something wrong with every man she got involved with: his height, employment status, lack of motivation, too many kids ... "Yeah, it could be," Autumn stated solemnly. "Anyway, let me get to this shop to relieve Summer. Her graduation is tomorrow. You still opening the shop for me?"

"Of course. I'm so proud of you and Summer. Your journey has been one heck of a ride, but you did the damn thing, Aut. Seriously, I don't know how many people would have been able to do that. Summer, with an MS in nursing, she is going to be making more money than you and me combined," Karashae said.

"Tell me about it. I'm so proud of her. Thanks again for all your help. If it weren't for you and your mom, it would have been that much harder. See you tomorrow after graduation."

Autumn ended the call with Karashae and headed straight to Mouth to Mouth, her adult novelty shop. Today, her sister had opened up while she attended the early-morning speed-dating event. Now, she couldn't wait to tell Summer just how much of a waste of time it was.

During the drive to the shop, Autumn lowered the windows of her BMW and let the wind blow her hair. The last few days had been rainy and cool, but today was gorgeous, and she wanted to soak in as much of the sun and warm breeze as she could. She reached her shop at eleven o'clock exactly. Her timing had been right on point. She was great when it came to timing, always accurate. She parked next to Summer's car and entered through the back door.

Summer smiled brightly when she saw her sister walk through the door. After handing the customer her bag and thanking her for shopping at Mouth to Mouth, she greeted Autumn. "So, Sunshine, how'd it go?" Summer watched as Autumn's face rapidly transformed from focused to frustrated. "Oh no. Again?"

Autumn nodded. "Worse! Because it seems like I'm more anxious than ever to get a man. And of all the twenty men in attendance, none of them felt right for me."

"Autumn, listen to me carefully. I'm not being mean, but men can smell desperation on a woman like a rotten cooch. I know you're a great catch for any man, but sometimes we have to reevaluate ourselves. Did you ever think it could be you?"

"What? Summer, no. It's not me." *Or is it?* I don't think that my guidelines are unreasonable. I'm not compromising what's important to me just for the sake of having a man. Am I ready to be sexed? Yes! Do I want that happily ever after? Hell yes! Did I not go outside of my comfort zone and adamancy to try speed dating?" The last question, just like all the rest, was rhetorical. Autumn had given up on physical sex long ago. She had been celibate for almost seven years and vowed that the next man to enter her would be her husband. She was tired of false promises and failed commitments.

"I'm not saying settle, Autumn, but compromise. The likelihood of you finding a man your age or older, with no kids, a great source of income, with entrepreneurial skills, and the physical package you're attracted to is very, very un-fucking-realistic, sister."

The sting in Autumn's heart caused a tear to threaten to fall, but she stopped it. She asked her sister to stay a while longer while she ate the breakfast that she had grabbed on the way to the shop and conducted some business. While checking emails and responding to text messages, Autumn ate her food and made a note to call back a couple of the people who had inquired about renting the LIPStick Lounge. She had created the LIPStick Lounge because she wanted her store to be more than the average adult toy store. She wanted to add some sensuality to the place. Her novelty shop had a funky layout. The first floor narrowed as it lead toward the back, almost to a peak. In the middle of the store, near the checkout counter, was a staircase that led to the top floor, where Autumn's office, a meeting room, and the lounge were located. The lounge featured a stripper pole, which was posted in the middle of the floor and rested on two feet of platform with a single step running the full parameter. Full-length mirrors ran along the sides of the walls, and red and black seats were carefully placed around the room. The walls were painted a soft gray. Her electrician had installed a sound system, dimmer, and strobe lights. Black and white paintings of the most intimate female and male body parts graced the walls. She even showcased smaller pictures of some of her more popular sex toys. The room oozed sex, just the way Autumn liked it.

Autumn checked her private and professional Facebook pages and responded to a couple of posts she saw. She kept a business page for Mouth to Mouth to advertise all the new gadgets and novelties that her store sold. She also posted reminders about sales and advertised upcoming events. That was how one woman knew she had a room to rent. She'd seen pictures that Autumn had posted of the LIPStick Lounge and instantly fell in love. Since then, she had been renting the place once a month, teaching women how to pole dance as a form of exercise.

Now, Autumn got more inquiries from other people who wanted to do the same. She logged off Facebook and pulled up her calendar in Microsoft Outlook before making calls. She wondered if her parents and grandmother were proud of her and her sister. Every day, she thought about them and whether she had made the right decision to leave home, especially the way she'd left. But that was twelve years ago. And although she felt guilty about the way things happened, she didn't regret any of it. Her thoughts wandered as she bit into her breakfast sandwich.

When Summer and Autumn had gone to get their identification documents from Grammy's, the first thing Autumn did was run down her list of things to get to Summer. The two of them moved swiftly through the house, gathering their belongings. Autumn thought about how they would leave the house. She didn't want it to become a boarding house for the wandering homeless nor did she want their family's belongings to be auctioned off when the house was resold. She mentioned her plan to Summer, and together, they agreed that there was only one real option. The two of them walked outside. Autumn placed her two suitcases next to Summer's and went back inside, alone. She turned the gas on for all four burners on the stove and lit several candles throughout the house. She said a silent prayer before blowing a kiss into the air and turned and left the house—for good.

Swallowing the last bite of her meal, she cleared her mind of her somber thoughts and placed her calls before returning to her sister.

"Took you long enough," Summer said when she heard Autumn walking down the stairs. "I need to pick up a few items before I leave here. I see you got some different products. I was helping a customer find lube and saw the cherry throat numbing spray. Ajamaal's ass gonna be open tonight," she said with too much giddiness for Autumn's taste.

"Ugh, I don't want to know about your raunchy rendezvous with your boyfriend, Summer."

"Whatever, Autumn. Your ass is more of a freak than me. I used to hear all your conversations with Karashae. You were a little hoe in college."

"What? Summer! You eavesdropped?"

"Girl, when you went in your room and closed that door, I knew juicy topics were on the way. You thought I was the stupid one, and you were the one who was naïve as hell. Talking about, 'Summer do your homework; I'm about to make a call.' Yeah right. I was right on the floor outside your door, listening to everything. I even heard you talking to *and* doing the nasty with Kasir."

"Shut up, Summer!

"Oh, and remember that time you asked God to forgive you for letting your cute male professor, what's his name ... oh, Professor Milton, go down on you in his office? Yup! My sister is a super freak!"

"You are one sick chick, you know that?"

"I've been told," Summer stated matter-of-factly. "You got to teach tonight?"

"Yes, right after I leave here. This is my last class of the semester, but I opted to teach an online six-week course over the summer. Why, what's up?"

"Oh, nothing. I was just wondering what big sis was getting into tonight, or better yet, who was getting into big sis. You work too damn much. Won't you give up that teaching gig, anyway? It's not like you need it."

"I like teaching. And I enjoy teaching anatomy. But most of all, I love educating these young kids on their bodies. I teach in hopes of showing them that they can do more sexually for themselves than some sex-crazed boy or girl can. And besides, the more folks who realize they can get better sexual pleasure without the risk of catching a dirty disease, the more who may follow in my footsteps and become celibate," Autumn said, looking at Summer suggestively.

"I don't know why you looking at me like that. That's

your path. I chose the one with plenty of men along the way, and I don't mind stopping to get a tune-up from one of them from time to time. I'll grab my spray and be on my way."

"You better not let Ajamaal hear you talking like that. He just might leave you."

"That fool ain't going anywhere. I got the clincher, literally," Summer said. She walked into the restroom and closed the door.

A customer was checking out just as another was entering. Having dropped a coin during the transaction, Autumn bent down to pick it up and hit the back of her head on the bottom of the checkout counter on the way up. "Ouch!" she fussed, rubbing the spot of impact.

"That must have hurt," her customer said. When Autumn locked eyes with him, she was mesmerized. The finest, dark-skinned, baldheaded, tall, handsome hunk of a man she had seen in a long time displayed a smile of perfection as he stared at her. Autumn's voice and breath were still trapped inside her body. It wasn't until he placed his right hand atop her left hand, which was resting on the counter, that she caught her breath and found her voice. But she quickly came back to reality. She had seen his type before. Men who were just as fine, but wound up being no sharper than a no. 2 pencil.

"Uh, um, pardon me," she said, shaking her head as if trying to clear her mind and regain her poise. "Yes, I'm fine.

Thanks. Welcome to Mouth to Mouth. Can I help you look for anything today?"

"Actually, yes. Can you tell me where you keep your costumes and accessories?"

"Yes, sure, follow me." Autumn led him to the middle of the store, where she kept her costumes and other naughty garments. "To the right is the men's gear and to the left is the women's attire."

Autumn watched as he went right, where she kept the male "assexeries," as she called them. She couldn't deny that the man was fine. *I'mma call him Mr. Sexy! Yeah, that fits him.* Autumn felt the flesh taking over and checked herself. Fleshly desires had led her to nowhere in the past.

Minutes later, Mr. Sexy approached the register. While scanning the merchandise and placing it in a bag, she used the opportunity to steal another glance. She nervously peeked up at him, and when she did, she was shocked to see him looking at her, expressionless. His head was slightly bowed and his eyes tenderly peeked up at her. His left hand rested comfortably in the left pocket of his slightly baggy jeans, and his right hand was propped on the counter with his wallet secured inside as he awaited his total. She hadn't noticed before, but he had the most alluring, sexy bedroom eyes, eyes that could undress her without him ever lifting a finger, the kind of eyes that had a chick ready to rape her own vajayjay if he didn't sex her willingly. Autumn didn't know if she should stare at his face or admire his well-defined arms. She hoped he couldn't read the indecisiveness in her eyes.

"That'll be sixty-nine, sixty-nine." Autumn said and Abaki smirked. As soon as the words left her mouth, the color drained from her face. Autumn was sure that her beautiful mocha complexion was now ashen. *You've got to be freaking kidding me. No way!* She had every mind to ring the items up again, but didn't want the awkwardness to last any longer than it needed to.

Mr. Sexy smiled. He handed her seventy dollars. Before the cash register could pop open, he grabbed his bag. She handed him thirty cents and when she tried to give him the remaining penny, he held up his hand. "A penny for your thoughts." He winked and walked out. She couldn't even locate her voice to thank him for shopping at Mouth to Mouth.

Autumn hadn't noticed Summer exit the bathroom and retrieve something from the shelf, placing it on the counter. "Who the fuck was that fine-ass brotha?" she asked.

"Summer, watch your mouth! I know I let you slide earlier, but I told you about talking like that in my place of business. You lucky there weren't any customers in here."

"Or what?" Summer challenged.

Autumn peeped Summer sliding the same item she had placed on the counter into her bag. "Uh un, miss thang;

you will be paying for that."

"Seriously, Aut? You own the place; why do I have to pay?"

"Because this is a business. Don't take it personal. Eight forty-seven, please." Autumn cashed her sister out and told her she would call her later. She had ignored her sister's inquiry about the "fine-ass brotha," mainly because she didn't know who the guy was, but also because she didn't want to mentally relive the embarrassment of ringing up sixty-nine dollars and sixty-nine cents, the most notorious number associated with sex, and at an adult novelty store at that. In keeping it honest with herself, she secretly hoped he would've paid with a credit card so she could have at least gotten his name. She'd reprinted the receipt after he'd left, wrote a note on it, and reminded herself to place it in the top drawer of her office desk. If and when she told this story, she wanted to be sure she had proof, because no one would believe her otherwise.

Chapter 2: Abaki

When Karl had told Abaki about the cute girl that his friend's lady hangs with, he'd dismissed him immediately. As of late, it seemed that each of his friends was trying to hook him up with someone they thought was worthy of settling down with. After witnessing the trouble he was beginning to have with his current girlfriend, his friends wanted better for him. In being completely honest with himself, he knew Inez wasn't right for him too. They'd suggested several women to him, but he'd had no interest in pursuing them.

Abaki wasn't born in America. Undesirable circumstances had led him here, but as he got older, he realized that his father's reasons were legitimate. And now, after twenty-three years as an American, he still didn't operate the way he felt most American men did: causally sleeping with multiple women, having babies out of wedlock, and dealing with girl drama. He steered away from those things. However, nothing could have prepared him for the instant attraction he felt for the woman he'd seen opening the adult novelty shop last week. He was going into the nearby hardware store when he'd seen her. He was allured by her simplistic beauty. The way she walked, smiled, and gestured while talking on the phone drew him to her. She had the grace of a lady and the confidence of a woman, with a splash of sass. For the past seven days, he had tried to get her off his mind, but he couldn't. He would catch himself daydreaming about her during the most inopportune times, wondering what it would have been like to be on the other end of her phone call. When he'd woken up today, he knew that nothing would stop him from getting a closer look.

Abaki had entered Mouth to Mouth with no other intention than to have a closer encounter with the woman who had been consuming his mind for the past week. Had he not seen her opening the shop that day, he probably would have never seen her again. Adult novelty shops weren't his thing. And even as he entered the shop in search of his new interest, he wondered what was happening to him. He didn't go after women. He definitely didn't have any real desire for the kinds of things sold in those stores, but he would pretend to if it meant another glance. What he wasn't prepared for was the effect he'd had on her. Sure, women goggled over him and professed their attraction regularly. Those were the kinds of women he wasn't interested in. Her behavior would determine whether he would pursue her or let her perish in eternal lust, just like the others.

When she had greeted him, her attraction to him was obvious. While she spoke, he took notice of her facial features and couldn't pick up on one flaw. Unbeknownst to her, he was mesmerized by the way her tongue peeked from between her beautiful lips and moistened them both at the same time, how her eyebrows furrowed above her perfectly-shaped russet eyes while she simultaneously wrinkled her cute, pointy nose. During his pretend shopping indulgence, he used every opportunity he could to steal glances at her. When she had finished helping her other customers, he seized the moment to cash out.

When he had first walked in, he hoped he would have her attention; however, his confidence wasn't so high after he'd left. He didn't want her goggling over him, but he did expect a little more of a reaction from her. After all, he had dressed in his favorite shirt, the one that complemented the ridges of his upper body very well. Her lack of interest didn't sway him though; he had already moved on to plan B.

Chapter 3: Autumn

Autumn locked up the shop, hopped in her car, and headed to her campus. She liked to be in the room and ready to go when her students arrived. Tiant was the first one to show up.

"Hey, Professor Hughes."

"Hello, Tiant. You're early this evening."

"Yeah, I stayed on campus to study for a final, so I decided to just come on over."

"Nothing wrong with that! I love when folks are punctual. There's nothing tackier than people who can't be on time. Good luck on all your finals. You've done quite well in my class."

"Thanks, Ms. Hughes. The last thing I'm trying to do is screw up my education. It's like I'm already here and paying for it, so why not do my best and only do it once, feel me?"

Autumn smiled. "Tiant, you're going to make a woman real happy one day."

"Yeah, and that woman could be you," Tiant flirted.

"Excuse me? Boy you know better than to be coming at me like that," Autumn stated firmly.

"Nah, on the real, why you not dating anyone, Ms. Hughes? With all due respect, you are a good-looking sista.

You're smart, cool, sweet, down-to-earth, and you appear to be doing quite well for yourself. You da kind of lady any man would want. I was just wondering why a guy hasn't snatched you off the market yet."

"And how do you know I'm not dating, Mr. Johnson?"

"Because, I can tell. You always here and on time. You regularly stay late. You own your own business, adjunct, and you facilitate online courses during the summer. That's a lot for a woman with a healthy dating life."

Autumn flushed. This twenty-year-old had just pulled her whole card. "Mr. Johnson, not that it's any of your business, but if you must know, I haven't met the right man yet. When he comes along, trust me, I'll know, and he will be pleased that he was the lucky man to get me. Let's just say I'm perfecting Autumn so that the next man I give my heart to will have no doubt that I am the real deal. Now, enough about me; get your head in the books and out of my personal life." Autumn smiled politely just as her other students began to arrive.

She set up her PowerPoint presentation and began organizing her lesson plan until it was time for class to begin. Her final presentation for the semester was on the effects STDs have on our bodies. Autumn loved her students and wanted them to understand the importance of loving themselves first. As she lectured, she tactfully hinted at self-pleasure as being the healthiest form of sex.

"So with that said, ladies and gentleman, you guys have a safe summer and enjoy your break. Before we know it, another semester will be upon us. It's been a pleasure teaching all of you. Oh, and be sure to log into the student portal this time next week. I will have all the final grades posted."

Every one of her students stood in line to give her a hug or just to say a personal farewell. She was nearly moved to tears that they seemed to take to her just as much as she had been taken with them. *Isn't life about rewards?* she thought. She packed up her belongings and left the lecture hall.

When Autumn arrived home, it was close to 9:30 p.m. She hopped in the shower, threw on a cami and some stretch pants, and turned her stereo on rotation mode. After leaving campus, she had stopped at the ATM and then gone to FYE to buy some CD's. She loved music. There was something about moving lyrics over a tight beat that did something to her. No matter her mood, she could always find the right song to complement it. The genre didn't matter. If she heard it and it sounded good to her ears and rattled her soul, she listened to it. In the midst of checking her mail, "Drift Away" by Uncle Kracker played. The chorus of the song reminded Autumn of her subtle desires to "drift away," up toward heaven, so she could visit her loved ones. She thought back on the dreadful day that she and Summer had gotten a call from their parents the morning of their fateful flight back home from The Dominican Republic.

The phone had rung several times before their grandmother had a chance to answer. Roxanne had told Grammy and the girls how relaxing and exhilarating their trip had been. She thanked her mother for sending them away. Six months prior to their vacation, they had lost their younger twin daughters, Spring and Winter, to SIDS.

Mrs. Chandler had been married to her husband, Henry, for over forty years until his death. He was at a nearby lake, enjoying his favorite pastime, fishing, when he suffered a fatal heart attack and fell over the boat. Together, they'd had five children, two boys and three girls. One of the boys had died at birth, and the oldest daughter had suffered a brain injury after a terrible car accident and never recovered. The youngest daughter had passed away several years later from diabetic complications, and the youngest son had died of a drug overdose. Only Roxy was left, and Mrs. Chandler had done everything she could to ensure her daughter some happiness. Mrs. Chandler wasn't an emotional person, but she fought to hold back the tears. Raising her children was a struggle, especially after her husband had passed, but by the grace of God, they had been able to make ends meet.

Roxy had handed Chauncey the phone and he chatted with his daughters. He called Autumn and Summer

"Sunshine" and "Blue Skies" respectfully. He adored his two little ladies. He told people that they brightened his day and he couldn't think of more appropriate nicknames. Autumn loved her father's nicknames for them. It made her feel special.

If Autumn had known at the time that it would be the last conversation she'd have with her parents, she would have said so much more. She had so many questions for her father, so many more poems to share with her mother. Here it was, eighteen years later, and the pain was just as strong as the day they'd left her.

Autumn's ringing house phone brought her back to the present. She wiped the tears from her face and cleared her throat before answering. "Hello," she said, trying to sound normal.

"Hey, sis," Summer responded, also crying.

"Summer, what's wrong? Why are you crying?"

Summer could barely get her words out because she was sobbing so hard. Autumn began to worry.

"Summer! Sweetie, tell me what happened."

After a few moments, Summer composed herself. "Nothing happened. I was just sitting here, polishing my toenails, and I started thinking about Mommy. She always polished our fingers and toes. I thought back to how she constantly drilled us: 'Girls, now remember to always keep your hair and your feet looking good, and everything else will fall into place.'"

Before Autumn knew it, another blanket of sadness swept over her. That was one of her mom's favorite lines, and it had proved to be true. Autumn and Summer would run to the market in just t-shirts and sweat pants and would still receive numerous cat calls. She attributed it to the fact that they had cute faces, their hair was always neat, never covered by bonnets or scarves, and their footwear was on point.

"Aut, I miss them so much." Summer squeezed out the last of her words before she started bawling again.

This time, Autumn said nothing and just cried with her sister. As sad as both of them wanted to feel, they knew that they couldn't pity themselves too much. Any other pair in their situation would have succumbed to the devil by now. Autumn raising Summer was like the blind leading the blind. She had to grow up fast and make grown decisions. She just wished she'd had someone or something for reference. But with her parents and Grammy gone, she knew the only person she had was herself, and she had refused to fail or let her little sister down.

"Summer, I was feeling the same way. I actually was in the moment when you called, and I tried to compose myself before I answered," Autumn admitted. "Is anyone there with you?"

"No. I'm by myself,"

"Good. I'm packing an overnight bag and coming to

stay with you tonight."

Autumn ended the call with her sister, gathered her things, and was on her way to be comforted by the only family she had left in this world.

Chapter 4: Abaki

Abaki had the same routine every morning. He would wake up, walk his dogs, and then go to the gym. He was a firm believer that the body was God's gift, and he needed to make sure he took great care of it. He committed himself to eating right, working out, and being in the best possible shape. Abaki was the oldest of five children. Being the only boy, his father constantly drilled into him the essence of being a man. At the tender age of five, he was required to do things for his family that children his age in other countries probably couldn't fathom. "Son, part of being a man means doing as men do. As a man, you have to be the provider, protector, and possessor. No real man can live without a woman. You must find a wife and nourish her, create a family of your own with her. You have to, at all times, provide for them and protect them at any cost." The only problem with his father's statement was that finding a wife was harder than Abaki had thought it would be.

After the tragic circumstances that led to his forced presence in America, Abaki still found himself burdened by the ills of his past. Of course he wanted to live up to his father's standards, but living in America hadn't yielded him a woman with qualities he'd seen in his mother. She was soft, gentle, loving, and kind. His father was the disciplinarian, firm and unrelenting. Having one parent to balance out the other had made him the man he was today. He didn't think he was asking for too much. He simply wanted a woman who knew her role, who understood that the man was supposed to lead the family, and it was his job to put food on the table and keep them safe from harm. He loved black women, and the darker the skin, the better. In America, there were plenty of beautiful, attractive, and successful black women. The problem was that it seemed that none of them were willing to relinquish some of their independence just to be with a man. That was the reason he hadn't married.

When he'd met Inez, he'd thought she was the one. She wasn't of a dark complexion, but she had all the other qualities he wanted in a woman—or so he thought. She was kind-hearted and always willing to do things for others. She volunteered at soup kitchens, donated to various charities, and even devoted some of her free time to reading to sick children at local hospitals. He liked that she was attentive to his needs. She gave him his space, always cooked, and would support him by coming to the basketball games he coached, never making it seem like what he did was a waste of time. Now, after four months of dating, it seemed as if she had become a different woman.

At first, Inez would come to his games and bring home-baked cupcakes and enchiladas for the team. She would stay late and offer rides to anyone who didn't have one and was even nice to the parents. But after a few months, that all changed. She became more aggressive and possessive. She didn't want Abaki talking to any of the moms: "She likes you. I can tell. I don't want to catch you talking to her again." She began telling him what to wear and, at times, attacking his manhood: "Baby, I don't think you should wear those shoes. They make you look gay." It seemed like all the things she had done and said in the beginning to attract him had totally vanished, replaced by attributes that completely turned him off. Although he would never admit it, the realization of it hurt him inside. Abaki was ready to have kids. He was ready for a wife. He was ready to finally be the man his father raised him to be. The only thing missing was the right woman.

He pulled into the school parking lot but hadn't noticed any of his friends' cars. Once a week, four of them got together to play a friendly game of basketball. Since he spent most of his spare time coaching basketball and doing odd jobs for people in need, he typically tried to dedicate some of his time to more social activities. He wasn't really a people person, but the few people who knew him got to see every side of him.

"Abe!" he heard a female voice call out.

Abaki stopped and cringed at the sound. It was Inez. She knew his schedule and was aware that every week, on the same day, at the same time, he would meet up with the same friends at the same place to play ball. He turned around and greeted her out of respect. "Hello."

"I thought you were going to come by and get me last night so we could hang out."

"Inez, I never said that," Abaki stated. He was frustrated. She constantly came up with things she had configured inside her head, making it seem as if he'd made a promise. He heard someone walking nearby and his vigilance made him look to see who it was.

Inez followed his eyes and sucked her teeth. She folded her arms in discontent. "What, you know that bitch? Is she meeting you?"

"What?" Abaki asked in disbelief. "I don't even know that woman. Look, this is getting way out of hand."

"Oh, really! Don't try to play with me, Abaki. Is she here to see you? I mean, you've been very distant lately. Maybe she's your new interest," Inez spat. "In fact, since you seem to be so closed-lipped, let me ask her." She started to walk in the woman's direction, but Abaki grabbed her arm.

"You are really beginning to upset me. Do not go ask that woman anything. I don't know her, nor am I interested in her. Inez, the best thing for you to do is leave."

"Why? Why do I have to? So you can go talk to that slut? I'm not going anywhere!" she yelled back in a thick Spanish accent that seemed to only surface when she grew angry.

Abaki saw his friends pulling up and wanted to end

the altercation with Inez as quickly as possible. "Go home, Inez." He began to walk away from her. He heard her walking behind him and turned around briskly. "Go! This conversation is over. Do not continue to follow me. You are really pissing me off, and if you think this is the way to get my attention, you're sadly mistaken. Now leave!"

He'd made his statement with such force that it caused Inez to halt. "But Abe baby, I miss you ... okay, I'm leavin'. Call me later, okay?"

Her words fell on deaf ears. Abaki was fed up with her antics. This would be the last time she showed her butt in his presence. The next time they spoke, he'd be telling her goodbye forever.

Chapter 5: Autumn

Autumn sat in her office at the shop. She decided to stay a little after closing so she could do inventory, and look over her class's grades before posting. Once she'd tallied all the scores, she posted the final grades to the student portal, feeling better about welcoming the weekend. Even though she had nothing special planned, she was still glad when Friday and Saturday rolled around. The weekend just had a different vibe to it. It had been a while since Autumn had spent time with her godson, Sebastian. She tried to get him twice a month, and the last time was three weeks ago. She picked up the phone to call Karashae, but it rang in her hand. She saw Jerrell's name pop up on the screen and contemplated not answering. *He's just going to call right back anyway*, she reasoned.

"Hi," she answered curtly.

"Hey, baby. I miss you. Guess you been kind of busy lately. You ain't been answering my calls," he said in his southern accent.

"Yeah, you're right. I've been very busy. In fact, I was just getting ready to make a call. Can I call you back later?"

"Uh, uh, un. You said that before and never called me back. You home? I'm coming over."

"Umm, no you're not. I'm getting ready to leave.

Besides, why you always have to come to my place? Have you realized that you have yet to take me to your house?"

"C'mon, sweetheart. Don't be like that. I told you I have some things going on right now. I'm getting my new place in a couple of months, and guess who's coming over."

"I don't know, your parents?"

"No, baby, you are. I'm going to wine and dine you real good. We gonna have some dinner and some drinks. You know, get you nice and ready for this dick."

Autumn pulled the phone away from her ear. "Excuse me? Jerrell, how many times do I have to tell you that I'm celibate?! I don't have sex anymore."

"Oh, stop. Everybody has sex. And you've waited too long, sweetheart. The next time I see you, I promise, I'm going to do that pussy real good!" he boasted.

Autumn was exasperated. She had continuously told him that sex between them wasn't going to happen. But whenever they were together, he always initiated sexual contact or implications. Driving by hotels and parking in the parking lot "just to talk" was only one tactic of many. He was turning her off and didn't even know it.

"I'm sorry, Jerrell, but that won't be happening. But I'll call you later, okay?" Autumn didn't even give him a chance to answer; she just hung up.

She had intended to call her best friend, but she decided to call her sister first. Because it was just the two of them left, they maintained a bond that was unmatched by any other siblings she'd ever met. When she had run away from the group home and kidnapped her sister from foster care, she had no idea what would lie ahead. She was just determined that they were going to be together, and there wasn't a judge, social worker, or legal authority who could tell her otherwise.

"Hey, sis," Summer answered on the third ring.

"Hi, Summy. What you doing?"

"Nothing, why?"

"Oh, good. I'm getting Sebastian tonight and thought maybe we could go to the mall. I want to find a couple pairs of sandals."

"I'm down. I need to find something to wear for tomorrow anyway."

"Where you going?" Autumn asked.

"My coworker invited me to this male review down on Northwest Highway. You should roll."

"Nah, I'm good. What time you wanna meet up though? Is this your weekend to work?"

"Hell no. I worked all last weekend and even picked up three more shifts this week. I'll be enjoying myself these next two nights, that's for sure. We can meet around six. That's cooh?" Summer felt that the proper pronunciation for "cool" was too nerdy, so she dropped the "L" and added an "H." It became a common expression between them.

"Yeah, that's perfect, actually. Meet me at Stephon and Karashae's house."

"Okay, cooh." They both hung up.

Autumn closed her shop at five on Friday and Saturday nights. Sundays were her lazy days, so the shop wasn't open for business. That gave her enough time to balance her till, lock up, and get to her girlfriend's place in time to meet her sister.

"Hi, Aunt Lully!" Sebastian screamed, running into Autumn's arms as she came through the front door.

"Hey, Juicy Pooh, how's it going?" Autumn asked, hugging him tightly and rocking him side-to-side.

"I'm good. Mommy said I was pennin' the night with you."

"Yes, Mommy was right. You got all your stuff?"

"Mm hmm, yup!"

"Hey, Autumn," Stephon said, finally able to greet her as he gave her a friendly hug and kiss on the cheek.

"Hi, Stephon. Where's Karashae?"

"Oh, she's finishing up in the kitchen. Go on in."

Stephon and Karashae had been together for seven years and still hadn't tied the knot. Every time someone asked what they were waiting on, neither of them had an answer. Stephon had proposed to her when she was five months pregnant with Sebastian. Karashae had delightedly agreed. She loved Stephon and he loved her. They were the cutest couple ever. Anyone could see that the two of them were crazy in love, and it trickled down to their brilliant two-year-old.

"Hey, boo," Karashae said, finally seeing Autumn.

"Hey, you," Autumn replied while hugging her friend.

"Your godson is all packed up and ready to go."

"I know. Y'all wasn't playing, huh?"

"Girl, I told you we were holding you to your promise. Now that my mother has moved back to Indianapolis, our QT has been cut short. So anytime we've got a willing sitter, we take advantage." Karashae laughed and winked.

"Nah, that's fine. I miss my baby anyway. What you and Stephon got planned?"

"His friend is having an album release party for one of his new R&B artists, and he invited Stephon and me."

"Oh, which friend is this? You know y'all know more people than a little bit."

"I told you about him before. His name is—" The doorbell rang and Karashae went to get it. Autumn heard her and Summer exchanging pleasantries.

"Hey, Stephon, Aut. Hiii, Sebastian!" Summer sang.

"Hi, Aunt Summer," Sebastian replied.

"You coming with me and Aunt Lovely?" Summer asked him.

"Mm hmm, yup," he confirmed. Autumn smiled. She loved how he said "yup" so matter-of-factly, emphasizing the

"P."

"Aunt Summer, can you stay the night too? I like when you stay. We stay up longer than Aunt Lully."

Everyone laughed. It was no secret that Autumn was the early bird and Summer was the night owl. The two of them were like night and day but got along just as well as sunshine and blue skies.

"Yeah, lil' man, for you, Aunt Summer will stay too, okay?"

"Yaaay!" Sebastian squealed with joy.

"Okay, Sebastian, time for us to go," Autumn said. "Kiss Mommy and Daddy goodnight, Juice."

Sebastian ran over and hugged his mom and gave her a kiss, and then he reached for his dad.

"Alright, Shae and Steph. You guys enjoy your night. Karashae, just call me tomorrow when you ready for him," Autumn stated. They said their farewells, and Autumn, Sebastian, and Summer were off to the mall.

~~~

Summer eyed Autumn suspiciously. She watched as her sister laid out the blankets and popped in a movie. She waited until she had Autumn's full attention before speaking. "Okay, Aut! I saw you checking out that guy in the sneaker store."

"I know, right? He was attractive," Autumn replied, "I'm celibate, not blind, so it's natural to sneak a peek sometimes. Hopefully, I'll meet some prospects before my eggs turn to dust."

"That won't be the only thing turning to dust," Summer quipped.

"Shut up," Autumn chided, looking over at Sebastian. "My body is not deprived. I just choose to please myself instead of having a man do it."

"See, I need to feel the D up inside me and some strong hands all around me. There aren't enough toys in the universe that could take the place of a man. Un, un, un, girl, you just don't know what you're missing," Summer said, standing up. "I'll be back. Start the movie without me. I'm going to take a shower." She headed to the bathroom.

Autumn snuggled up next to Sebastian on the floor. She thought back to her sexual tryst from the previous night and shuddered. She'd had a meeting with a new supplier a couple of days ago. Before she sold any new products in her shop, she preferred to test them out to make sure they were of good quality. When she first opened her business, she would just search online for products and order what she thought would sell. After several customer complaints about merchandise of inferior quality, Autumn started requesting samples before purchasing the brand. The vendors would give her the samples and welcomed her feedback. This time, she had received a new dildo and vibrating nipple stimulators. The dildo had a suction cup at the end and five speeds, three different vibrating modes, and a clit teaser attached. In addition to vibrating at many different speed, rhythms, and intensities, it also swiveled both clockwise and counterclockwise. She had been eager to try them out.

Since her encounter with Mr. Sexy that day he had walked into her shop, she had been masturbating every night and thought of no one but him. Prior to that, the star of her fantasies had been Professor Milton and sometimes her first, Kasir, or whoever else she could think about to help her get her rocks off. She'd even thought about President Obama and came hard that time. The guilt of lusting over a married man bothered her, so since then, she'd made sure the men in her fantasies were single.

That particular night, Autumn had been on a mission, double O, operation orgasm, and she had no time for subpar activity. She'd lit some candles to set the mood for herself while her bath water ran. Autumn loved taking baths. She was sure to take a bath at least once a week, preferably Sundays. A woman had to soak every now and again. She would add a little vinegar to her bathwater to help get rid of any bacteria. Plus, she'd heard that it helped keep the vajayjay nice and tight. She had turned on her bathroom stereo right before easing into the steamy, warm water. All of the lights were off in the bathroom. The only light in the room emanated from the burning candles that released the sensual scent of garden rain.

Autumn had started off soaping her body with oatmeal body wash. She lathered every part of her skin until she was covered in ecru-colored suds. Elle Varner was crooning "Refill" through the speakers. The lyrics were intoxicating, the instrumental stimulating, and it gave her just what she needed to make herself feel good.

Autumn had used both her hands to stimulate her nipples. She squeezed and pulled on them simultaneously until the forces between her legs sprung to life. She used her left hand to rub her bulging clitoris and her right to massage her nipples. Once she felt the space between her thighs moisten, she gathered her assexssories and put them to work. First, she slid the mini-vibrating butt plug from her collection inside her wet vagina. Using her natural lubrication, she eased the butt plug into her anus and turned the vibrator on slow. "Mmm," Autumn hummed. She eased the new dildo slowly into her mouth for a different form of lubrication. Autumn had never sucked a real dick. But she developed and perfected her skills by using her toys.

Holding the base of the dildo, Autumn had turned and twisted it while gliding it in and out of her mouth. After performing fellatio worthy of a gold medal, she slid the massive faux cock into her moistness, attached the suction to the tub under the faucet, turned on the preferred vibration setting, and activated the swivel. She was already on the brink of an orgasm. The dolphin snout tickled her love button masterfully. She placed the vibrating nipple stimulators on each of her nipples and turned it on. She reclined further into the tub and let her toys take her there. The various stimulators created unfathomable sensations. She closed her eyes and envisioned Mr. Sexy in there with her. She felt herself cumming just as Elle Varner asked for a "Refill." Once her body stopped convulsing, Autumn had slid back so that the dildo was no longer inside her. She removed the butt plug, but kept the nipple stimulators intact. Autumn turned around and slid back on the rubber cock. She bucked and rotated her hips and imagined that Mr. Sexy was perched behind her. The dolphin snout was in the right place to slightly penetrate her anus. She rubbed her love button aggressively until she felt herself coming again. This time, the release made her scream out in ecstasy. Mr. Sexy had helped her achieve one of her biggest orgasms to date, and she didn't even know him to thank him.

Autumn smiled inwardly at the memory. She'd made sure she told her supplier to send plenty of those suction cup dildos. She peeked down at Sebastian, who had fallen asleep. She eased the blankets over his little body and placed gentle kisses on his face. She'd heard stories and saw on the news how children turned to demons, hating and harming their parents. On the flip side, she also saw how parents harmed innocent babies, which broke her heart every time. She couldn't imagine anything like that happening to Sebastian. Parenting was hard; that she knew. Autumn pondered motherhood and wondered if she would make a great mom. Her thoughts carried her off to sleep before Summer rejoined her after her shower.

Chapter 6: Autumn

Autumn awoke to the morning sun and chirping birds. To her, there was nothing more beautiful than sunshine and blue skies. Her father had always told her that, which was why he'd given her and her sister the respective nicknames. Seeing that it was only seven o'clock in the morning, she used the quiet time to say her prayers, brush her teeth, and prepare breakfast for her two favorite houseguests. Autumn snickered when she saw Sebastian walk over to Summer and pull the covers back.

"Aunt Summer, wake up!"

Summer awoke to Sebastian staring at her face. "Sebastian, what time is it?"

"It's three-four-eleven," Sebastian said confidently.

Summer chuckled. "That's not even a real time, Sebastian." She peeked at the clock that read 7:45 a.m. "Shit! Just when I thought I could sleep a little later."

"Ooh, watch your mouf," Sebastian chastised Summer.

"Oh, sorry." She only half meant it. "Where's Aunt Lovely?"

"Her in the bathroom, brushing her teeth."

Summer smiled at him. "*She's* in the bathroom," she corrected him.

Autumn's cell phone rang, and Summer answered it.

"Hello?"

"Good morning, beautiful," the caller said.

Summer pulled the phone away from her ear, wondering who it was on the other end. The number was blocked.

"Um, I'm sorry. Who is this?" she asked skeptically.

"Oh, excuse me. I was calling to speak with Autumn."

"Who's calling?" Summer asked again.

"This is Jerrell."

"Hold on, please. Autumn, the phone!"

Autumn picked up her cordless, but was taken aback when she heard the dial tone.

"Summer, no one is on the phone—" she started until she realized that Summer meant her cell phone. She walked from the kitchen to the living room and snatched the phone from her sister before going into her room to hold the conversation. When she was done talking, she exited her bedroom and went to address Summer. "Can you please not answer my cell phone? That's an invasion of my privacy."

"What privacy, Autumn? You get one personal phone call, and now you acting like I breached your rights, or something."

"I don't care how many calls I get. The point is that's *my* personal cell, and I don't want you answering it. The house phone is cool, but my cellular is off limits. Don't forget it," Autumn stated.

Summer made an ugly face and threw up her hands in surrender. "Was that the guy from the mall last night?"

"No. I didn't give my number to him. That was Jerrell. I told him we could meet up Saturday."

"Saturday, as in May thirtieth, Saturday?" Summer asked.

"Yes, and?"

"Autumn, you know we're all getting together to go bowling and out for drinks, so why would you make plans to go on a date?"

"Well, I didn't make separate plans, if that's what you're worried about. I invited Jerrell to join us. This man has been hounding me for more time. He creeps me out, and I don't want to be alone with him, so I just invited him to tag along with us. He's annoying, but I haven't gathered the courage to cut him off completely," Autumn clarified. After Jerrell started being so pushy about sex, she didn't trust him enough to be alone with her.

"Oh, okay, as long as you weren't making other plans."

After her failed relationship with Kasir, Autumn continued to date. Everyone had promised her the silver lining in the sky, right up until they got the goods, and then they crushed her hopes as if promises were never made. She had slept with others off and on after that and soon realized that she was allowing men to sample her goods, but no one intended to make a purchase. At the age of twenty-two, she'd made a promise to herself and God that the next man to penetrate her would be the one who married her.

Her phone rang again. This time, it was her house phone.

Summer answered. "Good Morning. Hey, Karashae. Uh huh. He's up, bright eyed and bushy tailed. Okay, cooh. See y'all in a few." Summer hung up. "That was Karashae. She and Stephon are on their way. Let me go freshen up before they get here." She walked toward the bathroom.

When the doorbell rang, Sebastian was right on Autumn's heels as she answered it. As soon as he saw his parents, he jumped into Karashae's arms and planted kisses all over her face; then he reached for his father and did the same thing. Karashae and Stephon kissed Autumn on the cheek and walked into the living room.

"So, how was the event?" Autumn asked.

"Oh, Autumn, it was so nice. The venue was real classy. We're gonna have to go there for drinks one night. The artist was real good too. She has a beautiful voice and her music is something that you will definitely be feeling. And girl ..." Karashae said, peering at Stephon, "there were some good looking brothas there, not as good looking as my man, but they were cute."

"Yeah, yeah, don't change it up for me," Stephon joked. He kissed his wife on the lips and rubbed her thigh, letting her know that she could finish her statement.

"Nah, but for real; there were a couple of nice-looking guys there, who didn't have dates. I asked Stephon's friend's wife if they were single, and she said they were. So I had Stephon have his friend invite this one in particular to hang out with us next week when we go bowling," Karashae said excitedly.

"Oh God, Karashae," Autumn groaned. "I hope you didn't mention me."

"I started to, but I didn't, why?"

Autumn was relieved. "'Cause I kind of already invited someone to hang out with us next week."

"Get out!" Stephon and Karashae said at the same time.

"What? Why is that so shocking to you all? I've been seeing Jerrell for a couple of months."

"We know, but you don't even like him. And you haven't liked a guy in so long that we thought after Jerrell, your ass was joining the convent," Karashae chuckled, eliciting the same reaction from Summer and Stephon. Autumn didn't find it funny.

"Ha ha. I'm ready to start a relationship, but only if the guy is worth my time." Autumn looked on admirably at her best friend. She loved the relationship she and Stephon had. They meshed so well. She was sincerely happy for her and hoped that one day she could have a similar family of her own. But judging from the way her love life was going, she feared it would never happen.

~~~

Autumn's kickboxing class seemed to have gained some popularity since she had started two weekends ago. The class had grown to about thirty people, up from twelve when she'd begun. She was walking past the free room on the lower level, on her way to the ladies locker room, when she spotted a guy inside, pounding on the punching bag. He was bobbing and weaving as if he were in a professional fight. She couldn't see his face, but she didn't care. His back, shoulders, and arms gave her a view that caused her mouth to water. She missed the touch, smell, and feel of a man. Seven years was a long time to go without having sex. She hadn't even cuddled with anyone, not because she didn't want to, but because no one had made it to that point. She had either caught him in several lies, found out he had two kids too many, was unemployed, or lacked the drive and motivation she was looking for in a life partner. None of them were worth her reneging on her promise to remain celibate.

She watched as the man's muscles twitched with every punch he threw. Autumn secretly fantasized that those strong arms were wrapped around her body. She felt that familiar tingle in her hidden treasure. As if she had tapped him on the shoulder personally, the subject of her attention turned around, looking her dead in her face. Autumn's eyes grew large when they connected with the eyes of the man she had molested in her fantasies so many times: Mr. Sexy. She knew it was him. She recognized that nose, those lips, and his eyes. She had memorized his features and permanently stored them in her mind. Neither broke the stare. It wasn't until her water bottle fell from her hands that their trance was broken.

"Let me get that for you," he offered as he stepped out of the room and bent down to pick up her bottle. "Abaki."

"Huh?" Autumn asked in confusion.

"Abaki. My name is Abaki Lemande. Nice to meet you."

"Oh, uh, I'm sorry. My name is Autumn. Autumn Hughes. Nice to meet you, too."

"Well, here you are." He handed her the water bottle.

"Thank you. I appreciate that." She wondered what he would think if he knew that she'd had sex with him fifty times in her mind.

"Please, think nothing of it. I must resume my work out."

"Oh, of course. Bye. I mean, see you later. Uh ..." Autumn's voice trailed off to a faraway place, and she followed it, turning away from the room to make her way toward the front door. Abaki had impacted her in ways that no other man had, leaving her speechless. She couldn't wait to get home and have a flashback of his sweat-riddled naked upper body while she used her gadgets to bring her to an orgasm.

She had noted a subtle accent. That day at her shop, she hadn't detected it. But this time, it was more profound. He was different; she could sense that. But despite how sexy he was, he was much too poised for her taste. Abaki came off as aloof, disinterested even, and Autumn didn't want that. She didn't want to have to break down barriers to get someone to open up. She had invested time in others and it had brought no fulfillment to her life. She still felt empty. Her spirit was craving a distinct love, a deeper love, one that traveled beyond fantasies and wishful thinking.

Autumn wanted a husband. There was only so much love she could get from her sister and her friends. She had too many emotional gaps. Her need for her mother seemed to have heightened since her college years. She'd give anything to be able to call heaven and seek her guidance. Her father's absence was just as vital. If he was around, the likelihood of her seeking comfort and protection from a man would have been minimal at best. Her father would have filled a gap that only a real dad could. And Grammy had wisdom beyond any folktales. She had operated on simple but poignant principals: *"You get more bees with honey than you do with shit. Bite your tongue to keep the peace."* Autumn had taken note of everything her grandmother had said. She knew that her words were products of years of experience. Since Autumn no longer had her family there to speak unto her ears, she would continue to close her eyes and look to the sky, allowing them to speak to her heart.

Autumn turned on the car radio and Fantasia's "When I see you," played softly in the background and at that moment, she couldn't think of a more appropriate song. During her ride home she thought about how much Abaki had been on her mindsince their first encounter.

Chapter 7: Abaki

Abaki couldn't really focus on his workout after his encounter with Autumn. He wasn't sure, but something told him that she was an American woman. He was from Sierra Leone. He wanted a woman similar to his mom, who was raised from birth to obey, respect, serve, and worship her husband. American women, on the other hand, seemed to have the opposite view. They were raised to be, or at some point, chose to adopt complete independence and refused to relinquish it. Abaki couldn't go for that. He knew that his wife had to allow him to rule in three areas. He had to be the provider, protector, and the possessor. The woman he chose to be his wife had to know that he possessed her; she would be his, and she would have to allow him to provide for her and protect her at all costs, even if it meant death. Of his twenty-three years in America, he had not met one woman whom he could see himself loving for the rest of his life. From CEOs to receptionists, women threw themselves at him in ways that showed they had no respect for themselves. He didn't want that kind of woman in his life.

Abaki could see that Autumn was mesmerized by him the same as all the other women he encountered. It was all superficial in his mind. No one knew him, the man inside. They basically reacted from his shell, and sometimes, that was all it took to gain their interest, and that turned him off. He was a different kind of man. His culture allotted him a different moral upbringing. His friends reminded him of just how unusual he was, but he didn't care. He had standards and didn't plan to alter them for anyone, especially a woman.

Lately, he wasn't sure what was going on with him. He had yet to be as fascinated by any woman as he was with Autumn. He saw nice looking women on a regular basis. In fact, the gym he had attended before hers was full of them. He had assisted women with workout plans at their requests and could have been with any of them. But he didn't want them.

Once he'd found out what gym Autumn attended, he quickly canceled his membership at his old one and signed up at hers. He wasn't stalking her. He had just taken notice of her gym key tag while at her shop that day. He'd seen her keys dangling from her back pocket when she'd assisted him. The early cancelation fee at his previous gym was well worth his intent.

When Autumn had spotted him, he had no idea that she would be there that day. He was certain he would eventually see her there, but he didn't think it would be just two days after joining. He was changing. He was sure of it. It was totally out of character for him to pursue a woman. Even if he was attracted to her physically, like he was to Inez, he still wasn't the type to blatantly approach a woman. Getting closer to Autumn was essential. Since he had broken things off with Inez a few days ago, he felt comfortable about his unrelenting feelings for another woman. He cared for Inez, but he wouldn't go as far as saying he loved her or was in love with her. And if he ended up falling for Autumn, then he'd have to deal with his unfinished business back home sooner rather than later.

Chapter 8: Autumn

Whenever Autumn was experiencing a rough patch, the next person she turned to, other than her sister and God, was her frister. Since the day Karashae had befriended her, they shared a unique bond. She stood on her best friend's doorstep, waiting for her to answer the door. Today was one of those days when she was experiencing love blues.

"Hey," Autumn said as soon as Shae opened the door.

"Hey, boo! What's going on?" They made there way to the kitchen, and sat at the island.

"Oh God, Karashae. Jerrell is *so* getting on my nerves. I am in the right mind to tell him never mind about going bowling tomorrow and just change my number."

"Well, damn. What he do?"

"He's clingy as hell, he brags about himself, and he has no substance. It's like he's a little kid. Lately, it seems like all he wants to do is get me in a secluded area and sex me. That's why when he called the other day, wanting to hang out, I declined and invited him to come bowling with us instead. Now, he calls me every other day to confirm for Saturday."

Karashae burst into laughter.

"It's not funny, Shae!" Autumn said, pouting.

"I'm sorry. Well, Autumn, maybe he's really excited to be going out with someone like you. After all, you can't blame him; he totally hit the jackpot with you."

Autumn sucked her teeth. She knew her friend's statement was two-fold. Karashae was referring to her being a good catch and to her portion of her family's inheritance. Autumn had figured that she had some money coming to her after she and Summer had left Albany for good. Even though they'd left their grandmother's house as nothing but burnt frames and ashes, it was paid off. Once the life and homeowners insurance companies had discovered that Mrs. Chandler had passed, they had released the funds to her estate. Autumn's search in NYS unclaimed funds had yielded results for both her and her sister. Autumn had waited until Summer turned eighteen before contacting anyone. She couldn't risk them being caught and sent back to group homes and foster care in New York. Not only did they have the proceeds from Grammy's home and life insurance, but also their parents' retirement benefits, plus their share of the airline lawsuit settlement. Altogether, Autumn and Summer had over one and a half million dollars each.

Karashae waited for Autumn to laugh, but she never did. "You know I was just joking, right?"

"Yeah, girl. I'm not tripping. Karashae, be honest with me, do you think there's something wrong with me?"

"Hell no, girl. Why would you say that?"

"Because I'm almost thirty, with no man. I mean, I own a business, I have my own house, and I'm college educated. People say I'm fun to be around. I have a great sense of humor, and I'm personable, yet I'm single. Maybe it *is* me."

Karashae walked around the kitchen island and sat next to her friend. "Autumn, listen to me, there is nothing wrong with you. You have your idea of what you want in a man, and you just have to be patient and wait for him to come. The Bible says 'He who finds a wife, finds a good thing.' Don't feel you have to find the right man; let the right man find you. I'm sure he's searching. Waiting on a great man is better than waiting for a man to be great. With the first one, at least you know what you will get. With the second one, you may never get what you hoped for because he wasn't what you wanted in the first place. You just accepted him and hoped that he would mold into your ideal man. If you go that way, we will be sitting here having a different kind of talk, one that entails leaving him instead of finding him. Give yourself time. He will come. Everybody finds love at different times."

"I am giving it time! Shoot, at this point, I have no choice but to wait. I know God hears my heart. I want a strong God-fearing man. I'm not saying he has to be religious, but spiritual, yes. He has to believe in God, a higher power. He has to trust that there are forces beyond our control that help guide us through life. I just want him to be wholesome, honest, loving, and supportive. He has to be goal oriented and able to communicate his thoughts and feelings. Is that too much to ask? I'm not even asking for him to be rich or powerful, that's a plus though, just as long as he has a good heart and is healthy and hardworking, I'm good."

"Autumn Hughes, your day is coming. The man of your dreams will snatch you up so quick that you'd think you were dreaming."

Autumn hugged Karashae affectionately. She knew Shae was being a true friend, and even though she made it sound good, Autumn was still skeptical. "How did you know Stephon was the one?"

Autumn could tell that Karashae was thinking about her question. She also knew that Shae had met Sephon through a mutual friend. They actually weren't even attracted to each other at first. Constant interaction because of mutual friends had caused them to gravitate toward each other. One day, they had exchanged numbers and never separated thereafter.

"I don't know. You just kind of know. You get this feeling that's indescribable. You contemplate life without the other person, and it just doesn't seem right. You can't envision not being with him. It's a burning attraction, something that just draws you to him with no provocation at all. It's in the spirit, the soul. Once the two halves join, there is no denying the connection. In essence, the mind, body, and spirit receive confirmation that the soul has located its other half, and the heart embraces it."

Autumn sat quietly. She had never heard anyone explain or confirm love like that before. That's what she wanted. She longed to feel that same completion Karashae had just spoken of. "When are you guys getting married?" Autumn asked.

"Soon. We've already been talking about it. We're thinking maybe by the end of this year."

"Really?!" Autumn squealed as she hugged Karashae giddily. "Oh my gosh, Shae. I can't even contain my excitement."

"Yes, we feel the same as everyone else: 'What's taking so long?' We aren't getting any younger and wanted to make our union official. We've even been tossing around another idea: giving Sebastian a little brother or sister."

"Dammit ,Karashae! I'm your best friend. Why am I just finding out about this now?"

"Because we literally just discussed it, Autumn. We were talking about it last night, and when he woke up this morning, he told me to start planning. He's ready for me to be his wife."

Autumn placed her hand over her heart. "Aw, that was sweet. Stephon is such a good man. I truly look up to him. I want to be like you guys when I grow up."

"Oh, shut up, silly." Karashae swatted at her playfully. "My mom has been hounding us to move to Indianapolis.

She misses Sebastian and said she wants more time with her grandson. Stephon's company has offices in her area, so he could request a transfer if we decided to go that route."

Autumn was sad and happy. She was glad that her friend was evolving in life and doing amazing things. She had just revealed plans to tie the knot, expand her family, and possibly relocate. Those were big changes for anyone. She was truly happy for all the wonderful things happening in Karashae's life, but her heart also ached at the thought of the widening gap between her and her closest friend. Her heart couldn't deny the pain it felt at the thought of no longer having her best friend close by. Karashae was more than a friend, she was like a sister, her "frister," as Autumn often referred to her.

Autumn felt her demeanor flatten, and she knew Karashae could sense it. She was aware that Shae understood that her departure would bring her heartache. Through it all, Autumn had never displayed an ounce of jealousy toward Karashae. Even though she had no parents or family, she relished in the happiness Karashae felt from having her own. Even though Autumn didn't have any kids, she still loved Sebastian as if she had birthed him herself. Autumn was a rare breed, and Karashae loved her like the sister she never had.

"Autumn, you are my best friend, my frister. I have never met someone as genuine as you. You have great qualities, and I promise you that your day for happiness is near. Please don't be sad. *If* we do move, we'll still visit each other and keep in touch. Besides, my mother loves you like her own, and you will have another place to visit when you want out of Dallas for a while."

Autumn knew Karashae's mom cared for her and Summer. It was evident when she'd discovered their secret and helped them instead of turning them in when she and Summer were younger. Ms. Jackie was the admissions coordinator at Maya Angelou High School and had sensed something wasn't right with the girls. It had taken her two weeks to find out what it was, and when she did, her heart melted. Autumn still hadn't turned in the physical forms that were needed for them to stay in school. Each time Ms. Jackie would inquire about it, one of the girls would always reply that they'd forgotten them. Autumn had dreaded that the day would come. She had just hoped that it was later in the school year. She was honest with Ms. Jackie and told her everything, from her parents and grandmother dying, to them running away. She was careful to leave out the part about setting the house on fire. Ms. Jackie had been stunned. She couldn't believe that Autumn had pulled all of that off on her own and had instantly developed a soft spot for them. Autumn knew that if it wasn't for Karashae and her mother, she and Summer would have had a harder time navigating a new environment.

Autumn smiled at her friend. Karashae was such a sweet person, and the last thing she wanted was for her somberness to eclipse her frister's happiness. "I don't mean to be a Debbie Downer. It's just that I will miss you guys. You are the only real family Summer and I have had since losing our own, and the thought of not having you around ..." Autumn's eyes stung and her throat burned. She fought back the tears threatening to fall.

Karashae wrapped her arms around Autumn and held her close. "Autumn, your soul mate is out there, and he's looking for you. When he finds you, God bless, because when a man loves a woman, he loves harder than she does."

Chapter 9: Autumn

It never failed. As soon as Autumn was in the middle of doing one thing, her mind took her to something else she was supposed to do. Like now, as she was preparing to meet her supplier, she realized she hadn't confirmed reservations with her sister. Every year for the past eight years, Autumn and Summer traveled back to Albany, NY for either Mother's or Father's Day, just to pay respects to their family. And so far, neither of them had made the final arrangements. Autumn placed a call to her sister.

"Hey, Blue Skies. What you doing?"

"Making A.J. and me breakfast." Summer usually didn't do the domestic thing, so, for her, cooking was a rarity.

"Mmm, you up and cooking ... with just your heels and panties on? This must be my lucky day," Autumn heard A.J. say.

She heard Summer snicker like a giddy school girl. "Girl, call me back," she told her.

"No, Aut, hold on." Summer pulled the phone away from her mouth and whispered something to A.J. before turning her attention back to Autumn. "Ooh Autumn, I really like him. He is so awesome. He's all man. The brotha knows how to change a flat tire, cook, and will even do the dishes. Mm, mm, mm," she cooed. "But any who, I was going to call anyway about our trip back home."

"Yeah, I know. That's why I'm calling. We still haven't decided on how long to stay."

"Oh, that's right. I don't know. Shit, a few days later is my birthday, and I don't know if I want to celebrate there, with our friends from home, or if we should just come back here."

"I don't know either. I thought the same thing. My summer course doesn't start until after the Fourth, so I'm good either way. Let's just stay for the week and come home Saturday. That way we can celebrate your birthday on Friday, and you can be home by Saturday evening, in case Ajamaal wants to do something," Autumn suggested.

"Yeah, that sounds like a plan. Go ahead and book the flights, and I'll reserve the hotel. You know what you wearing tonight to the bowling alley?"

"Yup, something comfortable. Probably a pair of jeans, a tank top, blazer, and a pair of sandals I purchased from the mall when we went."

"Okay, cooh. I'm going to do something casual too. Aiight, big sis. I'll see you a little later."

Autumn was anxious about her date with Jerrell tonight, and not in a good way. She was already turned off by his latest antics and couldn't see how this night could be any better. She didn't even know why she just didn't cancel on him altogether. Then Karashae had invited one of Stephon's friends for her, and that was unsettling as well. She didn't think she could handle it emotionally if the guy turned out to be a dud, and she didn't want to get her hopes up, thinking that he could be the complete opposite. *I guess time will have to tell*, she thought.

~~~

Autumn and Jerrell were the last ones to arrive at the bowling alley. When they got there, everyone had already chosen lanes and was getting their bowl on. Autumn was pissed. She hated being late. Jerrell had insisted on picking her up and then claimed he'd gotten tied up and lost track of time.

Karashae spotted Autumn first and went to greet her BFF. "Hey, boo. This is Jerrell. Jerrell, this is my best friend, Shae."

Karashae told her there were two teams of five, from a total of ten people in attendance. But only nine were there.

Stephon placed his hand on Autumn's back. "Autumn, this is my man, Karmichael, but we call him Karl. And this is his wife, Chaianne. This is Fred, Karl's cousin. And everybody, this is like my sister; please meet Autumn." They all exchanged handshakes and Autumn introduced them to Jerrell. She rolled her eyes as soon as he started talking about his collection of antique cars that his uncle Bubba had left him. She left him there and went to the counter to get her bowling shoes.

Karashae followed, laughing. "Girl, why you just walk away from him like that?"

"Shae, he is so annoying. He didn't even wait until the introductions were fully made before he started running off at the mouth. And he's the reason we arrived late. You know I don't play that."

"Well, don't tell him about drinks later on. After we're done here, tell him you enjoyed and send him on his way."

"Ahh, I like that."

"Did you see him?" Karashae asked, switching gears.

"See who?"

"Karl's friend. The one I was telling you about."

"Eww, Karashae. That boy looks way too young and hood for me."

"No, not Fred, silly, Abe."

"No I didn't—"

"Oh, here he is, right here. Hey, Abe. I would like you to meet my friend, Autumn. Autumn, this is Abe."

Autumn turned around to greet him and was stunned. *No freaking way!* She couldn't believe her luck. She had shown up with a loser, and standing beside her was her secret lover. Atlantic Starr had it almost right, except Autumn knew about their imaginary love affair and he didn't. Karashae heard Stephon calling her, letting her know it was her turn to bowl, so before she walked away, she gently nudged Autumn with her shoulder.

"Abaki, right?" Autumn asked. Who was she kidding? She'd pretty much tattooed his name on her brain.

"Yes, that's right."

"Well, uh, um … it's good seeing you again."

"Likewise."

Autumn let her eyes linger for a few more seconds. She wanted to stand there all night and just stare at the statuesque man before her. Once she soaked in all she could, just before she turned to leave, she heard Abaki telling the employee behind the counter that his size twelve bowling shoe was too small. *Big feet, big …*

She felt awkward the whole two hours they were there. Jerrell thought he was making people laugh, when actually, he was the reason people were laughing. His country dialect and corny dialogue was not working to win over his audience. She wanted to tell him to chill out and be quiet, but she had already made up her mind that there wouldn't be another date. There was a much better woman out there for him than Autumn. It didn't help that Abaki was there. Every time she stole a glance at him, he was looking at her. She thought that he would turn his head when she caught him staring, but he never did. It was like he wanted her to know he was looking.

Jerrell had just returned from the bar with two beers, a tap beer for him and a Corona for her. Autumn loved an ice-cold Corona, topped with a lemon. They all made a toast and started their second game. For the second game, they switched up the teams. Karashae, Stephon, Chaianne, Karmichael, and his cousin, Fred, were on one team. Autumn, Jerrell, Summer, Ajamaal, and Abaki were on the other team. Stephon and Karl were bowling like they played for a league. Abe and Jerrell were being very competitive, trying to make as many strikes and spares as they could.

Jerrell was now on his third beer and behaving even more strangely. He started grabbing Autumn's waist, trying to pull her in for hugs and kisses. She knew that seeing the other couples interact had him feeling territorial, and he wanted the same. All the guys would high-five their ladies or bring them in for kisses when they did well or even if they did badly, like in Karashae and Stephon's case. But she and Jerrell weren't on it like that, and she had no problem denying his advances.

When the final frame was done, Autumn was ready for Jerrell to go. She told him that she enjoyed his company and thanked him for accompanying her.

"I was hoping we could finish the night elsewhere," he stated, moving his groin into hers suggestively.

"Oh, no. Sorry, but I promised my sister I would go with her," Autumn said, backing away.

"Oh, okay. I'll go too, then."

"Uh, no you won't."

"Come on, baby. Why you ackin' like that?" Jerrell

leaned in and tried to kiss her. Autumn pushed him back, but he grabbed her hands.

"I believe the lady said no," Abaki said to Jerrell.

Autumn looked at him in shock. He'd said absolutely nothing for most of the night, and the first time he spoke, it was in her defense.

"Man, mind your damn business. If the lady wants me to stop, she can tell me her damn self," Jerrell shot back, grabbing Autumn at the hip.

Before Autumn had a chance to move his hands, he had fallen to the ground. She looked down at Jerrell and then up at Abaki and saw him massaging his left knuckles with his right hand.

"Now this time, she didn't have to. And don't contact her again." Abaki looked at Autumn and his eyes told her to confirm his statement so there was no confusion.

"Jerrell, do me and you a favor and lose my number," she said.

Everyone had watched in awe as Abaki knocked Jerrell to the ground. Summer couldn't believe her eyes, Karashae was stunned beyond belief, Chaianne was thrilled, and Stephon, Fred, and Karl were used to it. They knew that Abaki hated to see women being mistreated. He didn't care where he was, who he was with, or who the offender was; if he witnessed some funny stuff, he intervened. Karl and Stephon told the others how Abe had seen a lady being assaulted by her boyfriend, and he went right over and started beating on him. By the time Abe was done with him, the guy was a bloody mess. Abe had told the girl that she could and should do much better before someone had to plan her funeral.

Abaki asked Autumn where she'd parked, so he could walk her to her vehicle. "Um, I rode with Jerrell. He picked me up," she said. "I'll just ride with my sister."

"He's like a super hero or something," Summer said just as Abe and Autumn approached her car.

Everyone watched as Jerrell stumbled out of the door, holding the right side of his face as he made his way to his car. When he pulled off, Autumn turned to Abaki and thanked him.

"So, are we still going to the beer hall, or what?" Karashae asked.

Everyone was still in agreement, except Fred. His baby momma had been texting him all evening, so he was going home. The rest of them got into their prospective vehicles and drove to the second part of their evening. Leaving Jerrell as a distant memory.

Chapter 10: Abaki

Abaki had seen Autumn as soon as he'd exited the restroom. Although he couldn't see her face, her hair, shape, and attire told him that she was the same woman from the adult toy shop. Even as he'd headed to the counter to change the size of his bowling shoes, he got butterflies. Typically, women didn't do that to him, but Autumn Hughes was proving to have a different effect on him. When his homeboy's wife had made the introductions, he'd waited to see if Autumn would acknowledge their recent encounter or act as if the introduction was their first. It was obvious that she hadn't told her friend about him, and it kind of disappointed him. Women were known for babbling to their girlfriends about the cute guy they'd met, or crushed on, or whatever. Surely, the way Autumn had behaved when she'd seen him had him thinking that she was interested. That was partially why he'd waited for her to say something first.

After that first awkward moment, he couldn't keep his eyes off her. That tongue thing she did with her lips turned him on more than he'd admit. Her face looked so soft and pretty, angelic. Her personality was warm and welcoming. Her demeanor was cool and inviting. So far, everything about her screamed his kind of women, except her date. Abaki typically didn't judge people based on who they chose to date. After all, Inez was of no direct reflection on the type of man he was. He hoped Jerrell wasn't a reflection of Autumn. Nothing about him gave Abaki the impression that he was her type of man. In fact, even her actions had said so. When Jerrell had gotten close, she moved away. If Abaki had been Jerrell, he would have been totally offended by her actions. From childhood, his father had taught him the essence of observations and perception, how it was always important to watch people, how they spoke, interacted, and carried themselves, as that would tell him more about the person than what initially met the eye. And something about Jerrell just didn't sit well with him. That's why he'd felt the need to keep a close eye on Autumn and her date. Autumn seemed uneasy around him, even unsafe. Everything inside of Abaki just wouldn't allow him to leave until he knew she was okay.

When he'd seen Jerrell grab Autumn, he was up on them in a matter of seconds. He didn't like men who hit women. He would never hit a woman, ever, nor would he allow such a thing to take place in his presence. Men were placed on this earth to provide the three P's, and a man who did otherwise wasn't a man in his eyes at all. When Autumn hadn't hesitated to tell Jerrell to get lost, Abaki's attraction to her grew stronger. Now, all he had to do was find out one more thing: if she was the type he was hoping she would be. Was she conforming, compassionate, and catering? If so, his trip back home to resolve unsettled problems would have to come sooner than later.

Chapter 11: Autumn

The beer hall wasn't as crowded as they'd expected for a Saturday night. Summer saw a sign for a mechanical bull and brought it to everyone's attention. "Yeah, let's go!" all the ladies said in unison. Karl ordered a round of drinks for everyone and the waitress said she would bring them up. The eight of them sat around, shooting the breeze. Abe was the quietest of them all.

"So Chaianne, how long have you and Karl been married?" Karashae asked, noticing the nice rock sitting on her left hand.

"Three years now."

"Yeah, me and my babe plan to make it official by the end of this year. We've been together seven years already," Stephon said.

"Dang, my boy, that's a minute," Karl responded. "To black love," he said, raising his glass for a toast. Everyone followed suit.

"Autumn, I apologize if I'm coming off as too forward, but where are you from?" Chaianne asked.

Autumn had noticed Chaianne staring at her all night. It wasn't a mean look but one that Autumn hadn't figured out yet. She thought Chaianne might have been admiring her jewelry. Autumn loved diamonds. She had a diamond-studded nugget ring on the middle finger of her left hand and a heart-shaped diamond ring on the ring finger of her right hand. A sterling silver diamond link bracelet sat on her right wrist, and a pair of one-carat studs adorned her ears. She was definitely icy, but classy. "I'm originally from Albany," she finally responded.

Karl looked at Chaianne, but she ignored his gaze. She looked at Summer and then back at Autumn. "St. Anne's?" she asked Autumn.

Summer and Autumn exchanged quizzical glances, wondering how the hell Chaianne knew the name of the group home where Autumn had lived when they were young. Autumn swallowed. She didn't know why this girl was asking, but she was definitely intrigued. "Yes, briefly," she admitted.

"See, I knew I recognized you as soon as you walked into the bowling alley. I seldom forget a face, especially in my line of work. You probably don't remember me. I lived at St. Anne's for a while before being sent back to Parsons."

"Yeah, I was only there for about two months before we moved here," Autumn replied, hoping Chaianne didn't mention anything else, at least not at that moment. Autumn relived her past often, even if she didn't want to. Being all the way in Dallas had her feeling a bit eerie about meeting someone from New York. She didn't know Chaianne and hoped Chaianne didn't know her too well. She feared that someone had witnessed their escape, or worse, her setting her Grammy's house on fire. But it had to be done. Otherwise, they might not have been where they were today.

"When I left there, I left Albany for good," Autumn said.

"I ain't mad at you," Chaianne said. "When Karl made me a promise I couldn't refuse, I packed up and moved down here, and I've been here for the past three years."

"Wow, such a small world we live in," Stephon added.

Ajamaal, who was normally quiet, jumped in. "I didn't know y'all were from Albany. I got peoples in Brooklyn and Jersey. That's not too far from your hometown."

"Nah, not at all. Brooklyn is like three hours south of Albany," Summer said.

"So, what do you do for a living?" Autumn asked Chaianne.

The waitress arrived with their orders and set everyone's in front of them.

"Mm, that looks good, Chaianne. What is that?" Summer asked.

"Oh, this is a kiss, the only thing I drink. Bacardi with cranberry and orange juice."

"Yeah, she's been drinking that since I met her and hasn't deviated from it yet," Karl added.

Chaianne turned to Autumn to answer her question. "I'm a private investigator. What do you guys do?"

Summer spoke up first. "I'm a nurse."

"I teach at a local college and own an adult novelty shop in the Main St. District. You guys should come by some time," Autumn suggested, handing Chaianne a business card.

"Oh, okay," Chaianne stated approvingly. "I love when a sistah is doing her thing."

"My wife started her own business fresh out of college," Karl bragged, giving his wife props.

Abaki spoke next, stunning everyone. "So, are you what they call an independent woman?" he asked Autumn.

Autumn didn't know how to take his question. She wasn't sure if he was complimenting her or scolding her.

"I'm independent, yes, but only because I have to be. I have no man, no brothers, and no father to do things for me and be at my every beck and call. Right now, I've got a laundry list of things that need to be done that I just can't do. My lawn needs to be mowed, the railing on my back porch is loose, my fence needs repairing. I mean I do what I can on my own because I have no one else, and for the other things, I pay to have them done. My sister and I are all we have. Trust me, if there was someone who was willing to do all that in the name of love, or just because, I'd be more than happy to lose the title. Until then, I'm on my own," she said honestly.

"I hear that fly shit," Summer said. "My sister is my role model. If I told you how she got us to where we are, you'd think I was lying. Autumn is a rare breed. She definitely held things together, considering how everything went down."

Summer was referring to their court hearing back then and Autumn's speech to convince the judge to remove Summer from a foster home and give her custody of her little sister. She had everyone in tears; even the judge was choked up. But when her compelling words hadn't been enough, she'd taken drastic measures. Nothing or no one was going to stop them from being together. When they'd arrived in Dallas, they had their challenges, but like other hurdles, they prevailed.

"But answer me this," Abaki spoke up again. "If you have a business, a career, and your own home, what is there left for a man to give you?"

Autumn didn't need to think too long. She knew the answer. "His heart," she said, looking Abaki dead in his eyes. "Yes, I have accomplished a lot on my own, but that's because I had no choice. I was forced to do what I had to do to take care of me and my sister, and part of that meant securing our financial wellbeing. So when the opportunity presented itself, I opened my own business. Make no mistake about it; if the right guy came along and wanted me in his life, I would compromise, all in the name of love. I would even sell my home and allow him to buy us one, if that is what he chooses."

"And the business?" Abaki asked.

Now that, Autumn had to think about. "Honestly, I don't know. I birthed that business, and it would be like giving a child up for adoption. I would hope that any man that comes into my life wouldn't see my business as a threat, but more so an entity that I created that could benefit both of us. I still have to have repairs done at the shop, shovel in the winter, do inventory, play security, and all that. So I would hope that he would want to help me expand rather than dispose."

Everyone was listening. No one was sure why Abaki had asked Autumn these questions. But those that knew her knew that her answers were genuine, and Autumn was being true to herself. Abaki didn't ask anything more after that; he just continued his visual assessment of Autumn, the same as he had done all night.

"So, what do you do, Abaki?" Karashae asked, trying to take the heat off of her friend.

"I coach high school basketball."

"Nice! So, you like kids too, huh?" Autumn asked.

"You can say that." He didn't elaborate, and she didn't ask him to.

She knew how rewarding it was to work with young folks, so she had an idea of how fulfilling his line of work could be.

"Man, stop being so damn humble," Karl interrupted.

"Let me tell y'all, this man is a jack-of-all-trades and master of many. He can do more shit than people who get paid to do it. My boy here is of a distinct breed. He doesn't operate like most capitalists. He's a barterer at heart. One day, he showed up at my house driving a fucking Ferrari, son. I knew he wasn't getting that much on a coaching stipend. He told me he had paved the driveway of one of the players' rich uncles, and he loaned him the Ferrari while he went away on a business trip, all because he wouldn't accept payment. Then he took us for a boat ride. I'm thinking we gonna be cruising on a little sailboat, and this dude here brings us to a dock where a yacht was awaiting."

"Word is bond!" Chaianne cosigned. "That shit was official. I told Karl we're definitely getting one when we retire." They all laughed.

The waitress came again to take more drink orders. This time, all the ladies ordered Chaianne's specialty, and the guys got more beer. Autumn sat quietly, mentally assessing Abaki. *Why is he so composed?* she wondered. She hadn't seen him smile or laugh once since they'd been out. If it weren't for his single smile at her shop that day, she would have thought he was toothless. *Mr. Sexy is so obscure*, she thought to herself. Autumn silently hoped he would emerge from his shell by the time the night ended.

Chaianne whispered in Karl's ear and watched as he dug in his pocket and handed her some bills. She took the money and headed to the jukebox.

"That girl loves to dance," Karl said.

"Shit, I do too," Summer chimed in, and Karashae agreed.

"I hope she plays some good tunes because I'm up there with her," Autumn added.

Just as the words left her lips, Lil' Wayne's "How to Love" started playing through the speakers. Autumn was the first one on her feet, immediately followed by Summer and Karashae. The three of them joined Chaianne on the dance floor as the men looked on in admiration. Karl was checking out his wife. He'd known she had moves since their second date. Summer and Karashae both swayed their hips rhythmically, but Autumn had them all beat. Her moves were so graceful and tasteful that all the women gazed admirably at her, egging her on. Autumn continued to dip, sway, and roll her hips as she heard the words her heart had been speaking for so long: "See, you've had a lot of crooks tryin' to steal your heart, never really had luck, couldn't ever figure out how to love."

When "Irreplaceable" by Beyonce started playing, the ladies really got into it. "Wifey" by Next followed. Before they knew it, the guys were on their feet, joining them on the floor. Autumn noticed that everyone had gotten up except Abaki. Not wanting to be the odd woman out, she used that moment to go to the bathroom. She was beginning to feel sad for herself, but she stopped the feeling before it could invade her happiness. "No, I will not let my loneliness overshadow a good night with friends. Get it together, Autumn!"

By the time she emerged from the bathroom, the song was coming to an end and she was glad. Everyone was walking back to the table at the same time. Autumn caught Abaki staring, and she looked away as usual. She thought back to their exchange at her shop. *What the hell is he thinking?* Autumn was in the right mind to dig into her purse for change and hand it to him—a penny for his thoughts.

The third round of drinks had come and gone. "Come on, y'all, let's go ride this bull. I'm feeling frisky," Summer shouted. Karashae and Autumn laughed. Chaianne didn't move until Karl gave her the green light. He patted her on the leg and nodded his head in the direction of the other three ladies. Chaianne swallowed the last of her drink and followed suit.

Summer went first, but didn't last long at all. She flew off the bull after thirty seconds. Karashae tried next and did a little better, but she still couldn't ride it 'til the end. Autumn let Chaianne go next. Chaianne had done the best thus far. She moved fluidly as the bull bucked forward and backward and spun around. But on the second spin, she lost her balance and fell off. She got cheers and claps from the other patrons, who were watching. It was Autumn's turn, and Abaki moved his chair so that he was facing the bull.

Karl nudged Stephon on the low so that he could peep how Abaki was watching Autumn closely.

Autumn mounted the bull and gave her sister a nod. She took several deep breaths to calm her nerves. She closed her eyes and blocked out everything around her. She imagined that she was the only one in the room and all she could hear was Kelly Rowland's "Motivation." The bull jerked backward and then forward, and Autumn was in her trance. She kept both arms above her head, her waist loose, and her back arched. She didn't fight the flow of the bull; she just went with the rhythm of it. Most people went wrong when they stiffened up. Autumn had learned from countless nights on her pole that the body had to be as relaxed as the mind; otherwise, the two would compete. The sound of Kelly's voice "motivated" her. Autumn kept her eyes closed and fantasized that it was Abaki underneath her and not some plastic bull. She moved like a porn star but performed like a lady.

When the bull stopped, Autumn opened her eyes. She hadn't heard the catcalls and whistles while she was riding. She looked at Abaki, and he was staring right back at her, expressionless. She looked away. She couldn't tell if he was pleased or repulsed. She didn't want to try to figure it out. She owed him nothing, and he owed her nothing. *It is what it is*, she thought. Karashae, Chaianne, and Summer were all smiling and high-fiving one another. They couldn't believe that quiet Autumn had just beat the brute of the bull.

"Damn, girl, you gonna have to give me some pointers. See, it's those quiet ones you got to watch out for," Chaianne said.

Autumn smiled at her and stole a glance at the table. She saw Abaki get up from his chair and walk toward the men's room.

"Damn, sis, I had no idea you could do that. You know how many people I saw try their skills at that thing only to be defeated?" Stephon said.

"Yeah, that was good," Karl said.

Abaki returned from the restroom and announced that he was about to leave. He slapped hands with Karl, Stephon, and Ajamaal, kissed Chaianne on the cheek, and waved goodbye to Karashae, Autumn, and Summer.

Autumn felt slighted. "Yeah, we should be going too," she suggested to Summer.

Everyone said their farewells and went their separate ways.

When Autumn got home, she skipped the shower and, instead, pulled out the bullet, her trusted toy, and imagined it was Abaki's tongue assaulting her love button.

Chapter 12: Abaki

Abaki needed to talk, and the best man for the task was his friend, Karl. They had known each other for five years. Abaki was there when Karl had asked Chaianne to spend the rest of her life with him, and he felt there was no better candidate now that he was wondering what it would be like to spend the rest of his life with Autumn. He needed to know what was up with her, though. He had to know more. He pulled into the parking lot of Karl's recording studio and parked in an open spot. He took the elevator to the second floor and tapped on the studio glass. Karl turned around and saw Abaki and told his artist to excuse him.

"What's up, man?" Karl asked as he leaned in and slapped hands with Abaki, giving him a brotherly pat on the back. Karl led Abaki to his office and offered him a seat.

"Man, I don't even know where to start. First off, last night, Autumn definitely surprised me when she said she wasn't on that independent stuff these females holler about nowadays. I really didn't expect that. I'm feeling her, man, and I don't know what the hell to do about it. I thought, for sure, she was going to brag about not having or needing a man, how a man couldn't do anything for her that she could do herself, how nowadays men are good for nothing anyway. You know, that superwoman talk."

Karl smiled. "Ah, so you picked up on her

vulnerability. You was feeling that, huh?"

"Heck yeah, man! I've yet to meet a woman who has all the things she has but would seriously consider giving it up if it meant a shot at love. That's the realest thing I've heard in a long time."

"Abe, we've known one another for years, and you've always been cool around females. Chicks normally come at you all hard and aggressive, and you hate that. Now, you feeling Autumn, and I don't know what to make of that. Just when I thought you were going to make it official with a chick, you end up breaking it off instead. I just can't figure you out, man."

"I know, bro. I really did think Inez and I would last longer. But she ruined that, not me. Before I even had a chance to step my game up, she started acting up," Abaki stated.

Karl snickered. "Look, only thing I can tell you is go for what you want. I don't know Autumn personally. I've never met her prior to tonight, but if she's close to Karashae then she must be cool peoples. Next time we play ball with Steph, ask him about her. She and his lady have been friends for a minute. So if anyone has the D's on her, it's him."

Abaki stood. "Thanks, man. I needed that. I'm going to try to find out what I can on my own first," he said, smiling.

Karl and Abaki slapped five again, and Abaki exited

the studio. Although it was out of character for him, he had to see what was up with Autumn. Deep inside, he felt like she was perfect, too perfect. After the bull ride, he was a bit uneasy though. He felt there was more about her than what met the eye. And if he was going to go through all the trouble of going back home and risking his life, he had to make sure she was worth it.

Chapter 13: Autumn

Normally, being at her shop was the highlight of Autumn's day. She loved everything about sex. There was nothing wrong with it when experienced between two consenting adults. She looked forward to assisting people with their sex lives by offering quality enhancements. But today was just one of those days. She vowed to do a quick work out and go straight home. After letting the last customer out, she was about to lock the doors and head up to the lounge when her cell phone rang. She raced back over to the counter and looked at the caller ID. Although it wasn't a number she recognized, she answered anyway.

"Hey, beautiful."

"I'm sorry, you have the wrong number," Autumn said, about to hang up.

"This is Autumn, right?"

"Yeah, who is this?"

"It's me, baby, Jerrell."

Autumn wanted to throw up. She kept getting calls from blocked numbers and she never answered. Now, when she'd answered the phone for a normal number, she wished she hadn't.

"Jerrell, just in case you were unconscious when I said it before, I will say it again; lose my number!" she spat, hanging up before he could utter another word.

There was nothing attractive about Jerrell. The face she once thought was cute now repulsed her. She wanted absolutely nothing to do with him. She texted Summer and told her she was going to be at the shop late just in case she went by the house looking for her.

When Autumn got to the lounge, she placed her phone inside her gym bag, turned on her stereo, and assumed the position. She enjoyed her solitary workouts and the tranquility that came with being alone in her shop, listening to her favorite songs, while keeping her body in great shape. Autumn did a final glide down the pole and looked around. While doing her dance she always kept her eyes closed. She liked to be in the moment, undistracted by outside influences. During the dance, she had sensed that she was being watched, but when she opened her eyes and looked around, no one was there. It had dawned on her that she'd never locked the shop doors or bolted the security gate. She immediately began to worry that someone was inside with her. She did a quick scan of the lounge and then did the same in her office and meeting room before checking downstairs. Once she'd given the premises a thorough survey, she locked the outside door, lowered the gate inside, and locked the inside door. She grabbed her things and set the alarm before heading out the back.

Chapter 14: Abaki

Since discovering that Autumn owned Mouth to Mouth, Abaki rode by all the time. He couldn't deny that he'd enjoyed the limited interactions he'd had with her. Even though she wore her thoughts on her sleeve and let it be known that she wanted a man, she still tried to be cordial and friendly without being flirty and forceful, or better yet, desperate. He was starting to think he had discovered a real lady. He'd enjoyed watching her that night at the bowling alley. He saw that she had a great sense of humor and was down to earth. She appeared to keep an equal balance of work and play. She was fun without being sloppy, energetic, minus the goofiness, and sweet and carefree, without being annoying. But just when he'd thought he might have found a woman worthy of his time, he'd watched her display a level of seductiveness that made him uneasy.

The way she danced and rode the bull left him feeling confused. Abaki wasn't sure how to take her performance. It was one of those things that could be interpreted as hypersexual, or she could just be secure with her sexuality. He'd had to leave before he said or did something that he would have regretted. He could tell she was comfortable with her body, but he wanted to pry, ask questions, just to see how comfortable she was. Did she sleep with a lot of guys? How many men had felt up her body? Abaki had questions he wasn't even sure he wanted the answers to.

After leaving Karl's studio, he raced home so he could walk his dogs and make it back to Mouth to Mouth before Autumn closed the shop. He wanted to talk to her and find out more about this lovely lady, about whom he'd grown quite intrigued, and he preferred to do it without a crowd of people. He had pulled into the parking lot just in time to see Autumn let the last customer out. He had watched as she hurried back to her counter and answered her cell phone. After several moments, she made a disgusted face and pulled the phone from her ear. She then picked up a bag, and he'd watched as she walked upstairs.

Abaki waited about five minutes to see if Autumn would come back down to lock up, but she didn't. Curiosity had gotten the best of him, so he exited his car and tried the door. Just as he'd expected, the doors were unlocked. He stepped inside and looked around. He heard the light sounds of music coming from upstairs, so he took the steps two at a time until he approached an open door. He could see that it was an office with two doors on either side. He walked to the left, from where he heard the music, and watched. He saw Autumn wrapping every limb seductively around a stripper pole in the middle of the floor. There was a song playing that he hadn't heard before, but it was obvious that Autumn was familiar with the tune. Every time the beat dropped, she did a funky move. When the music lingered, she waved her upper body while maintaining her hold on the pole with her legs. He watched in awe as she slid all the way down, twirled at the base, climbed back up, slid down again, stopped in the middle, and seductively moved her bottom half up and down the pole like she was gyrating on a penis.

Abaki's dick jumped. His dick had never jumped at the sight of a woman—ever, not even when he had attended strip clubs with his friends. And then he had a reaction he'd never felt from watching a woman. He couldn't tell if it was anger, jealousy, disgust, or lust—or a mixture of all four. He knew that he had to leave before one of two things happened: he'd despise her or sleep with her. And if he was being honest with himself, neither was a viable option. Abaki took a final look before leaving just as quietly as he had entered.

He got inside his car and slapped his hand on the steering wheel, gripping it tightly in frustration. Here he was thinking she had potential to be his wife, and she was humping a stripper pole. *I knew it! I should've known she was too good to be true.* He should have known that the good girl/businesswoman talk was a front for her *real* freaky occupation. She was like the other women he had heard about, the kind who used what they had to get what they wanted.

Autumn was gorgeous in his eyes. He could see that she had the body to be a stripper, even if it wasn't perfect. He figured she must have begun stripping to take care of her and her sister when they were younger. *She probably still strips to maintain her lifestyle.* He wasn't counting her pockets but he doubted that her business brought in enough money to maintain what he assumed to be a lavish lifestyle. He had noticed the diamonds she wore in her ears, on her wrists, and finger. Her sister drove a Benz jeep, so he figured that Autumn probably drove something comparable. *They probably strip at the same night club*, he reasoned. He banged his fist on the steering wheel again and started his car. Although he probably wouldn't admit it to his boys, the revelation of her freaky lifestyle pained his heart. He wasn't sure what his future wife would be like, but he definitely knew she wouldn't be a stripper. Abaki drove off, thinking that his desire to have Autumn would be just that—a desire. Nothing more. As far as he was concerned, he wanted nothing to do with her from here on out.

Chapter 15: Autumn

Autumn wasn't psychic, nor did she claim to be, but throughout the years, she had learned to pay more attention to that inner voice, the one that forewarned. And tonight, as she headed out the back door of her shop, she had a feeling that something wasn't right. The phone call from Jerrell had slighted her a bit, but she still was unable to shake the feeling that she was being watched. There had been a presence in her shop, and she'd felt it. Now, as she set out to leave, her uneasiness wouldn't wane. Being cautious and vigilant as she walked toward her car, she looked inside her purse for the mace she had purchased some time ago. Just as she lifted her head to check her surroundings, a familiar yet unwelcome face was staring right at her.

"Oh my goodness! You scared me half to death!" Autumn screeched. Although she tried not to show it, Jerrell's presence was making her increasingly nervous.

"Does that mean you're happy to see me then?" he asked as he leaned in for a kiss.

Autumn used both hands to gently, yet sternly push him away. "Jerrell, not now, okay? You've been drinking, and this is not the time for a conversation. I'll call you later," she lied and started to walk closer to her car. Her hands were shaking as she sorted through her keys to find her key fob and push the unlock button. *Just a few more steps, Autumn.*

Just keep walking, she told herself.

"No, you gonna talk to me now. You think I'm playing with you, bitch? Yo' ass ain't gonna keep avoiding me like I'm some sucka or sumthin'."

"Jerrell, please don't do this. I promise, this time, I will call you. Just go home and give me twenty minutes," Autumn pleaded in a shaky voice.

"I ain't finna go nowhere until you tell me why you been ackin' all distant. What, that muthafucka from the bowling alley doing ya real good, now? You fucking him, huh? Betcha he got this sweet pum pum, huh?" He forcefully grabbed Autumn's butt and crotch and starting licking on her neck.

"Stop, please, Jerrell! Please, stop. Help!" Autumn yelled. She knew it was in vein because all the other shops had closed over a half hour ago.

"Oh, don't whine now, baby. Wait 'til I stick this good thing up inside that stingy little pussy. You gonna be purring like a little kitty." Jerrell shoved Autumn to the ground, and when she tried to get back to her feet, he fell on top of her. He fumbled for his belt buckle to try to get his pants loose, but Autumn's constant kicking and clawing was making it difficult. She managed to get off one good swing that landed squarely on the left side of Jerrell's face.

"You bit—" he started to shout, but before he had the chance to finish his statement and his attack on her, his body went flying into the air.

Autumn sat crouched in the corner with her knees drawn to her chest, her body quivering. She watched in horror as Abaki landed punch after punch upon Jerrell's face, head, and body. He fought him like he was fighting for the heavy weight championship. After a good thirty seconds of continuous beating, Autumn finally reacted. She rose to her feet and went to pull Abaki off Jerrell.

"Abaki, please stop! You're going to kill him, please!" she cried.

Abaki looked at her tear-stricken face and seemed to melt at the sight of her fear and vulnerability. After hitting Jerrell one more time in the face and kicking him in the side, he backed away. Now his fury had a different target: Autumn. "Let go of me!" He snatched away. But even though he was upset with her, he still seemed to follow an instinctual desire to make sure she was okay. "Is this your car?" he asked as he glanced at Autumn's BMW.

Autumn was taken aback by his demeanor and wondered what she had done to deserve that kind of response. She was only trying to stop him from committing murder.

"Yes, this … this is my car," she stated, still a bit shaken by the whole ordeal. Autumn pressed the button to unlock her car doors. Abaki quickly grabbed her belongings off the ground and placed them in her back seat. As if a light bulb went off, Autumn asked, "Wha-what were you doing here? I mean thank you … for helping me, but how, how did you know?"

Abaki stared into her eyes for a brief moment. "None of that matters," he said. He opened her car door and waited for her to be seated. Once she was safely inside, he told her to get home, and then closed the door. She watched from her rearview mirror as he stood in the dark alley, apparently waiting for her to get a safe distance away.

During the drive home, she cried, contemplating and convulsing at the thought of what had just taken place. Was she grateful that someone had come to her rescue? Yes. Was she glad that it was Mr. Sexy? Yes. Was she happy that her celibacy wasn't compromised? Hell yes! But what she couldn't figure out was how the hell Abaki had managed to be at the right place at the right time. There was a reason, and tomorrow, she planned to find out. But right now, Autumn was having a difficult time fathoming her luck. Abaki was proving to be her knight in shining armor, yet he seemed so detached. He had shown no pity that she had just been attacked and no remorse for the way he'd beat Jerrell down. *What kind of man is he?*

Once inside the safety of her home, Autumn closed and locked the door and slid down the wall until the floor and her rear connected. She felt like she needed to cry more to cleanse her wounded soul, but no tears would form. Her heart palpitated and her mind wandered. She couldn't wrap her head around what had taken place. Naturally, she wanted to call around and get Abaki's number; she had questions. But she knew that wasn't appropriate. It was late, and she was tired. She wanted so badly to just crawl into bed and go to sleep. However, the reality of tonight's events had left her feeling like last week's garbage—dirty. She knew it was too late to call anybody and tell them what happened. Although she knew she should, she didn't even report what Jerrell had done to her to the police and she wasn't sure if she would. Autumn was exhausted, so she took a shower, said her prayers, and climbed into bed.

Chapter 16: Autumn

Typically, every night before falling asleep, Autumn would remove her bullet from her nightstand drawer and use it to bring her to an orgasm. But with all the craziness that had taken place that evening, the last thing on her mind was making herself cum. She tossed and turned as she slept. Her ringing cell phone jarred her from her restless sleep.

"Open the door," a man's voice said to her as soon as she answered. Autumn recognized the voice instantly, and she followed his command. When she undid the second lock, her door swung open, and he pushed her up against the wall in the foyer. In one swift move, the door swung closed and locked. He lifted her off her feet and carried her into the kitchen. With one swipe of a hand, papers, unopened mail, keys, and other miscellaneous items were now on the marble floor. Her tongue moved in an intense tango with her guest's as he pinched and twisted her nipples. Normally, it would have been painful, but the stimulation, coupled with the pleasure of an oral war, was arousing.

Autumn tried to wiggle out of the lock she was in, but it proved pointless. She gave up and succumbed to being a prisoner of ecstasy. When they were both tired from their tongue battle, he carried her body over to the island that centered the kitchen, and he forced her to lie flat. She heard her refrigerator open and then close, and she felt the sensation of something cold pouring up and down her midsection. She then heard a can shake and felt the contents dispensing all over her love box. The coldness of the condiments, mixed with the warmness of his tongue, which devoured everything that was spread over her body, was mind-blowing. Just when she thought the tongue torture was coming to an end, he lifted her legs into the air and extended them to a near-perfect 180-degree angle. The pleasure her body had received just moments ago was no comparison to the phenomenon cascading inside her now. He must have known she was on the brink of an orgasm because he stopped the oral abuse on her love button and watched as the muscle continued to swell and pulsate.

She almost caught whiplash as he quickly lifted her off the island and placed her on the counter by the butter rolls. Autumn's mind appropriately played R. Kelly's "In the Kitchen" as his massive cock greeted her love tunnel. "Yes!" Autumn called out. "Fuck me hard. Please, fuck me harder, harder. Yes. Don't stop. I need this!" Just when she was about to cum again, he pulled out of her, took her off the counter, and turned her around, placing both hands on top of it. He lifted her legs so that each one rested comfortably in the crook of his arms and penetrated her once more. This time, Autumn didn't need to say a word. She couldn't. His dick had her clenching muscles she hadn't used in a very long time. She felt her vaginal walls grasp his dick in a way that she thought maybe only virgin pussy was capable of. She began to moan loudly, and her breaths became more labored. "Oh, sh— ... I'm cumming! Don't stop. Plee-e-ase. Don't. Fucking. Stop. Oh, oh, oh yes ..."

Autumn jumped up, bewildered. She heard banging on her front door and her phone ringing. She looked around frantically while listening intently to see if someone was trying to break into her home. She hopped out of bed and grabbed her cell phone on her way to the door. She answered the phone just as she peeked through the peephole, and she hung up when she realized that it was Summer both at her door and on her phone. Before opening the door, Autumn looked around her living room and over into her kitchen. Everything she had placed on the kitchen counter the night before was still intact. No papers, keys, or mail was strewn about on the floor as her dream had illustrated. Autumn was disappointed and relieved at the same time. She swung the door open as Summer and the morning sun greeted her simultaneously. Normally, she was happy to see her sister, but this wasn't one of those moments. Anyone who ruined a great sex dream right before orgasm should be shot with shit and then killed for stinking, in her opinion.

"What?!" Autumn snapped.

"What you mean, 'What?' What the fuck did I do?" Summer asked as Autumn left her standing in the open doorway and walked into the kitchen.

"Oh, I see," Summer said. "I must have ruined a wet dream."

Autumn was stunned. "Yeah, right. What makes you say that?"

"Because there's a big-ass wet spot on the back of your nightgown."

Autumn flushed.

Summer bent over laughing.

"Shut up, Summer!" Autumn went into the bathroom and slammed the door.

"Don't be mad at me because you'd rather dream about dick than feel it."

When Autumn came out of the bathroom, Summer was going through Autumn's cell phone. Autumn snatched it out of her hand.

"What did I tell you about my cell phone? Do it again, and I will break your fingers."

"Okay, gee! Why you gotta get violent?"

"What you want, anyway? Ain't it a little too early for you to be up?"

"Well, I just got off work at seven-thirty, and then I dropped Ajamaal off at work. When you didn't text me back last night, I got curious and decided to swing by afterwards. Just wanted to check on big sis. Sorry I did," Summer said with no sincerity.

"Oh my God!" Autumn exclaimed. She'd almost

forgotten about last night.

"What?"

"Hold on. Let me get Karashae on the line. I only want to tell this story once." Karashae answered the phone groggily. "Shae, it's Autumn. Wake up. I got something to tell you."

"What, girl? What is it? Everything okay?"

"Well, kind of, I guess. Last night after closing the shop, I was attacked."

"What?!" Summer screeched.

"Are you serious?" Karashae asked, sounding fully awake now. Autumn heard Stephon ask what happened. "Autumn, Stephon just got out of the shower and wants to know what happened. I'm putting you on speaker, okay?"

"Okay."

"Go ahead, Autumn."

"When I was leaving the shop last night, Jerrell's crazy ass was in the back alley. He started talking all crazy about me not calling him and ignoring his calls, talking about how he wasn't letting me leave before he took the you-know-what. He must have been drunk as hell, because I smelled alcohol on his breath. "

"Oh my god!" Summer squealed.

"He knocked me to the ground and got on top of me. When I saw him reaching for his belt buckle, I started freaking out. I kicked and punched him so hard, but I couldn't get him to let up to save my life, literally."

"What the fuck?!" Stephon bellowed. "Damn, Autumn, I'm sorry that happened to you. Why didn't you park in the front?"

"I don't know," Autumn answered honestly. "I really didn't think about it. I'm so accustomed to pulling in the back that I didn't even consider safety concerns."

"So, what happened? How did you escape?" Summer asked.

"I didn't," Autumn admitted. She heard Summer and Karashae gasp. Stephon grumbled.

"Oh no, Autumn! He raped you?" Summer asked, almost in tears.

"No, he didn't. Abaki beat the crap out of him."

"Abaki?!" they all exclaimed in unison.

"How the hell—" Karashae started to ask.

"I have no idea what he was doing or why he was there. I even tried asking once I gathered my thoughts, but he dismissed me. Honestly, it seemed as if he was almost upset with me for being the victim. I don't know, y'all, but it was really strange."

"Oh my," Karashae shrilled.

"So, what happened next?" Summer asked.

"Nothing. He picked my things up and placed them in my car, held the driver side door open for me, closed the door, and watched me drive off."

"How fucking romantic," Summer said sarcastically.

"Yeah, real romantic. He didn't even ask if I was okay to drive, if I wanted him to take me home, nothing! He just walked me to the car and watched me drive away."

"Wow, he's like a superhero, walking around saving women," Karashae commented. "So what happened to Jerrell? Did you call the cops?"

"No, I didn't. I'm sure that after how Abaki handled him, he learned his lesson. Abaki was still standing there when I left, and honestly, I have no idea what happened to him."

Stephon finally said, "Yo, I guess that dude really is exceptional. I haven't met anyone of his caliber, ever! That's some wild shit. Wait 'til I tell Karl this one."

"Girl, we got to find out his deal for real, for real," Summer said.

"And I know just who we can ask," Karashae added.

"Chaianne!" Summer and Autumn said at the same time.

"Yup," Karashae confirmed, sounding like Sebastian.

Karashae called Chaianne and invited her to spend the day with them, and she gladly accepted. They made plans to hang out that Thursday instead of Saturday because Summer had to work the weekend shift. Chaianne had a business seminar, and as an event planner for a well-known Dallas-based company, Karashae had an event coming up, and she wanted to use the whole weekend to prepare for it. They decided that they would go to the spa and then out to eat.

Autumn couldn't get Abaki off her mind. She wanted to personally thank him for protecting her chastity. Although she wouldn't say exactly that, she did want to tell him that she appreciated his voluntary intervention. She couldn't wait any longer; she had to see him. She had already determined that after closing the shop on Friday, she would find out where he spent most of his time and pay him a surprise visit.

Chapter 17: Abaki

The past few nights had been rough for Abaki. On one hand, he wished he'd never shown up at Autumn's shop unannounced, and on the other hand, he was glad that he had. His intent was to get to know more about Autumn, just not in that way. Seeing her had totally crippled his good girl image of her and confirmed his suspicions. She just wasn't the girl for him. He erased the thought from his mind so he could get his head back into the game.

"D up, Abe, man," Karl told Abaki.

"Nah, don't say anything, K. I'm about to take it to the hole on him," Stephon boasted.

Stephon dribbled the ball a few more times before making his move. He traveled up the court and attempted to fake a left-hand layup and switched last minute to make the shot with his right. Abaki had read the play and already knew what move Stephon was going to make, so as soon as he did, Abaki was right there with the block.

"Yeah!" Karl yelled, giving Abaki a high five.

Stephon's partner wasn't enthused. "Yo, Steph, man, how you let him style on you like that?" he whined.

"Whatever, man," Stephon said. "He coaches ball for a living. What you expect?"

"Yeah, I guess. You got that," Stephon's friend gave everyone dap and announced that he had to go.

Stephon, Karl, and Abaki walked over to the bench and took a break.

"I heard you was playing superhero again," Karl said to Abaki.

Abaki just looked at him, knowing exactly what he was talking about.

"Yo, man, that was good looking. Autumn is good people. She's like my sister, and the thought of something foul happening to her fucks me up. But let me ask you, what the hell were you doing there?"

"I was driving down that side road when I spotted a man being overly aggressive with a woman. At first, I couldn't tell that it was Autumn, but as I got out of the car and took a closer look, I reacted. So ..." He let the rest speak for itself.

"Sooo, you just happened to be in the area?" Karl questioned.

Abaki wasn't one to lie, and Karl knew it. He wanted Abe to admit that he was feeling Autumn. "Honestly? No, I didn't just happen to be in the area. I knew she owned the joint because I stopped by the hardware store one day to grab some stuff, and I saw her unlocking the shop. After watching her at the bowling alley and then at the beer hall, I grew an attraction or a curiosity, I should say. So, that night, I swung by her shop to see if I could catch her leaving. I saw her let a customer out, but she never locked the door; she ran back inside. When she didn't come out after about five minutes or so, I got out, tried the door, and it was unlocked. The rest doesn't matter. I thought she was someone I would be interested in, but I don't do strippers."

"Stripper?" Stephon gave a confused look. "What makes you think that?"

"Yeah, man. I figured she was into something kinky by the way she danced and rode that bull. That was quite impressive."

Stephon and Karl looked at one another and smirked, remembering how Abaki had turned his chair around to face Autumn at the beer hall.

"Then when I go into the shop, I hear music playing, so I followed the sound. Upstairs, there was an office that led to two rooms." Abaki didn't know if he should share what he saw. Even though he had decided Autumn wasn't the woman for him, he didn't want the image of her dancing on the pole in the heads of his homeboy and homeboy's friend. "In one of the rooms, she had couches, chairs, and ... a *pole*."

"A pole?" Karl asked.

"Yeah, man, a damn stripper pole."

"Oh, hell no, man," Stephon interjected. "Autumn ain't a damn stripper. Believe me when I tell you she's wholesome. That's not her style at all. I never been upstairs, but my lady and I have been to the shop a couple of times. Shae told me that she rents the room out for certain functions, like bachelorette parties, ladies nights, and for private lessons. I can assure you that Autumn is not an exotic dancer. She's definitely a good woman. Her and her sister were dealt a fucked up hand in life and they made the best of it without compromising their integrity or disgracing their family name."

Abaki didn't know what to say or how to respond. He had been sure that Autumn lived an alternative lifestyle. Now that he was hearing the exact opposite, he didn't know how to deviate from his premature convictions.

Karl looked at him and placed his right hand on Abaki's left shoulder before speaking. "Man, if there's a part of you that likes shorty, then you need to holla at her, for real. From what my man, Steph, here is saying, you might be close to finding the one. All the years I've known you, I have yet to see you this interested in a woman, not even your girl, Inez. Stop being so guarded and give love a try. I can promise you, it's the best feeling in the world. Trust me, I know."

"Me too," Stephon added.

Abaki didn't respond. He decided that if he was going to give Autumn a chance, he had to make sure she was the *one* before announcing his decision to pursue her further to his boys. He picked up the ball and threw it competitively toward Karl and Stephon. "Let's see what you two can do with little ol' me," he challenged.

Chapter 18: Autumn

All the ladies met at Destiny's Day Spa and greeted one another with genuine hugs. Their hostess welcomed them into the reception area.

"This place is really nice," Autumn said.

"Yeah, I can get used to this," Chaianne chimed in.

Summer nodded in agreement. They all opted to have private rooms for their massages. They didn't want to ruin the relaxing experience with girl talk. After the massage and before their facials and pedicures, they all agreed to meet at the sauna to chat. There was information to obtain, and Autumn couldn't wait to get it.

"I swear I'm about to lose ten pounds by the time we leave here," Karashae said.

"Girl, that makes two of us. Since I've been with Karl, I've packed on at least ten pounds. He swears it's all in the right places, but I just feel so … so fat," Chaianne whined.

"Don't I know it. Since I've been dating Ajamaal, all we do is go out to eat. If it wasn't for all the sex, my ass wouldn't be able to fit into any of my jeans."

"Autumn, if you want to stay fit, stay single," Karashae suggested.

Autumn wasn't interested in any talk about being single. She had been alone far too long. She needed info on Mr. Sexy, so she cut straight to the point. "Um, Chaianne, do you mind if I ask you about Abaki?"

"No, girl, not at all. I don't know much about him, but I can tell you what I do know. What's up?"

"Well, what kind of person is he? Is he dating? Does he have kids? You know, the basics."

"As far as I know, Abaki is pretty much to himself. He's quiet, observant, and calculative. He coaches basketball at one of the local high schools, resides in North Dallas, and basically lives a modest life. From what Karl said, he has some 'unfinished business' back home that he's been mentioning lately."

"How old is he?"

"Oh, he's thirty-three, I believe. No kids at all, and he was dating this crazy chick, Inez, but once she showed her true colors, he started distancing himself from her. And that's all I really know. He's extremely laid back."

"Yeah, until he's pissed off," Karashae added.

Autumn chuckled. She knew Karashae had a point. Autumn hadn't missed Chaianne's mention of "unfinished business," but she had decided not to inquire about it at that time. Some things she simply wanted to extract directly from him.

"So Autumn, do you mind telling me a little more about you?" Chaianne asked.

Autumn thought about her question and how much she wanted to reveal. "Well, let's see. I am the oldest of four girls. You've met Summer, and we had twin sisters, Winter and Spring, but they passed away at the same time when they were only six days old. SIDS, they called it. My parents gave us a good life, and just like any other family, we had complications, but we were well taken care of. We moved here about twelve years ago. The last of our family passed away, and we stayed, choosing to make a life here," Autumn told her. She hadn't lied; she just hadn't told the story in sequence or with much detail.

"Oh, okay. How old are you, if you don't mind my asking?"

"No, not at all. I'll be thirty in October. And you?"

"I just turned thirty in March. I was born and raised in Albany. My mom went to prison when I was in the third grade, and I grew up under DCYF custody until I aged out at eighteen. That's how I recognized you. Once you've been in the system for a while, you kind of recognize new faces. Did you go to the local schools?"

"Middle school and most of high school. I still have friends back in Albany though. In fact, my sister and I are going in June."

"Oh, really? When in June?"

Summer joined the conversation. "For Father's Day. We go every year to visit our family's plots."

"I'm going to be there around that time too. I usually bring my daughter, Quay, every summer. She stays from

June to August, and I stay for a few days or so. My closest friend still lives there, so me and my other friend, who flies in from Cali, meet there every other year," Chaianne stated as she adjusted her bottom to get into a more comfortable position.

"Well dang, everybody don't leave at once!" Karashae jumped in, feeling a bit left out.

"Seriously, Karashae, you should come. Chaianne, did you book your flight yet?" Summer asked.

Chaianne raised her eyebrows in realization. "Actually, no, and I need to. I've been putting it off for the past two days. So if you really want to roll, then talk to Stephon and let me know. I can hold off booking me and my daughter's flights until tomorrow."

Shae got excited and smiled. "Okay, yeah I'm going to do just that."

"Heyyyy, it sounds like a party back home." Summer threw her right hand in the air, waving a few times and snapping her fingers. "Now let's get out of here before our skin melts off," Summer joked.

They all laughed.

Chapter 19: Abaki

Abaki was out back, tossing the ball with his two dogs, Yin and Yang, when he got a text from Karl, letting him know that he was going to swing by to check him out. He rarely had company, and although Karl did stop by sometimes, something told him that his visit was going to be more about Autumn than anything. He couldn't front, she had been heavily on his mind since she was attacked. Unbeknownst to her, since that night, he did go to her shop every night, just to make sure she made it to her car safely. Each time he saw her, he just wanted to reach out and hug her, to let her know that he was sorry for misjudging her. Except, to do so would leave him feeling vulnerable. Plus, he wanted to know more about her. There were things about him that he chose to keep private until he absolutely knew a person. Some people were too caught up in material things, and Abaki didn't want to be associated with those kinds of folks. Even though Autumn seemed to have made a good living for herself, he wanted to know how she'd made that happened.

He watched as Karl exited his car and met him at the front door. The two of them exchanged pleasantries and went inside.

"What's good, my boy?" Karl said once they were seated.

"Nothing much, man. What's going on with you?"

"Same ole. That new artist I signed last month is doing well. Her shit blowing up the charts. Other than that, you know, everything regular. I haven't seen you or talked to you since we played ball. What's good?"

"You know, same old stuff, man. I have my team in the gym a lot more this week. We got a game later this evening. I'm heading to the school in a couple of hours to do some warm-ups. You should come to the game."

"I just might do that and bring the missus and the kids. What time?"

"It starts at seven-thirty tonight."

"Okay, I'm there. Let me ask you something; what you doing the week of the seventeenth?"

"Of June?" Abaki asked.

"Yeah."

"Nothing that I know of. Why, wassup?"

"My wife called me while I was on my way here. She said that Autumn and her sister go back to New York every year to visit their loved ones' gravesites. You know my wife goes every year too, to drop Quay off. I guess Karashae is trying to work something out to go. I'm going to be in New York City that same week, checking out a new artist and promoting current ones, and I want you to roll."

Abaki gave it some thought. It would be a great opportunity for him to get up close and personal with Autumn. "Aiight, cool, man. I'll book my flight tomorrow.

Text me the dates."

"Aiight, brotha. I'll do that!"

Abaki walked Karl to the door and waited until he reached his car before closing it. He wasn't sure what would come of this trip, but he hoped to gain a better understanding of Autumn and for her to get the same from him. As a man, he rarely spoke of his inner feelings to people. When rebels had killed his mother and sisters, he'd seen, firsthand, the anguish his father had felt at the realization that he wasn't able to protect his family the way he had advised his son a man should. Even after their deaths, he had never heard his father speak of the hurt, guilt, and void that he'd felt, nor did he see him show it. But Abaki knew. His father had spent way too much time with him, teaching him the three P's for him not to be able to identify the slightest change in his demeanor.

Mr. Lemande was a warrior, a man of great stature and respect. He never drank or smoked, and he stayed in good shape, mentally and physically. "Son, the enemy will try to attack you from all angles. You must always be prepared, mind, body, and soul." He'd told him to always keep his hand close to his chest. "Real men don't show emotion. We're logical creatures." His father's principles had been drilled into Abaki's head so much that he didn't even mourn the loss of the only women who were ever close to him.

During those many times when he was home alone, he

thought often of his family. He missed the scent, touch, and gentleness of his mother. He missed the giddiness, graciousness, and innocence of his little sisters. He missed the structure, tenacity, and greatness of his father. Abaki missed his family, and at this stage in the game, he craved one of his own. That was why he needed Autumn to be more than he had imagined. He needed her to be the woman he dreamed of. He needed her to be the best woman for him. He needed a wife. He needed Autumn.

He had to make certain that she was the one before risking his life to go back home. He regretted what had taken place so many years ago, but as he knew, and as his father had told him, the problem needed to be addressed. Abaki didn't want to feel like he owed anyone any longer, nor could he fully commit to the woman with whom he chose to share his last name until it was settled, Then there was the issue of his family's assets. He hadn't been back to Sierra Leone since his father had brought him to America, where he was told he would remain forever, unless the situation was handled. The thought of going back to a place he hadn't been in so long disturbed him, but the thought of *not* going back concerned him. If things worked out well while he was in New York, the next thing he planned to do was book a flight to Africa.

Chapter 20: Autumn

Autumn heard her phone buzzing, but she was assisting a customer, so she let her voicemail take the call. After locking up shop, she waited until she reached her car to check the message: *"Hey Autumn, it's Chaianne. I got your number from Shae. I hope you don't mind. This is my number. Please store it. I was calling to invite you to join me and my family for Abaki's game tonight. If you're interested, call me back. Later."* Autumn was excited and anxious. She had intended to find out how to locate Abaki, but she had no idea that his whereabouts would just fall in her lap. She called Chaianne back and got all the necessary details and agreed to meet her at the game.

Autumn went home to take a shower. During the ride home, she had decided to wear one of her everyday blazers, a pair of jeans, and some peep-toe pumps. She wanted to be casual *and* cute. As she took another spin in the mirror, she concluded that her mission was accomplished.

The parking lot of the school was packed, and for a second, she got nervous about not being able to find a spot until she spotted someone pulling out. She quickly parked and walked briskly toward the school. She was digging inside her purse for her phone to call Chaianne when she spotted Karl walking back into the gym.

"Hi, Karl!"

"Hey, Autumn. Good seeing you again. Glad you could make it. C'mon, follow me. Chaianne and the kids are right over here."

Abaki's team was playing at home tonight, so the bleachers were on the other side of the gym, opposite the entrance.

"Hey, girl," Chaianne greeted her with a broad smile and warm hug.

"Hello," Autumn said, reaching out to return the gesture.

"These are my kids. This is Quay. She's eleven. And K.J. He's two. Kids, this is Mommy's friend, Autumn."

"Hi, Ms. Autumn," the kids said in unison.

Autumn could tell that they were good kids. Chaianne didn't even have to tell them to use a title when addressing someone older; they did it automatically. She was digging Chaianne's parenting skills already. Her children were beautiful. Quay looked just like Chaianne, while K.J. was an even mix of his mother and father.

Autumn looked onto the court nervously to see if she could spot Abaki. She didn't know what to expect since he surely wasn't expecting to see her—or was he? "Um, Chaianne, did Abaki know I was coming?"

"I didn't tell him. Babe, did you tell Abe that Autumn was coming to the game?"

"Nah, I didn't tell him. Why? You uneasy?" Karl asked

Autumn.

"Kind of," she admitted. "He's just so standoffish and I don't want him to be upset that I'm here. This is his domain, you know."

"Nah, you good, ma," Karl reassured her. He may come off that way, but he really is a cool guy. He just plays his hand real close when he doesn't know people. He likes to keep folks guessing."

The announcer got on the mic and introduced the two competing teams. The away team's starting five and their coach were introduced first and were welcomed by the fans that had shown up to support them. The same was done for the home team, and they received thunderous applause. Autumn couldn't take her eyes off Abaki. He looked quite debonair in his slacks, button up, and tie. The last few times she had encountered him, he was dressed casually. Today, she was able to see him in a different fashion, literally.

His tall, muscular frame, baldhead, and poised stature made him that much more alluring. Autumn couldn't keep her eyes from visually molesting Abaki. He was unlike any other man she had encountered. Sure, she'd met men who wanted to stand up for their lady, only to be knocked down right in front of her, men who played tough guy, but really weren't. She could see that Abaki wasn't an act. He was the real deal. She could only imagine what the future would hold for the two of them, if anything at all.

From the beginning of the game through half time and right up until the final minutes, she had witnessed several of the players' mothers from both sides trying to get his attention. She watched as the ladies whispered to one another, giving flirtatious stares and suggestive gestures. During halftime, they had so much to say to their sons, when, in her mind, there wasn't that much to be said. They seemed to be overzealous toward a man who didn't appear to be fazed or interested in the least. He took it all in stride and remained focused on the game. Autumn silently wondered why he didn't take the bait that was so easily available. She was certain that he wasn't gay. Autumn could sense that he had a certain standard, but she couldn't fathom exactly what it was.

With twenty seconds left in the game, Abaki's team was down by four points. He called a time-out, and his players formed a huddle. From where she was, Autumn couldn't make out what was being said, but she knew that whatever he'd told them must have motivated them, because she noticed a change in the players' demeanors after the huddle. One of his players threw the ball in. He did a couple of dribbles, moved forward a few feet, stepped back, and tossed the ball in the air for a clean three-point jump shot. The home crowd roared and was now on their feet. With less than ten seconds to play, the opposing team had the ball, and one of the players dribbled one bounce too many, allowing

Abaki's lead man to steal, run it back to his side of the court, and dunk it on one of the opposing players, winning the game by one point: 68-67. The crowd roared, and the players celebrated by slapping high-fives, jumping on each other, and embracing Coach Abaki. Autumn stood and clapped too. She was proud and nervous. She wanted so badly for the man whom she had waited all week to see to show a little bit of interest in seeing her as well.

After the game was over, Autumn and Chaianne made small talk until most of the crowd had left. Of course, there were about three women still lingering and Autumn knew why. Not wanting to step on any toes, Autumn waited for Abaki to emerge from the locker room. She wanted to see how he would react to seeing her before she approached him. When he exited, he immediately noticed Karl and threw him a head nod. It took him all of two seconds to lock eyes with Autumn; he held her gaze for several moments. Autumn watched as the three women approached Abaki. They bore overzealous smiles and did more talking with their bodies and eyes than with their mouths. She peeped how he kept glancing at her. She wasn't sure if he was trying to read her reaction or make sure she hadn't left. She watched him thank the ladies and make his way over to where they were.

He gave Karl dap, kissed Chaianne on the cheek, and hugged the kids.

Karl reached his right hand out to shake Abaki's and

dapped him on the back, "Yooo, good game, bro. Y'all definitely came through those last few seconds. The way you tear shit up when we play, those kids are lucky to have you, man."

"Yeah, that was a great game," Chaianne complimented.

"Thanks," Abaki said.

"Well, aiight. We gonna get going and get these kids home. It's past their bedtime, and they're cutting into our time," Karl said, grabbing Chaianne around the waist.

"Alright, brotha. Thanks for coming through and bringing your family. The love is appreciated."

"Don't even mention it. Handle ya business." Karl briefly glanced at Autumn, who was standing there, waiting.

Autumn wondered what he made of her presence. She knew they would run into one another again because of their mutual friends. But she was almost certain that it probably never crossed his mind that she would show up at one of his games.

Autumn spoke first. "Hello."

"Hello, to you, too," Abaki responded.

"I hope you're okay with me showing up here ... at your game like this. I hope I didn't intrude too much."

"No intrusion at all. It's a surprise, but a pleasant one."

Autumn's heart skipped a beat. "Um, I just wanted to

personally thank you ... for helping me that night. If you weren't there, I—"

"But I was. No need to worry about if I wasn't."

They shared an awkward silence for a brief moment before Autumn spoke again. "Great game. Your team played very well."

"Thanks," he replied humbly.

Another pregnant pause.

"Well, I just wanted to personally thank you. I'll be going now."

"Wait. I'll walk you to your car."

He shook hands with the two officials and walked back to Autumn. "After you."

Autumn wasn't good at making idle conversation, but it would take a few moments to make it back to her car, and she didn't want there to be dead silence. "So, how long have you been coaching?" she asked him.

"I've coached basketball for five years," he responded, watching as she used her tongue to tickle the corner of her mouth and then lick her lips. "I enjoy what I do. The boys are great kids, and with a little guidance and discipline, they'll go a long way. I've actually had several of my players earn either full or partial scholarships all because they excelled at what they liked. That's how life should be, ya know. Someone can tell if they love what they do because they will continue to do it with or without reward. My boys love to play and would do so whether a scholarship was on the line or not. That's what I like about them. They're passionate about this sport."

Autumn was taken aback by how vocal he was. This was the most she'd heard him say in the couple of times they'd encountered each other. Autumn told him about her teaching gig and how she enjoyed a similar passion. She told him that she, too, had been teaching for five years. When they reached her car, she tripped the alarm and Abaki opened the door for her and waited until she climbed in. She lowered the window before allowing him to close the door.

"Drive safe, Autumn."

That was the second time she'd heard him say her name. And although he pronounced the 't' harder than he needed to, she liked the way it rolled off his tongue. It was masculine, yet gentle, the same way he interacted with her.

"I, um, uh ... Would you mind catching a movie one day?" There, she'd said it. She'd finally gotten up the nerve to ask Abaki on a date. She wasn't sure if he would agree, but she wasn't about to let another night end without making an attempt to get to know Abaki, the man inside.

He didn't answer right away. Autumn watched his eyes closely for any signs of apprehension or lack of interest.

"We will see," he said, closing the door. "Goodnight, Autumn."

Chapter 21: Abaki

Abaki stood there and watched as Autumn pulled off until her vehicle was no longer visible. He hadn't hesitated because he was uncertain, he hesitated because he was caught up. He was intrigued by the way her tongue expertly moistened her lips, captivated at how her eyes caressed his face, and moved by how her well-manicured fingers added to her hands' gracefulness and beauty. He hadn't realized he was holding his breath until his body forced him to exhale. The last thing he expected was for her to ask him out. He wouldn't say that Autumn came off as shy, but she had given him the impression that she was femininely reticent. He definitely liked that about her. Friendly, but not forceful. He pictured her licking her lips and wondered just how many guys had felt those lips in more ways than one. How many men had she rubbed all over or how many had rubbed all over her. He wasn't necessarily looking for a virgin, but he didn't want a woman who had been around and back again. He expected that any American woman who had what it took to capture his heart would be sexually active to some degree. He just hoped that it wasn't more than he was willing to accept.

Autumn was the first woman in a long time to sexually arouse him as quickly as she had, but not the first to capture his attention. He had met Inez six months ago and had been mesmerized by her lady-like ways. She dressed, walked, and spoke with class. She was a lady, or so he'd thought. Just when he was beginning to think that she had what it took to make him consider settling down with an American woman, she had started acting jealous, coming to all his games, trying to intimidate his players' mothers. It had gotten so bad that she'd almost had a few scuffles. She popped up at his home, even after he'd asked her to let him know when she was coming. He had even caught her snooping through his wallet, cell phone, and pants pockets. After that, he knew she wasn't the woman for him. He was honest and had told her that they could no longer date. She'd seemed to take the news well at first, but after a while, he would see her driving by his house and riding past the school after practice. Women like that brought drama, and at this stage in his life, Abaki had no time for drama.

After only a brief comparison of the two, he noticed genuine differences between Autumn and Inez. Inez hadn't initially come off as forceful, but after he'd shown interest, she had changed. Autumn seemed a bit more reserved with her attraction. Inez had mentioned wanting to settle down, get married, and be a housewife. Abaki had no problems with that, but because of his family's status back home, he preferred a woman with a little more ambition. America was the "land of opportunity," and he liked a woman who knew how to take advantage of that. Although his wife would never have to work a day in her life, he still wanted her to have goals of her own, things that he could help her work toward, possibilities that would afford abilities to their kids for many years to come. There was a lot he had to consider. And before he revealed himself fully, he had to make sure that Autumn was a woman of substance. Abaki started his car and buckled his seat belt. Instead of turning on the music, he let the memories of his encounters with Autumn be his entertainment during the ride home.

Chapter 22: Autumn

While walking on the treadmill, Autumn thought about how she hadn't heard from Abaki all week. Once she'd put herself out there and asked for a date, she had anticipated a response. If it wasn't for him showing up at her shop yesterday to make a purchase, she would have thought he'd skipped town. She had been truly surprised when he'd walked through the doors. She didn't want to, but she greeted him just as she would have any other customer and let him go about his business. She tried her damnedest not to watch him as he moved about the store, but she knew that at some point they would come face-to-face because she had to cash him out. She also knew that she wasn't going to offer again. If Abaki wanted to go on a date with her, he would have to ask, plan, and pay for it.

She had put herself out there in the past only to get hurt. She'd ask for a date and the guys would accept only to cancel on her. Or they would call her to "hang out," get the goods, and then only call her when it was time for the next nut. Those kinds of situations had ultimately led to her decision to become celibate.

When Abaki had approached the register, she'd done all she could to avoid staring at him. "Did you find everything okay?" she'd asked, maintaining her professionalism, but managing not to look up at him.

"Yes, I did," he answered.

Autumn had noted the blindfold, handcuffs, and massage oil. She placed the three items in the bag just as she'd told him his total. "That'll be twenty-three, twenty-nine." Again, he'd paid with cash, giving her a twenty-dollar bill and a five. She gave him the penny first. "For your thoughts," she'd said and then handed him the rest of his change and receipt. "Thanks for shopping at Mouth to Mouth."

Autumn was glad another customer was waiting in line. She and Abaki had no time to say anything else. He took his change and left her store just as smoothly as he had entered. She couldn't help but wonder who the lucky lady was who benefited from his purchases. The only other way she could justify his shopping at her establishment was to conclude that he was either a porn star or a stripper. She couldn't imagine him being the former. It just didn't fit his personality. Plus, she had seen almost all the porn videos featuring black stars, and she'd never come across his face. And surely someone as sexy, handsome, and masculine as Abaki would have been featured in almost every video made.

Autumn increased the speed on the treadmill and began sprinting. She turned the music up on her headphones and allowed the beat of the song to match the beat of her feet. Mary J. Blige crooned about searching for a "Real

Love," just like Autumn. Autumn just hoped and prayed that she would find hers too.

Chapter 23: Abaki

Abaki hadn't expected Autumn to react to him the way she had when he'd stopped by her shop. His intentions were to explain his distance, but he didn't think she would go for it. American women tended to develop an attitude that only a sista could conjure. He didn't want that, so he didn't do or say anything to provoke it. His plan was to let her know that he was more than interested in a date with her. If he could've had it his way, they would've gone somewhere right after the game. But between his coaching and volunteering for Habitat for Humanity this past week, he had very little time to devote to anything outside of that.

Just as he had done with the other purchases he'd made at her shop, he'd left the bag on the side of a road, hoping that someone who could actually use the items would pick them up. He had no use for them. He thought it would be rude to just go into her shop and not purchase anything. He could tell that Autumn was getting fed up with his antics. He had to make a move soon or risk losing her altogether. He vowed that once they made it to New York, he'd put his best foot forward and see to it that Autumn Hughes knew that Abaki Lemande was interested in getting to know her outside of their small circle.

Chapter 24: Autumn

Summer's birthday had finally arrived, and the girls were looking forward to the celebration. They had landed in Albany, NY shortly after two o'clock in the afternoon and went straight to the cemetery before checking into a downtown hotel. They asked the cab driver to wait while they paid their respects. Their grandfather and Grammy, three uncles, Aunt Rose, their twin baby sisters, Winter and Spring, and of course, their parents were all buried on the same grounds. Summer and Autumn would visit each relative separately, placing a single rose on each of their graves, except their parents and Grammy. On Mother's Day, they'd bring a bouquet for Grammy and their mom, and they did the same for their father on Father's Day. Even though it made them both sad, every time they went back to New York, they looked forward to visiting the gravesites because they felt connected with their family.

Summer went to her grandparents' plots first. They were buried side-by-side as were her parents. She kneeled and began cleaning the dirt and other debris from the gravestone. She sang her grandmother's favorite hymn, "At the Cross." Autumn heard her sniffling but she didn't go over to comfort her. This *was* their comfort. Whenever they went to the cemetery, they were emotional. Neither of them tried to prevent the other's tears. They just allowed them to fall freely and focused on feeling the presence of their loved ones' spirits.

Autumn had made her rounds and was now kneeling at her parent's plots and cleaning them off the same as Summer had done with their grandparents. She used the opportunity to talk to them.

"Hello, Mommy and Daddy. I always feel silly talking to you two out loud because I know I won't hear your responses, but I *do* feel them. I know I tell you guys every year how much I miss you, but that's because it's true. I know they say time heals all wounds, but I don't find that true. Even though the pain of losing you both is not as intense, the void from you not being here is ever so present. It is a void that no one could ever fill, ever. Summer is developing into a wonderful woman. She met a man, and he seems great for her. But I won't say anymore because I want her to share her good news. Me, on the other hand, I'm still waiting on my king. For heaven's sake, I'll be thirty in a little while." Autumn broke down into tears.

"Mommy and Daddy, I think something is wrong with me. I can't seem to secure a boyfriend if I locked him away. As you watch over me, you see the countless dates I've been on, yet no one seems to tickle my fancy. There is a guy that I kind of like, but he is different. I know that for some reason every man seems to be different. Chaianne said that about her husband. Karashae said it about Stephon, and of course,

Summer will tell you just how different her boyfriend is, but this guy is *really* different. Well, I don't have to tell you guys; you see what I see. When I go to Grammy next, I'm going to ask her to meet with the two of you so you guys can work together to send me a good man, who is heaven sent, literally." Autumn snickered and then wiped the tears from her eyes and the snot from her nose. "I don't know, maybe I'm being hasty. It's just that it's hard to watch everyone close to me enjoy the fruits of a great relationship while I'm still single. It makes me question my worthiness. I don't know. I won't complain, or at least I'll try not to. I would love nothing more than to have what you two had or still have. Are you guys still together up there? I miss you so much."

Her heart grew heavy again. "Summer and I are actually staying here until the end of the week. She wants to go out and celebrate her birthday. That girl is a party animal. I have trouble keeping up. Any who, as always, it's a pleasure to come and visit. It brings joy to both of us, knowing that we can still connect with you guys after so long. I know the Chandlers are up there rocking out. How many Luther and Whitney concerts have you guys been too? I'm sure they are magical, but I'm in no rush to get there. As much as I miss you guys and would like to hug and hold you, I am enjoying my time down here. We shall meet again. I love you, Mommy and Daddy, and as always, I hope I am making you proud."

Autumn slowly stood, but not before placing a tender

kiss on each of their gravestones. She walked past Summer on her way to her grandparents. She missed her Grammy dearly and she prepared herself to have a long talk with her as well. If anyone could make her dream of happily ever after closer to a reality it was her Grammy.

~~~

Autumn propped her foot on the edge of the hotel bed and leaned in as she polished her toenails. Summer was in the shower, singing loudly. Autumn thought about going through her phone, just like Summer did hers, but thought better of it. *She probably got some freaky stuff in there, too. Always talking about me,* Autumn thought. The hotel phone rang, pulling her from her thoughts. The first call was from Shae, telling her that they were "in the building." By the end of the conversation, Summer had gotten out of the shower, and they all agreed to go to the new hip-hop club, The Riverfront, in Troy, the neighboring town. Shortly after Autumn hung up with Shae, there was a knock at the door, and Summer went to get it.

"Oh, hello," she greeted room service.

"Good afternoon, ma'am. I have a delivery for Summer Hughes."

"That's me." Summer sounded surprised.

The service man grabbed a bouquet of roses from his tray and handed her a card. Summer thanked him and closed the door.

"Aw, who sent that, Blue Skies?" Autumn asked.

"I have no clue."

Autumn waited until Summer read the card and watched as her eyes watered.

"It's a card from Ajamaal. It says, 'Summer, I wanted to send you a small birthday offering. I know this doesn't replace my presence, but I wanted you to know I am there in spirit, and these flowers are a reminder. I hope I am lucky enough to be able to spend more birthdays with you and celebrate life with you in general. Always on my mind and forever in my heart. Yours truly, Ajamaal.'"

Now Autumn was tearing up. "That was beautiful, sis. He must really like you. I am so happy with you." Autumn rarely said that she was happy *for* people. She usually said that she was happy *with* them because she understood that she couldn't be happy for someone else; the other person would have to achieve that on her own, but she could share in the joy and be happy *with* them.

"Thanks, big sis. I'm growing fonder of him by the day. He really does bring joy to my life. I miss him already," Summer admitted.

"I'm sure, girl, but don't get mushy on me already. We have to celebrate tonight."

There was another knock at the door, and this time, it was Karashae.

"Hap-py birth-day to ya; hap-py birth-day to ya; haap-py biiirth-daaay!" Karashae sang the Stevie Wonder rendition so well that Summer and Autumn started dancing.

"Aw, thanks Karashae!" Summer squealed.

"So, y'all ready to partay, or what? Chaianne just called me, and she said that her two friends Shakyra and Chanel want to hang out, too. You guys cool with that?"

"Sure. The more the merrier," Autumn stated.

"Are they cool chicks? I don't want to have to deal with bullshit on my birthday," Summer added.

"Girl, don't get me to lying. I haven't met them yet. Chaianne speaks highly of them, though. How you guys like her?"

"Oh, she cool as hell," Summer said.

"I really like Chaianne. She's really down to earth. I can tell she's a little hood, but hey, aren't we all at times? I don't do ghetto, and she's not that, so it's all love here."

"Okaay," Karashae sang. "So it's a party. Shit going down tonight."

They all agreed that they would meet at the club early so they could secure their spots and establish a bond with the bartenders. They had plans to really enjoy themselves and wanted the drinks to be strong.

~~~

When they arrived at the club via taxi, the only people

that were there were the bartenders, the DJ, and a couple of other partygoers. Chaianne led them upstairs, where there were seats and tables, and they all got comfortable. Since everyone had ridden in different taxis, no one had been formerly introduced.

Chaianne stood between the two sets of women and made introductions, "Summer, Autumn, and Karashae, these are my friends, Shakyra and Chanel. Chanel and Shakyra, this is Summer, the birthday girl, her sister Autumn, and our friend Karashae."

Summer and Autumn then introduced everyone to their friends from middle and high school, who had stopped by to celebrate with them. Everyone said hello and wished Summer a happy birthday.

"Summer, I hope it's okay. My daughter's father and his fiancé planned to come out tonight, and I told them we would be here. Do you mind if they join us?" Chaianne asked.

"Girl, no. Not at all."

Chaianne got a text from Karl, asking where they were. Moments later, Stephon called Karashae, asking the same thing. Karl and Abaki had left the city early and arrived in Albany a day earlier than Chaianne had expected them too. Unfortunately for Abaki, the hotel was booked due to a banquet, but rooms would open up tomorrow night. Karl knew that Chaianne had the option of staying with her friend, so he'd told Abaki he could share the room with him for the night.

It was just after midnight, and the DJ had stepped the music up a lot. The girls were getting their drink on and feeling nice. Summer was enjoying her birthday, glad that she had some wonderful people there to celebrate with her. Her cell phone vibrated, and she walked away to answer the call.

"Hey, A.J.!" Summer's words were slurred.

"Baby, are you drunk already? It's just after midnight."

"Baby, I was drunk when you called me right before midnight, just to be the last to wish me a happy birthday," she said, giggling.

Ajamaal laughed with her. "So, where you say you at again?"

"I'm at this club in Troy called the Riverfront. Baby, it's really nice. It has two levels with a bar on both floors and ..."

Summer turned around to see who was tapping her on her shoulder, and when she did, she was staring her man in the face. She had no idea he had hung up on her and entered the club in a matter of seconds. "Oh my gosh! Baby, what are you doing here?"

"I couldn't miss celebrating your birthday with you. Autumn sent me a text once she found out where you guys were going, so I came to surprise you."

Summer cried. She hadn't expected him to travel all the way to New York just to spend time with her for her birthday. He'd said he had something come up, but actually, he'd gone to visit some family down in the city and had planned on meeting Summer at the club the entire time.

"Don't cry, baby," he said. "Wipe those tears and let's have fun."

Summer and Ajamaal joined the rest of the gang. Summer was introducing him to everyone when Vaughn, the father of Chaianne's daughter, showed up. Their party was growing bigger and Summer was loving it, especially now that A.J was there. Chaianne could spot her husband a mile away, and a different town or scenery couldn't hinder that. As soon as she spotted him on the lower level, she jumped to her feet and ran to greet him. He had shown up with Abaki and Stephon. Chaianne led them upstairs, holding Karl's hand. Now, it was Karashae's turn to get excited. Neither of them had expected the men to show up at the club tonight. Everyone had thought that Saturday night would be the night for them all to get together and chill, but it was a pleasant and welcomed surprise.

Chaianne went around and introduced everyone. Karl and Vaughn greeted each other without Chaianne's assistance because they were already cool. Karl introduced Vaughn to Stephon, Abaki, and Ajamaal, and all the men went to the bar and ordered several bottles of whatever the ladies were already drinking plus a couple bottles of champagne for Summer's birthday toast. Autumn felt out of place. It appeared that everyone was coupled up; even one of their old friends had come with a date. Although Chanel and Shakyra had come alone, Autumn watched as they linked up with people she assumed they already knew. She sat back and took inventory of everyone who was there.

She noticed that Vaughn and Karl were really close, considering that one was Chaianne's husband and the other her baby's daddy. She actually liked that they got along and there was no tension between them. She wondered how and why they were so cool. Vaughn was good looking. She could see from where Quay got her features. In fact, all the men in attendance were very attractive. But in her eyes, no one was as fine as Abaki. Maybe that was because she didn't have eyes for other people's men. The more she thought about it, the more she reasoned that Abaki was definitely the finest man in the club, just not *her* man. She didn't have one, not one prospect, whom she could call on to snuggle with her at night. She felt herself getting emotional, so she eased out of her seat and headed to the restroom.

Karashae knew her frister well. She could tell when something was eating Autumn, and tonight was no different. Even after all the drinks they'd consumed, she was still aware of her surroundings; so when she saw Autumn get up, she was right behind her. Karashae waited until everyone left the restroom, and then she locked the door. She could hear Autumn's subtle sniffles. "Autumn!"

Autumn opened the stall door, briefly looked at her friend, and walked over to the mirror to get herself together.

"Autumn, you okay?"

"Yeah, I'll be fine. You know, I'm just going through the motions."

"Well, if it makes you feel better, Abaki really does like you."

"Yeah right," Autumn said, trying to sound uninterested.

"No, seriously. They went to play ball a couple of weeks ago and he admitted that he *did* like you, but he thought you were a stripper."

"A stripper? Why would he think that?"

"The way you danced at the beer hall that night and your amazing bull riding skills impressed him and scared him." Karashae laughed.

Autumn snickered too. "So, did Stephon tell him I'm not like that?"

"Of course he did. You know we got your back."

Autumn's mood lifted a bit.

"Chin up, girl. Now, let's go out there and enjoy ourselves. Now that he knows you're not a stripper, you can shake that ass and blow his mind."

Autumn hugged her friend. She was so glad that the

two of them had met. Karashae was exactly what she needed at that moment. "I love you, frister."

"And I love ya back," Karashae replied, imitating Martin Lawrence.

Karashae and Autumn returned to the upper level and rejoined the group. Autumn was pleased that her sister was having such a good time. She looked down at them on the dance floor and smiled inwardly. *At least one of us is happy.* She walked over to the table, and Abaki handed her a drink.

"I heard you like this," he said.

Autumn contemplated taking the drink. As much as she liked him, she was feeling some kind of way toward him for mislabeling her. "I'm good," she told him and went to the bar to get her own drink.

Abaki watched as she walked off in the direction of the bar and followed her. "Did I offend you?"

Autumn wanted to scream "Yes!" but she answered with a curt "No."

The bartender recognized Autumn from earlier and quickly came to serve her. Autumn rested her elbows on the bar. "I'll take a shot of tequila and a Corona with a lemon, please."

Abaki didn't say anything.

"Twelve dollars," the bartender announced.

Before Autumn could reach into her back pocket for her money, Abaki had already put the money on the bar.

"Enjoy," he said as he stared at her.

Autumn didn't respond. She licked the salt off her hand, threw back the shot, and sucked her lemon, feeling the heat of Abaki's stare penetrate her face before he decided to step off.

Two mixed drinks, a glass of champagne, a shot of tequila, and a Corona later, and Autumn was feeling nice! She saw her sister, Karashae, and Chaianne, and all of her friends on the dance floor, getting their two-step on. It was only one in the morning, and the club was just starting to fill. The DJ saw that he had a better audience and started playing better music. Autumn reached the dance floor just as Remy Ma's "Conceited" blazed through the speakers. Some songs that just took her there, and this was one of them. Chaianne was a beast on the floor. She could switch from lady to hood in the blink of an eye. The way she rapped the lyrics and dipped and rocked her body were evidence of her rougher side. Autumn stayed pretty mellow, but she still knew every word to the song. The DJ didn't disappoint when he began playing Fantasia's "When I See You." Now Autumn was really in the moment. She had worked the pole to that song several times before and loved the feeling it gave her. She closed her eyes for a moment to feel the effects of the song that Fantasia sang so well. Autumn was in her zone. She loved that song and she let her movements express it.

Abaki was now on his feet, leaning over the railing,

watching Autumn dance. He recognized the song from that night in her shop when he'd seen her dancing on the pole. Autumn looked up and met his eyes. This time, she didn't break the stare. Normally, when she caught him looking her way, she would look away first, but not tonight. Maybe it was the booze, or maybe it was her hormones; she wasn't sure. But she was sure that Abaki was getting a glimpse into her heart. She just hoped that he was keen enough to know it. She caught Abaki looking at her and her insides softened.

The DJ noticed all the couples on the floor and told the crowd he was going to mellow it down. Zap and Roger's "Computer Love" boomed through the speakers. Some walked off the dance floor and just as many stepped on. Autumn was side-stepping her way off the floor when someone grabbed her hand and reeled her in until she was wrapped in an embrace, her back to his front. She tilted her head upward to the left and was surprised to see Abaki behind her, doing the two-step. She stiffened.

"Dance with me, Autumn, please?" he asked.

She didn't answer verbally; she just leaned back against his chest and swayed with him. She closed her eyes and relished in the moment. She even discreetly pinched herself to ensure that, this time, their interaction wasn't just a dream.

Chapter 25: Autumn

The chemistry between Abaki and Autumn was undeniable. Autumn was certain that Abaki knew how much she liked him. However, she had no idea if Abaki liked her or not. She was wearing her heart on her sleeve and she knew it. The older she got, the more vulnerable she became. She didn't consider herself to be a pushover, but she was a love bug at heart and had no problem giving love a try.

Autumn looked over at Summer and could tell that she was wasted. She had made several attempts to take Ajamaal right there on the dance floor. Another drunk man must have thought Summer was up for the taking because when A.J. walked away, he grabbed her ass and tried to press his groin against her. Summer stepped back and slapped him. The guy gripped the side of Summer's face and mushed her with his palm.

Stephon and Karashae were standing the closest, so Stephon hauled off and punched him in the face. The guy launched his arm backward and was about to punch Stephon when A.J. came back and caught him right on the jaw. Now the drunk man's friends were ready to brawl. Security had quickly jumped in and started filing them out of the club. The drunk man and his entourage started threatening A.J. and Stephon. By that time, Karl, Abaki, and even Vaughn were right there, ready for whatever. They had all moved the women to the side and were prepared to back their friends up if shit hit the fan.

"Are you okay, Summer?" everyone asked her.

"Yeah, I'm good. Why can't people come out and respect others. I didn't know him, but he had the gall to violate me."

"You know how people can be," Karashae said, sweeping her hand down Summer's arm.

Chaianne threw her right arm in the air. "No, fuck that. He got what he was looking for. That muthafucka don't know!"

At that moment, everyone was ready to go. They'd had enough to drink and had really enjoyed themselves before the altercation. Everyone gathered their things and headed outside to hail a couple of taxis.

"Now what, punk muthafuckas?!"

They all turned around to see the drunk man standing there holding a gun. Four of his friends stood behind him, ready for war. Stephon, Abaki, Karl, A.J., and Vaughn all pushed the ladies back inside.

"Karl, no! Please come in," Chaianne begged.

"Chaianne!" Karl said, keeping his eyes on the men in front of him.

The tone of his voice let her know that it was not up for discussion. Karashae grabbed her by the hand and pulled her back inside, where they all stood by the door to see what would happen. The drunk man made the mistake of stepping closer, and when he did, Abaki did some warrior shit and grabbed his arm, bent his wrist, and took the gun in the blink of an eye. He then used the butt of the gun to bust the man in his face, cracking the bridge of his nose. He disassembled the gun, threw the pieces at the drunk, and held the bullets in his hand. The man was bleeding profusely. Abaki, Karl, Stephon, Vaughn, and A.J were all in fight mode, ready to move if the others were feeling frisky. But after what they'd witnessed, none of them wanted to fight. They held up their hands in a truce and reached down to help their drunk friend. "Man, I told you to leave that shit alone. You don't listen," one of the guys said.

Two cabs pulled up. A.J. held one and Karl held the other. The ladies didn't exit the club doors until the men told them it was okay. Karashae, Stephon, Chaianne, and Karl rode together, while Autumn opted to ride with Summer and A.J. Abaki didn't want to leave Autumn by herself after that ordeal, so he rode with them. Vaughn was parked right in front, so he and his lady hopped in his car. On his way to the cab, Abaki dropped the bullets in the sewer.

While inside the cab, Chaianne called Autumn to let her know that Karl had made arrangements for Abaki to stay in their room, but now that she wasn't going to her friend Shakyra's house, she wanted to know if he could stay in

Autumn and Summer's suite. Karashae had told Chaianne that Autumn and Summer had a two bedroom suite and probably wouldn't mind if he'd slept on the pullout couch. "Sure, that's fine. I'll let him know," Autumn replied. She turned to Abaki. "That was Chaianne. She said she's going back to the room with Karl. We have a suite, so I don't mind if you stay with us. Do you, Summer?"

"Hell no. Not after what he just did."

"Yo, man, that was some wild shit. Where the hell you learn that at?" Ajamaal asked Abaki.

"My father was a warrior. His father was a warrior and his father before that. I guess I have it in my blood," Abaki said and then looked over at Autumn.

They all arrived back at the hotel at the same time, but everyone chose to go to their separate rooms. Abaki had told Karl that he would get his bag in the morning. As soon as Summer and A.J. got inside the suite, they went straight to their room. Autumn wanted to take a shower but didn't want to leave Abaki alone or give him any ideas. She decided to go freshen up instead and excused herself. Once inside the bathroom, she reflected on the evening. Abaki had captivated her and confused her all at the same time. He seemed uneasy around woman, yet he defended them at every point. He kept his feelings to himself but seemed to be in tune with hers. She was shocked that he'd danced with her. She thought for sure that he would have just watched her from afar as he had done many times before. She hadn't forgotten the conversation she'd had with Karashae. In fact, it pissed her off all over again.

She exited the bathroom and walked right up to Abaki as he sat on the couch, flipping through channels. "How dare you?" she snapped.

Abaki stood. Autumn used her right hand to slap him in the face but he blocked it with his left hand and held onto her wrist. She tried to do the same with her left hand but he grabbed that wrist with his right hand and leaned into her.

"What have I done to deserve this abuse?"

"You are a hypocrite, Abaki. How dare you not want to date me because you thought I was a stripper when you do the same thing!"

He gave her a perplexed look but said nothing. When he released her arms, she went into her room. Abaki followed, but he didn't enter. "A stripper? I'm no stripper, Autumn," he said as he stood in the doorway.

"You can come in," Autumn granted, defeated.

"I take it you may have some questions about me. I know I am different than the average man, but I can assure you my intentions are good and I am no stripper."

Autumn had so many questions, but she didn't know where to start. She figured that she could start by asking him what made him think she was a stripper and why he'd purchased those things from her store.

"The night that guy attacked you, I was there in your shop, watching you move about the pole. I saw when you let the last customer out and ran back inside. I was waiting for you to come out, but you didn't, so I went in. I heard the music and followed it, and it led me to you. So, then I guess I jumped to conclusions."

"The wrong conclusion," she retorted.

He proceeded with a heavy sigh. "I had only come into your store after seeing you open up one day. A week before I had first entered your shop, I had spotted you and you piqued my interest. What makes you think I strip?" he asked, perplexed.

"Uh, maybe the things you purchased when you came to my shop."

Abaki smirked. "Oh, those were 'just 'cause' purchases. Now, I couldn't just walk up in there and not buy anything. That would have been wrong."

Autumn smiled shyly. She was a bit embarrassed but quickly dismissed the feeling because it was legitimate.

"I know, I'm different, as you say. I see how women throw themselves at me and offer to sex me without knowing me. It's very degrading. I value women, and the thought of them acting like less than ladies is repulsive. I've reached a point in my life where I would love to settle down and have a family, but I refuse to settle for a woman who doesn't know her worth."

"And what if a woman felt that way about you?"

"Then that would be her prerogative and my loss. But I have yet to meet a woman who would turn a man down because of a less than desirable lifestyle."

"I would," Autumn admitted.

"You know, for some reason, I believe that, which is why I find myself growing more interested in you."

Autumn's heart smiled. His admission to liking her left her in disbelief. "What kind of woman interests you?"

"Know this, you're a female by genetics, a woman by nature, and a lady by choice. To answer your question: in short, a lady. To elaborate, I like women who are beautiful, like you, smart, driven, caring, loving, supportive, focused, and ... willing."

"Willing to what?"

"Willing to let me be the man."

She noticed that he didn't say "*a* man," he'd said "*the* man." Abaki wanted full control, but Autumn wasn't sure what that meant. It was late and she was tired, but she wasn't too exhausted to get more information from him.

"Abaki, can I ask you a question?"

"Absolutely."

"Have you slept with a lot of women?"

Abaki had never been asked that question, probably because most women didn't care. They just wanted to see if they could try their hand at him. Abaki welcomed the honesty. "Would it matter?"

"Kind of."

"In due time, you will know. Now let's go to bed; I'm tired, and so are you."

Autumn was tired and she knew it, but she was also curious and her hormones were raging. This was the closest she had been to being intimate with a man in a really long time, and her body was begging for some sexual stimulation, but her mind knew that she had to be true to her heart and stick to her celibacy. "Abaki, I have to tell you something. I, um, I haven't had sex in seven years ... I'm celibate." She hoped her revelation didn't scare him off.

He was expressionless. She wasn't sure if her admission had turned him on or off and she started to feel anxious. Abaki removed her shoes and then his own. He placed them neatly along the wall. He grabbed a pillow and told her he was going to sleep on the couch.

"Abaki, please, can you just lay with me?" She wanted to feel the touch of a man. She didn't want to have sex with him; she just wanted to be held more than anything, especially tonight. Abaki started to remove his shirt but thought better of it. He lay on the bed and positioned himself. He motioned for her to lie next to him. When Autumn lay with her back to his front, he told her to turn around so that they were face-to-face. Once she'd cuddled comfortably, he leaned into her ear.

"Autumn, I haven't had sex in thirteen years. Let's sleep."

He kissed her neck and held her. If his eyelids weren't closed, he would have seen that her eyes and mouth were wide open. *No way!* Autumn was beyond stunned. But nothing compared to the myriad of emotions that stirred inside. Tonight felt good, right, content. She allowed her mind to recite the poetic lyrics of her heart.

Finally, something for which I've longed

It's hard being right when good feels wrong

I'm listening to a song, and it's not by chance, that it's carrying me along

The words penetrate my soul and touch my heart

Could this be a new beginning, a fresh start?

I think he's the one, but I've got to be certain

Could this man be him, for whom I've been searching?

Chapter 26: Autumn

Autumn slept comfortably, peacefully, like a freshly bathed baby. She had no idea that having a man share the bed with her would yield that much pleasure. Abaki wasn't inappropriate at all. She slept with her head close to his chest and his chin atop her head. The whole night, his hand rested respectfully on the small of her back. She lay there wondering how he'd gone so long without having sex. She thought seven years was long, but thirteen? That was almost double the time. *No double way!* No way could a man of his stature abstain from sex for thirteen years. She couldn't wait to hear why. Autumn remained still in the bed next to him. She always woke up early, even after a night on the town. Not wanting to wake him, she just lay there, taking him in. His features, his scent, even the smell of his morning breath turned her on.

"Watching me, are you?" Abaki asked, never opening his eyes.

How the hell did he know that? I never moved a muscle, Autumn thought. "I, um … Well, yes, I was. Does it bother you?"

"Not at all. I enjoyed watching you as you slept," Abaki admitted, opening his eyes.

"You were watching me too?"

"Of course, Autumn. This is a first for me as well. A

woman as beautiful as you would capture any man's eyes."

Autumn blushed. "When are you leaving?" she asked him.

"I guess tomorrow. That's when I was informed we were leaving. How about you?"

"Tomorrow," Autumn answered.

"So, what's the plan for today?"

"I have none."

"I would like to take you on a date today, if you don't mind."

Autumn sat up. *Yes, yes, yes!* She was surprised that Abaki had made a move. She hadn't been sure of what today would hold, but now that she knew, she was all for it. "I don't mind at all. I would like that," Autumn replied, her heart fluttering. "What did you have in mind?"

"I want something low-key. I want to enjoy our time together and give you the opportunity to ask me anything you want. I know there are some things that need clarifying, and I won't deny you that."

Autumn was elated. Finally, she felt like she was getting somewhere. Here was a guy that she could not seem to get enough of, and now, he was asking for her time. Autumn wondered where they would go or what they would do. Abaki wasn't from Albany, so he wouldn't know where to take her. She had heard that he was quite resourceful, but she doubted that he knew his way around her hometown.

As if reading her thoughts, Abaki said, "Have you been to the observation deck?"

"What observation deck?"

"I can show you better than I can tell you. Come, let's get up."

It was a little after eight in the morning, so Autumn knew that Summer was still asleep. She figured she and Abaki could use the shower and be long gone before Summer and A.J. woke up.

"My bag is in the room with Karl. I'll go get it and see if there's an available room. Maybe someone checked out early and the wait won't be too long."

"Abaki, you don't have to spend the money on a room. I don't mind if you stay here another night," Autumn offered. Although she wanted him to stay, she had to admit that having him in her bed felt too complete for her comfort. She could tell that he, too, didn't want to risk them getting too snug. Women were driven by emotions, and Autumn's actions had made it clear that she had feelings for him.

"Autumn, that is very gracious of you; however, I must decline. You and I have come so far, and I won't let us risk that."

Autumn knew exactly what he was referring to. They both had spent many years of their lives celibate, and if they shared a bed for a second night in a row, surely the flesh would win the battle. She had argued with herself about whether she should kiss him in his sleep. But in her heart, she didn't want to be rejected or accepted. If Abaki rejected her, it would have been awkward, and if he accepted, well, Autumn knew how it would have gone. She was glad he was being rational.

"I understand. Thanks for always looking out for my best interest." She meant that in more ways than one.

"I'll go take care of things and ring your room when I'm all set."

Autumn nodded. She walked him to the door and locked it behind him. She stood there a moment with her eyes closed, holding her breath, trying hard to imbed his scent into her brain, her body, and her soul. She wouldn't dare admit it to anyone, but Autumn Hughes was really feeling Abaki Lemande.

Chapter 27: Abaki

By the time Abaki made it back to Autumn's room, she was dressed and ready to go. He greeted her with hug and noticed how she deeply inhaled the spicy oriental scent of his Davidoff Hot Water cologne.

"Mmm ... you smell nice," she said.

"Where you two love birds going so early?" Summer asked, stepping into the room.

"Abaki is taking me on a date, if you must know," Autumn responded.

"A date, huh? Autumn Hughes, you never cease to amaze me. Just when I thought you had given up on men," Summer teased.

"Summer, I have never given up on men, and I never will. Now, if you'll excuse me, I have a date with Abaki."

Abaki held out his arm so that Autumn could slip hers through.

"Enjoy the day, Sunshine."

"I will, Blue Skies."

The first place Abaki took her was to the observation deck. Autumn professed how intrigued she was by the Albany skyline, and that pleased him. She told him that she had never been to the observation deck of all the years she had lived in this town. Her parents had certainly showed her and her sister good times. They'd gone to Hoffman's

Playland, Bleeker Stadium to ice skate, the Altamont Fairs, and all the local festivals and amusement parks. They had done it all, including visiting the museum on occasion, but per parents had never taken her to the rooftop.

"Abaki, thanks for bringing me here. Of all the years I've lived here, I've never visited this spot before. I appreciate this."

"Autumn, the pleasure is all mine. My uncle lived down in Westchester County. He had a political position, so we traveled to Albany a lot. He would take me around to explore the town. So that's how I came to learn about a few of the attractions here. Let's walk; there's more I would like to do."

They left the observation deck and walked the compound. Spotting an early morning vendor, he stopped and purchased two fruit cups for both of them. Autumn opted for the one with more pineapples.

"Pineapples, huh?" Abaki asked.

Autumn didn't respond right away. He thought that maybe it was because she was aware of the same folklore he'd heard from some of his friends: women who ate a lot of pineapples tasted fresher "down there."

She just smiled slyly. "I love pineapples. I'm not going to say that's the only fruit I eat, but it definitely is one of my favorites."

"What else do you enjoy?"

"Well, let's see. I like other fruits such as oranges, preferably sliced, apples, strawberries, grapes, cherries, and peaches."

"That's it? No mangos, melons, or cantaloupe."

"Yuck, I don't do melons or cantaloupe. I may eat a mango or a piece of kiwi every now and then, but the others are my favorites."

"What else interests you?" he asked. He wanted to know as much about Autumn as he could, from the foods she liked to eat to the places she wanted to visit. If things turned out his way, he'd be willing to give her everything short of the solar system.

"I enjoy reading, love listening to music, traveling when I have the chance, writing poetry, and spending time with my sister, frister, and godson."

"Frister?"

"Yeah." She giggled. "That's what I call Karashae. She's my friend but more like a sister."

Abaki nodded. "I see. You said you enjoy spending time with your godson. So, does that mean you want children of your own someday?" Abaki had to know. He wanted children of his own and any woman he was serious with had to want the same; otherwise, they would have no future together. Marriage and a family was what life was about, and if a woman wasn't about that life, he couldn't make her his wife.

"Abaki, to be honest with you, I'm not sure." Autumn seemed to be oblivious to his disappointment. Although his expression remained unaffected, his feelings were definitely impacted. She had no idea how her words had just pierced his heart, deflated his spirit, and wounded his soul. Autumn's hesitation was enough to make him second-guess his interest in her.

"I mean, I love kids. Karashae and Stephon's son is the closest I've ever been to being a parent. I will admit that the feeling is like no other. I guess I'm just not sure if I am capable of providing that unconditional love, ongoing support, and guidance. What if I'm a horrible mom? What if I don't do a good job and they turn out to be bad kids?"

Abaki went from feeling defeated to hopeful. She wasn't against having kids; she was nervous about being a mother—a good mother. He reached over and placed her hand in his. "Autumn, there is no manual for parenting. It's a natural process and one that we develop the moment we create life. Selfishness goes out the window and the only thing that matters in the whole world is making sure that child is safe, loved, and cared for. Everything else, we learn as we go. It's instinct. Nobody's perfect. All parents make mistakes. That's how we learn and grow. Besides, you will not be alone. It takes two, remember?"

He hoped she took heed to what he'd said. Every first-time parent had to learn how to parent from scratch; that was just the way things went. Whether naturally or through adoption, parenting was a learning process. He just hoped that she would be open to the idea; otherwise, everything they were doing was futile. He had to find out the basics from her. He wanted to see if they were equally yoked in terms of faith, family, and future plans. He didn't think he was moving too fast. He was simply too old for games. He dated for a reason, not just to wine and dine a woman, but to determine just how much they had in common, and right now, he wanted to maximize his date.

"Is marriage something that you welcome?" he asked her. To some, it may have seemed like a silly question, but Abaki had met women who didn't care to ever marry. They were fine just shacking up with a man, never taking the step to have God bless their union through marriage.

"Hell yeah," Autumn responded with more enthusiasm than she had the question about children. "I *so* want to get married. I wasn't able to witness the love my grandparents shared but I saw firsthand how much my parents valued and loved one another. I would like to experience true love like that."

This time, Abaki's heart fluttered. Autumn's words touched him deeply.

"How about you?" she asked.

"Yes, I would love to find the right woman to make my wife and for us to have lots of babies."

"Lots?"

"Yes, I would like about five children."

"Five children, Abaki? Gee, that's a lot."

Abaki laughed. It was the first time Autumn saw him laugh. "How many would you be willing to bear?"

He saw that she was thinking about his question; her response was delayed. "You have a nice smile, ya know... and an infectious laugh. I enjoy seeing that opposed to your expressionless side," she admitted.

"Duly noted."

"But to answer your question: I would like three children."

"Why three?"

"Um, I don't know. In my mind, three is completion. I love that number. I don't see the point in people having one child. It just seems way too lonesome. I don't know what I would do without Summer. Besides, naturally, we are expected to age, and typically, the children help care for the aging parents. If it takes two parents to care for a child then why only have one child to care for the parents?"

Abaki liked her rationale.

"Two is a good number as well; it's company for the other child, but three just seems so much more family oriented."

He wasn't sure how to respond. For someone who was unsure of her future as a parent, she had provided damn good justification for the number of children she wanted to bring into this world. "Three, huh? I think that's a compromise."

"So, how do you feel about marriage?" Autumn asked him.

"Autumn, I don't believe in having children before marriage. I know people do it, but that's not what I want for myself or my kids. When I do it, I only want to do it once, with one woman. That's why I have to be sure she's not only the one, but the *right* one."

Abaki was grounded. He was a man who knew what he wanted out of life and was not willing to settle for anything less.

"And your faith?" Autumn asked.

He didn't hesitate to answer. "She has to believe in God. Christian, Catholic, Baptist. It doesn't really matter. I just want to be sure that when we kneel to pray together, we are praying to the same savior and praying for similar things."

Autumn expressed that she was raised as a Christian and believed in God. So far, they were headed in the right direction. He just hoped they would continue walking the same path.

Chapter 28: Autumn

Their walk led them to a playground not far from the base of the observation deck. Like two puppy-love teenagers, Autumn and Abaki swung on the swings, rode the seesaw, and even took turns descending the sliding board. Autumn was really enjoying the time they spent together. She hadn't enjoyed a date this much since she had dated during her college years. Most guys wanted to do the typical dinner and a movie, and she was fine with that, but their conversations never really took on any real significance. Autumn had revealed to Abaki all that interested her. Now, she wanted him to reveal the same.

"So Mr. Sex—, uh, Abaki, what is it that you like to do in your spare time? You know, when you're not saving women from the male jerks of the world."

Abaki snickered. "Well, Ms. Hughes, if you must know, I enjoy working out, coaching basketball, of course, I love watching movies, traveling, eating, and relaxing."

"Oh, so you're a movie geek, like I'm a music freak? Well, let's test your knowledge, shall we? I'll quote a line from a movie, and you give me the title."

Abaki agreed with a nod.

"'You had me at hello.'"

"Well, that's kind of tricky since it appeared in several

movies, but I believe the first was *Jerry Maguire*," Abaki responded.

"Okay!" Autumn was impressed. "How about 'You are the perfect verse over a tight beat'?"

"That's easy. *Brown Sugar*," Abaki said confidently.

"Okay, Mr. Know-It-All. Here's another one for you: 'Don't forget, I'm just a girl, standing in front of a boy, asking him to love her.'"

He stepped closer to her so that he could whisper in her ear. "A romantic are we? *Notting Hill*." His breath wisped across her ear. "Nineteen ninety-nine," he added for good measure.

Autumn's nipples perked and her heart skipped a beat. His impact was so forceful yet gentle. She couldn't explain it. He was the man of her dreams, literally. "Abaki, damn you." She laughed. "And, yes, I am a hopeful romantic. One more?"

"Sure," he welcomed.

Autumn had to keep from smiling and laughing. It was a silly quote, and she wasn't sure if Abaki would get it or not, but she was going to put it out there. "Okay, ready. 'Do something to make me feel better.'"

Abaki acted as if he was thinking hard. She knew that he knew the answer, but he was pausing to throw her off. "Uh, *Players Club*?"

"Abaki!" Autumn squealed. She was shocked and

impressed as she playfully hit him on the arm.

He wrapped his arm around her shoulder in a friendly embrace. "I told you I love movies. I'm sure you could do the same with music."

She looked up into his eyes. He was right. They had just learned so much about each other in such a short period of time.

"All this talk of movies makes me want to watch one. Down to go to a theatre?" he asked.

"If it means more time with you, of course."

They didn't go to the movies right away. Abaki spotted an Aquaducts bus tour sign and decided that he and Autumn would do that before seeing a movie. She learned even more about the small town, about the buildings and their significance and other lesser-known historical facts. Her day was turning out to be better than she'd expected. Autumn was aware of the small theatre not too far from where they were. It would be a bit of a walk, but the day was beautiful and it just meant more time with Abaki. She would do anything to be able to be with him all day and just take in all the man he was.

She chose the Spectrum Theatre but allowed him to select the movie. She could tell that he chose the *The Vow* because she loved a good love story. A man and woman fell in love. She had an accident and suffered memory loss, forgetting everything she'd ever shared with her husband. He knew what they had and wasn't willing to give up on them, so he remained persistent, and eventually, he got her to fall in love with him all over again.

"Wow, was that coincidence or fate?" Autumn asked after the movie had ended.

Abaki thought. "Fate; it had to be. The chance of an individual falling in love with the same person twice, with no recollection of the first affair, is no coincidence, Autumn. That's destiny. It was exactly what it was meant to be. When one has located the other half of their soul, they have it for life, even if it gets lost; it will always come back."

Autumn had heard Karashae give a similar explanation about love. She wanted that and was hoping that Abaki would prove to be her better half. As they walked, Autumn used the silence to pray. She prayed to God, to Jesus, to her parents, and to Grammy. She prayed to Cupid and all of his love angel friends. She wanted, no, she needed Abaki to be hers. She needed a man like him, to laugh with, to love, to share a family with, and most importantly, to grow old with. Autumn didn't just need any man; she needed Abaki. She needed a love like his.

Chapter 29: Abaki

After the movie, both of them were hungry. Neither had eaten much since the fruit cups they'd had earlier and popcorn during the movie. They walked to the bistro next door and were immediately seated. Abaki allowed Autumn to sit first and then sat next to her. Once they had placed their orders, he said, "Autumn, do you mind telling me about your family and how you came to live in Dallas?"

She sat quietly for a moment before talking. He hoped she didn't plan to hide anything from him. He just wanted her to reveal intimate details about herself to a man who hoped one day to become a permanent fixture in her life.

"Well, I was born and raised in Albany. I grew up in a neighboring town and attended the schools out there until my parents passed away in a plane crash. We lived with my grandmother for five years, and then she passed away. Now, it's just Summer and me. We had twin sisters, but they passed away when they were infants. My father, Chauncey, he was an only child. His parents had died when Summer and I were little. His father passed away from cancer, and then four weeks later, his mother died. My father always said it was from a broken heart. My maternal grandparents had five children, and they all passed away as well. My mother, Roxy, was the last of her kids, and when she died, I think a big part of Grammy went with her. She tried to hang around until Summer and I were of age, but she was tired and ready to be with the Lord and the rest of her family. So when Grammy went, I was placed in a group home and Summer went to a foster home. It wasn't ideal for any kid and definitely not for us, so we packed up everything we could and got on a bus and found our way to Dallas."

They both sat in silence, Abaki replaying and Autumn reflecting. He knew the impact of death all too well. He had lost those most dear to his heart. He knew firsthand what it felt like to feel lonely and not have any real family around for comfort. Unfortunate circumstances had led him to where he was today. He usually didn't tell people about his background, at least not why he had to stay in America. Abaki missed home but definitely not the nightmare he'd left behind.

"So, that's my story. What's yours?" Autumn asked.

"I moved to America when I was ten years old. My mother and father had an arranged marriage, and when she was fourteen, she had me and then four others after. My father was a powerful man. He owned one of the most profitable pieces of land back home in Sierra Leone. He always told me that I had to understand the art of war. From the time I was a toddler, he'd drilled into my head that men are the protectors of our property and it's up to us to defend it. From an early age, I was taught basic self-defense tactics and hunting techniques as well as archery, carpentry, blacksmithing, and anything else my father felt I needed to know to become a well-grounded man. He told me that I had to be the provider, protector, and possessor. The only way we could have a family was if we were well suited to care for one. My father was only fifteen when he had me, yet he was a jack-of-all-trades and a master of many. I don't think there was anything my father couldn't do. I remember him building my mom a new house because the family was expanding. She was a wonderful mother. Even though my father was tough on us, Mom always balanced it with the emotional side that only a woman could give. When he scolded, she soothed; when he yelled, she hugged. She gave us that balance, showed us that we had to be more than fighters; we had to be lovers as well." Abaki paused for a moment. He was thinking about the next phase of his life.

"In my country, the families would arrange marriages. My father had made a deal with another very powerful family, The Buhari's, from a neighboring township. Mr. Buhari had one daughter of seven kids. He wanted her to marry into a family with the same level of affluence as she, so he made a deal with my father to marry her to me. We were nine years old when she allowed me to penetrate her before we wed. Her brother caught us in the act and threatened to tell her father. I ran away from her and off his property, back to the safety of my family. When I arrived, my mother was panicking because she had been looking for me. I recall my father telling me that the local village men had started warfare to take over everything they could, and they were going after everybody. My mother had to hide herself and us as a direct order from my father. We were hidden away for five days when my mother left to go find food. Being the only boy, she had me stay behind because she felt that if she and my sisters went, they would be safe from harm, probably because they were women and would be seen as less of a threat. I remained hidden beneath a trap door, under the floors by myself for another five days, without food and with little water. My father finally came for me and took me somewhere safe, where he fed me. He told me that my mother and sisters had been captured and killed by the enemy and that Mr. Buhari wanted my head for disgracing his daughter. I was his only living child *and* son, for that matter. He couldn't risk something happening to me, so he made arrangements for me to come to America to live with his older brother. I've been here ever since."

"Is your father still ..."

"Hey, you two!" Chaianne called to Autumn and Abaki.

"Hey, Chaianne!" Autumn waved.

"I see you guys are out and about. Do you mind if we join you?"

"No, not at all."

Chaianne and Karl sat down to join them for a meal. Karl greeted Abaki with a brotherly dap and Autumn with a handshake. He was glad to have them there with him and Autumn but he could tell that Autumn wanted to hear the rest of his story. He reasoned that it would have to wait until another time. He was glad that she didn't try to bring it up again. He didn't want to hide anything from his friend, but certain things were sacred. And even though he and Autumn hadn't made it official, he felt comfortable enough to give her details of his past that he normally would have kept to himself.

Chapter 30: Autumn

Although Autumn was in tune to what was going on around her, she was still thinking about Abaki and the little girl he had been intimate with. She figured there was more to that story, but she wasn't sure if it would be good or bad. She wished they hadn't been interrupted; she needed to know more. After they finished their meals, they all agreed to go back to the hotel and meet up with the other four for some fun by the hotel pool. This was their last night in Albany, so they wanted to chill and take it easy while enjoying the company of good friends.

After they all waded in the pool and shared some drinks and laughs, Abaki walked her to her room. He was a perfect gentleman. If she grabbed his hand, he held it; if she was talking, he was sure to listen attentively. No matter how cozy they got throughout the day, he still respected her and her personal space. He was receptive to her but had yet to initiate anything intimate. Autumn's body was craving a kiss. She wanted nothing more than for Abaki to push her up against a wall and tongue her down. There was nothing sexier than a freak-romantic, a guy who could love her, romance her, fuck her, and spank her at the same time. She had tried to give him signs that she wanted him to touch her but he either ignored it or was just oblivious to the obvious. She'd brush her hardened nipples against him in the pool or use her foot to tickle his calves, but she didn't get a response. So when he only walked her to the hotel door, ensured her safety, and left, Autumn was disappointed. She took a shower to wash the chlorine from her body and hair and thought about Abaki and his perfect body until fatigue overpowered lust.

~~~

Autumn stirred in her sleep. Her body was yearning for the feel of a man. If Abaki wasn't going to make the first move then she surely would. She eased out of her bed and located a pair of her stilettos. She slid them on her feet and threw on her trench coat. Even though it was June, the temperature had a tendency to drop at night, so Autumn always made sure she brought a jacket with her when she visited.

Autumn knocked on Abaki's room door and stood there, hoping for the best. When he answered the door, she didn't wait to be invited in. She slid inside and closed the door on her own. Abaki wore a pair of cotton boxer briefs and nothing else. His feet were the prettiest she'd ever seen on a man. They looked like they had been dipped in a bucket of chocolate syrup and wrapped in silk. She allowed her eyes to travel up his legs, past his muscular calves, over his perfectly formed knees, and across his toned thighs, settling on the extremity that centered his pelvis. She could tell that he was well endowed. Even flaccid, he was the same size as some men when they were at their hardest. It turned her on.

She pushed him gently against the wall and used her tongue to invade his mouth. When he didn't resist, she kissed him harder until she provoked a response. Abaki wrapped his left arm around her waist and grabbed the back of her head with his right hand. He used his body to move her body to the other wall. He broke away from her mouth and used his lips to pull on her nipples. Autumn felt her body temperature rising. She pulled Abaki's head from her breasts, grabbed his hand, and led him to the bed. She sat him down and opened her coat to reveal the skin she was in. Abaki's eyes never left hers. It was as if he was willing himself to be respectful, even in the heat of the moment.

Autumn was tired of playing Ms. Nice Lady; she was ready to be Ms. Freak Lady. She squatted in front of Abaki and eased his manhood out of the comfort of his underwear. She hid her surprise at seeing his size firsthand. She started off licking the head of his dick. She slurped every little drop of pre-cum that surfaced from her tongue's teasing. When she felt she had gotten him as hard as she could, she skillfully began sucking and massaging, taking him in little by little until she felt the tip of his manhood greet her tonsils. Because of its length, she was unable to take him completely into her mouth. She would slide it out and kiss, lick, and gently nibble from the tip down the shaft and to the base of his manhood until the whole thing glistened from her saliva.

Abaki couldn't hide his pleasure or excitement. The harder and stronger her oral hold became, the louder his moans grew. She used the sounds to gauge her performance. When he hissed, she slurped. When he gasped, she bobbed deeper. Autumn had practiced extensively on her dildos and she knew that even though she never allowed another man's penis in her mouth, the skills she had accumulated from practice were enough to compete with the best porn star. She continued to suck, slurp, and massage his member. Abaki began to whimper louder and more aggressively. His thighs stiffened and his hands gripped her head in a tight hold with subtle attempts to pull her mouth away from his member. Autumn never let up. Abaki's struggle to resist proved feeble compared to Autumn's expertise. No longer able to hold off, he tried pulling Autumn's head from the one between his legs, but she wouldn't let up. She kept him in her mouth until he emptied his pleasure completely, and then she swallowed.

He opened his eyes and looked at her.

Autumn smiled.

He scowled. "Get up and get out!" he commanded.

She wasn't sure if she was hearing him correctly. Surely, he wouldn't be talking to her like that after the performance she'd just given.

"Stand on your feet, put on your coat, and get out of my room. You disgust me. If you could do that to me after only a first date, I can imagine what you will do or have done to others." Abaki grabbed her coat and threw it at her. He walked to the door and held it open.

She slowly put on her coat, trying to remain composed. She got to the door and stopped.

Abaki held up his hand to silence her. "Goodbye, Autumn."

Nooo, she thought. Didn't he know that goodbyes were forever? She never said goodbye to people she cared about. Her heart felt as if it had gone through a shredder and was then thrown into a dumpster. The last thing she wanted to do was lose the man she felt she could love forever.

Chapter 31: Autumn

Autumn openly sobbed. She was feeling a pain that was different than what she'd felt from losing her family, but it was just as intense. Her body trembled as she cried.

"Autumn, Autumn, wake up, honey. It's okay. I'm here."

Autumn was sweating and her heart was racing. She looked at her surroundings and was relieved that she had been dreaming—no, having a nightmare. She looked at her sister and took another glance around to confirm that she was still in her hotel room, wrapped in the towel she'd used to dry off after her shower. She exhaled. "Damn, sis. I had the worst dream."

Autumn heard A.J. approaching the bedroom door. He asked if everything was okay. Summer got up before he could make it to the threshold and told him everything was fine; she would rejoin him in a minute. She closed the door and sat back on the bed to talk to Autumn.

"Well, what the hell were you dreaming about? You scared the shit out of me," Summer stated.

"Abaki," Autumn whispered. She placed her hand on her chest then ran it across the front and sides of her neck.

"Well, shouldn't you be moaning and not crying?"

"Summer, I'm so confused. Abaki is so restrained, and

I'm not used to that. I have to fight most guys to keep them off me, but with him, I'm damn near begging for him to touch me. It's not that I want to break my celibacy, but some form of intimacy is okay, isn't it?" She had never really shared her intimate feelings with Summer before but she needed an outlet. She needed to talk to someone about the battle between her heart and mind; surely, one was smart and the other, blind. She had heard that somewhere before and was now starting to fully understand its meaning.

"Autumn, you are a beautiful and amazing woman. You are someone that any guy would love to have on his arm and invite home to meet his momma. Maybe Abaki is just protecting his heart. You may not know his struggles and what led him to be the man he is today. Give it some time; I'm sure he'll come around. Any man who spends enough time with you will fall for you, for sure. What is there not to adore about Autumn Hughes?" Summer smiled.

Autumn smiled back. She was glad to hear her sister say those words. For so long, she had awaited a man like this. Although she didn't want to admit it to her sister, or anyone, for that matter, deep inside, she could see herself loving Abaki. But for now, she just wanted to be held. She wanted Abaki to wrap her in his strong arms and tell her how much he cared for her and wanted to be with her. Autumn struggled with whether she would feel that strongly about his lack of intimacy if she were involved with other men. Was it

Abaki she wanted or just any man. She couldn't answer that question for now, based on their recent interactions, but he possessed most of the things she was attracted to. His physical appearance, his conversation, and protectiveness all contributed to a well-rounded, but at times obscure man. The thought had crossed her mind to fall back from him altogether and see where things would go when he led. She didn't want to be the aggressor any longer; she wanted to be pursued. Autumn decided that she would leave well enough alone. If Abaki wanted things to move further, it would be his call and on his timing. She had come too far to rely just on her heart to make decisions.

"Thanks, sis. I think I'll just follow his lead. Let him guide this thing we got and see where it goes." Autumn hugged her sister goodnight, and Summer exited her room, closing the door behind her. She stole a glance at the clock and saw that it was after one in the morning. She contemplated going to Abaki's room or even calling. She wanted to talk to him, to hear his voice, but she reasoned that she would follow her former state of mind and just go with the flow—his flow.

The phone rang, startling her. "Hello?" she answered skeptically.

"Autumn?"

Her voice was caught in her throat. Had she talked him up? "Abaki?" she managed.

"Yes. Did I wake you?"

"No, not at all. You okay?"

"Yes, of course. I was calling to hear your voice. A part of me now wishes I would have accepted your offer to share your room with you tonight."

Autumn wasn't sure if her heart had dropped or risen. His voice and words were the melodies she wanted to hear but she remained quiet. *Let him lead.*

"Autumn, there are some things you don't know about me, some things I have yet to reveal. I am not a complicated man; it only seems that way." He was silent for a moment. "I enjoyed spending the day with you."

"I did too," Autumn finally said.

"When we get back to Dallas, I would love to have more days like the one we just shared."

"I would like that as well, Abaki."

They used the opportunity to exchange cell phone numbers.

"Have a good night and a safe flight," Abaki said.

Autumn wished him the same and they ended the call. Now, she felt complete and was able to go to sleep, hoping that this dream would be much more pleasant than the last.

Chapter 32: Autumn

The flight back to Dallas was peaceful. Autumn couldn't wait to get back home and just relax for the day. On Monday, it would be business as usual. She daydreamed about her date with Abaki, and for the second time in a long while, she used the time on the plane to write a poem about love.

> *Love, what does it mean and how does it really feel?*
> *Is it a passion or a mirage? Is it fake or real?*
> *Does one dream about love, and if so, how deep?*
> *Is it the kind that haunts them at night while they sleep?*
> *Or maybe it's delightful and evokes daydreams.*
> *Love, what is it and what does it mean?*
> *Will I have it for me, or will it always be just a dream.*

When she got back to her house, she placed her things on the floor and checked her mail. She threw bills, advertisements, and solicitations on the counter and proceeded toward the back of the house. She was greeted by the smell of old garbage. She had forgotten to set the trash bag out before she'd left, and now, it had the whole back of her house smelling. Autumn opened the door to deposit the bag into the trash bin but ended up dropping it on the ground instead.

The backyard looked beautiful. Her lawn was nicely mowed, the bushes neatly trimmed. Her railing had not only been fixed but it was also painted the same color as her back porch. The fence was mended and painted a color that complimented the porch as well. Mulch bordered the fence, and some colorful foliage tied it all together. There was only one of a few people she could think of who would have done something so nice, and all but one would have told her. She had mentioned the laundry list of things that needed to be done at her home that night at the beer hall, but the last thing she'd expected was for Abaki to do them.

Her insides melted. Her vision became blurry from the tears, and she had a hard time locating his number in her contacts.

"Hello?" his baritone greeted her.

Autumn couldn't stop crying. No one had ever done something so nice for her without even acknowledging they'd done it, let alone without asking for anything in return.

"Autumn, what's wrong? Did something happen to you?" Abaki asked, his tone heavy with worry.

Autumn sensed the protectiveness in his voice and she tried to gain her composure quickly. She didn't want him to think she was in danger. She stopped crying and dried her tears. "Abaki ... oh my goodness. Thank you so much!"

He let out a sigh of relief.

"I ... I ... I don't know what else to say. I cannot believe you did all this. When?"

"I did it when you went to New York. Finding out where you lived wasn't hard. It's actually public record. I had a couple of my friends help me. We got it done during the couple of days you and Summer were in New York before I got there. Your neighbor allowed me to use her electricity. The only thing I had to do was mow her lawn and set out her garbage."

Autumn laughed. She knew what neighbor he was referring to. The little old lady next door was something else. "Abaki, I really can't thank you enough. You have no idea what this means to me. I'm truly grateful. How much do I owe you guys for this?" she offered, uncertain of whether he would accept payment from her.

"Nothing. When I do things for you, it's because I want to, not because I need to be compensated. You've worked hard for what you have, and from what I see, you have done tremendously well. Look at it as a blessing from above for all the hard work and sacrifices you've made for you and your sister."

"Can I at least treat you to dinner or cook you something? Please allow me to do something," Autumn begged.

"Autumn, in due time, you will have repaid me and

then some. Now that I know you are pleased, I feel better. Some people don't take too well to surprises."

"Well, this one was well received. Thank you again."

"Think nothing of it. Good day, Autumn."

"Thanks, Abaki. Same to you."

She would need a Richter scale to measure her gratitude. She called her sister and Karashae immediately and told them what Abaki had done for her. They told her they were on their way because they had to see what had her so emotional. Autumn got some wine glasses ready so they could sit out on her refurbished deck and take it all in. As she waited for them to get there, she allowed her heart to swell with joy.

~~~

Autumn missed the normalcy of her everyday life but a vacation was always welcome. She would normally have Shae open and close the shop when she and Summer went away, but this time since Karashae was with them and they were gone for almost a week, she'd posted a sign, letting her customers know that the shop was closed for vacation and when she would be returning. Business was back to usual and she couldn't be happier.

It was the week of Independence Day and Abaki had called to invite her and Summer to his house for a barbeque.

Autumn was happy that he had called her personally instead of inviting her through their mutual friends. She was looking forward to spending more time with him. Since they had been back, they really hadn't had a chance to go on any dates. Abaki was busy doing what he does and she was busy running her business, preparing for her final summer course, and spending time with Sebastian. She missed him while they were away. Stephon had a family member watch him when they went to New York. She had picked him up every Saturday since she had been back. He was such a smart kid for his age. The things he did and said amused her, and she felt blessed to have such a wonderful body of spirit in her life.

Autumn heard the door chime and looked up to see Karashae and Chaianne coming into her shop. "Hello, ladies! Welcome, Chaianne."

"Hey, girl," Karashae replied.

"Hello," Chaianne greeted jubilantly.

"So, to what do I owe this surprise visit?" Autumn gave a skeptical smirk.

"Well," Karashae began, "did Abaki tell you about the Fourth of July cookout at his place?"

"Yes, he called me about it a few days ago. You all are going, right?"

"Um hm. We go every year," Chaianne said. "He throws the best events. Just in case he didn't mention it, he lives near a bike trail, and there's also a pool in the backyard.

The house is nice, let me tell you."

"Yeah, I heard," Shae said. "We were invited last year but were unable to go. I'm really looking forward to it this time. You're bringing the kids, right?" Karashae asked Chaianne.

"Yeah, they'll be there."

"By the sounds of it, he lives in quite the digs. How can he afford such luxuries from just coaching?" Autumn asked.

"Like Karl said before, he does these really nice things for people and never charges them. They pay him back in favor," Chaianne answered.

"That's it? Nah, there's something more to it. No way are people going to just loan him Ferrari's, yachts, and freaking large homes," Autumn stated. "I'm telling you right now, if I find out he is part of some type of African organized crime or that he's a drug dealer, his sexy, fine, handsome, illegally rich behind can go. I don't do illegal of any kind!"

Chaianne giggled. "I'm sorry. I don't mean to laugh, but I highly doubt Abaki's a criminal. Seriously, it doesn't fit his demeanor. He's quiet about his financial status but I don't think it's because he's dirty."

Autumn's thoughts showed on her face. "Well, maybe you're right. But I have yet to see. I'mma pay close attention from here on out though."

"As you should, frissy." Shae smiled and nodded,

drawing laughs from the other two ladies.

"So, are you guys planning on swimming? I ain't trying to be the only one in the pool," Chaianne said.

"Hell yeah, I'm swimming. I love the water," Karashae said. "And Sebastian does too. About how many people usually come?" she asked Chaianne.

"The last few times I've been, it was about twenty of us. A couple of Karl's artists, Abe's assistant coach, his family, a couple of his friends, and us. We have a nice time. Oh, and that chick Inez was there last year. If he invited you, I doubt she will show up this year," Chaianne added.

"What's her story?" Autumn asked.

"Who, Inez?" Chaianne replied.

Autumn nodded.

"She's Hispanic, about our age, no kids. I'm not sure where they met but I don't think they even dated six months. She's a little off from what Karl tells me. When she started acting all jealous, Abaki fell back, said he didn't want someone like that."

Autumn usually didn't prejudge people, but based on what little Chaianne had shared, something about Inez didn't sit well with her. She hoped she didn't show up at the barbeque. The last thing they needed was drama. "I think this calls for a new swimsuit. You ladies down to do some light shopping?" Autumn asked. They all agreed. Just in case Inez did show up, Autumn wanted Abaki to have eyes for no one but her.

Chapter 33: Autumn

Autumn was feeling uneasy. She had called her sister three times in one hour to find out what she was wearing, what she should wear, and how she should style her hair. Summer was giving her a hard time and threatened to hang up on her, but she knew this was all new to her sister.

"Sunshine, don't fret. You'll be fine and you'll look fine. Shit, the way that swimsuit hugged you, your ass will be the envy of all women. Just chill. Wear the dress you purchased and have your swimsuit underneath. Bring your cover-up to wear when you're not in the pool, and it'll be all good."

"Yeah, I guess you're right. Thanks, Blue Skies. I'll be there by three to get you, okay?"

"Sounds good to me, sis."

"Oh, is Ajamaal coming?"

"Yeah, he said he'll meet us there. He's working the morning shift, so when he gets off, he's going home to get dressed and will just catch a cab."

"Why don't you just let him drive your car?"

"Because, fool, nobody drives my car, nobody."

Autumn laughed and fared her sister well.

When Autumn and Summer arrived, there were already people in the pool and food on the grill. They could smell the barbeque a mile up the road. Abaki greeted them as they entered the yard. Chaianne was right; the house was beautiful. It wasn't too large or too small. The backyard featured a nice-sized underground pool that could easily accommodate everyone in attendance, plus pool accessories.

"So glad you guys were able to make it," Abaki said, greeting Autumn with a kiss on the cheek and doing the same for Summer. Their trip to New York had everyone on a friendlier basis. The days of handshakes and head nods were over.

"Is there anything I can help you with?" Autumn asked Abaki.

"Well, I see you brought more ice and beverages. I have another cooler inside the house on the back porch. Do you mind bringing it out? I can fill it up and add the beverages. I just want to turn the meat so that it doesn't get too charred on one side."

"I don't mind at all. In fact, it would be my pleasure," Autumn said, eyeing him pleasingly.

She was glad that Abaki was opening up and allowing her to play a role.
She thought he was going to decline her offer to assist, but maybe he was coming around. When Autumn reappeared on the porch with the cooler, Abaki was standing there, waiting to relieve her of it. He poured the ice inside and added the alcoholic and non-alcoholic beverages she had purchased.

When he was done, he looked into her eyes. He had a

thing for boring into her eyes. "You know you didn't have to do that, right?"

Autumn looked up at him. "Abaki, it was the least I could do. You wouldn't let me purchase any meat, so I took it upon myself to at least get the drinks. Get used to it. I don't show up anywhere empty handed."

"Aunt Lully, Aunt Lully!"

"Sebastian! Hey, sweetheart. How's my Juicy Pooh?"

"I good. Mommy said I can go swimming. Can you get in the pool with me, please?"

"Of course I can, baby. Mommy and Aunt Summer will get in too, okay?"

"Yaaay. Mommy, Aunt Lully said you getting in the pool, too."

"Oh did she, now?" Karashae walked up to Autumn, balancing a dish in her left hand and hugging her best friend with her right. "What's up, girl?"

"Hey, Shae. Hi, Stephon," Autumn said, releasing Shae and hugging Stephon.

They greeted each other with the usual kiss on the cheek, as did Abaki and Karashae. Stephon and Abaki gave the universal brotherly love dap and hug.

"Let me get these beers on some ice, and I'll come relieve you of the grill for a little while," Stephon offered.

"Man, I won't argue with that," Abaki accepted.

Summer made her way to Karashae, Sebastian, and

Stephon. She was greeting them when Chaianne and her family arrived.

By four o'clock, the cookout was in full swing. The music was playing, mostly all the food was cooked, people were in the pool, and everyone really seemed to be enjoying themselves—that was until unwanted, unexpected company arrived. Autumn had never seen the women before, but female intuition told her that she was someone to keep an eye on. Summer and Karashae must have sensed something too because they went and stood next to Autumn. Chaianne seemed to recognize the guests. Autumn and Abaki were standing by the grill, removing the last of the food when the three ladies walked up to him. One of them boldly tried to give him a kiss on the lips. Abaki side-stepped the kiss and quietly asked what she was doing there.

"What do you mean? I came last year. Was I not invited?" She snickered, turning toward her friends.

"Chaianne," she said.

"Inez," Chaianne acknowledged out of formality rather than cordiality.

"Am I interrupting something?" Inez asked.

"Actually, you are," Abaki said. "If I didn't tell you to come, why would you show up?"

"Abaki, you invited me last year, and since you didn't tell me about it this year, I figured there was a reason," Inez explained, giving Autumn the side eye.

Autumn didn't want to add fuel to the fire, so she opted to walk away and give Abaki the privacy he needed to handle the situation at hand. As she started to turn away, she heard Inez say, "So is this the bitch that's been getting all your attention?"

Autumn turned right back around. "Excuse me? Bitch? I'm sorry, but whatever issue you have with Abaki is between you and him. There is no need to call me out of my name. Let's not make a problem where there doesn't need to be one, alright?" Autumn may come off as docile, but she was far from it; she just masked it well.

"Autumn, please. I will handle this," Abaki assured her. "Listen, Inez, you need to go. You weren't invited, and quite frankly, you are ruining a good time and making my guests uneasy."

"Uneasy? You think I give a shit about your guests? You don't return my calls or initiate any, for that matter. You stopped hanging out with me, and I barely see you anymore. So don't talk to me about uneasy, Abe."

Abaki's frustration seemed to grow by the minute. "Listen, why don't you and your friends leave the same way you came, and let's leave well enough alone. Goodbye, Inez." He turned to walk away, ushering Autumn deeper into the yard.

"Fuck you!" Inez spat. She swung to hit Abaki.

No way was Autumn having that. Abaki had defended

her on more than one occasion. There was no way she was going to allow a woman to put her hands on him. Autumn swung around so quickly that even Abaki didn't know what was happening. She grabbed Inez by the throat and pushed her against the side of the house. "I believe he said leave. Like I said before, don't create a problem where there doesn't need to be one," Autumn warned before releasing Inez's throat.

Inez snorted as much phlegm as she could muster and spat at Autumn, almost catching her in the face. Autumn was livid. She back-handed Inez with her left hand, and then punched her with her right, and then another left. She kneed her in her midsection and slapped her with her right hand. "Bitch, don't ever try to spit on me or anyone else, for that matter."

Inez's friends attempted to step to Autumn, but Karashae, Summer, and even Chaianne had stepped up too, daring them with their eyes to do something stupid. "Y'all bitches might just want to pick your girl up off the ground and get to stepping quick, fast, and in a hurry," Summer warned. Her two friends must have sensed that Autumn and her crew weren't to be taken lightly because they helped Inez up and walked her out of the yard the same way they'd come in.

Autumn was a bit shaken up. Once she was sure that Inez and her friends were long gone, she walked into Abaki's home and stood in the kitchen near the door, holding her chest. She couldn't believe what had just happened. Autumn had never been in a fight before. Up until now, she had managed to stay away from drama. Who would have thought that the most reserved man would have dealt with someone as ignorant and disrespectful as Inez. In a way, she felt sad. She was upset that she had reacted the way she had. She was also upset that she had been put into a situation where she had to react that way. She heard the back door open and close. Abaki stood in front of her.

"You know you didn't have to do that," he said.

"Do what, Abaki? Hit her?"

"Well, no, not that. I mean defend me."

Autumn looked up into his eyes in disbelief. "As many times as you came to my defense, you really think I was going to stand back and let a woman hit on you. Yeah right." She waited for Abaki to ask her if she was okay, to make sure she was fine, but he never did. He just grabbed her hands and looked into her eyes, not uttering a single word.

He held her hands and her gaze for a long moment. "Come, let's enjoy the rest of the night."

When they exited the kitchen, Autumn could tell that the incident was the talk of the crowd. She felt a need to apologize for her behavior. The last thing she wanted to do was embarrass Abaki and his guests.

Summer walked right up to her and hugged her. "Sis,

you okay?"

"Yeah, I'm fine. A little embarrassed, that's all."

"Embarrassed? For what?" Karashae asked as she and Chaianne joined them.

"Because I'm about to be thirty years old. I shouldn't be out here fighting like some unruly teenager."

"Shit, she deserved exactly what she got. She fucked up twice: once for trying to swing on your man and again for trying to spit on you. Hell, that alone shoulda cost her an ass whooping," Chaianne stated.

"You got that right," Karashae chimed in.

"Word! That is the ultimate disrespect. I wanted to slap the piss out of her just for general purposes," Summer added.

"And don't even feel like you have to apologize, either. Everyone out here witnessed what happened. We all agree that Inez was completely out of line and you did what you had to do," Karashae reassured her.

"Yeah, remind me not to piss you off. I don't want to get Inezzed out," Chaianne said, and they all laughed. She was good for cracking a joke to lighten the mood. It became an inside joke amongst them.

Autumn felt Abaki watching her the whole evening. She couldn't tell if he was admiring her for standing up for him or scrutinizing her for her behavior. He didn't seem pleased that she'd done what she had, but he didn't shun her either.

Sebastian came running over to where they were. "Aunt Lully, you okay? Daddy said because her spit on you, you had to kick her ass."

"Sebastian, boy, watch your mouth!" Karashae yelled, laughing as she scolded him.

"Yeah, Sebastian, that's nasty. Don't ever do that to anyone, you hear me?" Autumn advised.

"Um hm, yup. Can we get in the pool now?" he asked, his big, bright, innocent eyes willing her to say yes.

"Sure, come on, baby. In fact, we're all getting in. Let's go, y'all."

Autumn, Summer, Chaianne, Karashae, and even the fellas got into the pool, bringing the kids with them. They played volleyball and Marco Polo and just enjoyed the night. Some of the guys started discussing sports. They bickered about Lebron winning another ring and made predictions about the upcoming football season. It was now after dark, and the kids were asking for the fireworks. Abaki had purchased a ton of fireworks for the kids. They all seemed to be enjoying the sparklers, snappers, and how the little fire worms shriveled when lit. The guys took turns lighting everything they had in the boxes: bottle rockets, aerial repeaters and shells, firecrackers, ground spinners, and wheels. They had over two hours' worth of fireworks to display. The kids and the adults got a kick out of it.

Once they were done with all the fireworks, it was well after ten o'clock. Parents began gathering their children and saying their goodbyes. The night was wonderful. Chaianne and Karl and Karashae and Stephon stayed a while longer to help Abaki put things away and straighten up before leaving. Chaianne and Karl had agreed to take Summer and A.J. home so they could leave Autumn and Abaki alone. They thanked Abaki for the invite and told him how much they enjoyed themselves.

The weather was still mild and Autumn wanted to enjoy the pool alone with Abaki. "Take a swim with me." It was almost a command.

"Sure. I'll race you there," Abaki said, taking off his shirt as he raced to the pool, diving head first into the deep end.

Autumn jumped in after him, and he swam to her. "I really had a good time today. Thanks again for inviting me and my sister over."

"Think nothing of it. I enjoyed having you here."

"So, what's the deal with you and Inez? Apparently, she still has feelings for you."

"Inez and I have been over. The writing was on the wall and she chose to ignore it."

"But Abaki, sometimes we women need to hear it. We can't always assume that a guy wants nothing to do with us. We have to hear you say it, even though you may think your actions are speaking loud enough. Rest assured, verbal communication is best to eliminate misunderstandings."

"Duly noted. However, if a man says that he is no longer interested in pursuing things further and he only wants a friendship, then isn't that enough?"

"Maybe, but not all the time, as you can see. Why did you end things with her?"

"At first, Inez was everything I wanted in a woman. She was smart, sweet, attentive, loving, and the list goes on. Then, the more we became involved, the more obsessed she became. She started coming to my games, harassing the mothers, going through my phone, questioning my every move. I started easing back from her because that wasn't the kind of woman I wanted in my life. I am a one-woman man. When I decide to commit to a woman, she has all of me, not part of me. I gave her no reason to question my loyalty, yet she acted in a manner that was unflattering. So I slowed things up and eventually ended our courtship. She seemed to get it at first, but I'm not sure exactly how much she got. She still stopped by my home uninvited, sat in the parking lots after the games. It just became too much to bear."

Autumn listened intently. She definitely didn't want to make the same mistakes Inez had made. It sounded as if Abaki was a fair guy who wanted to be trusted because he gave no reason not to be. She didn't respond to Abaki because she didn't need to. Her ears were listening, her mind was processing, and her heart was embracing. He was everything she wanted in a man and then some. Autumn was tired of suppressing her attraction. She wanted intimacy. She leaned in and kissed Abaki, not just a peck; she went full throttle. She used her tongue to spell out just how much she craved him. She was ready for him to grope her and reciprocate his feelings, but he didn't. He just pulled back and looked at her.

"We can't."

We can't? Autumn thought. "Why not?" she asked, feeling rejected.

"Because we've both came so far."

"Abaki, it's a *kiss*, for crying out loud. A freaking kiss! Give me something ... anything. Just show me you like me!" Autumn snapped.

She was hurt and upset. She feared that this would happen, yet she'd put herself out there despite her resolve to sit back and let him lead. She didn't say anything else; in fact, she didn't even look at him. She just eased out of the pool, retrieved her things, and headed to her car without a wave or a goodbye. Abaki had deflated her spirits and crushed her hopes one too many times. She refused to give him more ammo to do it again.

"Autumn, please!" he called out, following her.

Autumn never turned around. She got into her car, started it up, and pulled off, leaving Abaki standing there in his wet swimming trunks, water dripping to his feet. Countless times, she had made it clear to the men she'd dated that she was ready for more. And it seemed like the more she gave, the less she got back. She was done trying. Trying to get a first-grade kiss from Abaki was starting to feel like an eighth-grade science project. There was only so much her heart could take. She began to think that this love thing was overrated. For those who had it, they were simply lucky. But deep down inside, Autumn knew her worth. And if Abaki wasn't wise enough to see that he had something good, he would lose her to someone who could.

Chapter 34: Autumn

Autumn cried a quiet, painful sob. Everything she didn't want to happen had happened. *Why won't he just kiss me?* she wondered. *Am I that bad? For sure he kissed that crazy woman, Inez.* Autumn was tired of trying to make things right with Abaki. He was sending her mixed signals and she didn't like it. She decided that she would just move on with her life, allow herself to explore other men, give them a chance they may not have otherwise received. Maybe she was being too picky. Tomorrow was a new day, and she vowed to make it the beginning of better days to come. After all, she was responsible for her own happiness.

Autumn needed to clear her mind. A good, solid workout in the LIPStick Lounge would be the perfect fix. To avoid a repeat of the incident she'd had with Jerrell last month, she parked out front. When she entered her office, she put her things down before changing into some spare workout clothes that she kept there. She turned on her system and played Foxy Brown.

Since college, Foxy's track "I Can't" had been a surefire way to get Autumn's mind off a man and focused on what was best for her. It was as if the lyrics gave her the adrenaline she needed to kick a guy to the curb and move on with her life. She made the lyrics her own. Track after track, she twirled, climbed, and slid, encompassing the pole with more energy in the next move than she'd exhibited in the last. After an hour of doing what she did best, she called it a night. She grabbed her things and headed home, ignoring the icon on her phone indicating that she had missed calls and a voicemail message. She was tired, and anything that had nothing to do with sleep would have to wait until the next day.

~~~

It was the first day of her online class and five days since she and Abaki had spoken. He had tried calling her but she'd refused to answer. He had even come by the shop, but she had ignored him and was glad that, on that day, she was at her busiest. She had shipments coming in, people stopping by to look at and inquire about the lounge, and a steady flow of customers. After an hour of waiting, he'd realized that it wasn't a good time and left.

After she closed up shop, Autumn swung by the campus to grab some things for her upcoming class. When she exited her car, she ran into her old Anatomy professor, Professor Milton. Although he had gotten older, he still looked just as good as he had when she was taking his course in college. If the fourth finger on his left hand was still sans a ring, then she still had a shot. Abaki had made her begin to question if she still had what it took to capture a man in that way. Since Professor Milton had shown interest in the past, she wanted to know what effect she would have on him now, so many years later. If Abaki wasn't going to step up and give her what she needed then she would move on. There had to be one person in the world who held the other half of her soul.

Chapter 35: Abaki

The trip to Albany ended up being one of the best decisions Abaki had made. His connection to Autumn had grown drastically while they were there, and he was really glad they'd connected the way they had. It was only right to invite her to his annual Independence Day cookout. His suspicion that Inez would show up had proved to be correct. Despite breaking things off with her, she had still managed to interrupt an otherwise perfect event. But what was he to do, get security to police an intimate barbeque? He should have sensed bad things to come when she had handled their breakup too well. All she'd said was, "I knew this was coming. Fine!" and told him to take care.

When he'd seen her enter the yard, his stomach twisted into coils. He knew Inez could be a hot head and wouldn't hesitate to ruffle feathers. But he hadn't expected Autumn to react the way she had. So far, with Autumn, he had managed to avoid the American-woman attitude that he had witnessed so many times with other women he'd encountered. But now, he had seen a different side of her. But he figured that she only behaved that way when provoked. The two of them had been exposed to each other enough for him to know that she hadn't displayed typical behavior. He got the sense that she was defending him, someone she deemed worthy of her intervention, and she wouldn't have thought twice about doing it again.

Although he didn't blame her for what happened, he hated that it had. Now, he had really pissed her off by not reciprocating a simple kiss. Her sudden departure had made him realize that if he wanted what they had to work, he had to be willing to give a little. That was why he'd swung by her shop. He had to win her back.

Abaki wasn't naïve. He had been inside Mouth to Mouth for close to an hour and she still hadn't acknowledged his presence. She had blatantly ignored him and had done a good job, while he waited patiently to talk to her. He'd heard the saying "drastic times call for drastic measures" on a number of occasions and reckoned that this situation with Autumn was one of those times. Although he had left, he'd gone back to the shop when he knew she would be closing. Unfortunately for him, he had gotten there a little too late and saw her pulling out of the parking lot. He had followed her to the parking lot of the campus where she taught, parking two parking spaces away from her car. He'd watched closely as she exited her car and listened intently as she spoke to a man with whom she appeared to be very comfortable.

"Autumn Hughes, how are you?" the man said, wrapping her in a friendly embrace.

"Hello, Milton. I'm good, and yourself?"

"I'm good. Long time no see," he said, eyeing her seductively.

Autumn's back was toward Abaki, but Milton was facing him. Abaki was able to see firsthand the lust Milton held in his eyes for Autumn.

Autumn turned her head slightly and caught a glimpse of Abaki's physique heading in her direction. She leaned into Milton for another hug, this time, letting it linger a little longer. "Oh, you have no idea how long it's been," she said flirtatiously, just as Abaki stood at her side, poker-faced.

"Excuse me, Autumn," Abaki interrupted, "can I speak with you for a moment?"

Autumn took her time averting her gaze to Abaki. "Um, excuse me. I *am* in the middle of a conversation," she replied sharply, turning back to Milton with a zealous grin.

Abaki's patience was wearing thin. He wasn't stupid. He knew what Autumn was trying to do, and he was trying his best to keep his cool.

"So, how are your classes going? Any juicy news to share this semester?" she asked Milton.

Milton glanced at Abaki and back at Autumn. He gave a quizzical glance with an arched eyebrow. "Well, not really. My students have done quite well last semester, and as you know, the summer session just started, so we'll see in the next six weeks how things sizzle up." Milton looked at Abaki again and shifted his briefcase to the other hand.

Abaki was annoyed now. His patience was gone. He was about to make an ass out of himself, and he didn't care. "Autumn, I said I need to speak with you."

Autumn must have been aware that he was no longer interested in her antics, and he noticed that Milton was beginning to feel uncomfortable. She wrapped up the conversation with Milton and fared him well. When he was a good distance away, she finally addressed Abaki. "What? What the hell can I do for you now?" she snapped. He couldn't blame her after the way he had rejected her that night in the pool.

"Listen, I'm sorry. My intentions weren't to hurt your feelings. I was ... maybe I shouldn't have refused you."

"Maybe you shouldn't have, but you did. Now if you'll excuse me, I have things to do." She turned on her heels to walk away from him.

Abaki gently grabbed her by her arm and swung her into his. He thought back to Autumn's words, *"Give me something,"* and he leaned her against a parked car and kissed her with more fervor than he had ever felt with anyone in his life. He wanted Autumn to feel his connection to her so she would never have to doubt herself or his attraction to her again. She tried to break away, but he wouldn't let her. He didn't stop until he could feel her lower her defenses.

When he finally pulled away, he said, "I said I am

sorry. Please, Autumn, forgive me. These past five days have been hell. It's like someone stole my sunshine, and I've been living in complete darkness since you've walked away from me. Give me another chance to make it right, please?"

He exhaled in relief as he watched her lips spread into a beautiful smile.

~~~

Since their reconciliation two weeks ago, Abaki and Autumn had been inseparable, speaking to or seeing each other every day. One night, they met up with Summer and A.J. and played a few hands of Spades. The other night, they met at his house and played Scrabble and watched movies. It was the first time Autumn had been fully inside his home. She'd told him that she had never seen such a nice layout. It was a two-story house. The first floor featured one big master bedroom with an ensuite bathroom, a living room, kitchen, dining room, and sunroom off the backyard. Two more bedrooms were on the second floor, along with another large bathroom and a den. A spiral staircase connected the two floors. Abaki brought her downstairs to the finished basement, where there was a bar, pool table, a large sixty-inch television, and a contemporary sectional.

"Autumn, I want you to meet two of my trusted friends. My dogs, Yin and Yang."

Autumn didn't know that Abaki had pets. When they

were there for the Fourth of July, she had never seen or heard them. "Dogs? Are they new?"

"No, I've had them for about three years. I don't introduce them to just anyone. They are never to get too friendly with anyone other than me and those I introduce to them. Do you want to meet them?"

Autumn looked nervous. "What kind of dogs are they?"

"Pure bred American pit bull terriers."

"You mean pit bulls, as in the most aggressive dogs known to man?"

"Yes and no. Yes, they are pit bulls, but no, they are not the most aggressive dogs." Abaki chuckled. "But you must know that even though they are known to get aggressive, they are not violent by nature. Dogs are trained to be vicious."

"Did you train them to be vicious?" she asked.

"I trained them to be protective, and yes, that does require some degree of ferociousness. I will say this, my dogs are well trained. They only attack when I tell them to, if I am in distress and unable to tell them to, or when someone has entered my home unauthorized. I can assure you, they will not harm you. Do you trust me?"

Abaki hoped she didn't wait too long to answer. He had told her loud and clear that he had to be the possessor, provider, and protector. If she was going to allow him to fulfill that role, she had to start now.

Abaki watched as she raised her eyes to his and answered, "Yes. I do. I trust you."

He felt her words; he knew she was telling the truth. Abaki led her to a door, but before he entered, he said something in his native language.

He started to open another door, but Autumn stopped him. "What did you just say?"

"I told them to be at ease in my native language, Krio."

"Oh," Autumn replied.

Abaki sensed her nervousness. "Please, be at ease as well. You said you trusted me. I would never allow them to harm you," he reassured her, looking down into her eyes.

Autumn gripped his hand tighter, and he felt her palms getting sweaty. "But what happens if they don't like me and try to attack me?" she asked innocently.

Abaki didn't hesitate to answer. "Then they will die because that means they have failed to obey me, and what good are guard dogs if they don't obey their master."

He opened the second door, revealing two beautiful dogs. Both dogs sat perched on their hind legs as stiff as statues. Abaki didn't move Autumn any further into the room, giving Autumn and the dogs a chance to adjust to each other.

"Would you like an introduction?" he asked her.

Autumn looked at the two beautiful creatures before

her. One was brown and white and had a red nose. He was the bigger of the two. The other was dark gray.

Autumn swallowed. "Sure."

Abaki said something else in his native tongue, and the dogs got up and walked to him. He repeated the "at ease" command, and they sat. "Go ahead and pet them," he offered.

Autumn reached her hand out, going to the gray one first.

Abaki took notice. "Yin, Yang, this is Autumn. She is a very special lady. You are to accept her the same as you accept me. You are to protect her the same as you would protect me. You are to obey her the same as you would me." He reached out and placed his hand on top of Aututmn's, guiding her to pet Yang, and he did the same to Yin.

"Which is which," she asked?

"Names or sex?"

"Both."

"The blue nose is a female; her name is Yin. The red nose is a male; his name is Yang."

"I've heard those names before, never for pets though. What's their meanings?" Autumn inquired.

"Yin and Yang come from Chinese philosophy, meaning dark and light, respectively. These two vibe off one another and will go to great lengths to protect me and each other. One is feminine and knows her role when in the presence of the male dominant. I didn't want two boys, brothers or two girls, sisters. I chose a male and a female of no relation for a reason. In the natural world, there is no stronger connection than that of a man and woman, and the same holds true for animals. They are protective of each other just as spouses are. You should read up on it. The concept of yin and yang is quite interesting," he explained.

Abaki could sense Autumn's growing comfort. He gave the dogs another command and they began wagging their tails and sniffing Autumn. "No worries. Tail wagging is good," Abaki assured her.

"Abaki, how are they around children?"

"I don't have many children around them, but they do fine with kids. When I walk them around the neighborhood, the kids pet them and they do well. Even Karl's little man has interacted with them, and you know how pesky toddlers can be."

She laughed at that. Abaki gave the dogs varying commands in his native tongue. She watched in awe as each time he said something they sat, rolled, lay down, stood at attention, walked away, came back, and were right back at their feet. After a few more minutes of petting and getting to know each other, Abaki and Autumn left the room.

"Do you like animals?" he asked her.

"I do. In fact, I've always wanted a dog. I just don't have the time to donate to a pet right now. My schedule is quite busy."

"What kind of dogs do you like?"

"Well, I like dogs. Yours are just really big, and very intimidating. Cats aren't really my speed, too sneaky for my taste. I've always wanted a shar pei. Those dogs are the cutest ever."

Abaki had to smile. He had expected her to say something like a yorkie or another small dog, but a shar pei was a bit of a surprise. But he could see why she would be interested in them.

"They are just so adorable. They have those wrinkles and a mug only an owner would love."

"Isn't that what they say about pugs?" he asked.

"Yes, but I feel the same way about them." She smirked.

Abaki noticed her dimples. He loved them and wanted to do everything he could to see them on a regular basis.

"How many languages do you speak?" Autumn asked him.

"Fluently, seven. There are about twenty-five spoken languages in my country, but I have learned seven: Krio, Bassa, Gola, Limba, Susu, and Vai. There are eight if you include the Sierra Leone sign language."

"But you only named six besides sign language," Autumn said.

"Did I need to state the obvious?" Abaki teased.

"English." Autumn smiled with embarrassment.

He kissed her cheek, grabbed her by the hand and led her back upstairs, where dinner and a movie awaited.

Chapter 36: Autumn

Autumn lay in bed thinking about Abaki. The time she had been spending with him had heightened her attraction to him, but it also piqued her curiosity about his finances. She trusted Chaianne's opinion, and after last night, she, too, doubted he did anything illegal, but he definitely had access to more money than he led on. He had mentioned something about coming from a "powerful family," but Autumn needed more details. It was too early to go digging into his personal finances, but curiosity was getting the best of her. She wished he'd volunteer the info so she wouldn't have to ask. But Autumn knew herself; she could only hold her tongue for so long.

Mondays seemed to come faster than any other day of the week. Autumn had really enjoyed her weekend, mostly because Abaki had been a part of it. Now it was back to business as usual, which meant facing another work day. The beauty about being her own boss was that she had no one to answer to. She made her own rules and followed them. The down side was there was no one else there to help her handle the affairs; therefore, she couldn't call in for time off. It was raining really hard, and Autumn was in the mood to roll over and skip work. She was tired and wanted nothing more than to stay in her comfy bed and sleep the day away. She knew that wasn't an option. Days like this made her wish she would've hired employees, so that all she had to do was manage the business without having to work the retail hours. She told herself that at the beginning of the year, she would put out an ad for a couple of part-time workers.

She checked the time on her phone and saw she had a text message: *"Just letting you know that I went to sleep with you on my mind and woke up with the same. I find myself thinking about you more often than not. I hope you have a great day, despite the gloom.*

—Abaki"

Autumn smiled at the message. It was the first of its kind and she hoped there would be many more. She eased out of bed and headed to the bathroom. During her shower, she thought about Abaki and the dates they'd had since returning from New York. He had kissed her that day on campus and he'd even kissed her on the lips when they parted but they had yet to really engage in any real physical intimacy. They had cuddled and held hands, but Autumn wanted so much more. She wanted as much as she could get without actually having sex.

She turned on the water and stepped inside the shower. The water hit her skin with just the right amount of pressure, soothing her inside and out. She closed her eyes as the water penetrated her skin. She wondered what it would feel like to have Abaki's tongue tickling her love muscle. The kiss they had shared on campus was awesome. She imagined that his tongue would be just as experienced when it finally met her pearl. Her eyes remained closed as she fantasized about Abaki exploring her triangle with nothing but his mouth. As she lathered her body, she envisioned his hands roaming every inch of her. She silently cussed for not having any of her assexories handy. She had created the perfect environment for self-pleasure, but she was missing the key ingredient. *Necessity is the mother of all innovation.* She propped her leg up on the side of the tub, positioned the shower spout just right, and let the pressure from the water bring her to a climax.

After her shower, she grabbed a towel and went into her bedroom to dry off. She applied Rice Flower and Shea lotion, and the scent coupled with her own touch turned her on. The first orgasm wasn't enough; she was horny and wanted another. Autumn reached into her nightstand and pulled out her silver bullet. It never failed her. She needed a quick release, and the bullet was just the tool to get the job done. She let her eyelids connect and thought back to the fantasy she'd created in the shower.

She pictured her and Abaki in the pool at his house. Instead of rejecting her kiss, he accepted. He kissed her back with fierce passion. His hands explored every curve of her body, and he didn't seem shy. Abaki peeled her wet swimsuit from her body until she was in the pool the same way she had entered this world, whining and naked. He kissed her neck, sucked on her breasts, and rubbed her clit with the fingers on his right hand. When her hips moved and her moans increased, he glided his middle finger into her vagina while still massaging her clit, but this time, using his thumb. Autumn increased the speed on her bullet and pretended it was Abaki's fifth finger doing all the work. In her fantasy, he kept pressing her love button until she began to convulse. She turned the bullet to the highest speed and kept it there until she released all over her towel and cried Abaki's name in deep pleasure.

Pleased with herself, she quickly dressed and jumped into her car. She contemplated stopping to get some breakfast, but she didn't want to risk being late. Opening up was a process, and Autumn never wanted to leave her customers waiting. The shop opened at ten o'clock in the morning, and already, it was close to nine-thirty. Breakfast would just have to wait. Autumn parked in front, grabbed her bags, and hummed a song as she walked to the door.

Her heart fell to her feet when she saw "Home wrecking whore-bitch" spray painted in big, black letters across her storefront window. She wanted to faint. She didn't know what to do. Even though the weather was crappy, there was still a chance that customers could show up in a half hour and see this mess. Not only was it embarrassing, it was bad for business. It was too early in the morning to have someone come and clean it up before customers showed up.

She didn't know what to do.

After a few minutes of stunned silence, she retrieved her cell phone from her purse and called the cops. She went inside to put her things in her office after requesting that an officer come to the store so she can file a report. She grabbed a bucket and some water and went back outside to try to scrub the paint off. When that didn't work, she broke down and cried. She pulled her phone out of her pocket and called Abaki. She knew that he could either help make her feel better or make the situation better altogether.

Abaki answered the phone on the first ring. "Good morning."

"Abaki, can you come by my shop? My window was vandalized, and I'm supposed to open in fifteen minutes."

"I'll be there in three," he responded before hanging up.

When Abaki arrived, an officer was already there, taking Autumn's statement. Autumn told him what time she had gotten to the shop and who she thought could be responsible. Abaki walked up, holding a brown paper bag and two bottles of juice and stood next to Autumn.

"The only person I can think of is this woman named Inez. Prior to my encounter with her, I've never had this type of problem," Autumn explained.

The officer asked who Inez was and why Autumn thought she would be the culprit. Afraid to admit that she had assaulted Inez, Autumn told the officer about the incident at Abaki's home, but omitted the physical confrontation. Abaki told the officer everything he knew about Inez, including her full name, address, and contact numbers. The officer took all the information and told them someone would be in touch soon and where she could get a copy of the report. When he left, Abaki went to the hardware store several doors down. He returned with a solution and a rag and began cleaning the window. By the time he was done, the window was clean. No one would have ever known about the disgraceful slogan that once smeared the glass. Autumn was so grateful. She showed him to the bathroom so he could wash his hands.

He returned, approaching Autumn with caution. She hadn't said much the whole time he was there and hadn't even come outside to check his cleaning progress, not that she couldn't watch from inside. Inez was the only suspect. Both of them knew she was the one who had defaced Autumn's store.

"Autumn, I'm sorry you had to go through that. I'll handle her, I promise you."

Autumn looked up at him with red eyes. "Abaki, I don't blame you. And to be honest, I don't want you to get involved. Please allow the authorities to handle this. If she will stoop this low, I don't know what else she will do. Just promise me that you will stay as far away from her as possible," she pleaded.

Abaki conceded. He didn't leave right away. He stayed with Autumn to make sure she was okay before he left.

"How did you get here so quick?" she asked him.

"To be honest, I was on my way here anyway. I was up, so I figured I would surprise you with breakfast before going to the gym." He pulled a fruit bowl out of the brown paper bag, along with a blueberry muffin. He handed her the orange juice.

She smiled. "That was really sweet. Thank you so much. I kind of lost my appetite, but I'll put it in my office fridge and eat it later. Thanks for coming by and clearing things up, literally."

Abaki smiled. "I hope this never happens to you again, but if you ever encounter such a problem, you can use Goof Off, and it will correct the issue."

Autumn made a mental note. It was close to eleven, and the first customer had arrived. Abaki gave her a hug and told her he would call her later. She didn't feel like talking, so she sent a group text out to Summer, Karashae, and Chaianne to let them know what happened. She told them that she was at work and couldn't talk but they could swing by her place later and get the details. Karashae replied, explaining that her car was in the shop and asked if everyone could meet at her place. Autumn didn't close until eight Monday through Thursday, so she didn't expect everyone to meet at Karashae's so late, but they all agreed to it.

Chaianne picked her son up from the studio with Karl and then picked Autumn up from home since they were close by. Once everyone was at Karashae's, Autumn removed a bottle of Primo Amore moscato from her carrying case and poured them all a glass, except Summer. She said wine made her sleepy, and if she drank before going to work, she would be no good to her coworkers and patients.

Autumn told them the story, and when she was done, Summer was the first to comment. "Where does this broad live, so I can go bust that ass."

"Not before I dig my claws into her," Karashae said.

"But we can't be sure she did it," Autumn tried reasoning, but she knew otherwise.

"C'mon, Autumn. Of course Inez did it. You've had that shop for, what, five years, and nothing like this has ever happened. And now after taxing that ass, someone spray paints something like that on your shop. It was her!" Summer barked.

"Yeah, I'm with Summer," Chaianne finally said. "The bitch ain't all there, and by the way Abaki said she behaved after he broke things off with her, I'm sure she did this. She was handed a huge dose of reality that night at his place, and I highly doubt that she was going to just walk away ... calmly."

"Exactly," Karashae chimed in. "That was no one but

her ass. What did the police say?"

"He told me that the report will remain on file and if anything else happened, to call them back. He did ask me to provide them with a copy of the surveillance tape once the security company mails it to me. I have a camera at the front door, back door, and the register, so they should be able to get an image, seeing as how she would have been in plain view."

"Well that's a plus. What will they do to her once they confirm it's her?" Summer asked.

"I guess I can press charges. I do plan to do that and get an order of protection, so she can't come near me, my place of business, or my residence. I regret not doing the same for Jerrell, but after that beating Abaki put on him, I haven't heard from him, so I bet he got the picture."

"What did Abaki say?" Chaianne asked before taking a sip of her wine.

"He told me to press charges. He said I needed a paper trail just in case. He was upset when he found out I didn't do the same with Jerrell. I don't know. I just want to do the right thing. As soon as I find someone I'm interested in, something or someone comes along and tries to mess that up. I won't let it happen," Autumn stated with conviction.

All of the ladies just looked at each other. Each had thoughts of her own about Autumn's recent change of events.

Summer removed her balled fist from underneath her

chin and stood from the couch. "I can't believe Abaki would even deal with a chick like that. Home wrecker? Really?! She acted like you stole her husband away from her and the kids," Summer screeched.

They all laughed. It was the first time Autumn laughed all day.

"I know, right," Karashae added. "That girl is four kinds of crazy. I told y'all those Spanish people ain't right." They all cackled.

"If she ain't smoking, she need to start, and if she is, she need to stop. Gotta even that shit out," Chaianne joked.

Autumn thought about Abaki, how sweet he was and how protective of her he had become. The thought made her feel good inside. She decided to send him a poetic text. She didn't want to say anything too mushy, but she did want him to know what she thought about him and how she was feeling at that moment. While the other ladies chatted amongst themselves, Autumn composed her poem:

"A is for Abaki, my human sentinel

B is for brave, because that is what I think of you

A stands for my aptness to call you to my rescue

K represents the keen demeanor that amasses you

I really appreciate all that you do. I can't thank you

enough for being a friend who's true."

Autumn waited for a response as she daydreamed about what she and Abaki had shared thus far. She was really digging him, and she had a feeling that he was digging her too.

Jiggling keys jolted her from her daydream. She pushed Abaki to the back of her mind and tuned her attention back to her girls. The ladies exchanged farewells and Chaianne dropped her off at home.

As she walked up her porch steps, she turned in the direction of a moving car and spotted Abaki's black coup just as he pulled in front of her house. He had once told her how his car was his pride and joy. When he wasn't coaching, he spent hours in his garage, fine tuning and inspecting it. Now, as she watched him exit in his gray hooded zip-up jacket, black jeans, and a pair of gray and black ACGs, she thought he looked damned good.

Based on their previous text exchange, he knew Autumn had been out. And whenever she and the girls were together, wine typically was involved. "I hope you weren't texting and driving. And driving after drinking," he said in an authoritative tone when she opened the door.

"Abaki, no and no. I texted you the first time while I was at Karashae's, then again from the passenger seat of Chaianne's car. And … I only had wine. I am by no means intoxicated," she stated. She watched as he gave her a once over and asked if she enjoyed her time. She told him she did. He waited by her front door and talked to her for a moment. After gazing into her eyes, he pulled her in, kissed her on the tip of her nose and made sure she got inside safely before turning to leave.

Autumn went inside, locked the door, and stood behind it with uneven breaths. *A kiss on the nose? Why not the forehead, collarbone, hell, the lips?* But the nose was cute. She would take that. *Better the nose than nowhere*, she reasoned. Autumn looked at the clock and took note of the time. She hoped Summer wasn't too busy to take her call.

"Hey, sis," Summer answered.

"Hey, Summy, you busy?

"No, not yet. Wassup?

I called to tell you about Abaki, but how was your coworker's party last week. I forgot to ask you about that."

"Oh Aut, it was really nice. I soaked up tons of ideas for your thirtieth."

"Summer, I'm not interested in doing anything that serious for my birthday. Why can't we just go out and celebrate?"

"Because, Autumn, you only turn thirty once. Besides, you haven't had a party since you turned sixteen, when Grammy cooked all that food and invited your only two friends over to celebrate." Summer laughed.

Autumn had to laugh too. They didn't hang with many people back then but Grammy had insisted on cooking like they were hosting a block party. Autumn smiled at the memory.

"I've already talked to Karashae; she's so down. Chaianne even offered to help. Abaki wants to be a part of it too. We have more people in our lives now, and they all would love to share in the moment. Your birthday is in twelve weeks, so I have work to do before then. Karashae has a wedding to plan, so she is mainly helping me with the ideas, and of course, she'll do the invitations and favors. Other than that, it's pretty simple, I promise, sis."

"Okay, if you insist. Anyway, Abaki showed up tonight to make sure I made it in safe. I think Inez has him worried, but he hasn't said it."

"Shit, she has me worried. I swear I want to lay hands on that woman. I know it's her doing that dumb mess. Your problems didn't start until you knocked her ass out." Summer laughed then added, "You would have thought she learned her lesson."

Autumn thought back to that night. She wondered if she had gone too far. "Maybe I shouldn't have put my hands on her," she said.

"Autumn, seriously, outside of her swinging at Abaki, that nasty bitch spit at you. That is disgusting. She deserved all she got for that reason alone. Her trying to hit Abaki was an added bonus. Don't even go there. The fact that you were there was enough to send her over the edge. Please. You were completely justified."

"Thanks, sis. You might have a point." Autumn

sighed. She still didn't have a good feeling about all this. In the pit of her stomach, she felt like the worst was yet to come.

"I'm going to bring it down now. I'm fatigued."

"Okay, sis. Get that mess out your head. That girl cray, and it has nothing to do with you. Love you."

"I love you too, Summer."

Autumn took a shower and lay in bed. Her thoughts effortlessly wandered to Abaki. She thought of everything they'd done and how far they had come. Autumn knew that her parents, Grammy, and God were looking out for her. She wondered what the rest of her life would look like if she ended up spending it with Abaki. She imagined them having a few kids, a modest one-family home, and living life the way it's supposed to be, happy and free. She got on her knees and said her prayers. Her happily ever after was getting closer; she could feel it.

Chapter 37: Autumn

It had been a little over three months since Autumn and Abaki had first met, and even Autumn was surprised at how well they meshed. She got to see many other sides of him and she really liked it. He seemed far removed from the reserved man she had first encountered. He talked a lot more and even smiled more. Karl had warned her that it took Abaki some time to warm up to people, and now that he and Autumn were comfortable with each other, he had finally opened up to her. Autumn drove to her sister's house. Since she and Abaki had been dating more frequently, she hadn't spent as much quality time with her. Plus, she and Ajamaal had been going away almost every other weekend or doing something together, so there was very little time for her and her sister to bond. She parked in the building lot and Summer buzzed her in immediately. When she got off the elevator, her sister was standing at the door, talking on the phone.

"Okay, soror. I can definitely make this trip. I'll reserve my flight tonight, and make sure I'm roomed with either one of you. Okay, great. I can hardly wait. Later." She turned her attention to Autumn. "Hey, sis!"

"Hey, Blue Skies. What you getting into now?"

"Oh, that was my sorority sister. My chapter is having our next meeting in the Hamptons, so she was just confirming my attendance."

"Oh, when is this?"

"We leave next week and we're staying for two weeks. I should be back after Labor Day."

"Damn, two weeks, sis? That's long."

"Aw, honey boo, you gonna miss me?"

"Yes, of course. What did A.J. say?"

"Nothing, really. He knows I'll be gone for two weeks. He pulled the same thing you pulled. He would have come but he has to work and didn't know enough in advance to request the time off. He'll be okay. We've been dating for almost seven months. A little time away can only do us some good."

Autumn nodded.

"Come on, Aut, stop it. This is the longest you and I will have been apart, and I know this. I see you and Abaki have been getting cozy, so you'll be fine. If I felt otherwise, I wouldn't even go."

Autumn knew her sister was telling the truth. Summer had always declined her sorority's vacation meetings because she didn't want to leave Autumn alone. But now that Autumn was dating and seemed happy, Summer explained that she felt it was time for her to do more with herself and her life. "Sunshine, there's going to come a point in our lives when we have to go our separate ways. We're only getting older, and the demands on our lives will take us in different directions."

Summer could handle the separation, but for Autumn, it would be more difficult. It would be like losing a sister, a best friend, and a child all at once. "I know, sis. I'll be fine. I guess that's just me being me." She laughed.

Summer smiled. "So what's good with you? Do you not have anything planned? I mean the summer is practically over and besides going home, you haven't been anywhere."

"I know, right. I don't know. Abaki and I were talking about traveling together. I told him I like to travel but haven't been many places. He's actually taking me to the gun range with him, Karl, and Chaianne. He's picking me up from the shop tomorrow."

"Autumn, first of all, you haven't been *any*where. New York, Cali, and New Orleans don't count. Second of all, why the gun range?" Summer asked.

"Well, we went to Cancun."

"Autumn Hughes, are you serious? That was a one-day booze cruise and can't hardly count as a vacation. And the gun range?" Summer reminded her.

"He asked me if I knew how to shoot. I guess with my encounters, as he calls them, with Jerrell and Inez, he wants me to be prepared to defend myself."

Summer thought about it and could see his logic.

"Anyway, a summer trip might have to wait because Abaki has an end-of-the-summer inner-city tournament on

Friday, plus he invited us to cruise on his friend's yacht for Labor Day. But I guess you won't be here for either."

"I can go to the tournament. I ain't leaving until next week."

"Oh, goody!" Autumn perked up. She was glad to be able to spend some QT with her sister. She made a mental note to remind herself to book them both full-day services at Destiny's Day Spa. She planned to treat Summer before she left for the Hamptons. Summer eyed Autumn as only Summer could. She knew her sister was changing, but she wasn't revealing much.

"So, what's up with you, Ms. Hughes? Has Abaki gotten into that love tunnel yet?" Summer asked.

"Summer! Yeah right. I wasn't celibate for seven years just so I could lose it to a guy I've only known for three months. But we have been getting to know each other a lot more. We vibe really well. He's so cool. Way different from the man we met in the beginning."

"Oh, that's good. The last time I was around you two was when we all played cards that night. He seemed attentive then."

"Yes, he's coming around. He's been busy getting ready for the tournament, so our time together has been minimal. I'm really looking forward to it. I hear it's a big deal."

"What's to be expected?" Summer asked.

"Well, from what he's told me, I guess this is his first year coaching for it. The coach that normally works for the Inner City Community Center is unable to do it this year. One of the guys on his team mentioned it to him, and he went and spoke to the powers that be and he agreed to coach. Of course, he declined the summer stipend. He is such a missionary. I wonder about him though. How the heck can he afford to turn down paid gigs? I'm telling you, Summy, something is up with him and his finances. Either he's hella rich and is pretending not to be or he's getting money illegally. But Chaianne knows him better than me, and she basically all but guaranteed that he doesn't do anything illegal. I want to ask so bad. If he *is* rich, he may think I'm a golddigger for asking, and if he's not, he may think I'm shallow for doing so."

Summer shook her head. "Ya think? I say go with what Chaianne said and just leave it be. It'll reveal itself, promise. I don't think criminal shit is his style. I'd bet money he comes from money. No worries, sis, if the Feds are watching, it ain't for him!"

"I hope not! He doesn't strike me as the drug-dealing, money-laundering, bank-robbing type, and I really don't get the feeling he's up to no good. He's just so ... so perfect. I hope he doesn't turn out to be a bad guy. He's so awesome, Summer. I really, really, really like him!"

Summer smiled as she watched her sister gloat. "You

know what I think? I think he's going to be the best guy in the world for you, and you two are going to get married and give me some beautiful little nieces and nephews."

Autumn smiled at the thought. She didn't want to continue harping on it, so she changed the subject. "Anyway, are you excited about your trip? I think I'm going to need counseling while you're away. We've never been apart." Her eyes grew sad.

"Oh, c'mon, Sunshine. Don't go getting sad on me. I'm going to miss you too, and I promise to call every day." Okay, Momster?" That was a word Summer made up for Autumn's role in her life. She served as her mom and sister.

Autumn looked at her sister lovingly. She did have a sort of motherly love for her baby sister that stemmed from their troubled childhood. Summer's protection and wellbeing had been priorities one and two since the day their Grammy had passed. Her thoughts carried her back to the day when she'd pleaded with a judge to allow her to be Summer's legal guardian.

After her Grammy had died, she had been sent to group homes because no one wanted to foster a seventeen-year-old girl. Summer was with a family, but the disabled uncle had kept making passes at her, so her social worker had removed her. She was then sent to a group home for children her age, but she was fighting almost every day. At their final hearing before permanent placement, Autumn had asked the judge if she could speak.

"Your Honor, my name is Autumn Hughes. I am seventeen years old, and my sister, Summer, is thirteen. We are all we have." Autumn took a deep breath to compose herself. "My sister and I lost all of our family: aunts, uncles, siblings, parents, and most recently, our grandmother. I know that in the eyes of the law, I may not be fit to fully care for myself, let alone my little sister; however, I can assure you that no one person or facility could give us what we need, and that is the love and comfort we get from one another. Summer is not just my sister; she's my everything. We've lost the only people who have ever cared about us, yet we still have each other. Sir, if my sister is taken away from me, you might as well give me death. Summer is all I have, and I am all she has. I can and will get a job to support us. I have one more year of school left, and then I can work full time and see to it that my sister finishes as well. All I am asking for is the opportunity to prove myself, to show the court that I can be responsible enough to care for both of us. Your Honor, I am begging you from the bottom of my heart. Please, please don't allow us to be separated again. Please don't put us, especially Summer, back into an environment where she can be violated. All I am asking for is a chance. I can do it ... I know I can."

Everyone in the courtroom that day was moved. There wasn't a dry eye in the place. The stenographer, Summer, and even the judge had tears in their eyes. Everyone was emotional except Autumn. She had cried enough. She was done crying. It was time for her to be strong and show the people of the court her strength, mentally and emotionally.

After what seemed like hours, the judge finally spoke, but not before clearing his throat and composing himself. "Ms. Hughes, let me first say that I have never had someone as young, articulate, strong, and tenacious as yourself stand before me. I have three daughters, and I can only hope that they have your resolve when they get older. The law is very stringent about these kinds of things, and for good reason. We have a duty to ensure the safety and wellbeing of all minors in similar situations. As mature as you are, you still are not of legal age to care for a minor. It is with a heavy heart that I have to deny your request."

Autumn didn't hear anything he'd said after that, and she didn't need to. After the judge banged his gavel and finalized his ruling, she and Summer were given a private moment to talk before they were sent their separate ways. "Summer, look at me," Autumn commanded in a hushed whisper. Summer was a hysterical mess. Tears flooded her eyes and snot rolled from her nose. She didn't care. All she wanted was to be with her sister, and her only wish hadn't been granted. She hesitantly looked up at Autumn. "Wipe your eyes. I don't give a damn what that judge says; we will be together." Summer held her sister's gaze. Although she didn't know for sure what Autumn had in mind, she could tell that her sister meant every word.

Autumn had always been a strong willed person. Whatever she put her mind to, she accomplished. "I already know where you've been staying. They are taking you back there tonight. I need you to listen and listen good. Before you go to bed, I want you to make sure your window is up. Watch the clock. I'll be there at exactly two a.m. to get you. Have all your things packed, hidden, and ready to go. Do you understand, Summer?" Summer nodded. Autumn wasn't satisfied. "Summer!" she said with a little more force. "You will not spend another day in the system. I'm coming for you at two in the morning and I need you to be ready just like I instructed. Am I clear?" This time, Autumn knew that Summer understood. She meant business.

Summer dried her eyes and used the sleeve of her shirt to wipe her nose. "Yes, Autumn, I got it."

"Good. I will see you later, baby sis." Autumn kissed Summer on the cheek and gave her the biggest hug. She thanked the court administrators for their time, turned to her social worker, and told her that she was ready to go.

Summer's perplexed expression and waving hands brought Autumn back to the present. "Hello? You still there? she asked with a raised brow.

Autumn chuckled at herself. "Yeah, I'm here." She shook the memory from her mind. "Just thinking about us.

And hey, you better call every day while you're gone, like you said."

Autumn stood and gave her sister a long, tight hug.

Summer walked her to the door, promising to see her at the tournament.

Chapter 38: Abaki

Chaianne fired twelve rounds, and all twelve either hit the target in the chest, head, or neck. Abaki stood behind Autumn, showing her how to grip the gun and where to look to get better aim.

"Tilt your non-firing elbow at an angle like this. Yes, hold it just like that. Keep your shooting arm straight. Don't let it move. Better. Now look straight between those prongs. Steady, and fire. Okay?"

Autumn nodded.

Abaki couldn't deny how much he was into Autumn. In fact, he had developed feelings for her beyond what he'd expected at this point. So far, everything about her was heart gripping: her personality, looks, and aura. In essence, she intrigued him. His will to remain celibate had been diminishing since they'd met. Even though he couldn't confirm it just yet, deep inside, he felt like Autumn was the one. He found himself becoming more and more concerned about her wellbeing. Before, he had no problems going to sleep and talking to her a day or two later. Now, he couldn't go to sleep unless he made sure she was safe and sound inside the house. That was why whenever she was out with the ladies, he would go to her house and make sure she'd made it in safely before he made the twenty-minute drive back home. He found himself going through great lengths to ensure that she was okay. He'd even asked Chaianne to give her shooting lessons. He was aware of the fact that he couldn't be with her every moment of the day, so he was taking measures to make sure she would be okay, even if he wasn't around. Plus, he was sure that he was going to be going away soon, handling unfinished business, and wanted to know that she had the means to protect herself in his absence.

Autumn fired her pistol five times in a row, keeping her eyes closed the whole time. When she opened her eyes, she looked at her target and then at Abaki. He smiled. She had done well. Three of the five shots had hit the target in different parts on the body.

"Much better," he complimented.

Autumn passed the instructor her weapon and walked outside of the shooting area with Chaianne, while Karl and Abaki turned in the equipment.

When they were out of earshot, Karl asked, "You love her, huh, man? Why you going through all this?"

Abaki ignored the first question. He couldn't say whether he loved her ... yet, but he did care a lot for her. "I'll be leaving soon. I've already made up my mind. I have to go back home and take care of this situation and secure some things on my family's land for good. While I'm gone, I want her to be as safe as possible," he explained.

"Oh man, she'll be good. What you think, somebody's

gonna try to harm her?"

"That's just it, man. I have no idea. That would kill me! I just gotta make sure she's good."

They all left the gun range and drove a mile down the road to a diner to grab something to eat. After they placed their orders, Abaki addressed Autumn closing her eyes when shooting. "How do you expect to see your target if your eyes are closed?" He chastised her out of care, not anger.

"I'm afraid of guns. I don't like seeing them, touching them, or holding them. Plus, I don't plan on shooting one anyway."

"Afraid? Why didn't you tell me?" he asked her.

"I don't know. I guess I didn't want to disappoint you. I could tell you really wanted me to do this, so I did."

"Autumn, so many things have happened. Don't you want to know how to defend yourself if you have to?"

"But Abaki, if something is going to happen, it's going to happen. What good is knowing how to shoot if I don't plan on carrying a gun?"

"I think if and when you learn how to shoot, you won't be afraid to possess a firearm," he retorted.

"I just don't see the need, especially if I have you to protect me," Autumn stated, looking up into his eyes.

Abaki swallowed and looked at Karl. Karl gave him that "What you gonna do now?" look but offered his advice anyway. "You know, Autumn, Chaianne taught me how to shoot. She had her license before we met. I'm a felon, so I can't get a permit. But I still go to the range and fire off a few every now and again. Even though you don't want to possess a gun, you never know when someone may try to use one on you. Then you might have to use it on them. Survival of the fittest, ma. It's definitely better to know how to use it and not have to than to need to use it and not know how. Feel me?"

"Okay. I understand."

Abaki smiled and squeezed Autumn's hand, allowing his gratitude to show in his eyes. He hadn't expected Ms. Autumn Hughes to reveal how much she relied on him to protect her. It would make leaving her that much more difficult. She was already proving to be the woman he needed. She had accepted the fact that he needed to protect her. Now, he just had to make sure she was willing to let him provide and possess. Once he made sure of that, he'd be sure that he'd found his wife.

Chapter 39: Autumn

The crowd was live and people were standing on their feet. It was the last two minutes of the championship game and the score was tied. Between Abaki's team putting on a great show and the two sets of fans eagerly cheering their teams on, the noise level was so high that Autumn wondered how any of the players could concentrate. When it was all said and done, Abaki and the 'And One' players won the game by three points. They gathered in the middle of the court and received their trophy. The team opted to give the trophy to Abaki instead of the team captain. They all posed for pictures with jubilant smiles. No one seemed to beam with more pride than Autumn.

While she waited until Abaki was done with pictures and formalities, she used the time to see what the other ladies had planned for the evening. Chaianne leaned in and whispered to Autumn, "Nothing much. Did Abaki tell you that they were going to a strip club tonight?"

"Um, no. He's not my man, so he probably didn't feel the need to tell me. Are you okay with Karl going?"

"Yeah, I guess." Chaianne snickered. "See, I'm selfish. I love that he lets me go out and enjoy myself, but when he wants to go someplace, I get all funky. Like right now, I'm feeling some kind of way because I don't want him to go, but I know I can't stop him."

Autumn laughed. "I feel you. So, let's sneak up on them," she suggested, surprising herself.

"Really? That's a great idea! We can just play it off like we didn't know they were going to be at that one," Chaianne schemed.

Karashae and Summer heard them conspiring and joined in on the fun. "What you two over here whispering about?" Karashae asked.

"Yeah, let us know," Summer chimed in.

"Shhh," Autumn told them. "We don't want the guys to find out. Abaki and Karl are going to the strip club tonight, and we were talking about sneaking up on them," she confessed.

"Ooh, sounds like fun," Summer cosigned.

"Oh, hell yeah! Let's do that. Karl called Stephon last night and asked him to go. You know his ass was all for it," Karashae said.

"Well, you bitties have fun. I'm going away next week, so I have to give A.J. that good ole QT before I bounce."

"We ain't mad at cha," Chaianne commented. "I was going to stay home with K.J. and do a movie night. But since Autumn came up with this brilliant idea, I think I'll just call Karl's little cousin over to watch him for a couple of hours."

"Game on," Karashae cheered.

Autumn waited as Abaki finished talking and receiving accolades for a job well done. She watched as he retrieved his things and headed their way. She could sense his hesitance. The quick decision whether to approach Autumn or his boys first was not lost on her. Either way, she wouldn't have been upset. Abaki owed her nothing, so she wasn't about to front like she was his one and only. She knew where they stood and had no problem playing her position; she was a friend. Much to her surprise though, Abaki walked over to her first and gave her a big hug. She told him before that she liked affection and could tell that he was making an effort to provide it.

With his left arm still around Autumn, he reached out and dapped his boys, Karl, Stephon, and then A.J. There were some other people there he knew and he acknowledged them as well.

"Good shit, bro. You stay styling. You definitely handled business out there," Karl complimented. Stephon and A.J. agreed with nods of their heads. "You did ya thing," he said, giving him a high five.

"Aiight man, me and the misses outta here. You still rolling later, right?" Stephon asked him with a slick grin on his face.

"Yeah, of course," Abaki replied. He turned to Autumn. "Where did you park?"

"About two blocks away."

"Come, I'll walk you to your car."

"Abaki, it's broad daylight. You don't have to do that."

Abaki just looked at her, ignoring her rebuttal. Autumn knew not to argue. He was showing her that his decisions weren't up for discussion. If he wanted to walk her to her car, so be it. She wanted to pick his brain anyway. She had questions that only he could answer. Her feelings for him were growing daily, but so was her curiosity. She despised the thought of him doing illegal things for money. She decided to test his honesty.

"So, what you got planned for later?" she asked him.

He grinned and looked down at her. "I'm hanging out with the fellas tonight. Why?"

"Oh, just asking. You guys doing anything special?" she probed.

"Some male bonding, that's all."

"Abaki, can I ask you something?"

"Anything."

"Are you a drug dealer?"

He frowned. "No."

"Do you launder money or do anything illegal?"

"Autumn! Why are you asking me this?"

"I'm asking because you do so much, and I assume that someone living off a coach stipend couldn't afford all that you have, but you live in an awesome home and seem to be able to afford much more than the basics. Forgive me if I seem rude, but I can't be with a man who isn't legit." Autumn watched as his facial expressions morphed from surprise, to shock, and then neutrality.

"Autumn, I understand. I'm legit. That, I promise you," Abaki affirmed.

They reached her car and Autumn looked up at him. She still wanted to pry. *Why is he so damn secretive?* she wondered. She thought for sure that her question would have provoked more of a response, but it hadn't. But she quickly figured that she had no reason to worry. If he told her he was legit, she would have to believe him. Abaki opened her door and closed it once she got in. He kissed her on the nose and waited until she drove off, before heading to his car.

Chapter 40: Autumn

Autumn offered to drive, seeing as how it was her idea to crash their guys' night out, but Chaianne insisted on driving since she lived the furthest away. Plus, she knew that Karl wasn't to be messed with, and if she needed to make a quick getaway, she wanted the luxury of having her car handy.

"Ladies, I have an idea," Autumn confessed.

Chaianne and Karashae looked at her then each other.

"Oh lawd! What you got up your sleeve," Shae asked.

Chaianne laughed.

"Okay, y'all know how Abaki thought I was a stripper and didn't want to deal with me, right?"

"Yeah, but don't tell me you really *are* a stripper!" Chaianne exclaimed.

"No, but I kind of want to play a joke on him, test his sense of humor. I want to do a secret surprise pole dance. But the only people who will know it's really me are you guys."

"What?" Chaianne yelped.

"OMG!" Karashae screeched. "How do you plan to pull that off?"

"Well, I was hoping you two could help me. I have a genie costume and a mask in my bag. I'm going to pull my hair up so it's not visible. I'll do my little dance and reveal a part of my body that only Abaki would recognize."

Shae tilted her head and held up her hand, "Okay, Aut, you know I always got your back, but I don't know how I feel about Stephon seeing my BFF dancing on a pole and shit."

Chaianne agreed.

"Ladies, they've seen me dance and ride a bull, for crying out loud. There is no difference. Besides, I don't plan on taking my clothes off. That night at Abaki's home when we were in the pool together, he had asked me if I had tattoos. I told him I did and showed him the tattoo of a pair of lips on my pelvis, right below my waistline. The waistband of my genie pants stops just below, and I know as soon as he sees it, he'll know it's me."

"So what's the point of that?" Chaianne asked.

"No point at all. Just figured I'd tease him about me being a stripper."

"Okay, little miss sunshine. Let's see what you got," Karashae said.

Surprisingly, the club wasn't a funky hole in the wall. It was actually well manicured and seemed to have a touch of class to it. The ladies took a seat at the back booth and immediately started searching for the men.

"There they are, over there in the corner," Chaianne said. "I can spot Karl's ass with a blindfold."

"Now how in the hell are we going to sit here and not

be spotted? One of them will notice us for sure and blow our cover," Karashae mentioned.

Autumn went into her bag and pulled out some items. "Here, you wear these glasses, and you put on this hat. Both can help hide your identity a bit without making you look suspicious," she stated.

"But how are we going to get drinks?" Chaianne asked.

As soon as the question left her lips a waitress showed up to take their orders.

"We'll take three kisses, three shots of tequila, and a Corona," Autumn ordered.

"Kisses?" the waitress asked.

They giggled. "Three orders of Bacardi Light with cranberry and orange juice, light ice," Chaianne clarified.

"Excuse me, Rosa," Autumn said, reading the waitress's name tag. "My boyfriend is here tonight and it's his birthday. I wanted to surprise him with a special pole dance. Who can I speak with about that?"

"I'll send the manager right over."

In a matter of minutes, a short, stubby guy walked over to their table and introduced himself. "So, one of you lovely ladies wanted to see me about a job?"

Autumn gasped. "Uh, no sir, not quite." She explained what she wanted to do and promised that it would take less than four minutes. She asked if the DJ could make an announcement that there was a lucky guy in the building and his lovely lady wanted to perform. Autumn told him what song she wanted, and the manager agreed to let her do her dance.

"The ladies break in ten minutes. You can go up and do your thing during that time. If you're good, maybe you can work here," he offered.

"Uh, yeah, about that ..." Autumn said, and the three women laughed heartily.

Everyone tossed back their shots and chased it with their drinks. Autumn guzzled her beer in no time and had eased out of the booth to go change. When she came out, one of the bartenders showed her where she would make her entrance. Autumn asked for one more shot. Her nerves were acting up, mainly because she wasn't sure how Abaki would react to her performance. She didn't want to upset him; she simply wanted to play a joke.

The emcee got on the mic. "Okay fellas, there's a woman here who says her man is in the building, and she wants to surprise him with a dance. So if you got a lady, pay attention; this could be her."

When Autumn heard T-Pain's "I'm in Love with a Stripper," she took a deep breath and sauntered onto the stage. Every man looked on curiously, wondering if she was his chick.

"Yo, that's Fred's baby momma," Karl called out.

"Yeah right. That ain't my chick. She at home with them damn babies."

They all laughed. Karl and Stephon looked and confirmed that she wasn't either of their women. They heard roars and laughs coming from across the room and figured that one of the guys over there was the victim.

Autumn was a natural. She had the grace of a professional dancer. She twirled, wiggled, dipped, and swayed to T-Pain's beat. She climbed all the way to the top of the pole and swung her body around until the onlookers got dizzy. In a quick move, she flipped her legs over so that she was hanging upside down and moved down the pole slowly and seductively. She stole a glance at Abaki's table to see if he was watching. Satisfied that she had his attention, she turned right side up and rolled her midsection from front to back, in and out. When she caught him looking at the tattoo, she knew she had him.

Just as the song was ending, Autumn completed her dance with a full split at the base of the pole. She got up, dashed off the stage, and ran toward the bathroom. As soon as she finished, she heard thunderous applause and loud whistling. All of the men hollered for her to come back, waving her toward them. Autumn never stopped, not even to pick up the pile of money that lay on the stage after her sultry routine. Her main thought was to get the hell off that stage and out of the club before Abaki and the other guys caused a scene.

Autumn trotted into the women's room so she could change clothes. Once inside, she leaned against the door and inhaled deeply. *Whew, I can't believe I just did that!* She had to smile at her antics. She never thought she would have done that but it was something about Abaki that brought out the boldness in her. After quickly switching her attire, she exited the bathroom. She took a glance down at her shirt and pants to make sure everything was in place.

A familiar voice startled her.

"Is that your idea of some sick joke?" Abaki said, causing her to jump.

She couldn't even respond in her own defense. There, standing before her, was a blurry vision of Abaki. She couldn't tell what kind of mood he was in. She didn't know if he was cool, calm, and collected or annoyed, astonished, and turned off. She wanted to think he was okay because she'd seen him laughing and joking with the guys. Hell, they had all even enjoyed the sight of two women at their table grinding on each other, putting on a show of their own.

Autumn decided to feign ignorant. "What are you talking about?" She didn't know if it was the alcohol making her bold or not; either way, she wasn't backing down.

"Oh, so we're gonna play that game?" He was stone-faced.

"Abaki, I don't know what you're talking about. Now

please, excuse me," she said, trying to side-step him.

Abaki gently grabbed her by the arm and looked into her eyes.

"Who are you here with?" he asked.

Autumn swallowed. She wasn't sure if she should tell him the truth or avoid it. The last thing she wanted to do was get her friends in trouble, but she saw Karashae looking their way and was glad when she came to her rescue. Abaki's back was toward them, so Karashae and Chaianne walked on either side of him and stood next to Autumn so that all three of them were facing him as a united front.

"Yo Abe, why you holding my girl hostage?" Chaianne asked.

"What are y'all doing here? Matter of fact, don't even answer that for me; tell your husbands," Abaki told them as he stepped aside so they could go before him.

He waited until all three of them were walking back into the main room and followed. Chaianne tried to head out the front door but Stephon spotted them and called out to Karashae. Karl turned around and locked eyes with Chaianne.

"Oh, fuck!" Chaianne whispered. She and Karashae exchanged nervous grins and headed over to the guys' booth.

"Word, Chai?!" Karl asked.

Stephon didn't even say anything at first. He just looked at Karashae, smiled, and shook his head. Karashae walked over to him and sat on his lap. He leaned in for a kiss. "You spying on a brotha?" he asked her.

Autumn and Karashae made brief eye contact. "Actually, no. We were all on the phone and decided to do something."

Abaki pulled out a chair for Autumn. He stood close to her, listening to his boys.

"So, of all places, you end up at the same club your fiancé happens to be at?" Stephon inquired.

"Yeah, I guess. We didn't know what club y'all was gonna be at," Karashae answered with a straight face.

Chaianne looked at Karashae, trying her best to hold back a snicker.

"What's that look about? Who got lil man?" Karl asked his wife.

"I had your cousin come over and watch him. She's just going to sleep over," Chaianne answered him.

Fred finally chimed in. "Y'all here and y'all need to be home, cooking ya man a good meal and waiting in bed with a teddy on, or something."

Everybody laughed, including Abaki.

"That's what I'm talking about, cuz. I bet you didn't even cook before you left, huh?" Karl said, looking at Chaianne.

Chaianne shot him a guilty look. "Whatever! You know I ain't got to cook to feed you," she teased, twisting her lips and slanting her eyes.

Karl licked his lips and threw her a wink. "Come here, ma. Kiss Daddy." Chaianne gave her man a long, juicy kiss.

"If you're hungry, tell me what you want and I'll go to the bar and place an order," Chaianne said, when their spontaneous passion ended.

Karl told her to get him two cheeseburgers, one for himself and the other for Fred. He handed Chaianne his bank card. Stephon told Karashae to order him a dozen honey barbeque wings. He didn't need to hand her the cash in his pocket. She already had his bank card in her possession. That was how they rolled.

Autumn stood up and looked at Abaki. "What would you like?"

"You know you don't have to do this, right? I mean, not being my lady and all. I don't want you to feel obligated."

"Abaki, I'm grown. If I want to place an order for a friend, I can do that, okay? Now tell me, would you like something to eat?" She winked.

Abaki watched her lick her lips. "Yes, please. Wings, mild and on the crispy side." Autumn took a step to walk away, but Abaki called after her. She turned her head and saw him standing with his arms folded, cash dangling from his fingers. Autumn took a step backward, grabbed the money, and proceeded to the bar to order their food.

After they ate, Abaki ordered another round of drinks

for everyone and Stephon treated the ladies to lap dances. Karashae was having a ball. She had even danced for Stephon with one of the girls. They all laughed at the performance. Everyone enjoyed themselves. Chaianne spotted a stripper whom she thought was pretty attractive and met Karl's physical qualifications: thick and cute with big tits and a big butt. She waved her over and paid for her to give Karl a lap dance.

Abaki stole a glance at Autumn. She hadn't said too much to him since getting his food. "Did you drive?" he asked her.

"Nope," she said, finishing up the last of her drink. Autumn couldn't deny that the drinks had her feeling nice. She'd had two shots, a Corona, and two kisses. She giggled more, talked slower, and smiled harder.

"Who drove?" he asked her.

"Chaianne."

"So curt," he replied.

Autumn looked at him and batted her eyes with incredulity. She had the kind of eyelashes that women had to purchase to emulate and she used them to show Abaki just how bewildered she was by his demeanor. She still hadn't determined if he was upset about her performance or not.

Karl heard Abaki ask Autumn about how they had gotten there and then asked Chaianne the same thing. After his lap dance, he knew what time it was and was ready to leave the scene. "Yo Steph, my lady brought everybody here, and I don't think she's fit to drive." He chuckled, looking sideways at Chaianne.

"Aiight, man. That's cool. I got mine, and I can take Autumn home too."

"Fred, you can take my truck, and I'll get it from you in the morning," Karl said. "Fellas, it's been real, but I need to get my wife home while the getting is good." Karl dapped hands with Abaki and Stephon, and Fred followed suit.

Autumn was grateful that Stephon would give her a ride but she wanted a different chauffeur. She looked at Abaki. "Do you mind taking me home?"

Abaki looked into her eyes. "You have to walk the line first," he said to her.

Stephon started laughing.

"I'm joking. Of course I'll take you home. You ready?"

"Mm hm, yup," she said, imitating Sebastian.

This time, Karashae laughed.

They all stood. Karashae and Autumn hugged and Abaki and Stephon shook hands. They all fared each other a good night and safe travels. Abaki exited the venue with Autumn close by his side. He opened the passenger door for her and reminded her to buckle up. He climbed in, started the car, and buckled up as well. He turned on the radio to eliminate the silence. Autumn heard Zhane's, "Sending My Love" coming softly through the speakers. She turned it up and sang along with the song, feeling the lyrics and the melody penetrate her deep within. Autumn was killing it. The beat alone had her in a trance. She recited the lyrics with more fervor than she had ever performed. Maybe it was the alcohol, but right then, that song was everything to her.

Once it went off, Abaki said, "You like that song, I see."

Autumn looked up but didn't answer. She just looked into Abaki's eyes, hoping to find some reassurance that she was the kind of woman he wanted. But instead of finding answers, she found herself becoming more emotional. Before the lone tear could fall from her left eye and spiral down her cheek, Abaki had cleared it away with a swipe of his thumb. The alcohol had her emotions running on high, and the song had put her over the edge. She was feeling him, and she doubted that he even knew how much. All she wanted right now was for him to hold her, kiss her, and tell her that he loved her, even if he didn't mean it. Autumn Hughes was craving love, Abaki's love.

"So, Ms. Music Nerd," he said, smiling. "Can I quiz you lyrically like you did me theatrically?"

Now it was Autumn's turn to smile. "Sure." She wiped her eyes and the top of her lip.

"Name this song: 'Most of these girls be confusing me. I don't know if they really love me or they using me.'" Abaki did a nice job rapping the song. Autumn would never have taken him for the hip-hop type. "Don't sleep," he joked. "Name the song."

"Diddy, 'I Need a Girl, Part One,'" Autumn replied.

"Okay, good. Here's another. 'All them days that I reminisced about how I used to kiss them pretty lips. But as long as you happy, I'mma tell you this; I love you, girl, and you're the one I will always miss.'"

"Abaki, um that's the same song. Diddy, 'I Need a Girl, Part One.'" She laughed.

"Oh, my fault. One more. 'Ay yo, the sun don't shine forever, so as long as we here, we might as well shine together. Never mind the weather, go somewhere and get our minds together. Build a love that will last forever.'"

Autumn looked deeper into his eyes. Her smile faded. *He couldn't be.*

"When you talk, I listen, Autumn. Even when you don't utter a word, I still seem to understand. You like threes; that's a good number for you. Three times I've told you 'I need a girl,' so now I'm asking you, will you be my lady?"

Autumn wanted to faint. She wanted to pinch herself; better yet, she wanted him to pinch her. He was asking her to go steady with him. Abaki wanted to be her man! She wanted to fly all the way back to Albany just to kiss the plots of her family and personally thank them for answering her prayers. But for now, she would send them a love gram from her heart.

She didn't even remember the ride home. She was still stuck on the fact that Abaki Lemande had asked *her* to be his lady. She couldn't even recall if she had answered him. All she knew was that her heart was smiling like it had never smiled before. Finally, they were making progress.

Chapter 41: Abaki

It wasn't pleasing to see his potential lady put herself and their possible relationship at risk by dancing sexily in front of a crowd of men. Autumn wasn't concerned about his ego. He could tell that she was trying to tap into his emotions, and it had worked. He had already decided that he wanted to take things to the next level with her. When they'd made it to the car, he'd watched in awe as she swayed and sang so melodically. He had heard the song before, but right then it had taken on a whole new meaning, and he let her have that moment for as long as the radio station was going to let the song play. He was very well in tuned to Autumn's emotions; he knew what her singing meant. She was singing her heart out to him. For the past few days, he had been wondering what things would be like if they were a couple. So tonight, he'd taken the necessary steps to ensure it. Now, he was worried because Autumn hadn't even replied. Maybe he had been too late. Maybe her performance was her way of showing that she didn't care anymore, that she had given up on trying to get him to accept, touch, and want her. That alarmed him.

Abaki turned off the car and got out to let Autumn out and walk her to the door. He watched as Autumn retrieved her keys from her bag. "Are you coming inside?" she asked him.

"Are you comfortable with that?"

"I don't think I've ever been so sure of anything." Autumn opened the front door and was greeted by the darkness that waited inside.

"Autumn, you should leave a lamp or something on when you leave. It's not safe to walk into the dark. I also noticed there is no sensor light on the outside. Sorry, don't mean to be pushy, just suggesting safety precautions," he advised her.

"Duly noted. Come in. Make yourself comfortable," Autumn offered.

"How about we do a walk through, so you can show me the floor plan." Abaki wasn't being nosy. He was being safe. He needed to know his surroundings. Plus, he wanted to see if there was anything he could do inside her home that would make her safer.

Autumn led him through the house, showing him the bathroom, bedrooms, den, and even the basement. When she finished the tour, they walked back into the living room and Autumn turned on the television and her stereo.

"What's your favorite movie?" she asked Abaki.

"Oh, man. You can't ask me that. I have so many favorites. Let's see, some of the movies I can watch over and over are *Belly, Paid in Full, Takers, Italian Job, Scarface, Heat,* and the list goes on. But those are at the top of my list.

How about you?"

"I'm glad you asked," Autumn said, still smiling. "I like *In too Deep, Love & Basketball, Juice,* hell, anything with Omar Epps. I love that man. *Lean on Me, Women of Brewster Place, Fifty First Dates, Disappearing Acts, B*A*P*S;* that's my movie for real. Some of my old favorites are *Little Shop of Horrors, The Boy Who Could Fly, Teen Wolf, Teen Witch, Beetlejuice ...*"

As if just processing all that she'd said, Abaki asked, "Wait, you like *B*A*P*S*? That was a good movie. Not too many people were feeling that."

"Oh yeah, Niecey and Mickie were something else. But they loved that Mr. B, and he loved them."

Abaki observed her, how she talked, the way she smiled. His phone chimed, letting him know his battery was dying. "Do you have a charger I could use?"

"Is it a smart phone?"

"Yeah, Android."

"Okay, look in my room in the bottom drawer of the night stand. There should be a charger. I'm about to take a couple of Advil. I feel a headache coming on."

"Take it with warm water; it dissolves quicker," Abaki advised, heading into her bedroom.

Upon entering her room, he noticed that she had two nightstands and wondered which one she was referring to. Since she lived alone, both sides of the bed belonged to her, so he figured the charger could be inside either. He tried the one on the right side of the bed first because he noticed an outlet near it. When he opened the drawer, he was taken aback by her arsenal of sex toys. He saw dildos, bullets, oils, nipple clamps, handcuffs, and other items of which he wasn't sure the purpose. His temples pulsated. *Why does she need handcuffs?*

When he turned around, Autumn was standing in the doorway of her bedroom with her arms folded, watching him. "See something you like?"

"More like something I don't."

Autumn walked to the other side of the bed, opened the bottom drawer, and pulled out the charger. "Sorry, I didn't specify which nightstand."

Abaki was quiet. He didn't know how to address the handcuffs or if he even should. She went into the bathroom and changed into a pair of leggings and a thin tank top that she had left in there earlier before joining Abaki in the bedroom.

"You were right about the warm water. My headache is subsiding, and I just took them."

"Old trick. Now you know."

Autumn glanced at her nightstand. "Are you okay?"

She had opened the door by asking, so he walked in. "Why do you have handcuffs?"

Autumn smiled. "I own an adult novelty shop, Abaki. I

have a lot of things that I am unable to use right now. Sit," she invited him. Abaki sat on the edge of the bed. "Can you tell me why it's been thirteen years since you've had sex?"

He knew that at some point he was going to have to provide an explanation. Now was as good a time as any. "Like I told you before, during my college years, women seemed more interested in my flesh than they were me as a person. Besides the girl from back home, the first real sexual experience I'd had was with a cheerleader. We had sex a couple of times, but she told me that it pained her to do so, so we stopped doing it. Then one day, me and a few friends went to this campus party. One of the girls there was interested and seduced me. During sex, she too said that she was unable to handle it and pushed me off her. She told me I was some kind of freak because my penis was larger than any man's she had ever seen. After that, I felt weird. I didn't want to be subjected to that ridicule again. I decided that from that day on, I wouldn't engage in sexual intercourse with anyone other than my wife."

"Thirteen years, though? Do you at least masturbate?"

"Not really. I can count on one hand, maybe two, how many times I've done that."

"Wow! How old are you, anyway?"

"Thirty-three."

"I'll be thirty in October, the twenty-second."

"I knew your birthday was in October; I'd heard your

sister mention it."

"When is yours," she asked him.

"February, the fourteenth."

Autumn's eyes got wide and then teary. "Valentine's Day?" she whispered.

"Yeah, is something wrong with that?"

"No. I always loved Valentine's Day. It was a special day in the Hughes household. Every year, my father would come home with something for Summer and me and something even bigger for my mom. My mom would cook us a special meal and then usher me and Summer off to bed. Now I know why, but back then I just thought it was routine." Autumn's mood turned solemn. She looked back up at Abaki. "My parents' anniversary was on that day. My father's mother's maiden name was Love, so her husband married her on Valentine's Day, and he felt there was no better way for him to solidify his love for my mom, so he kept the tradition going. Even his parents' parents as well." She smiled.

"I guess that makes the day even more special," Abaki told her.

He felt the urge to kiss Autumn. Usually, she initiated a kiss on the lips, but seeing her so somber and beautiful made him vulnerable to her intimacy. But first, he had a question. "How many men have you slept with?" That was a personal question, and he knew it. He had just revealed that he had only been with two women, so he didn't think it was a big deal for her to disclose the same.

"Oh God. Are you going to judge me?"

"That depends," he said honestly.

"How much is too much?" she asked.

"One," he answered.

Autumn playfully punched him in the arm. "Eleven."

"Eleven?" He asked for confirmation, not letting his face show how he felt about it one way or the other.

"Yes. Does that turn you off?" she asked him.

He thought about her question. "Eleven, that's a lot, but not *too* bad. When we get into double digits, it makes me wonder a little. I know American women operate on different principles, but let me ask you, if you give yourself to a man who has no intentions of making you his wife, what have you saved for the man who actually does?"

"I guess I never looked at it like that. I've had men perform oral sex on me but I've never done it to them. No one knows what Autumn feels like raw, in the natural. I've never had sex without a condom, and never anal."

Anal? Abaki thought. *Oh, she must be a little on the freaky side.*

"Did I just gross you out?" she asked.

Abaki wasn't against anything in the bedroom, although he did have reservations about some sexual acts. But if she liked it, he had to love it, anything to make his lady happy. He just wanted to be sure that what they did stayed in the sheets and didn't spill out into the streets. When he got married, he would be more than willing to do anything his wife wanted insofar as it didn't involve other people. He was willing to hang her from a chandelier if she so chose, but they would be the only two in the room.

"So, you've never gone down on a man?"

"Nope. I've thought about it, but to me, that's such an intimate act that I just wanted to wait until I was in a real relationship with someone special before taking it there."

"Were you not in relationships with others?"

"I called myself dating four of them, but none made it to the one-year mark. Two of them were just fillers, two-date stands, if you know what I mean. The rest, casual."

"To be honest, I have never gone down on a woman, nor has one ever been down on me."

"Yeah right! You've never experienced oral sex as the giver or receiver?"

"Never. I hope the first woman I do perform it on is willing to teach me."

"I'm a professor; that's what I do best." She laughed. "I'm joking."

There were several moments of silence with Abaki and Autumn just staring at each other and then looking either down or around the room. Keri Hilson's, "Knock You Down" played on the stereo. *I never thought I'd fall for you as hard as I did. You got me thinkin' 'bout our life, our house, and kids.*" The lyrics couldn't be more telling of how he'd felt since meeting Autumn. Abaki watched as she tickled the corner of her mouth with her tongue in apparent deep thought. He leaned against her headboard and pulled her into his arms. Using his pointer finger and thumb, he guided her chin so that her lips were next to his, and he said, "You never answered my question. Will you be my lady?"

Her breathing became labored. "I would love to, Abaki."

He grabbed her so that she straddled him. His right hand gripped the back of her head and he pulled her in for a kiss. He didn't hold back. Autumn's subtle moans let him know that she was just as much into the oral embrace as he was. Penetration wasn't an option, but he was willing to please her in other ways. Flipping her over and laying her on her back, Abaki took off his shirt and began caressing her breasts, continuing to kiss her. Autumn started to remove her clothing, but he stopped her. Removing his mouth from hers, he placed his lips on her left breast and then her right, alternating between the two. He tenderly bit, nibbled, kissed, and licked her nipples through her thin top. Autumn's body squirmed with pleasure. The light pants she wore were thin enough for him to stimulate her clit without ever undressing her. Still teasing her nipples, he used his free hand to rub on her love button. Autumn gasped in pleasure.

Abaki was rock hard. He pulled his body up so that Autumn could feel his erection. He seductively grinded his pelvis on hers and watched as her eyes fluttered in ecstasy and her body moved to the same tune. He started to pull her on top of him, but she stopped him by grabbing his butt with both hands. She moved her hips underneath him and told him, "Don't stop." Her eyes were closed, her back arched, and head tilted backward.

"Oh Abaki, baby, please don't stop. This feels so good," she cooed as she massaged his back.

A light moan escaped his lips, and he began sucking and kissing on her neck.

"Yes, suck harder and move faster. Please, Abaki, baby. Yes, come on, baby. Faster. Yes, right there. Oh goodness. Please baby, faster. Yessss! Oh Abaki, I'm cumming! Oooh," she grunted.

Autumn panted for a few moments and then eased him off her, pushing him onto his back so she could climb on top. She straddled him and moved her hips slow and steady. Rocking back and forth, she applied just the right amount of pressure so that her love button was being massaged in a way that had her on the brink of another orgasm. She bucked back and forth, slow and fast, the whole time, teasing her nipples through her shirt. They had been at attention for the past twenty minutes and were still hard as missiles, just like Abaki's penis. The pinching and squeezing, twisting and turning had Autumn ready to cry out. Abaki grabbed her around her hips and helped guide her to her second orgasm. Talking wasn't his thing. He got his rocks off by watching and listening to Autumn purr like a kitten. She liked to close her eyes a lot. He liked to keep his open. He wanted to watch her in her glory and take in the site of her sweet sexual releases while she still remained chaste. Abaki watched as her body twitched and listened as she whimpered. He took note that she was vocal during times of intimacy. And the fact that he could make her feel that good without them having sex pleased him even more.

Chapter 42: Autumn

I cannot believe he just made me cum like that!
Autumn thought. Finally! Mr. Sexy was able to make her
orgasm outside of her dreams, and Autumn was beyond
pleased. Just as she was thinking about climbing on top and
straddling him, he had pulled her in for the same. She had
hesitated at first because she didn't think she could handle
his rejection. *Do it to me once, shame on you. Do it to me*
twice, shame on me. Her father had been known for saying
that, and it was applicable every now and again. When it was
all said and done, Autumn had cum once and orgasmed
twice, and all the while, her clothes never came off. That
hadn't happened to her before, ever. If someone had told her
that she could orgasm while fully clothed, she would have
sworn they were lying.

Curiosity was getting the best of her, and she wanted
to see his dick. She wanted to feel it, hold it, and caress it.
Leaning down to kiss Abaki, she used the opportunity to
massage him through his jeans. He was lengthy and thick.
Sliding down his mid-section, she stayed mounted but
stopped at his knees. She began unzipping his pants, but he
grabbed her wrists.

"No."

She snatched her hand away. "Yes."

Then it dawned on her that he probably thought she

wanted to sex him, but she didn't, she just wanted to see it and touch it. "Trust me, please?"

He answered with his eyes.

Once the zipper was fully descended, she located the slit between his boxer briefs and removed his member, licking her lips subconsciously. *Damn!* Reaching over to her nightstand, she opened the top drawer and grabbed a small bottle of baby oil.

"I just want to touch it. Is that okay?" she asked.

He nodded.

Abaki was definitely larger than any man she had ever been with. She figured that her fists were about three inches wide, so Abaki had to be about ten to eleven inches in length and two and a half inches in diameter. Her calculations were based on the fact that she had two hands around his shaft, and they were two inches apart. He still had about an inch underneath one fist and another inch or so above it, including the head. With her hands slick from baby oil, Autumn gingerly and expertly massaged his member until it stiffened more. The tip of his dick glistened from pre-cum. Autumn began massaging faster and harder. Abaki hissed with satisfaction. A hand job was new to her, so she wasn't sure if she was doing it right. She wanted to know what turned him on and asked him to show her.

Grabbing both of her hands, he guided her so that one of her hands was toward the top, just under the head, where it met the shaft, and he placed the other hand on the lower half, not quite in the middle, but not at the bottom either.

"Slow and steady," he instructed her. Autumn glided her hands up and down his shaft slowly and consistently, just as he had directed. Every time her top hand gripped the rim of the head and then went back to the shaft, he shifted and grunted. She had located a sensitive spot. Using that to her advantage, she added more oil and went back to methodically stroking his member. Twisting, turning, and gliding, Autumn found a rhythm and stuck to it. The more pre-cum that oozed from the tip, the more she wanted to lick it off. When Abaki closed his eyes for a brief moment, she threw caution to the wind and did just that. His eyes flew open and he looked at her in awe and shock. He didn't scold her or stop her, so when more reached the tip, she did the same, this time, licking it a little more seductively.

Her grip got tighter and her movements a little faster. She positioned herself so that her crotch was now on his shin. Autumn moved her hips so that her clit could grind against the muscle in the front of his leg. The faster she rocked, the faster she massaged, and the more there was to lick off the tip of his dick. Abaki kept his eyes open. He started shaking. He clutched the sheets, gritted his teeth, and grunted loudly as he ejaculated. Autumn never stopped massaging. She kept the rhythm until she felt she had emptied his balls. He pulled her on top of his chest and kissed her hard. Both of them were spent. Abaki tucked his penis back into his boxers and zipped his pants. He kissed Autumn on the forehead, and then the tip of her nose and cradled her in his arms. As they lay face-to-face, they both fell into a deep slumber.

Chapter 43: Autumn

The morning sun shone through the slits in the blinds and through the curtains into Autumn's bedroom. Last night had been magical, and she had one man to thank for it. She opened her eyes to see Abaki looking into hers. "Watching me sleep, are you?" she asked, recalling when he'd said that to her when they were in New York.

"An appraisal is more like it. Did you sleep well?"

Autumn stretched her arms, legs, and back, and then placed her right arm on his waist. "I slept very well, thanks. And you?"

"Never slept better."

Autumn's cell phone rang, as Abaki got up to go to the bathroom. She looked at the time and knew that it was probably her sister, but she second-guessed because it was too early for Summer. Checking the caller ID, she saw Karashae's number. She didn't want to be rude, so she figured she would answer and let her know she had to call her back. "Good morning," Autumn greeted.

"Oh, Chaianne," Karashae said, "she must have had a long night because she is usually up earlier than this."

"Is that right?" Chaianne added. They had Autumn on a three-way call.

"Ladies, what can I do you for?" Autumn asked.

"Oh, Autumn Hughes, you can start by telling us how

your night ended," Karashae said.

"Well, what if I told you it's still in progress?"

"Abaki stayed the night?" Karashae screeched.

Autumn whispered, "Yes, and he's still here. He just went into the bathroom, so if the two of you can swing by the shop around one or one-thirty, it's usually quiet during those times, and I can fill you in. I gotta go."

"Oh, we'll be there," Chaianne said before they all hung up. Autumn placed her phone on the nightstand and kissed Abaki on the lips when he reentered the room. As he was getting ready to sit beside her, the doorbell rang.

"Busy woman, aren't you?"

"Not usually. Rare moment." Autumn walked to the door and looked through the peephole. It was Summer.

Autumn greeted her. "Good morning, sis. What you doing here so early?"

"I was on my way to get some things from the market and decided to check on you. How did the strip club spying go?"

"Shhh," Autumn tried hushing her.

Abaki entered the living room.

Summer's eyes got wide. "Well, well, well ..." she teased. She eyed Autumn suspiciously. "Hello, Abaki. Good to see you again."

"Hello, Summer. Likewise. Excuse me." He turned to Autumn and wrapped her in his arms. She wanted to melt and stay there for eternity. "I know you have to get to work, and I have to pick up my bike from the shop. I will call you later, okay? Stay sweet, my chocolate angel."

Chocolate Angel? He had given her a nickname already, and she liked it. "Okay, I will." Autumn blushed. "And please do," she replied, referring to his promise to call her later. Autumn walked him to the door.

"I put your charger back in the drawer. Thanks for a wonderful night." He kissed her on the tip of her nose and left.

She closed the door and stood there for a minute, taking in his scent and relishing in the memories of their night.

"Uh, uh, un," Summer interrupted her thoughts. "I want details, now! You have to be to work in an hour, and I'm not leaving until you fill me in."

All too eager, Autumn grabbed her by the wrist and led her to the couch. "Oh my goodness, Summer. I can hardly contain myself. Abaki is the real deal."

Autumn told her about the strip tease she did at the club, how Abaki busted her, and then how they were spotted by Stephon when they were trying to sneak back out. "I asked him to drop me off and invited him in. We talked, and one thing led to another."

"You fucked him?"

"Geez! No, Summer. But he did make me cum and

orgasm twice."

"What? How the hell he do that without fucking you?"

"Summer, you are such a wet brain sometimes. He played with my love muscle and other sensitive parts of my body until I responded in a wet way." She laughed.

"Oh, well, alrighty then. I've yet to experience that," she admitted.

"Oh Summer, it felt so good to be able to have a human body help me do things I've done on my own for so long. I'm in awe. I really like him."

"Well, he must like you too, the way he embraced you and called you his chocolate bunny, or whatever he said."

"Get it right; he called me his angel, his chocolate angel."

"I'll give him that. That's cute."

"Oh, and he asked me to be his lady last night!"

"Get out! So you guys are an item now?"

"Yes, sis. Finally, I got a man!"

"Oh Aut, I am really happy with you, as you would say. You two make a really cute couple. I have no doubt in my mind that Abaki is what you need and will truly make you happy."

"Thanks, sis. I've prayed for this for so long. I think our visit to Memory Gardens helped. I told Grammy to link up with Mom and Dad and send me a man. Now look," she said, giggling.

"Well, they looked out for sure. I like Abaki. I think he is everything you need and then some. Congrats, big sis. Let me get my butt to the store. A.J.'s stomach is probably doing summersaults."

"Yeah, get going so you can feed that man. I'm going to hop in the shower and get over to this shop. Are you working tonight?"

"Yes, girl. Urgh! But I gotta get this money. I'm officially on vacation countdown."

"Don't forget that Wednesday we have appointments at Destiny's. Karashae agreed to run the shop while I go."

"Oh, I didn't forget, but I may not have time to do the full day. I'm thinking massages, full body wrap, facial, pedi, and mani. That's cooh?"

"Yeah, that's fine with me. I'm all about saving money. Have a good day, baby sis. Love you."

"Love you too!" Summer called out while walking back to her car.

~~~

Karashae and Chaianne entered the shop at one-fifteen. "Hey Autumn," Chaianne greeted her.

"Hi, frister. We came with food," Karashae said, hugging Autumn.

"Hello, ladies. Well, wasn't that sweet of you. Feed me

and then milk me for information."

They all laughed. "C'mon, we can go up to my office. Like I said, it's usually quiet until three, but my door will chime when a customer enters."

"Ooh, maybe now I get to see this LIPStick Lounge I've heard so much about," Chaianne said.

"Oh, this is your first time up here, huh? Come on, I'll show you. You guys can put the lunch bags in here." Autumn walked them to the meeting room and then back through the office to the lounge.

"Girl, this shit is nice. I wish I knew about this when I got married. Not that I had a lot of friends to fill it but I damn sure would have celebrated my bachelorette party here."

"Thanks, Chaianne. Anytime you want to use it just let me know."

"By the way, you gonna have to teach me some moves. I saw the way you worked that pole at the strip club, and I was impressed. Man listen, let me figure that shit out and I'm going to have Karl install one in our bedroom."

"It would be my pleasure. I learned from watching the ladies that come in to teach the pole dancing classes."

"So you never took classes yourself?"

"Nope, never. I really just watched the techniques and started practicing on my own. A form of exercise, ya know."

"Well, when Chaianne comes, I'm coming too. I might

as well add some tricks to my bag. Keep good ole Steph happy," Karashae added.

Autumn shut off the lights and they walked back to the meeting room. She brought her girls up to speed, starting from the time she and Abaki got to the car until the moment he left.

Karashae's mouth was agape at the revelation. "You guys made each other cum and never removed your clothes, ever?"

"Not one article. Oh, excuse me; Abaki did take off his shirt, but that was it."

"I'm impressed," Chaianne said.

Autumn saw Karashae looking at her and smiling. "Girl, what are you looking at?"

"I'm really happy for you, or should I say *with* you?" Karashae said. Autumn winked. "I've known you for just about twelve years, and I know how much you wanted this. I'm glad Abaki came out of that shell and gave you a chance. He's going to marry you, watch."

"Yeah right. That's still a ways away. We've just met, for Pete's sake. He just asked me to go steady."

"No, I'm with Karashae. I think he will definitely ask you to be his wife. When we left the shooting range that day, I got a kick out of watching the two of you interact. Abaki likes you. I mean, he likes you a lot. He really wants you to learn how to defend yourself. That whole Inez situation probably put things into perspective. I would bet he didn't know how much he liked you until that moment. Once he confirmed it, he wanted you to be able to protect yourself at all costs. I don't think he could bear having something happen to you. You guys look really cute together."

"Thanks, Chaianne. I think it really bothered him when she vandalized my store. He wasn't happy about that. I wondered if that whole situation opened him up to me. He's still a little ambiguous, but the way he hugged me this morning and kissed me last night, I think he is opening up. Ladies, I really like him. I just hope he doesn't hurt me. He is the first guy I've felt so strongly about since I became celibate."

"Well, this doesn't leave this room," Chaianne leaned in to share the secret, "but Karl told me that Abaki is definitely feeling you. He said to Karl that he thinks he may have found his future wife."

"Shut up!" Karashae squealed.

"No, really. After I hung up with you guys earlier, Abe had called Karl about twenty minutes later. When they hung up, Karl mentioned to me that you had Abaki's nose wide open, and his man ain't usually like that. Then he asked me what us women be doing to them." They all laughed.

"Power of the P!" Autumn said, and they high fived.

~~~

Autumn was locking up her shop, with her back to the parking lot, when she heard someone pull up to the curb. Looking through the glass door, she saw the reflection of a man on a motorcycle.

Abaki removed his helmet and greeted her.

"You have a motorcycle?"

"Yes. When I said I had to get my bike from the shop, what kind of bike did you think I was talking about?"

"A bicycle, not a motorcycle. Way cool. I like it."

"Have you ever ridden?"

"No, I haven't. They intrigue me but they seem too dangerous."

"They can be when a knucklehead is driving them. Come, take a ride with me."

Abaki saw that she was hesitant. He was finding out that she was a woman of many fears: guns, mice, squirrels ... motorcycles. Abaki put the kickstand down and got off the bike. "Are you afraid?"

She nodded.

"I have a helmet for you. I won't let anything happen to you, I promise. Do you trust me?"

"I told you I did."

"Well then, don't worry. Now will you ride?"

Autumn swallowed and nodded again.

Abaki pulled another helmet from the console under

the back seat. Placing it on her head, he tightened it and made sure it was snug, but not too tight. "Is this good?"

"Yes," she whispered.

He placed a soft kiss on her lips, and then took her purse and placed it in the spot the helmet had just occupied.

"What about my car?" she asked.

"It will be okay. As soon as we're done, I'll ride you back to get it, okay?"

"Okay."

"Relax, Autumn. Like I said, I got you."

Those three words resonated deep within. Once they left his lips, her fears subsided—a little.

"When I lean, you lean. Keep your arms wrapped around me and hold on tight." He eased off the side of the road, and Autumn held on tight, like he told her to.

Chapter 44: Abaki

The motorcycle ride was spectacular. Abaki drove them up the coast of scenic White Rock Lake to the Dallas Arboretum. The massive green space was home to some of the most exotic plants and shrubbery. He pointed out the small things that caught his eye. Even though it was closed, Autumn could see how beautiful it was and told Abaki she wanted to go there for their next date night. He stored the request in his memory bank. After finding a spot to park his bike, they both got off and walked closer to the shoreline. The two of them sat to watch the sunset.

Abaki reached out and gently grabbed ahold of Autumn's midsection, pulling her into him. "I like you, Autumn."

She smiled. "I like you too, Abaki."

"Am I the kind of guy you could give your heart to?"

"What if I told you that you already have it?"

Abaki was quiet. The longer he pondered her words, the sharper they tugged at his heart. Autumn definitely wore her feelings on her sleeve, but he didn't know that she had relinquished her heart to him already. He'd heard that women fell in love quickly, usually before the guy. As much as he liked Autumn, he wasn't sure if it was love or just a very deep attraction. Having had nothing to compare it to, he couldn't confirm whether what he was feeling was love, but he knew it felt good. He had feelings in areas that a mother, father, sibling, or child couldn't reach. Maybe he did love her. It had been three and a half months since they'd first met, and the times that they were around each other were pure bliss. And after last night, he knew that he wanted her around for a long time. A few forevers wouldn't be long enough. Without saying anything, Autumn turned around so that her back was now to his front and leaned into his chest. He thought she was going to say more, anything so he didn't have to, but she didn't. Perhaps her admission to him having her heart was enough. He smiled and squeezed her tighter, reminiscing on the day he laid eyes on his future.

Abaki and Autumn sat, enjoying each other's company until it was time to head back to her car. He made a left turn into the parking lot of Autumn's shop, heading toward her car, the only one still left in the lot. His body stiffened as they got closer. The right side of Autumn's head was resting on his back. As they approached her car, he felt her head rise only seconds before her hands tightened around his chest. The gasp Autumn released made his heart ache. Not only were all four tires flattened, her car was scratched from hood to trunk, all the way around, and every window on her car had been smashed. Before he could come to a complete stop and lower the kickstand, she had hopped off the back of the bike, hurrying to her car.

As if the damage done on the outside wasn't enough,

the whole interior had been torn to shreds. Abaki watched in agony as she placed her hand over her mouth and kneeled in defeat. She stood again and walked to the back of the car. Abaki looked on as she stared at her license plate. Walking slowly around her car, she placed a hand over it and dragged her finger along the scratches. Her eyes welled with tears and Abaki's heart cried. He felt bad for Autumn and responsible for this whole mess.

"I. Am. Killing. That. Bitch! I swear to God, I am going to kill her ass!" Autumn yelled.

Abaki was tense. He had never heard Autumn swear like this, nor had he witnessed her this angry. Even when she and Inez had fought, her temper hadn't flared this much. He didn't know what to say to comfort her, so he pulled his phone out and called the police. When he went to grab her, she yanked away.

"Look at this shit, Abaki. Look at it!" she yelled. "Why? Why would she destroy my property like this? My fucking car and shop have nothing to do with anything. Does she hate me that much? What the hell is wrong with her?!"

Abaki went to grab her again, and this time, she let him. He held her and hugged her tightly, letting her cry angry tears. His phone vibrated and he answered just as the officer arrived.

It was Karl. "Yo, Abe, what's good man? I know it's kind of late, but I had a question to ask."

"Hey, bro. Now is not a good time."

He knew Karl could sense the anguish in his voice. Abaki walked a few feet away from where Autumn and the officer were standing before speaking again. "Autumn's car is destroyed, man. That crazy woman flattened all four of her tires, scratched the car from bumper to bumper on both sides, smashed every last one of the windows, *and* shredded the interior."

"Get the fuck outta here! Yo, what the fuck is wrong with that crazy bitch? How's Autumn, man?"

"I can't even say. She just told me she planned to kill her. I know she probably doesn't mean it literally, but I can't say for sure. I've never seen her act this way before!"

"You need me to come through?" Karl offered.

"Nah, man. Thanks for the offer. When she finishes giving the report, I'll take her home and hit you up tomorrow."

"Aiight, Abe. Yo man, be easy and make sure Autumn does the same. Can you imagine what that broad would do if she knew where Autumn lived? She'd probably burn the fucking house down, with her inside."

The thought alone pained Abaki. "I don't even want to think about that. We'll talk later." He ended his call and walked back over to Autumn. He draped his right arm over her shoulders and squeezed her upper arm. When the officer finished taking Autumn's statement, he called for a tow truck to take Autumn's car. Once it was securely fastened to the bed of the truck, Abaki and Autumn left. During the whole ride, Autumn barely said anything. When they pulled in front of her home, Abaki got off the bike so he could help her off.

"Where does she live, work, or play? Just tell me where I can find her," Autumn stated.

"I can't do that, Autumn."

"What the fuck do you mean you can't do that? This sick bitch vandalizes my storefront window, and now this! And you mean to tell me you can't tell me how to find her? Fuck you!" Autumn stormed off and Abaki followed.

"Autumn, it's not like that. You're being irrational because you're angry. It's just that I don't want you to do anything stupid and then the tides turn. Her day is coming. Please don't go after her."

Autumn looked into his eyes. "Abaki, I will not ask you again."

He hung his head and then looked back up at her. "I won't condone you doing anything stupid."

"Goodbye, Abaki."

He looked on sorrowfully as she went inside her home, slamming the door in his face.

Damn! He cussed to himself. He empathized with her and could see why she would be so angry. His car was his pride and joy. He spent countless hours of his free time doing things to make it better. Now it looked as if she would have to replace her car. Repairs wouldn't be enough, and since he was the reason for this mess, he felt it was only right that he took care of it. Autumn's next ride would be newer and better. He would see to it. Now, he just had to confirm who did it and make sure that it never happened again.

Chapter 45: Autumn

Autumn had studied Abaki from the time they became acquainted. She paid attention to how he sat, the way he stood, his facial expressions, and even his subtleties. So the slightest change in his posture when they had pulled into the shop's parking lot had caused her to raise her head from his back. When she saw the damage, she wanted to pass out. She loved her car. It was her first major purchase and a gift to herself for accomplishing her goals. She was experiencing emotions she didn't even know were there. Of course she had been angry before, but this was a whole other level of rage. And when Abaki had refused to give her Inez's information, it sent her over the edge.

The fact that it was midnight didn't seem to prevent Autumn's phone from ringing off the hook. She knew it was either Abaki, Summer, Karashae, or Chaianne, but she didn't care who was calling. Her feelings were hurt in more ways than one and she didn't want to talk to anybody. She passed on the shower, stripped her clothes, and went straight to bed, crying herself to sleep.

When she awoke the next morning, her whole aura was off. She had cried so much that her brain felt too heavy for her head. Her imbalance was confirmed when she left her house to go to the shop and realized that she didn't have a car. She checked her phone and saw all the missed calls and her voicemail icon.

She called her sister first. "I need a ride to work, please."

"I'm en route as we speak," Summer confirmed.

Summer picked Autumn up in less than five minutes of them hanging up. Her sister didn't say anything the whole ride. Autumn knew that Summer knew what happened, and Summer knew that Autumn would fill her in. She was just giving her the time she needed; eventually, she would talk. Autumn was glad that Summer didn't interrogate her. Based on the voicemails she'd received, she could pretty much tell how the story got around. She was glad that Karashae had told Summer everything because if she had to tell the story again, she couldn't be so sure that she wouldn't go head hunting for Inez at that very moment. Autumn silently prayed on the way there that nothing had happened to her store. That would be the straw to break the crazy woman's back, and Inez would be guaranteed a death wish. They pulled up to the shop. She breathed a sigh of relief when she saw that her shop was fine.

She also saw that Chaianne and Karashae were waiting outside. Autumn opened the shop and all the ladies filed in. She placed a sign on her door, letting her customers know that she would be opening a half hour later.

Karashae was the first to speak. "Yo, fris, all I want to know is what time do I need to be ready?"

"If I didn't have to run my business, I would say now. But believe me, when I get off work, my number-one mission is to find and slay her ass. I promise you, I am fucking her up something terrible."

Chaianne was as hood as they came, but even she was taken aback by Autumn's vulgarity. Typically, Autumn didn't cuss, but today, she was full of expletives, and rightfully so.

"Well, I'm off tonight, so just let me know what time we rolling," Summer added.

"And do you know I asked Abaki to tell me where she lived, and he wouldn't? I could have killed him too."

Everyone looked at each other.

"Well, what did he say?" Chaianne asked.

"He told me he didn't want me to get into trouble by being hasty, blah, blah, blah. I wasn't trying to hear all that. This bitch has gone way too far. I'm busting her ass."

"Not trying to sway you, because I'd be the first one to knock a bitch the fuck out, but he does have a point. The last thing you want to do is go to somebody's house to fight them. That's an automatic arrest," Chaianne enlightened them.

"You know where she lives?" Autumn asked.

"No, but I know where she works. Just promise me that you won't start any shit at her job. Karl will kick my ass if he knew I gave up that info, knowing your intentions."

"I'll be with her, and I promise you she won't attack her at the job," Karashae reassured.

"Oh, no promises needed. I'm rolling too. Fuck that! This is the most excitement I've had since being here in Dallas. Plus, Inez is dead wrong. I live by the principle where you don't fuck with other people's property and that includes the five C's: children, cock, cars, cash, and cribs. When you violate in those categories, you're asking for consequences," Chaianne stated.

"We need to do this on some James Bond spy shit," Summer said.

"I have a car that I only use when I'm doing surveillance. The windows are tinted and everything. I can pick you up after you close and we can swing by her job. Maybe we can catch her coming out, and y'all can *talk*," Chaianne hinted.

"Bet!" Autumn said. She didn't know what she was agreeing to or what she could commit to. She just knew that she had to address Inez sooner rather than later. She hoped that Inez wouldn't act the way she had when they were at Abaki's place. If she even so much as uttered something inappropriate, Autumn was prepared to take her down.

~~~

Chaianne drove to the mall where Inez worked. On the way, Summer had called the travel agency to see if she was still there. When her coworker placed her on hold,

Summer hung up. "Oh yeah, she's definitely working tonight."

They waited almost a half hour for Inez to exit the building. They watched her walk to her car with several coworkers.

"Aut, I know you may have intentions to talk but just in case it goes beyond that, I don't think there should be any witnesses," Karashae reasoned.

"Chaianne, please follow her," Autumn directed.

As a private investigator, Chaianne was a master at her craft. She tailed Inez so well that they thought she had lost her. "Nah, I got this. If I follow too closely, she'll pick up on it. Shit, I know I would."

"But you might lose her," Summer said.

"Summer, I got this."

Chaianne was right. Even after Inez had turned corners, Chaianne still managed to keep her in view. They all watched as Inez pulled up in front of the Marriott, right outside the Main St. District, not too far from Mouth to Mouth. After a couple of minutes, a Hispanic man exited the building, wearing a hoodie.

"Who the hell is that?" Summer asked.

"I have no clue. No one I've ever seen before. He looks like my crazy-ass ex though." Chaianne laughed nervously.

"What are they doing?" Autumn inquired.

"I can't tell," Karashae said from the front passenger

seat.

"Oh, go, go! She's pulling off," Autumn blurted.

Chaianne waited until the car pulled back onto the main road and then eased off. After about ten minutes, they arrived at a brick ranch-style house. Inez pulled into a garage.

Autumn sucked her teeth. "Dang! I was hoping she just parked in the driveway."

"So you want to come back another day?" Chaianne asked.

"Nope! Chaianne, you stay in the car," Autumn directed, putting on her leather gloves. "If you hear sirens or see cop cars, you and Karashae pull off. Summer and I will be okay."

"Oh, hell no! I'm not pulling off and leaving you," Chaianne retorted.

"That shit ain't happening," Karashae added.

Autumn sighed. "Listen, Summer and I are single with no kids. You two have a family. The last thing I want to do is jeopardize that. I can't have y'all getting arrested and going to jail. You guys have children."

"What happened to just talking?" Chaianne asked.

"I'm going to talk," Autumn said, "but I'm also going to add special effects."

Chaianne looked at Karashae, and they both knew that it was out of their hands. She did have a point about them having families.

"Okay, but we ain't leaving. Fuck that. We can come up with a lie later," Karashae said and Chaianne cosigned.

"Alright, Summer. I just need you to ring the doorbell. It's after dark, so I presume she'll look through the peephole before answering. If she's smart, she won't open the door at all, but then again, the bitch must not be working with a full deck, so I'm going to bet on her opening. When she does, step aside and let me do what I do, got it?"

"Yeah, but big sis, I can't rock her a couple of times first though?" Summer asked excitedly.

"Nah, baby sis. This all me."

Autumn and Summer hopped out of the car and did as planned.

"Who is it?" Inez asked from inside the house. "Can I help you?"

"Yes, I was walking my dog, and I think he ran into your yard. I was going to go back there but ..."

Inez opened the door, and when she did, Autumn punched her squarely in the face and grabbed her by her shirt. She dragged her outside and down the steps and began beating on her. Inez tried defending herself by swinging back, but it was pointless. Autumn thought back to Abaki's picnic and how she'd spat at her, her storefront window, and the ultimate demise of her sweet 750i. Autumn caught her with right hooks, left hooks, and everything in between.

"Bitch, you want to destroy my shit?! I should kill your fucking ass. I told you not to fuck with me, but you didn't listen. All. This. Over. Some. Dick!" Autumn spat as she threw blows upon blows, hitting Inez in the face, arms, legs, chest, back, and head.

Inez must have realized who was giving her the beat down of a lifetime, because she started screaming for help.

"Sis, let's go before somebody calls the cops," Summer said, tugging on Autumn's arm.

Autumn was in a zone. She couldn't stop if she wanted to. Inez had stopped fighting back and Autumn kicked and stomped her in her mid-section. A guy ran from out of Inez's house and pushed Autumn off Inez so hard that she fell on her backside.

"Back tha fuck up!" he yelled.

Karashae and Chaianne got out of the car, ready to pounce on the guy, but the sound of police sirens in proximity halted them. Karashae called for Summer and Autumn to hurry up and get in.

During the drive back to Autumn's place, nobody said a word. Chaianne loved a good gangsta song, so she threw in Fifty Cent's *Get Rich or Die Trying* CD and let the second track rip as she tore up the pavement.

~~~

Autumn wasn't up for company or discussing the night's events. The drive home had given her time to think about her actions, and quite frankly, she was embarrassed. Remorse had kicked in quicker than she'd expected. Seeing Inez walking to her car and smiling as if she didn't have a care in the world had angered Autumn all over again and she'd gone back into beast mode. Her mind was void all rationality and the only thing in her eyes was revenge. *"Sunny days wouldn't be special if it wasn't for rain. Joy wouldn't feel so good, if it wasn't for pain. Death gotta be easy, 'cause life is hard. It'll leave you physically, mentally, and emotionally scarred."* That verse from 50 Cent's song "Many Men," had spoken volumes about her state of mind. Autumn was physically tired, mentally imbalanced, and emotionally drained.

"Do you want us to come in?" Karashae asked.

Autumn shook her head. "No, thanks. I need some time to think, to clear my head. I've never been so taken out of character. I just need to be alone. I need time to reflect. If this is the price I have to pay for love, then I'm starting to question whether I want it. Good night, ladies." Autumn got out of the car and closed the door. Summer told them to hold on as she climbed out behind her sister.

"Hey Aut, hold up." Summer looked into her sister's eyes and saw that they were teary. Summer knew Autumn better than anyone and she needed to make sure she was okay. "It's alright, big sis. Hopefully, this is the end of all this shit. That ass whooping was enough to make the craziest woman think twice about crossing you. But do yourself a favor; don't beat yourself up too bad, and don't cut Abaki off. If loving him was easy, it wouldn't be worth it. He's a good dude. You know that, and you've waited long enough for this. Chin up, Aut. I love you."

"Love you more, baby sis."

Autumn gave Summer a hug and waved to Chaianne and Karashae. They waited until she was inside before pulling off.

Chapter 46: Abaki

"Goodbye, Abaki!" Autumn's devastating words had been on repeat in Abaki's mind since she'd uttered them. She'd told him that she never fared her loved ones a goodbye. "That's such a final word," she had told him. Now, she had recited them to him and he didn't know if she'd meant it in that way or not. A huge part of him wanted to wait, give her the space he knew she needed, and see if she would call. But when he hadn't heard from her at all the next day, he had to make the first move. He tried calling Autumn throughout the day but she never answered. Of course, he wasn't protecting Inez; he was protecting Autumn. The last thing he wanted was for Autumn to get the shit end of the stick. He knew that Inez would someday pay for her behavior and the police would get her once and for all. His main interest was Autumn, only Autumn. He really intended to give her time, but the fact of the matter was that he missed her and longed for her dearly.

Her language and behavior the previous night had been new to him. He didn't want to label her as psychotic but he hadn't known her long enough to rationalize things further. The way she'd conducted herself up to this point was of the utmost reverence and to see her do a 180 was tough for him. Abaki couldn't deny the feelings he had for her though. Not willing to let more time pass, he got into his car and drove to her home. He hoped that she didn't hate him.

Chapter 47: Autumn

In the midst of searching for Band-Aids for her bruised, sore, and bleeding knuckles, Autumn's doorbell rang. She had just gotten out of the shower and thrown on some sweat pants and a tank top. When she answered, there were two police officers at her door, one much taller than the other.

"Autumn Hughes?" the taller officer inquired, watching her rub her hand.

Autumn knew why they were there and contemplated lying. "Yes?"

"Ma'am, you are under arrest for the battery and assault of Inez Garcia."

Autumn's heart sank. *Under arrest!* Now she really wanted to cry. She had never been to jail before. Her nerves were so bad she thought she would shit on herself. A tear threatened to fall from her eye but she quickly wiped it away and pushed her shoulders back. *You do the crime, you got to do the time*, she thought.

"Okay, can I at least call someone and lock up my place before you take me away?"

"Ma'am, we can allow you to secure your property but you can make a phone call when you get to the station," the shorter officer replied.

Autumn went into her room and grabbed her keys

from her purse. The officers followed her throughout the house while she turned things off and brushed her hair into a ponytail. They saw the look she gave them and the short cop responded. "Sorry, ma'am, it's protocol. Once we're on the premises, we can't let you out of our sight, for safety purposes."

Autumn reached the front door and turned on the lamp in the foyer. Abaki had told her to leave a light on when she left. The short officer reached for his cuffs.

"Do you really have to cuff me?"

He started to put them away, but his partner told him that he had to.

"We can cuff you in the front if it makes you feel better," he offered.

Autumn nodded. They guided her to the waiting patrol car. Autumn looked over her shoulder and saw the little old lady from next door looking on from her porch. She called out to Autumn and asked if she was okay. Autumn nodded. A few blocks away, Autumn saw Abaki's car heading toward her home, and she was glad that her neighbor had seen what happened. Autumn knew she would tell Abaki what she saw. After the way she'd treated him, she just hoped that he cared enough to see that she was okay. She sat in the back of the police car, still processing the fact that she had been arrested. She'd never worn handcuffs involuntarily.

Once she was fingerprinted and booked, they led her

to a desk and allowed her to make a call. "Summer, it's me, Autumn. I got arrested."

"What?! Oh my god, Autumn, where are you?"

"I'm down at central booking. They won't give me bail because they said it was a violent offense. I have to wait to see the judge in the morning. I need you to go by the shop and put a sign on the door saying I'll be closed for a week due to an unexpected emergency. Can you try and get me an attorney, please?"

"Yes, of course, sis. I—" Summer couldn't finish her sentence because she was sobbing.

The guard told Autumn she had another minute. Ajamaal took the phone from Summer when she started to break down. "Hey, sis, everything okay?"

"No, A.J., I got arrested. I need Summer to find me a lawyer. I go in front of the judge in the morning. I was told that I may be released on my own recognizance because I don't have a record. But I still want to be on the safe side."

"Say no more. Consider it handled," A.J. reassured her before they ended the call.

Sitting in the bullpen was the worst experience of Autumn's life. She reflected on how far she had come; she never would have thought she would see the day when she would go through something like this. The only thing that brought her solace was the realization that she would face the judge in just hours. She prayed that he would have mercy on her and release her.

~~~

"Hughes, let's go," one of the officers shouted.

Autumn opened her eyes and stood, running her hands over her hair. Even though this wasn't the place to be cute, she still wanted to look presentable; her mother wouldn't have had it any other way. When Autumn walked out of the bullpen, the guard led her down a hallway and through a door. As soon as she stepped into the courtroom, she was overcome with emotions. There, waiting in the room, were Summer, Ajamaal, Karashae, Stephon, Chaianne, Karl, and her man, Abaki. Summer instantly started crying at the sight of her sister, shackled like a criminal. A.J. reached over and wrapped his arm around her shoulder to comfort her. Karashae, too, was overcome with emotion, and Stephon had to do the same with her. When Autumn made eye contact with Abaki, that was when she cried.

She cried because he had come to support her, because he was at the center of all this mess, and most of all, because she missed him. The officer told her to stand in front of the table, and when she did, she was sworn in. The last time Autumn had stood in front of a judge was when she had to fight for her sister.

"Good morning, Ms. Hughes," the judge greeted her.

"Good morning, Your Honor." Autumn cleared her

throat and wiped away her tears.

He went over the legal jargon about her charges, what they were and in what degree.

Although the charges sounded serious, her attorney assured her otherwise. "Your honor, my client is an upstanding citizen. She owns property here in Dallas and she owns a business. As you can see, she has several friends and family members who showed up today to support her. My client has no criminal past, not even a speeding ticket." Her attorney started to elaborate but the judge silenced him.

"Okay, Counselor, I get it. Ms. Hughes, do you understand these charges as they have been presented to you?"

"Yes, sir."

"As your attorney stated, your lack of a criminal history is the main reason for my decision to release you on a personal bond of $100,000. Those are some very serious charges, young lady. I'll see you back in two weeks." The judge banged his gavel, finalizing his decision.

The bailiff removed the cuffs, and Autumn was free to leave.

"Autumn, stop by my office first thing Monday morning. I have some routine questions to ask you. I'm sure I can get this case dismissed at best," the attorney said.

Autumn gave a weak smile. "Thanks for coming on such short notice."

"It's what I do. Don't forget your property. Good day."
He grabbed his briefcase off the table and exited the
courtroom.

Everyone waited until they were outside to give hugs
and supportive words. Summer hugged Autumn first,
followed by Karashae. For several minutes, the three of them
stood there, crying and holding onto each other.

When they broke the bond, Chaianne went and
hugged her as well. "You okay?" she asked.

Autumn nodded. "Yes, I am. Thanks for coming."

Chaianne nodded in acknowledgement. One by one,
A.J., Karl, and Stephon gave her hugs and said a few words
of encouragement. Abaki was standing close by with his
hands in his pockets, watching her. He noticed the scratch
under her eye and near her chin and could see that her hand
had a couple of cuts. Autumn walked up to him with her
head down. "I'm sorry for the way I spoke to you. I shouldn't
have taken things out on you."

"Do you want me to take you home?" he asked, "or
have you made other arrangements?"

"I can have my sister take me if you don't want to."

"That wasn't the question."

"No, I didn't secure a ride. You can take me."

Autumn turned back to everyone and told them that
she was going home to take a bath and relax. They told her to
take it easy and call them if she needed anything.

Summer placed both arms around her sister and hugged her tightly. She pulled away slightly but maintained her hold. "Sis, I'm going home to get some sleep. Now that I know you're okay, I think my mind will let me rest. I'll be by later, okay?"

"Yeah, sis, thanks for getting the attorney."

"I didn't," Summer said. "Abaki did."

They hugged again. Autumn waved to everyone and went with Abaki. During the walk to his car, she grabbed his hand. Although it took him a moment to return the gesture, he eventually squeezed her hand in his.

Chapter 48: Abaki

As soon as they walked inside, Abaki told her to go get undressed and he would run her some bath water. "Are you hungry?" he asked.

"I should be, but I'm not. I just want to bathe and sleep."

While Autumn walked into the room to undress, he reflected. As he sat on the couch with his elbows on his knees, his head low, his thoughts were interrupted by her sweet voice.

"Abaki," Autumn called out. He slowly raised his head. "I'm really sorry for the way I spoke to you. My emotions got the best of me. I apologize. I hope you can forgive me."

Abaki struggled with his own emotions. So many times in the past twenty-four hours he'd contemplated walking away, out of her life. The fact that she had spoken to him the way she had, disobeyed him the way she had, and even doubted him the way she had, had him wondering if Autumn was *really* the woman for him. Granted, she was a great catch, but he had special needs and requests, and it was going to take a special kind of person to deal with him. There was no doubt in his mind that he cared for her. When her next door neighbor had told him that she had been taken away in a police car, he'd felt his whole world go black. As angry as she had been, he knew that she must have done something irrational. Once he'd gotten the call from Summer, letting him know that Autumn had been arrested, he immediately called a friend of a friend and gotten an attorney to take the case. Cost wasn't a factor. He would pay whatever was necessary to get her out of jail, whether he decided to stay with her or not. He admitted to himself that she was in this situation mostly because of him, so he would spend whatever it took to make it right. It wasn't until Karl called him and told him all the details of what had happened, that the depth of her troubles were solidified.

"Your water should be ready." He followed her into the bathroom, lit some candles, turned on her CD player, and left, closing the door behind him.

He was torn. Should he still deal with her, knowing that she could lose her cool at any time and risk her freedom for something so stupid and preventable? Or should he give her the benefit of the doubt, the benefit of knowing that she wasn't completely at fault. Had Inez not done those things to her, she certainly wouldn't have reacted like that. It wasn't like the first incident had gotten her riled up to that level of behavior. Hell, not even the second time Inez had violated her. She had behaved maturely through it all. "Damn," he said aloud. Autumn wasn't to blame. In that instant, he realized that she had reached her rope. Everyone had a limit, and this was hers.

Autumn was in the tub for over a half hour before Abaki went to check on her. He knocked but she didn't answer. When he entered the bathroom, he saw that Autumn was asleep. It wasn't evident whether she had washed, but he didn't want to wake her. Using her wash cloth, Abaki rinsed the remaining suds from her body. Autumn was beautiful and he took a few moments to take her in. He grabbed a big, plush towel and placed it over his shoulder. He lifted her from the water and wrapped her in the towel.

She woke up, slightly disoriented. "I'm sorry," she uttered, half asleep.

Abaki carried her into her room and lay her down. He dried her body and dressed her in one of her t-shirts. For the first time, he saw that her private area was dyed. She had shaved her pubic hair in the shape of the letter X and colored it red. Not sure how to interpret what he saw, he reasoned he wouldn't think too hard about it. He placed the covers over her and left the room.

Chapter 49: Autumn

The scent of spices and herbs filled Autumn's nostrils as she stirred in her sleep. She looked at the time and was surprised that she had slept almost eight hours. Autumn knew she was tired, but she hadn't known how tired she was until she'd eased into the bath water. She sat up in bed when she heard people talking. Slipping on some stretch pants, she opened the door and walked toward the voices. She could hear Summer and A.J. She turned around and went back into her room to put on a bra and a longer shirt.

When she reached the living room, her sister greeted her. "Hey, sleepy head. You feeling okay?"

"As good as can be expected. I didn't know I was that tired. Hey, A.J."

"What's up, Autumn?"

Abaki was at the stove, stirring a pot when Autumn walked up to him. "Smells good. What you cooking?"

"Cooked," he said, turning off all the burners on the stove. "I made some gumbo. You must be famished. Sit, and I'll make you a bowl."

Summer and A.J. had been waiting for the past hour to taste what he had cooked. So when Abaki offered them some, they happily accepted.

"How long you guys been here?" Autumn asked.

"We got here about an hour ago. I was calling you like

crazy but your cell kept going to voicemail and your house phone just rang. After a few attempts, we just decided to come over. Abaki said he didn't want to answer without your permission," Summer explained.

Autumn stole a glance at Abaki and smiled inwardly. "Mm, this tastes so good. I had no idea you could cook like this."

"There's probably a lot of things you still don't know about me, or you choose to ignore them," he retorted.

Autumn caught on to the underlying message. He didn't like drama, yet she'd gotten caught in it anyway. Summer gave Autumn the eye. She could tell that the air between them was thick. The eye contact was brief and then Summer went back to focusing on the meal before her. She and A.J. didn't look up or even speak the whole time they were eating. When Summer lifted her head, the bowl was finger-licking clean.

Autumn laughed. "Dang, sis! You want some more?"

Summer placed a hand on her stomach. "Girl, that was banging. He's definitely a keeper. What's up with these men throwing down in the kitchen?"

"I actually think men are better cooks than us women; they just don't want to cook," Autumn said.

"You might be right, sis. Remember how Dad used to throw down?"

Autumn became melancholy thinking about her

parents. She wondered what they would think of her recent behavior.

Summer noticed her change in demeanor. "Summer, I feel like a failure, like I let them down."

"Why would you say that, Aut?"

"Why not say that? I mean, for crying out loud, I've had more fights in the last two months than I've had in my whole thirty years on this earth. That's not me or my style. I'm the low-key type, cool, calm, collected. I can't believe I let someone take me out of my scene like that. I feel horrible. It was like I couldn't even stop myself or control myself. That's bad, really bad, and scary."

Summer placed her bowl in the sink and went to sit next to Autumn. "Big sis, I'm not going to justify your actions. Yes, what you did wasn't the best move, but you reacted out of anger. We worked really hard to get where we are, and you've worked even harder. I know you better than anyone, and I know that wasn't your style. But to be completely honest, home girl made her bed, so she had to lay in it. You did nothing to her for her to destroy what you've worked so hard for. That car was your baby. That was your gift to yourself for finishing high school, under grad, and graduate school, for maintaining a roof over our heads, feeding us, starting a business, and buying your first home all by yourself. And to have someone try to ruin that was really unfair. She had no right to violate you just because she saw you with a guy who is no longer interested in her."

Autumn held her head down. "That's what I keep telling myself, but the fact still remains that I assaulted someone, not once, but twice."

"Autumn, I get it, I do. First of all, that nasty bitch tried to spit on you. Even a saint would have slapped the piss out of her for that. I know I would've. And then she fucking totaled your whip. Like really, what was that for? She needs to be discussing things with Abaki and not taking it out on you and your possessions. If you weren't going to beat that ass, I would have. So chill; she had it coming. Hopefully, this was a lesson learned, not just for you but her as well. The police really need to get on their job and arrest that broad."

"Autumn, on some real shit. I can see why and how you would feel bad, but try not to beat yourself up too much. No disrespect, Abaki, but Inez should really be angry with you, not Autumn, so I'm not sure why she would take it out on her. Women do that sort of thing. Want to blame the other woman for shit when they need to be talking to the man about it," A.J. said.

"No, no offense taken. I tried calling her to tell her to leave Autumn out of it but she doesn't even listen. She denied having anything to do with everything and swore it wasn't her. I was hoping for a confession to give to the investigators but she didn't fall for it. That's why I shied away from American women. No offense to you all, but they're crazy."

A.J. snickered. "Yo man, you ain't never lied about that. Trust me, I know."

Autumn and Summer sucked their teeth at the same time. "Whatever!" Summer quipped.

Abaki looked at Autumn, and for the first time, he saw sorrow in her eyes.

Autumn turned to her sister. "Summer, do you mind praying with me?"

"May I join?" Abaki asked.

"I would love that," Autumn said.

Abaki, Summer, Autumn, and Ajamaal all stood together, holding hands. They silently prayed for themselves and one another. Autumn prayed for the obvious: forgiveness and peace of mind. She even prayed for Inez. Her heart wouldn't let her go as far as saying something was wrong with Inez, but she definitely knew something wasn't right with her either.

The house phone rang and Autumn went to answer it.

"Hey, girl, everything okay over there? I was calling you all day practically."

"Hey, Karashae, everything is fine. I just woke up about an hour ago and Abaki didn't feel comfortable answering the phone. Summer said the same thing, but you know her; she just shows up."

Summer stuck her tongue out at Autumn.

"Did you and Abaki talk?" Karashae asked. "I know Stephon said he was not pleased with what happened. I think he's upset."

"Oh, that's an understatement. I can barely get a full sentence from him. But he's still here. Can I call you later or tomorrow, when I leave the lawyer's office?"

"Of course. Call me if you need me."

"I will, frister, and thanks for everything," Autumn said, ending their call.

Summer stood, followed by A.J. "Hey sis, we're about to go, okay?"

"Thanks for coming by, baby sis. You and A.J. are the best."

"Think nothing of it. Do you want me to go to the attorney's office with you tomorrow?"

Autumn looked at Abaki, but he was busy tidying up the kitchen. "Abaki, are you able to go with me?"

"If you wish."

"Abaki will go, but if you want to, you can come with us."

"No, that's fine. I was just offering. We don't need to make a party out of it, but please call me as soon as you leave and let me know what he says, okay?"

"Okay. Good night."

She walked Summer and A.J. to the door. After locking it behind them, she inhaled deeply, mentally preparing herself for the much-needed dialogue between her and her man.

Chapter 50: Abaki

While cleaning the last of the dishes, Abaki felt Autumn ease up behind him and wrap her arms around his waist, placing the side of her face on his back. He inhaled the scent of her Rice Flower and Shea body lotion and inhaled deeply.

"Do you have to leave tonight?" she asked him.

"No."

"What about Yin and Yang? Don't they have to be walked?"

The fact that she'd inquired about his trusted sidekicks softened him a little. He rinsed the remaining dishes and turned around to face her. "They are fine. While you were asleep, I went home to check on them. I walked and fed them then. I also grabbed some stuff from the market so you will have some things to last you a couple of days."

"Thank you for everything. The lawyer, the food, the company, and the support."

Abaki nodded.

"Are you upset with me?"

"To be honest, I'm not sure who to be upset with. I want to be mad with myself for not handling Inez better. I want to be mad at Inez for behaving so immaturely, and I want to be upset with you for stooping to her level. I just don't know anymore. All this is new for me. If someone had told me this would happen, I would have thought they were lying. But now, here we are, dealing with teenage crap, and we're all supposed to be adults."

Autumn's head sank. "I really am sorry for what I did. Someone like her should've never had that much power over me to be able to control my emotions. Inez got the best of me, and I refuse to let that happen again. Sitting in that bullpen was a low moment. The last thing I want to do is disappoint those that love and care about me, and deep inside, your feelings matter a lot."

Abaki was touched. Now, that was the Autumn he was falling for. That crazy, deranged woman that she had transformed into was not the lady he wanted. "Let's talk." Abaki grabbed her hand to lead her into the living room. She winced from his touch. "I'm sorry. I forgot you had a bruise. How bad did you beat her, Autumn?"

"I don't know, but I think it was pretty bad. Some guy ran out the house and pushed me off her."

"What do you mean he pushed you?" Abaki bellowed. He felt his temples pulsate and his jaws clinch. "Autumn, don't lie to me. Tell me how he pushed you."

"Why, so the two of us can face assault charges? Abaki, just leave it alone. The push was justified."

He stood up. "Either you tell me now, or I'm going over there to find out who *he* is and do some shoving of my own."

Autumn's eyes shifted nervously. "I, uh, I was kicking and stomping on her when he ran down the stairs and pushed me off her. Summer was standing really close, so I think I tripped on her foot and fell back. That's all," she explained.

He'd seen her go into the medicine cabinet right before entering the tub. He had figured that she probably had a headache from all that was going on, but now he wasn't so sure. Abaki knew she was hiding something. He didn't want to create more issues than they already had, so he decided to let it go. If he ever came in contact with this individual, he would make sure that he would never be able to use his arms again.

Autumn took Abaki's hand in hers and looked into his eyes. "Can I ask you something?"

"Anything."

"Do you still love her?"

"Inez?" Abaki asked.

Autumn swallowed and nodded. Whenever she was feeling anxious, she would chew on the inside of her mouth as she was doing at that moment.

"No. I cared for her, but the love wasn't there."

"Do you care about me?"

"Of course, Autumn. Would I be here, doing all this if I didn't? I had yet to meet a woman who could make me love her until I met you. The feelings I have developed during the time we've spent together are the closest I've come to loving a woman. You are my main concern. The last thing I want is for you to go around beating people up and getting arrested. How can I protect you if you're putting yourself at risk and ending up in places where I have no jurisdiction? I can't. Autumn, promise me that you will not take any more matters into your own hands."

Autumn didn't have to think long. "I promise. It's just that when I saw the damage, I knew my car was totaled and it hurt. That really cut deep."

"Can you stop saying totaled? Your car was damaged, and yes, it will be an expensive claim for the insurance company, but it was a 2012 BMW with very few miles. It's worth more than the cost of the damage. Have you decided if you want it repaired or replaced?"

"First of all, it was worth *slightly* more than the cost of the damage, and no, I'm still undecided. Do you forgive me?"

"Of course. I won't hold a grudge. I want to apologize to you for having to go through that. Inez is the kind of woman I've tried to avoid all these years. Had I known she would turn out like this, I would have run the other way."

Autumn laughed. Abaki smiled, both glad that they were able to talk this through and not have things end the way it could have. Abaki started to lean in and kiss her when he thought about her dyed pubic hair. He hadn't known such a thing was possible.

"What did you do down there?" he asked, glancing down at her love tunnel.

Autumn blushed. "I dyed it. I was on the Internet one day and an ad popped up for Betty Beauty Pubic Hair Dye, so I ordered it and tried it. I fell in love with it, and for the past six months, I've dyed my area different colors. Does it freak you out?"

"To be honest ... it turned me on."

Autumn smirked. She didn't wait for Abaki to initiate. He had admitted to being turned on so she took full advantage. She gently pushed him so that his back was leaning against the sofa. She straddled him and planted small, sensual kisses all over his face, neck, and head before planting one on his lips. Abaki opened his mouth and used his tongue to gain entry into hers. Autumn moaned and moved her hips ever so slightly. The fight to remain celibate was becoming more and more difficult every time they were together. Autumn broke away from the kiss and looked into his eyes.

"Have you imagined the day when you would have sex with a woman again?"

"Every night since I've met you," he admitted honestly.

"When do you think we will have sex?"

Abaki hadn't expected her to come right out and ask.

He could tell she was feeling frisky, which was probably why she'd asked. If they did have sex, it would only be a prelude to the rest of their lives together, but Abaki still had to wait. "When you become my wife."

"How do you know I will be your wife?"

"I don't. That's why we're not having sex."

She was disappointed with his answer; he could tell from her expression. He knew that she wanted an answer that entailed him making plans to take the next step. But even if he asked her to marry him now, they both knew they couldn't make it happen now. They had just agreed to become exclusive. Plus, with Inez in the picture, things were still up in the air.

"Why are you asking about sex, anyway?" he asked. "Isn't your menstrual due?"

Autumn sucked in a breath. "How do you know?"

"I'm observant. Every month around the same time, you get that lone pimple on your face. Then for a week straight, you wear dark-colored jeans." Abaki had pulled her whole card.

"Oh my goodness! I had no idea you paid attention to that. Yup, every third week of the month, Aunt Flow sends me a postcard in the form of a pimple, telling me she's on her way, and the next day, she shows up. I adore you, Abaki Lemande."

"And me, you, Autumn Hughes. You in the mood for a

movie?" he asked her.

"Sure. What you got in mind?"

Abaki eased her off of him and went into his bag. He pulled out *Disappearing Acts* and showed it to her.

"Aw, one of my favorite movies. You *do* like me," she teased.

Abaki smiled and placed the movie in the DVD player. Sitting back on the couch, he pulled Autumn into his arms and kissed her on the nose as they snuggled up for a quiet night inside.

Chapter 51: Autumn

"Good Morning," the attorney's receptionist greeted Autumn and Abaki. Typically, Autumn wore a pair of jeans, stilettos, and a top layered by one of her everyday blazers. Today, she had on a simple fitted pencil skirt, a sheer blouse with a matching cami, and some peep-toe pumps. She looked like a woman who was ready to handle business, and Abaki was just as clean. His kaki slacks, brown button-down shirt, and matching brown hard bottoms completed his look.

"Good morning. Autumn Hughes here to meet with Mr. Kendal."

"Oh, yes, he's expecting you. Right this way." The receptionist led the two of them to the lawyer's private office.

Mr. Kendal was seated in his big leather chair behind an oversized oak desk. He stood to greet them. "Ms. Hughes. Abe, it's always a pleasure. Please, have a seat."

They took their seats. Autumn grasped Abaki's hand.

"As your attorney, it is imperative that you tell me everything that happened, even if you think it sounds bad. I need to know. My job is to defend you to the best of my ability, and the only way I can do that is to have all the chips on the table so I can be prepared for whatever the prosecutor throws at me. Am I clear?"

"Yes," Autumn said.

"From the beginning, tell me how this whole incident

came to be, leaving nothing out."

After inhaling deeply, Autumn told him everything from start to finish, from the encounter at Abaki's home in the backyard, to the moment she'd beat up Inez—the second time.

"And what made you so sure that she was the one who had ruined your car this last time."

"Honestly, I can't say. I just figured that if she was behind the other incidents then this was her doing as well. Surveillance from my shop's security system showed her defacing my storefront window. My problems didn't start until I'd had the first encounter with her at Abaki's."

Kendal nodded as he took notes. "Has surveillance been retrieved for this most recent incident?"

"No, I requested it from my surveillance company, though. They said it would take ten business days for me to receive it in the mail."

"This is the twenty-first century, and I'm not waiting on snail mail. With your consent, I plan to contact the security company and have them email the assigned detective and me a copy of the images and video. I'll have it within the next couple of hours. I'll be in touch as soon I get something. Since you have a solid work history and you're an upstanding citizen, my goal is to get the heavy charges dismissed. You may have to plead to disorderly conduct. Right now, with all the charges as they stand, you could be facing up to three years in prison and five years post supervision," Mr. Kendal stated.

Autumn gasped. Tears threatened to escape her eyes.

Abaki gripped her hand tighter. "Jail time is not an option for her. Neither is probation. Whatever we need to do to get the charges dismissed, we will do. Am I clear?" Abaki said to Mr. Kendal.

"Abe, as clear as you've always been."

We, Autumn replayed in her head. Abaki did care for her. His words meant that he was in it for the long run and she wouldn't have to deal with this alone. Her heart leaped at the revelation. The attorney jotted down Autumn and Abaki's contact information and let them know that he would call them as soon as he heard something.

For the most part, the drive to Karl and Chaianne's home was quiet. Autumn was thrown off guard by the charges she could face. Her whole demeanor had changed when the attorney had told them that. Granted, she had been wrong for physically assaulting Inez, that, no one denied, but she had been provoked. She didn't deserve jail time.

Karl had called Abaki before they'd left to meet with the lawyer. He wanted to invite the two of them over for brunch. They really liked Autumn and felt bad that she was in such a situation. Chaianne wanted to let them know that they were willing to help in any way they could.

"Hello, you two!" Chaianne sang when they answered

the door.

Abe and Karl gave each other a brotherly dap, and Autumn and Chaianne hugged.

Chaianne led them into the house, toward the family room, with a sliding glass door that connected to their patio. "How you doing, girl?" Chainne asked Autumn.

"I was fine until the lawyer told me that I could face up to three years in prison and five years parole," Autumn said as she sat down next to Abaki on the love seat.

"What?" Karl said. "Oh, hell no, ma. That ain't no place for you, and that parole shit is just as bad sometimes. The smallest thing will have them ready to lock you back up."

"Tell me about it. Inez could say anything, true or not, and that could mess Autumn up. That's why I told Kendal nothing of the sorts was even an option. Fines were cool, prison, probation, or parole, definitely not," Abaki stated with conviction.

"Well, what are the detectives saying?" Chaianne asked.

"I haven't heard from anyone. It's like they couldn't care less about what I'm going through. Maybe if she had been arrested after the first incident, I wouldn't be in the situation I'm in now."

"Who's on the case?" Chainne questioned.

"Some guy named Arthur Mac."

"Detective Mac? Tall, brown-skinned, balding on the

top?"

"Girl, I have no clue. I haven't met him yet. I was told that he was assigned the case and would be in touch if he needed to reach me." Abaki reached for Autumn's hand and she placed hers in his.

"I have a feeling it's the same guy. I have done a lot of work with Dallas PD. If it's okay with you, I'd like to reach out to him to see what's up."

Karl nodded in agreement.

"Be my guest," Autumn said.

"Cool. Well, come, let's eat. Karl grilled a few steaks, and I made some home fries, eggs, hash browns, and sausage. I even got some champagne so we can have mimosas."

"Ooh, my kind of girl!" Autumn got up and reached for Abaki's hand. The two of them followed Chaianne and Karl into the kitchen, to their awaiting meal.

After they were done eating, Autumn helped Chaianne clear the dishes and clean up. Karl, Abaki, and K.J. were out on the patio waiting on them.

"You ladies all done in there?" Karl asked, smirking.

"Whatever, K! If it was up to you, you'd have me in the kitchen three times a day, butt naked, pregnant, and barefoot," Chaianne yelled. They all laughed hard.

Autumn could recall her mother saying something like that. She figured that it must have been an old adage. She caught Abaki staring at her but saying nothing. "Is everything okay?" she asked him.

"Yeah, I was just taking you in. You look nice in a skirt."

"Thanks, Abaki. I really want to thank you guys for the love and support you've shown. It's been really difficult not having any family to lean on or call on in times of need. It was just Summer and me for so long, and to now have a healthy serving of friends who truly care ... it's really special to me."

"How old were you when your parents passed away?"

Chaianne had never gotten the full truth about her situation because Autumn had never revealed it. It wasn't that she was hiding it from her, but at the time of her original inquiry, Autumn wasn't as familiar with her as she was now. She now felt comfortable sharing her journey with them, all of it.

"Chaianne, I know I gave you a very brief synopsis of how we came to be in Dallas but there was a lot that I had left out," Autumn explained. She told them about their siblings passing away and then losing their parents in a plane crash when she was twelve years old and Summer was eight. Autumn went on to let them know that their grandmother had raised them until she, too, passed away five years later.

"The courts denied my plea to continue living in my grandmother's house. They said I was too young to carry on such a responsibility, so they placed us in state custody. Summer was depressed living in foster care, and someone had already tried to make a move on her. I decided that neither of us would be subject to such environments so we went AWOL. We went to my grandmother's home and packed everything we could, from photos to clothing. Summer had told me about a secret stash my grandmother had, so we used that money to make moves. The following morning, we caught a bus to Virginia and then another one to Dallas. When we got here, we found a sign in a window, advertising a one-bedroom apartment and a part-time job at the cleaners. The owner agreed to rent us the apartment for five hundred dollars, and he let me work there. Summer was still too young. I worked there for four years. The owner's health started failing, so his daughter came up from Georgia to handle his affairs and then she took him back to Georgia to live with her. They were nice enough to let us stay in the apartment for half the cost of the rent plus utilities. His daughter sold the business along with the building, so Summer and I had to look for work. I had a crazy school schedule, so finding a job conducive to my schedule was rough. For a whole six months, we went unemployed. I used the remaining cash from my grandmother's stash to cover rent. There were times when things got so bad that Summer and I often went hungry.

Karashae's mom was a blessing. In fact, she was the

one who introduced me to Karashae. Ms. Jackie knew we didn't have any friends or family here, so she told Shae about me, and we clicked instantly. She would invite us over for dinner most weeknights and there were times we accepted. Then there were the other times we had to decline. My grandmother always told us not to wear out our welcome and that there was no place for freeloaders in society. I don't think Karashae and her mom looked at us that way, but my upbringing wouldn't allow me to accept the offers all the time." Autumn swallowed and fought back tears. "We struggled to purchase books, buy food, pay the bills, and even get enough money to get back and forth to school. Summer talked about quitting school to look for work. When I told her that wasn't an option, she had contemplated stripping to make money." Autumn cut her eyes at Abaki. She wanted him to know that she had never considered such a thing. "And again, I told her that neither of us was going that route. We would shovel shit before I let us strip in anybody's club or sell our behinds for some money. Finally, after six months, both she and I were able to get jobs with a cleaning company. Eventually, Summer got an internship at the hospital she works for now, and they liked her so much that they hired her. I landed an office job and then applied to be an adjunct professor and got hired. Somewhere in between, I used my portion of our inheritance and opened Mouth to Mouth. I purchased my beloved BM shortly after that. And now, here we are."

No one said anything for a few moments; they just sat quietly, taking in the details of her journey.

"Wow, that's one hell of a story," Karl said.

"Yes. My heart goes out to you two. I commend you like crazy. You definitely held shit down for you and your sister. Up until now, I was under the impression that you moved here with your family and then they passed away. You are remarkable," Chaianne stated.

"Thanks," Autumn replied.

"So, what made you choose Dallas?" Abaki asked her.

"When we were on the bus going to Virginia, a woman was talking about Dallas and how she missed living there. Since we had no idea where to go, we came here. I follow signs. My Grammy always said, 'Trust in God, and He will lead a way,' so, that's what I did. And as always, she was right. Meeting Mr. Chandler was one sign. When we got here, our first job was at a cleaners, and the owner, Mr. Chandler allowed us to rent a small two bedroom apartment upstairs from the cleaners. Chandler is my grandmother's maiden name. Maya Angelou High School was another omen. Both my mom and I loved poetry. Everything, although we had some hard times, worked out fine ... until now."

"And it will get better; trust me," Chaianne said, trying to comfort her.

Autumn's phone rang and she excused herself. When

she was in an area where she could talk privately, she answered. "Hello? Yes, this is she. Oh hey, Mr. Kendal. Yes. Un huh." Autumn's mood flattened. "Really? Oh my goodness. I have no clue. Okay, please do. Thanks."

Abaki watched Autumn as she talked on the phone. In a matter of seconds, her disposition had gone from contented to concerned. Autumn went back to the patio, and everyone knew something was wrong. She grabbed her purse and told them she needed a minute. Abaki started to go after her but Chaianne offered, and he let her. Once inside, Chaianne slid the patio door closed and went to Autumn. "Hey, is everything okay?"

Autumn dried her eyes and shook her head. "No. That was the lawyer. He said he got the clip of the person destroying my car and ... it wasn't a woman. It was definitely a guy." Autumn cried harder.

Chaianne stiffened. "It couldn't be."

"What?"

"Oh my gosh! Come on. Let's go back out with the men."

Abaki and Karl stood when they came back out. Abaki saw that Autumn's mood hadn't changed, and Karl could see that Chaianne's had, for the worse.

"What the fuck, ma, I thought you went to help, and now you look crazy in the face. What happened?"

"K.J., honey, get your things and go inside with Quay

for a moment. Mommy has to talk to Daddy real quick."

"Okay," K.J. replied sweetly. He gathered his things and went inside. Once he was out of hearing range, Chaianne spoke. "Autumn's call was from the attorney, telling her that the perp seen destroying her car wasn't a woman, but a man."

"Oh, damn!" Karl exclaimed.

"Wait, but the plot thickens," Chaianne continued. "The night of the fight, Karashae and I had stayed in the car, but we kept an eye on everything that was going on. When Inez started screaming and yelling for help, some guy came running out the house and down the stairs and pushed the shit out of Autumn. When we saw how far and hard she fell back, Karashae and I got out of the car to jump his ass, but we heard sirens and called for Autumn and Summer to come on."

Abaki looked at Autumn, but Autumn ignored his gaze. She had lied to him, and she knew that he wasn't happy about it.

"Right before I hopped back in the car, I stole a glance at the guy, and you will never guess who he resembled," Chaianne said.

"Who?" Abaki asked.

Chaianne looked at Karl and swallowed. "Dom!"

"Dom! Dom? As in your ex, Dominic?" Karl was almost out of his seat.

"Yes," Chaianne said with a gulp.

Karl was incredulous. "No fucking way! What would he be doing with Inez?"

"That's just it. I have no idea. That's why I didn't make a big fuss about it. I figured it was a bad case of the lookalikes, and I left it alone. But now that they're saying that a man destroyed her car, I figured it had to be the same guy who came to Inez's defense."

Karl remained silent, just staring at Chaianne.

"What the fuck you looking at me like that for?" Chaianne screeched. "I didn't invite the muthafucka to Dallas!"

"That's not why I'm staring. I swore to myself that if me and this fool crossed paths again, I would put heat to his ass. I'm just praying for the sake of my family that this joker ain't him."

Abaki and Autumn were clueless as to what was going on. Chaianne had to fill them in. "Dominic is my ex-boyfriend. He and I were together right before I got with Karl. The two of them had a physical altercation that didn't end so well. Needless to say, he's one of our least favorite people."

Karl was livid. "Fuck that. Get on your Private EyE shit and find out if there's a muthafucking connection between them two. If it's that muthafucka, may God be with him. Yo Abe, let me holla at you for a minute."

Karl saw that Abaki was quiet, clueless, and curious. He'd told him how he needed to protect Autumn at all costs. He told him everything, even the gritty details about him and Dominic that he and Chaianne had vowed to never share.

Chaianne placed a hand on Autumn's shoulder. "Girl, have a seat. This shit is going to sound crazy, but it's something I think you should know. I plan to do some research to see if Inez really is connected to my ex, and if he is, we got two kinds of crazies on our hands." Chaianne's tense demeanor made Autumn even more intrigued. She explained to Autumn that her line of work had almost gotten her killed. And the one hired to carry out the hit was Karl, and Dominic was the one to reveal it to her. When everything had come to a head, she hadn't been sure if everyone involved would escape with their lives.

Chapter 52: Abaki

When Autumn gave Chaianne the real truth about her past, Abaki finally got the whole picture. Autumn had given him the short version of her story up until working at the cleaners. He'd had no idea how she and Summer had struggled afterwards. Now he could see why she was so hurt over what happened to her vehicle. She had put her blood, sweat, and tears into everything she owned, and for someone to try to destroy that was unfair. Abaki felt bad for being upset with her. Having now understood her plight, his heart went out to her and Summer. Her story had impacted him, and he wanted nothing more than to love her for the rest of his life and ensure that she wouldn't have to struggle again as long as he was a part of it. And being a part of his life meant that he had to protect her.

Hearing Chaianne reveal the truth about what had really happened that night at Inez's house upset him. He thought he had made it clear to Autumn that it was his job to protect her. How could he, if she lied to him about being harmed, by a man at that. He wasn't happy, and later, he planned to let her know just how unhappy her hidden truths made him.

"Yo Abe, let me holla at you, man." Once they were away from the ladies, Karl spoke his mind. "I need to go see if this is Chai's ex. I hate that muthafucka, and the fact that he's in my town makes me despise him even more. I need to go by Inez's crib, man."

"Let's go. I want to see him myself. Autumn told me that the guy pushed her but she tripped and fell. Your wife made it clear that he blatantly pushed her, trying to hurt her. I wanted to let it go, but now that you speak with so much passion about this dude, you've reopened a wound. I can't have another man putting hands on my lady."

"You preaching to the choir, bruh. Let's go!" They told the women they would be back, and although the ladies didn't want them to go, they trusted that they wouldn't do anything too foolish.

Karl knew what Dom looked like, so Abaki had no reservations about them mixing up his identity. When they arrived at Inez's place, Abaki and Karl got out and rang her doorbell. Inez took a minute to answer the door, but when she did, she kept the chain clasped.

"Can I help you?"

"Who's your company?" Abaki asked her.

"What company, Abe?"

"Inez, don't do this. You had a man destroy Autumn's car. And this same bastard had the nerve to put his hands on her. So I want to know who he is and where I can find him."

"I don't know what the hell you're talking about, and if I did, I wouldn't tell you shit. Ask your bitch!" Inez spat before slamming the door.

"Dammit," Abaki growled.

"She's lucky I'm a man; otherwise, I would have slapped the piss out of her," Karl said.

"Don't sweat it, man. Everything happens for a reason. He will get his," Abaki reassured him, referring to Dominic.

They didn't want to leave right away, so the guys opted to sit outside her home for a while. Karl felt that Inez may have tipped Dom off and either he wouldn't come by or he'd try to leave if he was there. He didn't show. They reasoned that they would leave but would check up on him regularly.

This whole situation was making Abaki more and more anxious. He had just made arrangements to travel back home and now that his travel plans were confirmed, he feared that he may have to cancel them. His intent was to go so that he could give his all to Autumn, but now he felt uneasy about leaving her. He worried about her safety.

"K, I have an issue," Abaki said as they drove back to Karl's place.

"What's up, man?"

"I'm leaving. Well, I'm supposed to be leaving. But there is no way I can leave with this situation still lingering in the air."

"Where you going?"

"Back home. I decided to take that trip. This is the only way I can have Autumn all to myself, without anything hanging over my head. Plus, I want to settle my family's estate. I always thought returning home was an option. To be honest, America is home now, especially with Autumn in my life. I'll have everything I'll need to live comfortably, freely, and happily."

"I hear you, bro. Do what you have to do. I got Autumn; you already know."

"Yeah, I know. It's just that she's *my* lady. I have to have her. All I need you to help me with is making sure that whoever is behind this will no longer be a factor—sooner than later.

"Bro, my wife already on it. We'll have answers soon. That's my word!"

Chapter 53: Autumn

When Autumn arrived back home from her much-needed spa time with Summer, Abaki's car and motorcycle were in her driveway. *How the hell did he get both of those here?* she wondered. He had been letting her drive his car when she had things to do or if he was busy and couldn't take her. Although she liked the way it drove, the race car look and feel wasn't her speed. She missed her 750i something terrible. That was the only car she'd fallen in love with.

Entering the house, she could hear the shower running and knew that it could only be Abaki. Her nipples perked at the thought of water glistening over his ripped body. After putting down her purse and keys, Autumn removed her shoes and walked into the bathroom. She eased the door open and was careful not to make it creak. The silhouette of Abaki's tall, muscular frame was visible from outside the shower.

"Autumn," he called out.

"Dang!" She wondered how he'd heard her when she was careful to be quiet. "Yesss?" she sang.

"Just confirming. Why you creeping?"

"Well, if you must know, I was trying to sneak up on you."

"How was the spa?"

"It was lovely. I have to treat us to a couple's massage soon. This girl, Hannah, gives the best massages."

"As long as it's a Hannah, and not him-a, then I'm glad you enjoyed."

Autumn pulled back the curtain and watched as he rinsed the suds from his body. Every muscle in her body clinched at the wonderful sight. Abaki looked at her as she subconsciously licked her lips and sensually tickled the corner of her mouth. His dick lengthened from the observation and Autumn's mouth watered in response. Without warning, she reached inside and massaged his extensive member. At first, Abaki seemed as if he wanted to stop her, but she held true to her intent. As far as she was concerned, this was just the beginning.

Once she felt his dick harden, she leaned in and wrapped her lips around it. Abaki recoiled, but she didn't relent. The thought of stopping crossed her mind. It wasn't that she was against giving head; she'd just had no desire to perform oral sex on the guys she was intimate with before him. Abaki's member was the biggest and prettiest penis she had ever seen. It was long, thick, smooth, and chocolate. Ignoring his feeble attempts to draw back, Autumn leaned in further as she sat on the edge of the tub. She didn't care if she or the floors got wet. Aunt Flow was messing up her flow, so even if she couldn't be pleased, she wanted to please her man.

After repositioning herself so that she was comfortable, she pulled on his shaft until he leaned toward her.

"You don't have to do this," he advised.

"I know," she replied softly.

Skillfully, Autumn wrapped her lips around Abaki's penis. She took him in as far as he could go, and he moaned at the sensation. His sounds of satisfaction gave her the confidence she needed to continue. She used her hands to massage the parts of him that couldn't fit into her mouth. All that practice on her dildos was finally paying off. Countless times, she had watched the women on pornos suck dick like true champions, and she'd rehearsed on her trusty toys. Abaki didn't need to say anything. His moans, gasps, and the way he gripped the side of her face let her know that she was doing it well. Autumn kept sucking, slurping, and buffing him until he was about to release. She didn't even remove his dick from her mouth. When he tried to pull out, her jaws gripped him tighter.

"Oh, damn. Autumn, baby, I-I can't hold it back," he moaned. And right after, he let out a loud grunt. Leaning against the shower wall, Abaki allowed everything he was trying so hard to hold in spill out. He was spent.

After taking a moment to recuperate, he leaned down and covered her mouth with his.

"You never cease to amaze me, Ms. Hughes."

"I aim to please, Mr. Lemande."

Autumn got up from the edge of the tub and left the bathroom. Abaki quickly washed again, rinsed off, and grabbed a towel to wrap around his naked body. When he left the bathroom, he found Autumn in her room, sifting through her closet. She jumped because she hadn't heard him enter. Abaki said nothing as he walked up behind her and planted kisses on the back of her neck, down to her collarbone. Her skin was smooth and smelled good. Sweet sounds escaped her lips. He picked her up and carried her to the bed. Removing her jeans and then her underwear, he told her to scoot back.

"Abaki, I'm on my period," she warned.

He took notice of the string hanging between her legs. "I know. I want to make you happy, Autumn, and if this will make you happy, then nothing else matters right now. Like I said, I've never done this before, so I want you to tell me when it feels good and let me know when it doesn't. Understand?"

Autumn couldn't speak, so she nodded. Normally, she wouldn't let anyone that close to her during her cycle. But because it was the last day and her flow was light, she gave in. She watched in awe as Abaki positioned his tall, brawny body in the best position. He looked at her and held his gaze as he lowered his head to her love box.

"A red X; how appropriate," he commented before

placing kisses all over her treasure. Abaki let his nose and lips travel up and down her lower extremities. "You smell nice. Always so fresh and clean; I love that."

After lip teasing her, he spread her pretty pussy lips and began tickling her love muscle with his tongue. He licked fast and she told him to slow down. He licked too slow, and she told him to speed up. Once he was performing at the perfect interval, Autumn's moans were stronger and more intense, providing the encouragement he needed to keep going.

"Yes, baby. Right there. Lick right there. Oh God, yes!" Autumn shifted her bottom so that his tongue could tease the spot right above her clit. "Yes, Abaki, baby that feels so good."

Abaki let his tongue tickle her clit and the area above it. The more he licked, the harder her clit got and the more she lost control. "Baby, I'm about to cum!" Abaki kept licking and grabbed ahold of the string from her tampon, gently tugging at the same time. Autumn leaned up on her arms and watched the magic happen. "What the fuh? Oh, Abaki, damn, baby, yesss!" Autumn cried as trickles of her love juices slid from her love tunnel, past the tampon and rested on the covers below. When she opened her eyes, she could see his beard glistening from the fruits of his labor. "You sure this was your first time?" Autumn inquired.

Abaki beamed, obviously proud of his performance. "I

guess chocolate does melt in your mouth, not in the hands," he said meekly.

"Come here, you."

Abaki leaned up and lay next to her.

"I love you," she whispered.

"I know," was all he said. "Now let's get cleaned up. I want to take you for a ride."

~~~

Autumn held onto Abaki like her life depended on it, and she felt that it did. But her fear of being on the back of a bike was subsiding. The more she rode the motorcycle, the more she loved it. With Abaki in her life, Autumn was overcoming fears that she once thought would be perpetual. First, guns and now motorcycles. She hadn't told Abaki that she had applied for her gun permit. She wanted to surprise him with it. And when it had come in the mail yesterday, she figured that today would be as good as any to reveal her surprise. She would even tell him about her very first pistol purchase: a .45 caliber handgun.

During the last ride they took, Autumn had revealed to Abaki that she was growing more comfortable and she was actually beginning to enjoy the rides. He offered to pay for classes so she could get her own motorcycle license. Every day they spent together was another day closer to the rest of their lives. She couldn't help but imagine the rest of her life with Abaki.

Recognizing the scenery, Autumn sat up. She recalled the time he last took her up the coast with the promise to bring her back. She just didn't think it would be this soon. "Are we going where I think we're going?" she yelled, trying to launch her voice over the whipping wind for him to hear.

Abaki nodded.

"I thought it closed at five."

Abaki said nothing. As he turned into the entrance of the arbor, a man came out and greeted them. "Abe, it's always great to see you. And this must be the lovely, Ms. Hughes. Ma'am, how do you do?"

"Hello. I'm very well, thanks. And you?"

"Life couldn't be better."

Autumn immediately took a liking to the nice gentleman before them. She could tell he was older, early sixties, but he took very good care of himself.

"Please, right this way," the older gentleman said.

Abaki took Autumn's hand as they followed the gatekeeper down a narrow concrete path, bordered by the most beautiful trees and shrubbery she'd ever seen in one place. Up ahead, Autumn could see that there was a private table for two situated in a nice garden area by a pond. The table was topped by a bucket of ice and a bottle of something inside, candles, and place settings. Even though she wasn't a cards and flowers kind of girl, she appreciated the two-dozen assorted roses on the table. She squeezed Abaki's hand in admiration.

"The park is yours for the next two hours. I'll be right over there in the arbor house. If you need me, just call."

"Abaki, this is so beautiful," Autumn said in awe.

Dusk was approaching, and it made the scene even more stunning. Solar-powered lawn lamps began to shine, causing flickers of light to grace the gardens that surrounded them. Several paths led to various places throughout the field. This location was the perfect backdrop to an amazing date. Autumn was pleased. Her man had shown her his romantic side, and he did not disappoint.

Abaki had hired a professional chef to put together the most decadent meal. Laid out in front of them was a fresh tossed salad, warm butter rolls, and shrimp scampi. To wash it down, they had water and her favorite moscato, Primo Amore.

"You *do* like me," she cooed.

For dessert, Abaki had the chef prepare an assortment of fresh fruit, but only Autumn's favorites: pineapples, strawberries, grapes, and kiwi. Some were chocolate dipped.

"When did you plan all this?" she asked.

"Yesterday. That's why you didn't see me the whole day.

Autumn smiled. She was ready to reveal her surprise.

"Whaaat I got for you?" Autumn said, imitating Sebastian. She missed her little guy so much. These recent events had her mind spinning in circles. As much as she wanted to get him, spend time with him, and have him sleep over, she couldn't risk Inez doing something irrational and having Sebastian caught in the middle. She would never forgive herself if something happened to him. Once this was all over, she and her godson were going to spend a lot of time together.

Reaching into her purse, she pulled out an envelope and handed it to Abaki.

"What's this?" he inquired.

She told him to open it.

When he pulled out the pistol permit, he looked shocked. "You really applied and were approved? I can't believe this. Wow! To be honest, I didn't think you and Chaianne were practicing."

"Yup. She made Karl promise not to tell you. We went three times a week for the past three weeks, and each time, I got better and better. Finally, I decided to apply. She used some of her contacts and was able to expedite the process."

Abaki leaned in and kissed her.

"Wait, there's one more thing." Autumn reached into the envelope and pulled out a photo. It was a picture of her target. It showed twelve bullet holes, all piercing what would have been vital areas. She watched as his eyes glowed. His smile appeared and then faded. She could tell that he was in thought. Instead of interrupting, she waited.

"Autumn, I have something I need to tell you."

Her heart sank, as she wondered what he had to say that had him sounding and looking so melancholy. She hoped it wasn't something bad, something they couldn't work out. *Does he love Inez? Does he want her back? Is he breaking up with me?* So many questions invaded her mind in just a short amount of time.

"I told you about the girl back home whom I was arranged to marry. But what I didn't tell you is that I was her father's second choice, but *her* first. Sekara; that's her name. She didn't like the guy her father wanted to betroth her to. Her sole purpose was to prevent that arrangement in hopes of her and I coming together. Sekara was very bright for her age. So at nine years old, she devised a plan that entailed me penetrating her and having her brother catch us. She knew that the first man to have sex with her would be the one who would have to marry her. After we were exposed, I quickly left, running from her side of town toward mine. I knew I had made a terrible mistake and needed to find my father to inform him. For almost the whole day, I was unable to locate him to tell him what had happened. By the time my father and I connected, he had already gotten word from Sekara's father, Mr. Bahari, of what I did. Marriage was the only way to rectify it. She was damaged goods, and no one would want her now that she was impure. My father and I had a talk, and during that conversation, I begged him not to make me marry her. He must have heard the desperation in my voice, because he conceded. He sent me away to live with my uncle and told me to never return unless I was willing to accept the consequences of my actions or pay a hefty fee, possibly my life. I left and never looked back.

Every two years, my father would come visit me and stay for at least a month. He would update me on how things were going back home and the status of the pink elephant that lingered. With each visit, he appeared to age more and more."

Abaki stopped talking for a second to gauge how Autumn was taking the information. When he saw that she seemed fine, he continued. "Whenever my uncle was in one of his political meetings, I would be with my father. He was a very influential man. His wealth yielded him great power but Mr. Bahari had the same, if not more. About five years ago, my father visited me. I didn't know then that the visit would be his last. I got word a few months later that he had passed. He'd made it clear, then, that I needed to settle things once and for all. The hefty price had been paid, but as a Lemande, it is imperative that I face the brute of the tiger and make clear my intentions or lack thereof. He wanted me to stand on my feet as a man and deal with Mr. Bahari as such. I later found out from my uncle that the woman I was being forced to marry was the same woman whose life my father had saved. Sekara had been kidnapped by one of Mr. Bahari's enemies, the Tiranis. She was Mr. Bahari's only daughter, so they knew that they had his most prized treasure, a bargaining chip. The enemy also happened to be indebted to my father, and my father was indebted to Mr. Bahari because of what Sekara and I had done. My uncle never told me what Mr. Tirani owed my father, but whatever it was, he settled the score by giving Sekara back to her family, which allowed my father to earn back my life.

Years before, Mr. Bahari had asked for a large chunk of my father's land as payment for what I'd done to his daughter. Trying to keep the peace, my father agreed to give him thirty percent of his land. He said that the other seventy percent would be for my use if I ever decided to return. Even though my father ultimately saved his daughter's life, Mr. Bahari didn't agree to return the land. He did agree that if I returned, he would give me a percentage, but I would still have to pay a dowry for his daughter. I guess that's my personal debt. In my eyes, Mr. Bahari is a greedy, greedy man. My father has paid him and then some, but that still wasn't enough."

Abaki looked at Autumn, who didn't know how to feel. So many questions ran through her mind, but she didn't know what to say or how to say it.

"So, are you saying that you have a wife back home?"

"No, what I'm saying is that I have to go settle a situation back home."

"So you're leaving?"

"Yes. But I will return."

Autumn started to cry. She knew it wasn't fair to Abaki, but hell, his pending departure wasn't fair to her. "Abaki, how could you? Why would you enter my heart and then tell me you're leaving? What kind of crazy game are you playing? I entered this relationship, thinking it was for keeps. Now you're telling me something that shows otherwise."

"Autumn, I promise you, this is no game. I have your best interest at heart; you have to believe me. Prior to meeting you, I was in no rush to get back home. Now that I've met someone who I can see myself with, I don't want this hanging over my head—our heads. I need you to trust me."

Abaki had yet to lie to her, so there was no reason to doubt him now. "When are you leaving, and how long will you be gone?"

"Soon. Very soon. I'll be gone for about a month."

More tears escaped her eyes. Abaki remained silent to give her a moment to process everything he had told her. When she finally stopped crying long enough to talk, she wiped her face and looked into his eyes. "Do you love me?" she asked him. It was a bold move, but Autumn needed to know. She knew that at some point he had to reveal his love for her and hoped it would be now because she needed to hear it.

Abaki used his forefinger and his thumb to lift her chin. "Autumn, if I told you I didn't love you, I'd be lying. And when I tell you no other woman has had me feeling the way I feel with you, I need you to know I am not lying. My trip home is not for pleasure; it's purposeful. It's imperative that I handle this so that I can make you my wife. This has to be done for me and us. Do you understand?"

Autumn took a few seconds but she nodded in affirmation. He hadn't told her he loved her and it hadn't gone unnoticed but the fact that he hadn't said no stuck with her as well. "Will you tell me when you're leaving, or will you just disappear?" she asked. For some reason, he struck her as the type to leave unannounced.

"Autumn, when I go, you will know. I promise you, okay?"

Autumn nodded her head slowly. "Yes." The thought of him leaving her for weeks and being so far away pained her deeply. She wanted to question the type of wealth his family had, but she decided against it. The last thing she wanted to do was give him the impression that she was a gold digger. When he was ready to reveal the source of his wealth, she reasoned that he would. Until then, she would let him communicate at his pace.

"Can I ask you one more question?" she said to him.

"Anything," he replied.

"What if that woman, Sekara, still wants to be with you?"

"I have no idea. I'm hoping that after all these years, another man has captured her heart. I'm certain that she has been married off by now, more than likely to a less than desirable candidate, which is why her father wants a hefty dowry. Even if her heart is still open to me, it will not change anything. As for me, my heart belongs to one woman, Autumn, and that's you. And the only heart I want is yours. You got that?"

Autumn nodded. Before their date ended, she told Abaki that she wanted to spend the night at his place, and he didn't hesitate to oblige. His lack of hesitation even surprised her. Her heart was smiling. Tonight, she was finally going to sleep in her man's bed, and she welcomed the joy that would come with that privilege. She hugged him and closed her eyes, silently praying that God wouldn't take from her something that she had waited so long to obtain.

Chapter 54: Abaki

As far as Abaki was concerned, the date with Autumn had gone well. She had handled the news as well as he'd expected. While she had taken in all that he'd shared, he took her all in. He had searched her eyes for reassurance, her body language for confidence, and her mental state for endurance. It pained him to have to leave her but this would be the one and only time he would ever leave her side. And as far as he was concerned, it was for a necessary cause. Autumn deserved all of him, and until he handled this, his integrity, future, and family name were on the line. Autumn's admission to loving him was something he hadn't wanted to hear, yet, at the same time, he had needed to hear it. This time, it seemed more genuine. What he hadn't anticipated was her asking him if he loved her. Although what he felt for Autumn was deeper than attraction, he still didn't think he was at the level she was. However, if he'd told her that he didn't love her, he risked losing her forever. If he'd told her that he did love her, there was still a small chance that she could lose him forever, and he didn't want his departure to hold her heart captive.

Being completely honest with himself, he had no idea how things would go when he went back home. Despite all that his father had done on his behalf, there was a chance that Mr. Bahari still wanted his head. The last thing his father had told him was to clear his name and know that "everything won't be what it seems, son. Research first." Those words had played in his head countless times. Now, facing reality bothered him just as much as it bothered Autumn. They had gone too far to have it all end now, but they hadn't gone too deep that they would never be able to move on. Since he wasn't able to tell her what she wanted to hear, at least he could adhere to what she wanted to do. If spending the night would make her heart happy, he was willing to do whatever it took to make her smile.

Abaki had grown fond of watching Autumn while she slept. She had a serene presence during times of rest. He was having one of those moments when Yin and Yang approached his side of the bed. They were trained not to bark at intruders. They notified him first, and again, they had demonstrated their trustworthiness and loyalty. Abaki eased out of the bed and stepped quietly toward the window with his trusted canines at his side. At the same time he heard Autumn stirring in her sleep, he heard rustling outside. He turned his attention back to Autumn and watched as she felt his side of the bed and then popped upright. The light from the moon provided just enough light for her to see him place his finger over his lips, signaling for her to remain quite. Easing out of the room, he headed toward the back of the house. Once he reached the back door, he opened it and motioned for Yin and Yang to go and explore. As soon as they were spotted, the lurker started screaming and yelling for Abaki to get them. He recognized the voice; it was Inez.

"What are you doing here, Inez?" he barked.

"I know you got that bitch up in there, Abe! I know it. I'm sick and tired of this shit. Either you get rid of her now, or she'll regret it."

"Are you threatening her? Because a threat to her is a threat to me," Abaki warned.

Inez folded her arms in defiance. "Well, you've been threatened," she spat.

Abaki heard rustling and muffled noises coming from upstairs. When he glanced at his bedroom window and then back at Inez, her facial expression confirmed his suspicions. Abaki raced back inside the house, up the stairs, and into his bedroom. The covers were on the floor and the dresser was swiped clean. He called out to Autumn but she didn't answer. He frantically checked every room, but to no avail. The sounds of screeching tires caused his heart to drop. Autumn was in danger again, and this time, it had happened right under his nose. He threw on some sweat pants, a pair of work boots, and a hoodie. Although he vowed that he would never physically hurt a woman, he swore that if Autumn was hurt because of Inez, she and her accomplices would get everything they deserved.

Abaki raced to his car and whistled for his dogs to join him. He had no idea where Autumn had gone but wherever she was, he trusted his dogs to be by his side. His first instinct was to notify the police. However, his internal voice made him wait. He wanted justice served, but not before carrying out a little of his own.

Chapter 55: Autumn

Autumn sat in the back of the car, gagged, tied, and blindfolded, listening to her two kidnappers discuss her fate. She recognized the female voice, and she assumed that the male voice belonged to the guy who had destroyed her car and practically injured her that night at Inez's home. Now, she was really scared.

"I don't give a shit what you want! I want her out of the picture. She stole my man and ruined my fucking life," Inez yelled.

"I understand what you're saying, but you ain't gonna be talking to me like that. I came here to do you a fucking favor. And now that I know what I know, it's not her I'm interested in anymore."

"Well, you better be if you want that other bitch. Remember, this comes first. Once you're done, I don't give a damn what you do."

The two went back and forth. Autumn sat in the backseat, struggling to get her hands free. She didn't know what she could or would do but she knew that without her hands, she was as good as dead. The car came to a stop, and Autumn could hear the sounds of a garage door lowering. If she was going to die, she would die trying to save her life. She wiggled her arms and twisted her wrists until the rope loosened enough for her to free her hands. When one of her assailants reached in to pull her out, she began fighting. She punched, kicked, and screamed in hopes of getting away or someone hearing her. He was way stronger than her and her attempts were futile. The last thing she remembered before she blacked out was a few hits to her face and one hit to her jaw.

When Autumn came to, her senses told her she was in a residential setting but she couldn't confirm exactly where. There was light; she could tell from the glow beyond the blindfold. She could smell cotton fresh air freshener. There was furniture in the room. She knew that based on the turns they'd made as her captors had dragged her half-consciously to her final destination. As much as she wanted to think of this all as a nightmare, she knew she wasn't dreaming. All these years on earth, she never would've imagined dying like this. She was frantic. Her hands were once again tied behind her back, this time a little tighter, so getting to a phone to call for help wasn't feasible. She wasn't even able to defend herself. Her body trembled, and no matter how much she tried, she was unable to stop the involuntary shakes. Her beautiful mocha face was now caked with dried and fresh tears. Blood flowed freely from her mouth and nose. Her russet eyes were bloodshot and practically swollen shut. Autumn did the one thing she always did when in compromising situations—she prayed.

Dear God. It's me, Autumn. I ask for a lot, I do. But

this time, I really need you, God. I need you bad, Lord. This man is going to kill me. I don't want to die, not like this. I just met the man of my dreams. Aren't we supposed to have kids and get married? Please, God. Please, don't let me die like this. My sister needs me. I'm all she has. I can't leave her, please. If I die, she will die too, inside. Her pain will be too great. I'm all she has left, and she is all I have. I can't leave her all alone, not like this. Please, please, please, help me out of this.

Autumn heard clicking heels and then nothing. The womanly scent of a floral musk permeated her nostrils.

"Well, well, well. I finally get to face the punta that has my man's nose wide open. You have no idea how you've ruined my life. I would have been set forever. But you fucking ruined that," Inez snapped, striking Autumn across the face again. "Undress her," she commanded.

Autumn's heart rate quickened. She tried to beg for her life, like she had when they'd first taken her, but to no avail. Her face hurt too much to talk, and she couldn't see. She still was able to think. *Think, Autumn, think.* Despite all her troubles, her brain still worked. She just had to give it time to concoct a plan. Just as that dreadful day twelve years ago, when she had to fight for her sister just to keep the two of them together, she would fight for herself. Her first plan was to free her hands. That was the only way she had a chance at defending herself.

A pair of man's hands traced the contours of her body, and she could feel his breath on her face before he whispered in her ear. "My cousin hates you, but I don't really want to hurt you. What I really want is your friend. Now if you can get Chaianne over here alone, I can make this all go away, okay?"

Grateful that he hadn't undressed her as Inez had ordered, Autumn nodded eagerly in agreement.

"I'm going to remove the tape from your mouth. If you do or say anything stupid, you're dead. Am I understood?" Autumn nodded again and he removed the gag. What's her number," he asked.

The truth was, Autumn didn't know Chaianne's number by heart. The only three numbers she could pull from the top of her head were 9-1-1, Summer's, and Abaki's, and her spirit moved her to have him dial the latter. Autumn silently prayed that things would turn out okay; it just had to.

Chapter 56: Abaki

The truth was Abaki had no idea where Autumn had been taken. All he knew was that time was of the essence; he had to get to her quickly. The first and most obvious spot for him to check was her home. Abaki raced to Autumn's house, getting there in record time. When he arrived, he ran up the steps, twisted the knob, and when it didn't open, he ran around back with Yin and Yang on his heels. Their lack of excitement confirmed that Autumn wasn't there. They knew her scent, so when he had placed her shirt to their noses, he was confident that they would let him know when they found her. He started to call her sister and his friends to help in the search but he didn't need more frantic people who would only add to the problem.

His next stop was Inez's place. If she wasn't there, then he would have to break down and notify the authorities. Although he wanted the assistance, he welcomed the idea of handling the situation to his liking. He made it back to his car in just enough time to hear his phone ring, but he had missed the call. He quickly pressed a couple of buttons to see who had called. When he saw that it was Inez's number on the caller ID, his adrenaline went into overdrive. Instead of calling the number back, he headed straight there. He knew someone was there, and the thought of Autumn being there too hurt him, but not as much as if he'd find out that she wasn't. He was aching inside. The thought of something happening to his lady would surely lead to a blood bath, probably the deadliest Dallas had ever seen.

Chapter 57: Autumn

The sound of car door closing let them all know that someone had arrived. When the doorbell rang, Inez's accomplice hopped up and Autumn started moaning. She heard Inez and Dominic whispering and plotting but she couldn't make out what was being said. All kinds of things roamed through her mind. She wondered if they'd somehow gotten ahold of Chaianne and got her to come over. She wondered if a neighbor had possibly heard or saw something and called the police. But most of all, she wondered if her call to Abaki had worked in her favor; however, the thought of him being on one side of the door with danger on the other frightened her.

She wanted to call out to whomever was outside to warn them, but every time she tried to move her mouth, her sounds were muffled and excruciating pain ran through her body. She tried to sit up but fell back down. The room was spinning. The only relief she got was when she remained still and closed her eyes. In that position, she prayed again. She prayed for their safety, more so for Chaianne's than her own. If he wanted to hurt her, he would have. But it was clear that he had other plans. Dom's trip to Dallas may have been to avenge his cousin's beef, but once he'd seen Chaianne, his game plan had apparently changed.

The pounding on the door and the ringing doorbell let

Autumn know that her first two concerns weren't accurate. In fact, the sound of her man's voice bellowing through the thick front door sent hope flowing through her battered body. The weakness and frailty she once felt was replaced by hope that strengthened her from within.

Chapter 58: Abaki

As Abaki approached Inez's block, he had no idea what he was up against. The only indication of the capabilities of his foes was what info he'd gotten from Chaianne and Karl. He reached into his glove box and grabbed his Glock. He made sure his clip was full and that there was one in the chamber. He had no intentions of killing anyone, but he was definitely prepared if the need arose.

When he walked up to the door, the dogs ran around the house, barking and growling. His banging and yelling weren't getting the results he needed. He wanted to go around back but feared that if he did, Inez and Dom would try to exit through the garage. With that thought in mind, he moved his car from the street and parked it in the driveway, hopped out, and ran around the back. He saw a few lights from the neighbors come on and knew that it would only be a matter of time before the authorities showed up. With a few hard kicks to the back door, it finally creaked open. His deep voice resonated through the modest home as he called out to Autumn. He heard shuffles and muffles, and he raced through the house in search of his lady. Yin and Yang's growls led him toward the front of the house. When he reached the living room, he saw Yin barking and growling at Inez as she curled up in fear near the front door. Yang was growling and biting Dominic, who was trying to drag

Autumn toward the door while fighting off Abaki's trusted sidekick.

With one giant leap, Abaki was up on Dominic, punching him. When he released Autumn, Dom used both his hands to defend himself. Autumn did her best to slide her body away from the scuffle and was able to put a little space between her and them. The dogs were trying to attack Abaki's opponent along with him. He was getting the best of Dominic, doing major harm to his upper body while the dogs did a great job attacking the lower extremities. Inez hit Abaki in the back of his neck with a hard object, causing him to fall over and land on his back. That gave Dominic the opportunity to get the upper hand, and he began pounding on Abaki. During the tussle, Abaki's gun fell from his waist and lay near the coffee table. Inez's swift move for the gun caused Yin and Yang to divert their attention to her. She grabbed some items that were in arms reach and began throwing them at the dogs. She used a pair of scissors that were on her coffee table next to the weekly ads as a makeshift weapon. When she raised her hand to try to attack one of the dogs, the other one jumped on her, causing the scissors to fly out of her hands and land close to Autumn. Autumn struggled to maneuver the scissors, but was eventually able to cut the shoestring-type material that bound her hands. She quickly removed the blindfold and grabbed the gun.

Inez's screaming and Abaki and Dominic's scuffling

were sure to draw attention. Abaki tried to keep Dominic from getting the best of him, while trying to make sure Autumn was okay, and then the sounds of the police entering the home stole Abaki's attention.

"Freeze! Put the gun down!" the officers yelled at Autumn while pointing weapons at her.

"Easy!" Abaki yelled as he scrambled to his feet. He didn't even know Autumn was holding the gun until they'd said something. "Please, don't shoot. She's the victim," Abaki pleaded. With his hands in the air, Abaki walked over to Autumn slowly and calmly. "It's okay, baby. It's over. I need you to put the gun down, okay?"

Autumn didn't respond or react.

"Autumn, look at me."

Autumn looked into his eyes.

"I need you to unwrap your fingers from the trigger and slowly lower the weapon, okay? It's over. Drop the gun."

Abaki stepped out of her way so the officers could see that she was doing as directed. When she released the gun, they went to arrest her, and Abaki stepped in front of her.

"What are you doing? I said she's the *victim*. The people you need to be arresting are her and him," Abaki yelled, pointing at Inez and Dominic. Dominic was lying on the floor in the same spot Abaki had pinned him. The dogs had paralyzed Inez with fear, and she was crouched stiffly near the coffee table.

"Sir, we are going to need you to move out of the way. Otherwise—"

"Get him!" one of the officers yelled as he noticed Dominic trying to flee the scene. Two officers ran after him.

More officers arrived along with EMTs, who began checking on the injured. Although everyone had suffered injuries, Autumn's were the worst. Her right eye was practically swollen shut, her mouth and nose were bleeding profusely, and her jaw was just as swollen as her eye. Abaki felt his heart leave his chest. His beautiful chocolate angel had been harmed, and he hadn't been there to protect her. He wanted badly to ride with Autumn in the ambulance but the authorities wouldn't let him. He begged them to allow him to call her sister to meet her at the hospital with promises to stay behind and give them all the information they needed. When they obliged, Abaki felt better. At least he knew that Autumn wouldn't be alone after what had just happened.

The fact that Dominic was still breathing bothered him. However, the comfort of knowing that Autumn was alive gave him a better feeling. He watched as Inez and Dominic were hauled off in police cruisers. He whistled for his dogs, who hopped inside the car. He got in behind them and headed to check on his lady.

Chapter 59: Autumn

When Summer walked into the hospital room where Autumn was being treated, the look on her face caused the two of them to break down. The sight of her sister, bruised and swollen, had practically brought Summer to her knees, and the sight of Summer's meltdown caused Autumn immense agony. Summer rushed over and hugged her with no regard for the nurse that was in the room, treating her wounds.

"What happened, Autumn?" Summer cried.

Autumn gave her a brief description of what happened, and Summer lost it.

"I will kill that fucking bitch. Do you hear me?"

"Summer, please calm down. There's no need to get all excited. The cops were there when I left, so I'm sure they'll be charged accordingly."

"This is bullshit. I'm suing the shit out of Dallas PD. They knew that bitch was crazy and was harassing you, and they did nothing, fucking nothing. Now look at you, Autumn. Look at your face!" Summer continued to cry. Another nurse entered the room and soothed her, explaining that everything would work out fine. She told her that Autumn's injuries weren't life threatening and she would be back to normal in no time. The damage looked worse than it was. Although the news helped both Autumn and Summer relax a little, Autumn could tell that Summer was still not pleased.

Moments later, Chaianne and Shae entered the room. Both grasped their chests when they saw Autumn. They all cried before anyone said a word.

"I can't believe things got this bad. Dominic just keeps popping up, and whenever he does, it's never good," Chaianne stated somberly.

"Tell them what you told me," Shae said.

"Well, last night, I discovered that Inez's father and Dominic's mother are brother and sister, both born in Cuba. Inez's father moved her and her mother to the States when she was six. Dominic and his mother came over when he was eight. Although he lived down there, when he turned eighteen, he began traveling back and forth to Albany to get money, and he did that for four years before we met. He and I were together for three years, and the whole time, it was nothing but drama. The last time I saw or spoke to Dominic was when I discovered the truth about Karl's *real* reason for pursuing me. Anyway, I left Dom alone and told him to never contact me again or he would regret it. Although, I gave up on him long ago, I don't think he ever stopped loving me, and that concerns me. I had a friend of mine hack into TSA, and he was able to confirm that he arrived in town the night before your car was vandalized."

"Basically, even though Inez didn't do it, she was behind the shit the whole time," Shae said.

Autumn was quiet and wondered what she had gotten herself into. The feelings she had for Abaki ran deep, so she wasn't willing to leave him. She loved him and she knew that he had feelings for her that ran just as deeply as hers. She wanted normalcy back in her life. A part of her wished she could go back to the days when she was just crushing on him. But although those times were peaceful, they weren't as fulfilling. Autumn prayed that his love would be worth all that she'd been through.

Chapter 60: Abaki

Until Abaki was sure that Inez and her crazy cousin where secured in jail, Autumn wasn't allowed out of his sight. When she moved, he moved. Although she'd told him it wasn't necessary, he begged to differ. After a week of turmoil, detective visits and written statements, the two of them were finally able to walk out of the courtroom with some relief. Both Dominic and Inez plead guilty to aggravated assault amongst other charges. Her attorney told her that they would be in prison for the next five to ten years. Abaki had been a big factor in helping her heal the wound, but it bothered him that he had to create another one. While Autumn bathed, Abaki called Karl, the one person who had been down for him all along. Although his mind was already made up, he needed a sounding board.

"What's good, brother?" Karl asked as soon as he answered his phone.

"It's hard to say. I'm glad that chapter is closed. Inez and Dominic were put away, and the DA dropped the charges against Autumn, but it saddens me to have to leave her so soon after all this crap. But I gotta do it, man. I have to make this move because it's either now or never."

"Damn, man. You taking that trip now? Shit. I know she won't take that too easy.

"I know! When I first told her I was going, she took it better than I thought she would. Her main concern was that I didn't love the woman and that I would be back. When I told her that I didn't love her and promised to be back, she was good. Now, I'm not sure how she'll handle it. K, man, she asked me if I love her."

"Get the fuck out of here! What you say?"

"I didn't say one way or another. I just couldn't tell her at that time, but being honest with myself, I do."

"So when you break the news that you gotta bounce, soften it with those three words, man. Trust me, every woman longs to hear it from the guy she loves."

"I know, but I can't, not now. Deep inside, I feel if something goes wrong while I'm there, not voicing that emotion will make it a lot easier for her to move on. If I do tell her I love her, I know it will hold her hostage. Autumn's an awesome woman and she deserves the best. So if I can't give it to her, I want her to be able to find it with someone else. But when I do come back, and trust me, I will or die trying, I'm not only going to tell her how much I love her, but I'm going to show her as well."

"What, you trying to take it there? You ready for that?"

"As ready as I'll ever be. She brings me out of my shell. Man, that girl got me doing things I thought I'd never do. I'm spruuung," he sang one of T-pain's songs.

Karl laughed.

"She's so sexy, sweet, carefree, loyal, grounded, and she's down for me. This whole situation didn't drive her away. In fact, I think it brought us closer. I've got to hurry up and get back to her. I need to, dawg. She got me."

"I feel you, man. Trust me, I know the plight all too well."

Abaki heard Autumn exit the bathroom and watched as she walked up to him and wrapped her arms around his waist. He ended his call with Karl and looked into her eyes. "Autumn, we need to talk."

Chapter 61: Autumn

Whenever someone said those four words, "We need to talk," it was never good, and that was how Autumn felt when Abaki had said those words to her. Although she'd just survived the worst experience of her life, she still hadn't lost sight of Abaki's pending departure. "You're leaving soon, huh?" she asked.

Abaki seemed a little taken aback. "What makes you say that?"

"Mainly because I feel it and partly because you just answered my question with a question."

He sighed heavily. "Yes, I am."

"When?"

"My flight leaves Monday."

"Monday? Abaki, that's in two days! When were you going to tell me?"

He watched as Autumn's disposition flattened. "Autumn, I swear I was going to tell you. But to be honest, it was killing me to have to. Are you okay?"

"Okay? Is that a trick question? Of course not! But what the hell can I say or do? It's something you feel you have to do, and I trust you and your judgment. It's just that I've wanted and waited for this for so long that now that I have it, I don't want to let you go."

"Trust me, Autumn, the feelings are mutual. In order

for me to be with you completely and openly, I have to take care of this. It's the only way."

"Well, can't you just call Mr. Bahari? I can buy as many calling cards as you need," Autumn offered.

Abaki smiled. "If only it were that simple. Look, this is just as hard on me as it is for you, trust me."

Autumn didn't speak. Her eyes got watery. She had put her heart on the table and told him it was his and he hadn't done the same for her. But certainly, he felt the same way if he was traveling across the world to handle his unfinished business just so they could be together. Abaki was doing what he felt he had to do in order to ensure their happily ever after.

"A penny for your thoughts," he said.

"Inside reflection, that's all. Abaki ... I'm worried that you won't come back. I don't know why I have that feeling, but I do. Who are you really doing this for, me?"

"No, Autumn, I'm not doing this for you. I am doing this for us. Listen to me carefully. I care about you deeply. In fact, my feelings have never run so deep for another woman. You mean a lot to me, and I can see us growing old together, with lots of kids and eventually grandkids. If I wasn't coming back, I would have told you. I swear on everything that has ever mattered, I plan to return."

Autumn watched as Abaki saddened. "What's the matter?" she asked him.

"You! I just hope that you'll still be into me then just as much as you are now. I can't have another man steal your heart from me while I'm away. Four weeks is a long time."

"Oh, Abaki! Seven years is a long time, and I'm still as single as a dollar bill. Plus, it will take a lot longer than a month for me to get over you."

"How long is too long?" he asked

"Don't show up after four weeks, and you'll see," she said, smiling.

Abaki smiled back. He scooped her in his arms and carried her to her room. He showered her with the romance and intimacy he knew she liked. They only had two nights to spend together, and she wanted them to be memorable.

Now that she knew he'd be leaving in a matter of hours, the time seemed to fly by. They both dreaded his upcoming leave. When they woke up the next morning, Abaki made her breakfast before they took a stroll with the dogs. Afterwards, the two of them rode together to drop them off at a boarding facility. Autumn planned a picture perfect picnic at a local park. They used that time to cuddle and talk about what lay ahead for them in the future. She loved him; he knew that. Although she was trying her best to be a supportive girlfriend, internally, she was having a hard time coping with his impending departure.

~~~

Later that night, Autumn prepared a romantic dinner for Abaki, complete with candles, wine, and a nice place setting. She made smothered pork chops, au gratin potatoes, and a vegetable medley. She skipped the dessert, hoping that the two of them would be all the decadence they needed. Autumn, of course, wanted to go all the way, but Abaki wouldn't allow it. She reasoned that if he was so sure of making her his wife, then there was no reason for them to wait. Abaki argued that that he didn't want something to happen, and then he couldn't make it back. The last thing he wanted to do was break her chastity ... and her heart. Autumn would just have to wait, and when he did come back, she hoped that he would make the wait worthwhile.

The next morning, neither of them wanted to get out of bed. Autumn held on to him as long as she could until he pried himself from her embrace. She had to go to work and Abaki's flight was leaving at eleven o'clock. Autumn was a wreck. Nothing he did soothed the ache. He left her place at eight thirty because he had to bring his car to his friend's garage and make it to the airport within an hour of the drop off. Plus, he had one phone call to make before he got on the plane.

Chapter 62: Autumn

Once Abaki left, Autumn sat on the floor by the door and cried. She cried because she missed him already, because she wasn't sure if he would really make it back. Her heart yearned for the only man she'd loved since losing her father. She cried just because she was sad. She had tried everything to make him stay, but nothing worked. Once she pulled herself together, she managed to take a shower and get dressed. Still without a car, she called her best friend to take her to the shop. Of course, Karashae agreed. During the entire ride, her frister witnessed the constant flow of tears falling from her eyes.

"I'm sorry for crying like this. It's just that I miss him already, and he's not even in the air yet," Autumn whined.

"Don't apologize. I can only imagine the pain you feel. He promised to come back, and I have no doubt that he will. I really love you and Abaki together. I think he is just what you need, and I don't think I could've picked a more suitable mate for you. Hang in there, fris. Things will definitely work out for you two. Why didn't you just go with him to the airport? It might've helped you feel better."

"He asked if I wanted to, but that would've only made things worse. It was like prolonging the inevitable. The sooner we separate, the quicker he'll come back, and the easier it will be."

Shae pulled up at the front of Mouth to Mouth. "I'll be back around seven-thirty, okay?"

Autumn nodded. Her heart was so sore that her mouth wouldn't speak. She hugged Karashae and got out of the car. She knew she had to get it together, and fast. Customers would be showing up soon, and as far as she was concerned, tears weren't good for business.

In a way, Autumn was glad that customer traffic was slow for the morning. It gave her the opportunity to sulk without appearing unprofessional. It was approximately one-thirty in the afternoon when a man walked through the doors, carrying the biggest, most beautiful floral arrangement she had ever seen. It stood about eighteen inches tall and was so bulky that he almost couldn't bring it through the door.

Autumn frowned in confusion but felt excited at the same time. "Hello, can I help you?"

"Yes, I have a delivery for a Ms. Autumn Hughes," the deliveryman said.

"That's me."

"Okay, ma'am, I just need you to sign right here, and these are for you."

Autumn grabbed a pen from her register and signed her name on the line. Her mind had been foggy since Abaki left, so she didn't fully read the details of what she was signing. The deliveryman watched as she leaned over and scribbled her name. He looked on in awe, unable to take his eyes off her luscious lips and beautiful, long lashes. When she was done, she looked up and smiled, handing him back the form. He ripped off the carbon copy and gave it to her.

"Lucky woman. Or should I say lucky man? Good day, Ms. Hughes," the delivery guy said while walking out.

Autumn blushed. She thought it was odd that his shirt tag read "Exotic Imports" since he had only delivered flowers. She could tell that he was flirting with her, but the only man she had eyes for was Abaki, and her heart wouldn't have it any other way. While marveling at the arrangement and sniffing the flowers, she opened the note that came with it.

"Autumn, I miss you already. My life would be so dull without you. Even though my trip is leaving a void, I hope that you can fill it with your beloved toy. Enjoy many rides and think of me. Yours truly, Abe."

Beloved toy? Autumn hadn't noticed the set of keys still wrapped inside the plastic near the massive arrangement. She grabbed the paperwork and read it thoroughly this time. "Oh my goodness. My car!" Glad that there were no customers in the shop, Autumn ran out front. Sitting there, looking prettier than the sunlight, was her 2014 BMW. Her insurance company had cashed her out to replace her damaged car, but she hadn't made a purchase yet. It looked as if Abaki had beat her to it. She jumped up and down a few times before she ran over to it and glided her fingers along the perimeter before unlocking it, getting in, and starting it up. It roared to life. *It smells like Abaki*, she thought. Autumn played with the buttons and gadgets before turning it off and going back inside her shop.

She started to call Shae and tell her not to come by because she had her car, but then she thought better of it and decided she wanted her friend to see her new baby. Karashae arrived around a quarter to eight. Autumn was straightening up the shop when she entered.

"Do not tell me that's your whip out there!" Shae exclaimed.

"Yesss!" Autumn squealed. "How'd you know?"

"First of all, all the other shops are closed, and there aren't many cars in the parking lot. Second of all, I know you had a BM before, so I figured the one sitting pretty and looking like a stack of new money just had to be yours."

"And you figured right. Abaki had it delivered this afternoon along with this massive bouquet of flowers, if you can even call it that."

"That pot is huge! I've seen those at the garden centers and thought they were just for decoration. I didn't think that someone would actually try to send an arrangement inside one. He's a keeper," Shae said.

"I know. I miss him so much. I wish I could just call him up and tell him thank you. But in the meantime, a journal will have to do. Then, when he gets back, he can read it so he'll have an understanding of how I was feeling in the moment."

"That's a great idea. We need a small road trip. I want to take a ride in your new car."

Shae waited until Autumn closed her shop so the two of them could leave together. She was glad that Abaki had her car delivered shortly after his departure. Somehow, she knew that he was already aware that her car would be just the mood booster she would need. She smiled at the gesture.

~~~

Some days, the hours seemed to fly by, and others appeared to drag. Tuesdays took way too long to end. Autumn had placed an ad on Craigslist for employees a few days ago and got a lot of calls. She was able to rule out many of the candidates by asking the right questions. When she finally met two women she really liked, she decided to hire them that day and train them the next.

Wednesday turned out to be a gloomy day and Autumn would have loved nothing more than to stay home. But she had her two new employees coming in for training, so she had to get up and take care of business. Both of the ladies were in school, so neither could commit to full-time hours. They arrived at one-thirty, like Autumn had requested. She gave them a tour of the store, including upstairs, before laying down the rules.

"So ladies, I've never had anyone besides my sister and friend run my store but me. I put my heart and soul into this place, so I value it dearly. I don't like liars or thieves, so all I ask is that you always be honest and never steal from me. You ladies got that?"

"Yes," they said in unison.

Even though the two girls seemed happy about their new gig, no one was happier than Autumn. She felt like she could finally have her store and more freedom to do as she pleased. Instead of going straight home after work, Autumn decided to go see about Yin and Yang. They meant so much to Abaki, which meant that if Autumn was closer to them, she'd be closer to him.

She stopped at the drug store and purchased some items for her car. Once she made it back to the car, she opened the glove box to place the hand sanitizer, lotion, and tissue inside. After moving some things around, she came across a folded piece of paper that seemed out of place. Autumn grabbed the paper and unfolded it. When she did, she covered her mouth with her hands and held her breath; it was a note from Abaki.

"If you are reading this then that means you have located a piece of my heart. It also means that I have left. Although at the time I wrote this, I didn't know how I would feel, I did know that I would miss you. The void I feel now

as I write this note lets me know that when I'm actually away, the feeling will be just as intense, if not more. Autumn, my love, you are the best thing that has happened to me in a really long time. I never want to lose you. Please wait for me. I hope you are enjoying your new car. Look under the passenger seat. I know some people who specialize in fragrances and had them create an oriental spice air freshner for your new car, similar to the one I wear that you like so much. By the time they run out, I should be back. Enjoy it, and every time you inhale, you will be breathing in a piece of me.

    Stay sweet,

    Abaki"

When Autumn got done drying her tears, she leaned over and reached under the seat. Low and behold, there was a package of about ten air fresheners. "Ten! That's more than a month's worth," Autumn said aloud. Her emotions returned, and she had to regain her composure before she drove. By the time she reached the dog shelter, her eyes were red and puffy. She masked the evidence of her aching heart with a pair of shades.

When she left the dog shelter, she felt slightly worse than she had when she'd arrived. She wasn't a dog expert, but Autumn got the feeling that Yin and Yang were just as sad when she left as she was when she'd arrived. She tried to be strong but she was losing the battle. She missed Abaki something terrible. Even a phone call would have helped. She thought about sending an email but wasn't sure if it would get to him. Until they met again, she would just have to settle for the notes and air fresheners to get her by. Before going to bed that night, she said a longer prayer than usual.

Chapter 63: Autumn

Several weeks had passed since Abaki had left, and Autumn anxiously awaited his return. The first week was the hardest, mainly due to Summer's absence as well. When Summer got back from the Hamptons, A.J. was waiting in the airport with an engagement ring that Autumn had helped him pick out. When he proposed, Summer happily accepted, and Autumn couldn't be prouder.

Thankfully, the second week wasn't as bad because the two sisters were able to do a lot of catching up. They went to the movies, to the mall, and had spa days. When Summer wasn't with A.J., she was with Autumn. However, week three was more of a blur. By that time, Autumn was really missing Abaki and wanted nothing more than for him to show up at her door. But until that day came, she made it a habit to do a lot of writing. To her, it was therapy for her pained spirit.

September 24th

My sweet Abaki,

Today makes twenty-one days since you and I last saw one another, and I realize that we never confirmed your return date. I do remember something about "four weeks" being tossed around, but you and I know how relative that can be. For both our sakes, I am hoping that by this time next week you are back in my arms. Tomorrow,

Yin and Yang will come stay with me. Hopefully, you won't be upset about that. It's just that when I'm in their company, it seems to ease the emptiness. Maybe that sounds weird, but it feels right, so I'm going with it (smile). Sebastian came with me to see them the other day. You were right; they took to him really well. That little boy surprised me. For sure I thought he would be scared of two large dogs, but he was just as curious as ever. Well, until next time ...

Love Always, Autumn.

October 1st

Abaki Lemande,

I'm sure you'll be able to tell that my tone has dulled as the days give way. Twenty-eight days is amongst us, which means that we're at the four-week mark. Not sure what exactly to expect in regards to your arrival, but every day, I find myself in a bundle of nerves. You left me with no arrival date, time, or flight information, nor have you contacted me with any! I tried emailing you several times, but they were undeliverable. My emotions are running rampant. One minute I'm crying, and the next, I'm laughing. Sometimes I'm nervous, and most times, disappointed. What are you doing to me? Please hurry up and come back. Feelings of abandonment are trying to invade my heart and mind, and it feels as if Autumn is

losing the battle. You said you were coming back to me, and
I am holding you to that! Patiently, but anxiously awaiting
your arrival.

Yours Truly, Autumn.

Rain, music, wine and candles were the perfect recipe
for poetry pie. Sitting on the padded window seat in her
room, Autumn pulled her eyes from the blurry outdoors and
began to write:

> *My days were once the brightest ever*
> *Not to be dulled by inclement weather*
> *If there were times of gloom, you'd brighten my day*
> *Without saying much, you had a whole lot to say*
> *Amerie said it best, what happens when eyes meet*
> *And when mine met yours, I swear they were talkin'*
> *to me*
> *Perhaps unbeknownst to you, your spirit seemed to*
> *reveal*
> *What your mouth wouldn't say but what your heart*
> *could feel*
> *I won't be burdened by a silent tongue*
> *Your emotions are familiar to me because we are*
> *intertwined as one*
> *So even if the words never left your lips*

The emotions you possess for me are released with
every kiss
    I keep reminding myself during times of gloom
    Not to fret too much, 'cause in my heart, you loom.

She wanted to write more, and there was more she could write, but she was tired. The wine, the loneliness, and the dampness of the evening made her feel drained, and to her, there was nothing better than a hot shower after a long, emotional day. After her shower, Autumn walked into the kitchen with her towel still wrapped around her. She retrieved the bottle of wine and poured the last few sips into her glass. The combination of nature's elements and her manmade vice was making her horny. She polished off the last of her wine and went into her closet in search of one of her many negligees. Choosing a white knee-length sheer nightie, Autumn removed her towel and let it drop to the floor. While combing down her shoulder length, brown hair, she thought about how things would be when she and Abaki finally reunited for good.

In the meantime, she decided to take some pictures of herself. Although she couldn't send them to him as a reminder of what he was missing, she could surprise him when he returned. Autumn put on her intimate apparel, spread some Mac lip glass on her lips, and set up her digital camera for some sexy shots. After setting the timer on her camera, Autumn performed one sexy pose after another. Wanting to spice things up a bit, she reached under her bed and pulled out her special occasion shoe rack.

She hadn't pulled it out in weeks. A square box with a little ribbon affixed to it was on top. A smile spread her lips instantly. It seemed that at least twice per week, she was finding little parting gifts that Abaki had hidden. He'd left the air fresheners, a nail salon gift card, a massage certificate, and then another note. The gifts were in the oddest places: the medicine cabinet, dresser drawers, linen closet, laundry room, and any other place he knew she would frequent. This discovery was no different, but just as special.

Abaki must be getting closer to home, she thought. She couldn't tell if her mind was playing tricks on her or if her heart was being gullible, but it seemed that each gift penetrated her soul more than the one before. Inside the package was Zhane's single "Sending My Love," the same song she had sung in the car the night Abaki asked her to be his lady. He must have recorded the song back-to-back because each time it ended, it would start all over again. He knew where she kept her dress shoes, so he'd placed a token of one of their most sentimental experiences in the soul of her soles. *How thoughtful.* Autumn placed the CD in her stereo system. She then adjusted her digital camera so that it was fixed on the center of her bed and turned on the video recorder. She crawled seductively to the center of her bed and stuck her index finger in her mouth. Zhane crooned about shipping love to the ones they love, and Autumn did a damn good job acting it out.

She dry humped the bed while separating her knees slowly, winding her hips suggestively. On key, Autumn moved her shoulders so that with each shift her breasts would poke out and then retract. She used the hem of her lingerie as a prop for the show she put on. Once she felt she had done enough teasing, she eased the gown over her head, leaned back on one elbow, and spread her legs. Autumn licked the middle finger on her left hand and placed it on her clit. She rubbed her love muscle slowly but with added pressure. She placed a pillow so that she could prop and support her back. Grabbing her silver bullet and vibrating butt plug from her nightstand, Autumn put them both in position and turned them on.

"Sending My Love" was still oozing from her speakers, adding to the intensity of her mood. "Oh, yes. Mmm, daddy, I want you to sex this pussy so bad. Abaki, I need you inside of me, baby," Autumn whined as she bucked her hips feverishly. "Yes, yes, that's it. Oh my good ... goodness. Baaaby, I'm cuuuming," Autumn whimpered. She kept the bullet on her clit and the plug in her butt until she thought she was going to faint from pleasure overload. She turned them off, removed them from her body, and tossed them on her nightstand, promising to clean them in the morning.

Drained but feeling good from the release, Autumn got up, turned off the lights and camera, and blew out the candles. She let the CD play as she drifted into the bliss of her memories.

Chapter 64: Autumn

Everyone had gathered at Karashae's home for an impromptu barbeque, thanks to the Indian summer they were experiencing. It was the second week in October, and the weather was gorgeous. Summer and A.J. were still on cloud nine from their recent engagement and were sharing stories about the same.

"Yeah, the people at my job are already planning us an engagement party," Summer said. "Even A.J.'s coworkers on his unit are coordinating a luncheon. Everyone seems to be pretty happy for us."

"And happy *with* y'all," Autumn interjected.

"Did you guys pick a date yet?" Chaianne asked.

"No, not yet. That's like the million-dollar question right now," A.J. answered.

"I was thinking some time next year. Honestly, we aren't in any rush. A.J. is almost done with school, so we already said we wouldn't do anything before then. Since he graduates in May, we thought maybe summer or fall, in honor of big sis, would be a good time."

Autumn smiled. That was her favorite season weather-wise, but not to get married. Her wedding had to be centered around Valentine's Day, for sure. As if in a far off place, where only her mind could travel, Autumn thought about her man. Her birthday party was next Saturday, and still no sign of Abaki.

Karashae noticed that Autumn had checked out. She interrupted her mental journey with a question. "Autumn, are you ready for your big day?"

"To be honest, I'm nervous. My emails aren't going through, which means that his probably aren't getting through either. He still hasn't called, and I'm not all that thrilled about celebrating my birthday without him. Thirty is such a big milestone, and I want my better half there to enjoy it with me. No, correction, I *need* to have him there with me," Autumn stated solemnly.

Chaianne saw how hurt Autumn appeared. Her heart went out to her friend, and it made her want to kick Abaki's ass for her. "Well, don't give up hope yet. Maybe he'll show up on or before your day," she said.

Had Autumn not been feeling so melancholy, she would have picked up on the glare that Karl threw Chaianne's way.

"I really hope so, guys. He was supposed to be back a week ago. As much as I want to give up hope, my spirit won't allow me to. It's like my mind wants to believe that he isn't coming back, yet everything inside me feels him near. He's studied me. My habits are imbedded deep within him. The places he hides little treasures are so on point and right on time. He may be close, but how close, I don't know. My true hope is that my birthday won't end without him there with me."

Now Karl offered his words of encouragement. "Autumn, Abaki cares for you ... a lot. My man is a man of his word, and if he said he'll be back, then he'll be back. I can't promise it'll be in the next seven days, but he will return."

Autumn smiled sincerely. Karl's statement did lift her spirits and gave her more optimism than she'd had all month. She hoped that he knew better than she did.

~ ~ ~

Flicking through channels, Autumn settled on a *Medical Mystery* episode. It was Sunday, her day to relax. Early that morning, she got up and took Sebastian home. When she'd left the cookout, he had asked to come with her, and of course, she had obliged. When she returned home, she took a shower and put on a pair of leggings and a tank top. Feeling comfortable, Autumn plopped down on the couch to watch TV. As soon as she was in a relaxed state, the doorbell chimed. She looked through the peephole and saw a man with a uniform on. With the chain still connected, she opened the door. "Can I help you?"

Standing on her doorstep was the same guy who had delivered her car to her shop along with that massive floral arrangement. "I have a delivery for Autumn Hughes."

"Delivery? Sir, today is Sunday. Deliveries aren't even made today."

"Yes, Ms. Hughes, I do understand that deliveries aren't normally made on Sundays; however, I don't make the rules; I just work by them. My boss told me that I had to make this delivery today, not yesterday, and not tomorrow, but today. Will you accept?"

"Hmm, Sunday delivery? For all I know, it could be a bomb."

The driver chuckled. "Would you like me to open the envelope for you?" he offered.

Autumn nodded. "Please!"

She watched intently as he pulled the envelope off the package and tore it open. "It says, 'To my chocolate angel—'"

Autumn gasped, closed the door to remove the chain, and then swung it back open.

"Read no more. Where do I sign?" she asked anxiously. The last thing she expected was to receive another gift from Abaki.

He showed her where to sign, and she quickly scribbled her name and went back inside. Autumn unfolded the note and began reading:

To My Chocolate Angel,

I can only imagine the things that have been running through your mind. If you are reading this then that means

I will be with you very soon. Things didn't go as smoothly as I would have liked, but my presence is near. We shall be together again. This is the first of many to come. There's nothing too precious for my special one.
Missing you dearly,
Abaki

She read the letter five times before she finally opened the box. Inside was a small, oval jewelry box with a pair of gorgeous diamond studs. They were perfect for the second hole. After placing them in her ears, she admired the glistening purity of the stones. She couldn't contain her excitement. Finally, she had heard from her man and he'd told her that he would see her soon. That night, she had one of the best night's sleep she'd gotten in a long time. But nothing prepared her for the days ahead.

All week, the gifts just kept coming. Monday, she received a two-carat diamond-cut gold bracelet: *"Autumn, my dear, here's twice the gift. It's to adorn your beautiful wrist."* Tuesday brought a pair of three-carat diamond studs: *"Three is a special number for you and me. Place them in your ears and let them be."* She put them in her first piercings and smiled at how well they complemented the first pair she'd received. Abaki was making up for his absence and his attempt at poetry wasn't lost on her. The gesture was more special than he'd ever know.

Wednesday's delivery offered some answers to her curiosity about his family's wealth. Abaki's family must have been in the gold or diamond business, because there was no way he could afford to send her such lavish gifts otherwise. *"Three, plus another one equals four. Are you tired of answering your door?"* A yellow gold pendant with a four-carat chocolate diamond, shaped like a Hershey's Kiss was situated on a beautiful yellow gold necklace. Above the tip of the kiss was a yellow ring full of diamonds, representing a halo. *"This is to be worn near your heart as a reminder of who you are. My chocolate angel, forever and always, know that your king is not too far."*

She cried. "Oh Abaki, what are you doing? I love you so much."

Curious, Autumn took the gifts to a respectable jeweler for appraisal. He couldn't believe she possessed such flawless stones. He went so far as to offer her over one hundred thousand dollars for all three pieces. Knowing that what she had was invaluable, she quickly packaged her jewelry and took it straight to her bank and opened a safe deposit box.

To her surprise, she had to do the same with Thursday's delivery: *"This is meant for the right hand, for on your left, I have other plans."*

I know diamonds are a girl's best friend, but damn! Autumn thought. Thursday's five-carat ring had Autumn awe struck.

As anticipated, on Friday, at nine o'clock in the morning, as she had done the days before, she opened the door to find the same deliveryman standing there with another delivery. She had tried tipping him, but during the first attempt, he'd made it clear that he couldn't accept. All expenses had been taken care of, including his tip. Friday's delivery was the biggest yet. The box was taller, wider, and much heavier: *"My blafrican queen, tomorrow is your day, so wear this proud. It is a custom-made royalty crown. I had it created especially for you. You are all I've ever wanted, a dream come true."* Autumn grasped her chest near her heart. She was afraid to touch it. The tiara glistened from every angle. Her eyes released tears. Very subtly, the words "Abaki's Love" were engraved in small stones in the middle of the crown. Autumn took a picture of it and texted it to Summer, Karashae, and Chaianne. They all seemed to text back immediately.

"Yo, that shit is hot! You are going to look splendid tomorrow!" Chaianne's message read.

"Oh my gosh, Sunshine. That is beautiful, just like you. Enjoy and rest up for your big day. We're working hard to make it memorable," Summer replied.

"Frister, I love it! You done put a spell on Abaki. Lol. Can't wait to see you wearing it," Karashae's message read.

Their reactions to her surprise weren't what she had

expected. Their responses only made her suspicious; she sensed they were all up to something. For the past two weeks, and especially these last seven days, she'd tried getting information from them, anything to help her piece together this puzzle in her head. But no one would tell her anything about the party, where it would be, the theme, how many guests would attend, nothing. They'd told her, "The only thing you need to know is the date and time. Leave the rest to us. Now stop asking questions." And she did. She showered and hurried to the shop so she could open up.

The Christmas season was quickly approaching, so both of her new employees wanted more hours. They asked to work today in addition to their regularly scheduled Saturday for the extra money. Using that time, Autumn decided that she would finally spend the gift certificates Abaki had left for her. The first stop was to get her feet and nails done, and then her full-body massage and facial. She then went home to get some rest. Something was telling her that tomorrow was going to be one of the biggest days of her life.

Chapter 65: Autumn

Awake and well rested, Autumn's stomach was in knots. Her body experienced a combination of emotions. She was nervous, happy, anxious, excited, sad, reserved, and blessed all at the same time. The queasy feeling in her stomach had to compete with the excitement she had in her spirit. Today was her thirtieth birthday, and she felt blessed beyond measure. Since so many of her family members had left this earth without celebrating milestones, she felt the need to thank her heavenly father that she lived to see an important one. Autumn got out of bed and kneeled on the floor.

"Dear God, it's me, Autumn. Thank you for waking me up this morning, but most of all, thank you for allowing me to see another year. Thirty is an age not many people get to see, and I am truly blessed for this gift. I guess that's why we call today the present. I know we talk often, and most of the time, I'm asking you to look after and protect others. Today, I am actually praying for something for me. If you are not too busy, can you find that man of mine and send him to me today? Nothing else can make my day more special than him holding me in his arms. No pressure though. I can only imagine how busy you are. So if you can't get to my request on this day, can you send him tomorrow? Yes, Lord, I'm desperate. Mommy, Daddy, Grammy, I love you guys. Not a day goes by that I don't think about you. Even though I have celebrated many birthdays without you, this one seems to be the hardest. Maybe it's because I'm older and wiser and I'm realizing the true essence of love. I think I've found it. I've never felt the feelings I have for Abaki before. It is so different from loving a parent, sibling, other relatives, or friends. I imagine that parenthood will bring a different kind of love as well, *if* I have kids. As always, I hope that I'm making you proud. Thanks for being such great role models in my life and guiding me in the right direction. Because of your love and upbringing, a man has fallen in love with me, the real Autumn, and I am certain that your parenting and guidance had a lot to do with it. The only gift I want today is Abaki. Can you guys help God make that happen? Forever in my heart, amen."

Autumn remained kneeling for several moments. She said her regular morning prayer and prayed for not only the ones she loved, but the lost, sick, disabled, and troubled. Just as she'd said the last of her prayer, her doorbell rang. Anxious that God had answered her prayers so soon, Autumn rushed to the front door and opened it without looking.

"Good morning," Autumn greeted the unknown visitor with disappointment evident in her voice.

A woman stood on the other side of the door. "Good

morning, Ms. Hughes."

"Yes, and you are?"

"My name is Taleesha. I'm your stylist for today. I was told to come by and get you picture perfect for your party. May I enter?"

Autumn was a bit hesitant to allow Taleesha inside.

"I have a hair appointment in an hour. Who arranged this?" Autumn asked.

Taleesha smiled. "Summer told me to come by and see to it that you get the works: hair, makeup, and wardrobe."

"That sister of mine. Sorry, Taleesha. Come on in."

Taleesha entered, carrying several garment bags and a makeup case, along with a rolling suitcase. "So what time does your party start?" she asked, making conversation, but mostly to gauge how much time she had to get Autumn ready.

"I was told the party starts at six o'clock. To be honest, I don't have anymore details than that."

"Okay, that's fine. Have you showered already?"

"Not yet. I took my time getting out of bed, and here you are." Autumn smiled politely.

"Well, it's almost twelve noon now. By the time I'm done with you, it'll be close to four. While you shower, I'll get everything set up. Is that okay?"

Not really, Autumn thought. *I don't want to be in the shower with some strange woman in my house.* Just as the words formed in her head, her doorbell rang again. *Abaki!* Autumn opened the door, disenchanted. Summer, Shae, and Chaianne were all standing there, waiting. As soon as Autumn opened the door, they all sang, "Happy Birthday!" They stood there and sang the whole chorus of the Stevie Wonder rendition.

Autumn couldn't stop smiling. "Aw, thanks ladies!"

"We are on a tight schedule, but we wanted to stop by and say happy birthday and make sure that you were being taken care of," Shae said.

"I was just about to hop in the shower," Autumn lied.

"Good, go. Time is of the essence," Summer directed.

Autumn came out of the bathroom after her shower, feeling refreshed. "Okaaay, I'm ready to be pampered," Autumn announced as she exited the bathroom in her robe.

All the ladies hugged and kissed her and told her they would see her later. Autumn called out to them to stop them at the door. "Guys, I think there is something you all are not telling me, and it's driving me crazy. What is up, for real? I see that, physically, there isn't a damn thing I can do for my own party to prepare, so can you guys at least tell me what's going on so I can prepare emotionally?" Autumn begged.

"Nope. Sorry. See you later," Chaianne stated as they all hurried out of the house.

"Wait! Who is going to go by and make sure the shop is closed up?" Autumn asked, still thinking of business as usual.

"Big sis, chill, I got this," Summer said, and they scurried out.

Summer scooped up all the dresses except the one that Autumn was going to wear in the limo. Shae already had her shoes at the venue, so there was nothing else they needed to do but wait and enjoy the night.

Chapter 66: Abaki

Abaki was anxious to get back to Dallas. His plan was to get back well before Autumn's party, but circumstances had dealt otherwise. When he realized he would be arriving on the day of her party, he made plans to surprise her there. Summer, Karashae, and Chaianne, had done a great job of helping him achieve his vision for Autumn's party. He wanted her to wear certain dresses at different times during the event. He was specific about her attire and how he wanted her to look. The rest, he had left up to them. They had complete creative control.

Abaki's plane landed in Memphis, Tennessee instead of Dallas. The pilot announced that they had to make an unexpected landing due to air overcrowding. The passengers were not fond of the surprise and their discontent didn't go unnoticed.

No one was more upset than Abaki. He had thought up the best thirtieth birthday party for his lady, and now that he was more than six hours away from her, he worried if he would make it there on time, if at all. The plan was for him to be dressed and in the limo, waiting when Autumn got in, but because of the issues with the flight, he wouldn't be able to see his beloved queen until he made it to her party.

It was twelve o'clock in Memphis, and the next flight wasn't scheduled to leave until five. If he drove, he could make it to Dallas no later than eight. If he waited, he would get there by seven, and that was only if the flight wasn't delayed further. He had flown too many times and was familiar with just how late flights could arrive. He couldn't chance it.

"Dammit!" He had no time to contemplate or plan. The best thing he could do was rent a car and hope that he wouldn't arrive at Autumn's party too late.

Chapter 67: Autumn

By the time Taleesha was finished with Autumn, her whole look was different. Autumn couldn't tell if she loved the makeup or hated it. Taleesha had done an awesome job, but Autumn didn't wear makeup regularly, so the finished product seemed too superficial for her liking.

"Do you like it?" Taleesha asked her.

Autumn thought for a second. "I-I don't know. It seems too heavy for my taste. I don't usually wear makeup, so less is best for me."

Taleesha stole a look at the clock and saw that it was four o'clock on the dot. Her job was to have Autumn ready by four, but now that she didn't like her makeup, they could possibly run over the time limit. Her hair design had taken up the bulk of the time. Autumn didn't like the first set of curls because they were too tight. The second set was too loose. Finally, on the third attempt, Autumn was pleased with the outcome and Taleesha went about showing her the alternate hairstyles she would wear throughout the evening.

"Are you going to be there to help me?" Autumn asked.

"All night," she reassured her.

After wiping Autumn's face clean, Taleesha restarted her makeup, hoping that the subtle application would be to her liking. Four-thirty had come in no time, and Taleesha had just finished applying Autumn's lip color. She gave Autumn the mirror. Now, Autumn risked messing up the makeup, not from dislike, but due to her tears. She loved it, and her eyes welled up at the beautiful sight before her.

"Oh no, no, don't cry! Please don't cry. We don't have any time for touchups," Taleesha begged, comforting her at the same time. "I take it you like it this time?"

"I love it," Autumn sniveled.

The house phone rang and Autumn answered it. "Hello?"

"Aut, what the hell are you still doing home? You should be on your way here by now!" Summer scolded.

"I just got done with my makeup. I'm about to get dressed now."

Summer could hear that Autumn was emotional. She was always emotional, and this time, it annoyed her. "Aut, pull it together. Save the tears for the party. Right now, we need you on your way, so get dressed and get outside. Your ride is waiting."

"Okay, sis. I'm together. I'll be leaving in five minutes."

"Good. Hurry up!" Summer said, ending the call.

Autumn put on the long, flowing dress that Summer had brought her back from the Hamptons. Since they'd told her that she would change at the venue, Autumn wanted to be as comfortable as she could during the ride, and the dress was perfect for that.

"Good afternoon, ma'am. I'll be your driver this evening," the chauffer said as he opened the back door. Autumn slid in. He grabbed the bottle of Primo Amore, opened it, and poured Autumn a glass. He set the bottle back inside the ice bucket, and then he reached into his inside jacket pocket and handed her an envelope.

Every minute she went without seeing Abaki was making her more anxious than the last. She expected to awake this morning and have him there. When her doorbell had rung, it had given her false hope. Just when she thought Abaki would have been in the limo waiting on her, it, too, proved to be a futile thought. Her nerves were getting the best of her, and it was starting to kill her happiness.

Opening the envelope, Autumn pulled out a card with a hand-written note:

Happy Birthday, angel. My plan was to provide this to you in person, but there must have been a snag in my agenda. One to always be prepared, trust that I am making arrangements to see you as soon as possible. Whether I make it to the party or not, I want you to know that I am there in spirit. Enjoy this beautiful evening that I have planned for you. When you see the amount of thought I've put into it, I hope it will make you smile. You mean the world to me, which is why I traveled half way across it to

make sure I never have to leave your side again. For you, I
will.

The guardian of my angel, Abaki.

Autumn had to will herself not to cry or scream. Was he telling her that he was not going to make the party? The letter, although sweet, had added a bitterness to her mood that she was trying to avoid. "Screw the party! I want *you*, Abaki. Dammit!" she exclaimed. She didn't care about the dresses, the makeup, or the birthday celebration. She would give it all up in a heartbeat if it meant being with her man again. Autumn let the flow of tears run down her face freely. She was done caring. If Abaki wasn't there to celebrate her birthday, then she didn't care how pretty she looked. Jeans and a wife beater would have been her choice of attire. Perhaps an evening at the bar, drinking her sorrows away would have been appropriate as well.

Noting that she had been in the car for over a half hour, Autumn asked the driver, "Where are you taking me?"

The limo driver wouldn't reveal the destination, but he did tell her that she would be arriving in less than twenty minutes. Autumn hadn't eaten anything all day. But the wine tasted way too good not to drink. "Might as well finish this bottle of wine. Maybe by the time I arrive, I'll be too drunk to notice that my man isn't there."

When the limo pulled up to the venue, Autumn was

greeted by Chaianne and Summer. "What the hell happened to you?" Summer barked.

Autumn's makeup was ruined. Eyeliner was running down her face. Her lipstick was smudged and her hair was a mess.

"Oh my God. We can't let the guests see her like this," Chaianne stated.

There was about ten or so people standing outside, smoking cigarettes, and rather than ask them to go back inside, the driver produced an umbrella, and they used it to shield Autumn from prying eyes.

"Come on, sis, we have to get you ready. You're already late!" Summer hissed.

The venue was a well-known banquet hall, used by many people to host wedding receptions and other high-end functions. They could use one of the private rooms, about the size of a hotel suite, to get dressed, primped, and pampered. The ladies rushed Autumn inside. Summer immediately went in search of Taleesha.

The hall looked beautiful. But to Autumn, even if David Tutera had decorated it himself, it wouldn't have mattered because the one key piece of the arrangement was still missing: her man.

"Autumn, honey, no more tears, okay?" Chaianne said. "I know how bad you want Abe here, and I'm sure he wants to be here just as much. If there is a will, there's a way, and I know Abe; he is doing all he can to make this day special for you. He put a lot of thought into this party, and he would love nothing more than for you to be happy. You have to try—"

Autumn looked up at Chaianne and interrupted. "Well, if he wanted me happy then why isn't he here? He is supposed to be here, Chaianne."

"I know that, and I also have faith that Abaki is doing everything in his power to make that happen. Pray for his safe return, and don't dwell on his absence."

Chaianne's words punctured her heart. All this time, she had been crying about him not being with her but had never stopped to think about his wellbeing.

"Oh my gosh. How selfish of me. You're right. I don't even know if he's okay. All I'm worried about is him not being here. Good grief!" Autumn exclaimed.

She sent up a prayer for her man and put her emotions in check. Taking a deep breath, she looked at Chaianne and gave her a weak smile before Taleesha and Summer stormed in.

"My God! What happened to you?" Taleesha asked, seeing all her work ruined.

"I had a meltdown in the limo, but I'm better now. Seriously, let's do this. Crying isn't going to bring him here any sooner. Might as well enjoy the fruits of his labor," Autumn admitted. She wiped her eyes once more and everyone relaxed a little.

Taleesha did her thing. When she was finished with Autumn, they both could have sworn she looked even better than she had earlier.

"You look amazing, Autumn. Your skin has more of a glow to it now than it did earlier. Simply stunning!" Taleesha complimented.

It was a quarter to seven, and cocktail hour was almost over. The three dresses that were selected for Autumn were laid out on the bed. The cocktail dress was long and black, stopping at her ankles. It was tailored perfectly to her body. One strap left one of her shoulders exposed, and embellishments adorned the neckline. It zipped on the side and dipped slightly in the back. When Autumn tried it on, she couldn't believe how amazing it looked. It oozed sexiness, and she wanted Abaki to be around when she wore it.

"I'm skipping the cocktail dress. Let's go straight to the dinner gown," Autumn stated.

There were close to seventy-five people waiting to see her and wish her well on her birthday, and they had already wasted so much time, so no one wanted to prolong things any further. "Girl, fine, whatever you want to do. We just need to get you to this party," Karashae declared.

The gold dinner dress was another beauty. When Autumn slipped it on, everyone sucked in their breaths, and

Summer started sniffling. Autumn beamed.

"Frister, you have just owned that dress, for real!" Karashae exclaimed.

"I see you, ma!" Chaianne cheered in delight.

Autumn did a twirl so she could see the back. The dress was fitted right down to the waist, along her hips, butt, and thighs. It flared at the thighbone. There was a small cutout in the back, and the front showed just the right amount of cleavage. A sweetheart cut with brown, gold, and red rhinestones adorned the neckline. Autumn felt like a goddess.

"Let me do one thing," Taleesha stated.

Autumn's hair was supposed to be down during the cocktail hour and then pulled up for dinner. However, seeing her in the dress, Taleesha's trained eye made her release Autumn's hair. With some twisting, tweezing, and twirling, she gave the style a whole new look.

"Exquisite!" Summer said, finally finding her words.

"Okay, ladies, let's get out there and mingle with everyone," Karashae directed.

Summer, Karashae, and Chaianne had also slipped into their final evening attire. What they wore for dinner would also be their party gowns, so they were sure to choose accordingly. They exchanged compliments before leaving the room.

~ ~ ~

When the ladies stepped out of the private room, guests were already heading into the banquet hall. Everyone smiled at them as the photographer took their pictures in the foyer. They took pictures along the double staircase near the entrance and underneath the massive chandelier. When the photographer was done with the ladies, Karl, K.J., Quay, Stephon, Lashae, Sebastian, Summer, and A.J. all joined in on more photos before they entered the banquet hall. Karl's friend, a DJ, who typically did the album release parties for his artists, had agreed to host the party. He announced that the birthday girl was in the building and everyone stood up and clapped upon Autumn's entry.

Soaking it all in for the first time, Autumn was able to absorb all the thought, planning, money, work, and love that went into preparing for her birthday. Red fabric draped the perimeter of the room. Golden spotlights shone upon the fabric. Red tablecloths sat atop round tables. Black runners topped every table along with centerpieces that exuded royalty. Crowns and heart-shaped balloons were placed strategically throughout the room. Opposite the DJ table, on the other side of the room, was a huge chair, with red velvet fabric, fit for a queen.

"Welcome to your Queen of Hearts thirtieth birthday celebration," Summer whispered in Autumn's ear.

Autumn looked around the room and at all the people. She had to fan the tears away. Her heart was filled with joy. The dim lights and large candle fixtures offered soft lighting. Stevie Wonder blared through the speakers as Autumn relished in the ambience created just for her.

The crowd sang the first verse of Stevie Wonder's "Happy Birthday."

As they sang, Autumn went from person to person, thanking each one for coming. The guests either handed her envelopes or small gifts. Summer and Karashae took them and moved them to the gift table. Folks had their hands in the air, singing "Happy birthday, to ya." It was an extraordinary party and Autumn was overcome with joy. Everyone she knew was there. Some of her colleagues from the school where she taught were in attendance. Karashae's mom had come to town to celebrate with her. The people she'd met at Abaki's Fourth of July barbeque had shown up, and even Karl and Stephon's relatives came to show love to the Queen of Hearts, Ms. Hughes herself. Summer and A.J. had invited a few of their coworker's too. The mood was great and love was definitely in the air.

The wait staff collected everyone's meal order: beef, chicken, or fish. Within a half hour of confirming orders, the entrees arrived. Autumn sat at a table with the three couples and couldn't stop the feeling of emptiness that overcame her as she glanced at the empty chair she knew was reserved for

Abaki.

Chapter 68: Abaki

Abaki turned into the car rental place at six-thirty. He had made better timing than he'd thought. His cell phone had died while in the airport, and not thinking about the possibility of having to drive, he'd opted not to bring his car charger with him. A taxi pulled up and Abaki had the driver take him to his friend's place so he could get his car. At least he could kill two birds with one stone. He'd get his vehicle and use the drive to Autumn's place to charge his cell phone so he could check his messages. Like he'd thought, Karl and Summer had called him several times and left numerous messages. He even had a message from Karashae. None from Autumn. Although he thought she would have called him, he figured that she had no reason to. Autumn was unaware of his return status. After listening to all his messages, he put the phone down and pushed the pedal to the metal. He had a woman to get back to, and he'd already lost so much time.

~~~

Abaki hurried and parked his car, rushing into the hall. When he got close to the banquet room, he saw Karl exit with his phone in his hand.

"Yo man, everything cool in there?" he asked in a panic.

Karl turned around to face an anxious Abe. "Oh shit, man. You had a muthafucka worried. I was just about to call you again. Where the hell you been?" Karl asked, reaching in for a manly hug with a pat on the back.

"Man, long story short, the plane got delayed, and I had to rent a car just to make it back to Dallas in a reasonable amount of time. How is she?"

"Sad," Karl said honestly.

"Damn, man. Alright, I'm going to go change real quick. I'll be in there shortly. I took a shower back at her place and grabbed my clothes, so it should only be a few moments."

"Bet. Hurry up. Ya lady ain't gonna be no good when she sees you."

Abaki smiled and nodded before rushing off to get dressed.

~ ~ ~

Summer, Karashae, and Chaianne had all given brief speeches about how much they loved Autumn and how good of a person she was. Even little Sebastian said a couple of words about his Aunt Lully. When the speeches were done, the DJ announced that the party was about to start, but first, the birthday girl had to cut the first piece of cake. Everyone who was interested gathered around the beautiful three-tiered cake. It was decorated with red, gold, and black icing and "Happy 30th Birthday" was written one word at a time on the front of each tier. A custom-made heart with a crown topped the cake. Pictures snapped left and right, and Autumn heard the guests commenting on how nice the cake was.

Karashae got the mic from the DJ. "Attention, everyone. We would like to thank you all for coming to celebrate my sister-friend's thirtieth birthday. In honor of the amazing frister that she is to me and the godmother that she is to my child, I would like to sing this song in her honor. If you know the words, please join in. If not, just listen."

Karashae started singing the *Golden Girl's* theme song and everyone joined it.

Abaki entered the room and saw the large crowd gathered in one area. He heard the *Golden Girl's* theme song and headed in that direction. As he traveled from the back of the crowd toward the front, the thirty or so people who had gathered around began to part to let him through. Folks were whispering and pointing, and he presumed that they were filling each other in.

"Wait, Sunshine. Before you blow out the candle, make a wish," Summer said. Autumn closed her eyes and stood still for several moments. Abaki was standing right behind her. He put his finger up to his lips to silence Summer, who looked like she wanted to hug him and slap him, Karashae, who looked like she was going to pass out, and Chaianne, who appeared to definitely want to slap him. When he showed his pearly whites and his sorrowful eyes, their expressions softened and they returned the smile. Autumn opened her eyes and blew out the candle. Everyone clapped.

"I can only hope that wish was for me," Abaki said.

Autumn stiffened. Those who could see her face were able to witness her bulging eyes. She closed them tight and reopened them. "Abaki?" she whispered, barely audible to those around her.

Abaki took a step closer and leaned down to whisper in her ear. "In the flesh, baby."

Autumn turned around, and there before her eyes was the love of her life. She jumped onto his chest and wrapped her arms around his neck. He couldn't allow himself to cry right then and there, but he surely felt like his heart had opened up and released its own tears. "I'm here, my angel. Sorry it took so long, but I'm back, and I am never leaving you again."

He pulled away from her and looked into her eyes. Even as a sappy mess, she was still cute. Autumn was wearing the chocolate angel pendant he'd sent her, and it made his insides melt. It looked perfect sitting around her neck, flushed against her chest. The crowd began to disperse. But Autumn, her man, and the trusted six remained standing there.

"Happy birthday, baby!" Abaki told her.

Autumn sniveled. "It's definitely much happier now."

The DJ played some line dance music to get the crowd hyped up and in dance mode. He played everything from the Electric Slide, to the Cha Cha Slide, and the Wobble.

"Okay, you two, it's time for Autumn to freshen up and put on her next piece. Abaki, she will see you shortly," Summer said, grabbing Autumn by the arm.

"No, I want him to come too," Autumn protested, still looking at Abaki.

"Alright, let's go," he replied, holding Autumn's hand.

When they made it back to the private room, Autumn asked the ladies, including Taleesha, to give them a moment. Finally alone, Autumn just stared at him. He assumed she was checking to make sure he didn't have any wounds or scars, the way she touched and felt his skin. Since nothing was out of place, he watched as she visibly relaxed. As much as he tried to stop her tears from flowing, he couldn't.

"It seems like forever," Autumn finally said.

"It felt like forever. I missed you!" he admitted to her.

Autumn gripped the back of his head and pulled him down for the sweetest, longest, and most passionate kiss they had ever shared. Neither of them wanted to break the hold before the other, so they continued to kiss for what seemed like hours. Abaki picked her up and carried her over to the buffet-style armoire along the wall and sat her on top. Autumn pulled on his suit jacket and loosened his tie so she could feel his bare chest. Still kissing, they continued to grope, physically exploring each other until their lungs begged for air.

When they finally pulled away, Autumn asked, "How did things go?"

"Things went better than I expected them to. To make a long story short, I avoided seeing Mr. Bahari. He's the kind of man who will do and say anything just to get a reaction. He's a man who doesn't back down, and neither does a Lemande. If I was to return to you in a timely manner, if at all, we could not meet face-to-face. What I came to realize about people like him is that if you allow them to feed you cow manure, they will, and they will go as far as to place it nicely on a platter and call it beef. He is the type of individual who would try to extract as much as he could from someone, even if he didn't need it. Anyway, when I arrived in my hometown, I met with the man who has been overseeing things. No one knew I was coming, so my visit was a surprise. I did, however, meet with a few of my father's trusted friends and they were told to keep my arrival clandestine.

My goal was to find out if Sekara had been married off. If she had, then for sure my dowry would be less than if she had not. Fortunately, I discovered that she had been married to a family of lower status, but was doing quite well for themselves. So I made arrangements for money to be transferred to his account with a memo, so that he knew that it would be the only payment he would ever receive from the Lemandes. I made the deposit only after weeks of watching him and his daughter's movements. Two days later, I was informed that he was enraged about the deposit because he knew that in order for it to happen, it had to have been handled from the inside. Mr. Bahari has so many connections and he expected that they would have told him about anyone trying to conduct financial business with his account. But my father, too, had connections, and my last name holds clout. The fact that I was able to make that happen without him knowing anything about it bothered him. I could have left after that, but I chose to stay. I wanted to be sure that he didn't do anything irrational, like try to destroy the family name, land, or those who were helping us mine it. On the final week of my stay, I did some soul searching, visiting, and a lot of praying before returning. Africa is a beautiful continent, with even more beautiful people. To say the most by saying the least, we should be living much better than we are. There is no other continent like it; however, it has been exploited and abused by both foreigners and natives alike."

"Would you ever go back?" Autumn wanted to know.

Abaki gave her inquiry some thought. "To live, no. To

visit, yes. Would you be interested?"

"Oh, Abaki, I would love to go to Africa. What person wouldn't, especially as an African-American?"

"Well, I shall make that happen at some point. Should we plan before or after the kids?" Abaki asked, grinning.

Autumn smiled. "I'll leave that up to you and God." She looked deeply into his eyes and kissed his lips again. "I need you so bad," she whispered.

"You still love me?" he asked her.

"More than anything in this world," Autumn confirmed.

Abaki stared at her long and hard. Autumn was at the center of his universe and he didn't operate well without her. "Go ahead and get changed. I'll be waiting for you when you're done."

Abaki helped her down from the buffet and kissed her on the forehead and then the tip of her nose before exiting the room. Once he opened the door, he held it open while Taleesha stepped in and immediately began helping Autumn out of her dress. He gave her one last smile and walked out of the room as she stepped into the bathroom.

He saw Karl and his cousin, Fred, and Stephon all standing in the foyer. He walked over to them. "Yo, K, man, I'm ready to do it. Tonight is the night."

"What? Do what? Propose?" Karl asked.

"Yes, *and* marry her."

"Get the fuck outta here!" Stephon exclaimed.

"Nah, fellas, I'm serious. I love her, and I'm ready to make her my wife. This is the perfect place and time. Everyone she knows is here, and everyone I know is here. I'm ready."

"Oh, shit. You really serious, huh?" Fred asked.

"As I've ever been," Abaki confessed.

Stephon went to get Karashae because he knew if anyone knew how to turn a birthday party into a marriage ceremony, it was her. Karashae wanted to break down and go screaming to Summer and Chaianne, but Stephon told her to pull it together.

"Autumn doesn't know. This is a surprise to her... and us, so let's make sure it stays that way, okay?" he said, and Karashae nodded. Her excitement was seeping through her pores, and it took everything in her not to run and tell Autumn the great news.

As discreetly as she could, Karashae went back to the private room and called Summer and Chaianne out, and Abaki told them what was about to go down.

"Who are we going to get to marry you guys on such short notice?" Chaianne asked.

"My mom's friend is an ordained minister, and she is here. I'll go talk to her. Summer, you make sure Taleesha gets Autumn in order and stall as long as needed. Chaianne, go with Abaki and make sure he has everything he needs:

music, vows, rings, everything," Karashae directed. She located her mom and her friend, and of course, her friend agreed to conduct the ceremony. One of the staff members went to the office and printed out some ceremony wording needed to make things happen.

Chapter 69: Autumn

Taleesha didn't disappoint with Autumn's up-do; it turned out marvelous. Her red party dress went well with the tiara that Abaki had made for her. She had planned to wear it during dinner but had forgotten to put it on, so when Summer suggested she wear it for a little while at the party, she didn't protest.

Autumn was finally dressed in a one-piece fitted red ensemble with her back and sides exposed, dangly earrings that Shae had purchased for her, and the bracelet Abaki had sent her. She felt like a queen. As promised, Abaki was standing outside the door when she walked out.

"You look lovely as ever, Ms. Hughes."

Autumn blushed. "And you look quite debonair yourself, Mr. Lemande."

Abaki went from a suit to a pair of black slacks, a black blazer, and a red button down shirt. He was so sexy that even some of the simplest outfits looked extremely good on him. Autumn and Abaki entered the ballroom as Trey Song's "Around the Way Girl" played. She dragged Abaki to the floor for a dance. Abaki was stepping, but Autumn could tell that he was trying his best not to get too sweaty. She saw Karl speaking to the DJ and assumed he was requesting a song. Autumn two-stepped into Abaki and wrapped her arms around his neck.

"Baby, I can't thank you enough for such a wonderful day. My sister told me you came up with the concept and money and had them execute it. This is the best day of my life, and I owe it all to you," Autumn said. She kissed his neck.

Abaki looked at her. "No, Autumn, this is the best day of *my* life."

The DJ got on the mic. "My man Abe asked me to play these series of songs for his lady, so partygoers, listen up. This is love at its finest."

He started out with KC and JoJo's "Last Night's Letter," then transitioned into "All My Life," and when Tyrese's, "Sweet Lady" began, Autumn knew something was happening. The photographer must have known it too because her camera was on the two of them the whole time.

"Autumn, my life hasn't been the same since we've met. The thought of securing someone to spend the rest of my life with was nonexistent until you came along. Your presence has made living that much more blissful. Autumn Hughes, will you do me the honor of being my wife?"

That was it. The moment of surprise hit Autumn like a Mack truck. She couldn't form the words to give him an answer. Instead, she covered her mouth and nodded her head incessantly. Their friends and family erupted in cheers.

Abaki pulled a box from his pants pocket and placed

the first ban on her ring finger. He stood up and looked Autumn in her eyes. "Now, Autumn Hughes, will you marry me?"

Autumn was a bit confused. Had he just asked her the same question twice? Surely, if she'd accepted his marriage proposal, then that meant she would marry him, right?

"Tonight?" he asked.

"Tonight?! You want to get married now?" she asked, and Abaki nodded. "Oh my goodness. On my birthday? Abaki I don't want to get married on my birthday. I dreamed of a beautiful Valentine's Day wedding and—" Catching herself, she instantly realized that having a Valentine's wedding would mean intruding on his birthday.

Abaki caught on to her realization. "Marry me on your day, and we can celebrate our marriage on mine."

Autumn thought about it and decided that it was a great compromise. "How are we going to do it now?" she asked.

"As if on cue, the minister walked up front and stood near the DJ. Summer, Karashae, and Chaianne served as her bridesmaids, and of course, Summer was the maid of honor. Sebastian was the ring bearer, and he knew exactly what to do because Karashae had been working with him on his moves for her own big day.

Karl was Abe's best man, and standing amongst them was another good friend of his and Stephon. The time came for them to state their vows. Abaki had his vows written down and went first. Playing softly in the background was Westlife's "I'll Be Loving You Forever." Abaki started. "Autumn, your name is evident of the beauty you exude and the love I've found with you. Just like the season, you are versatile and beautiful, and just like the leaves that fall from the trees, I fall deeper in love with you each day. I, Abaki Lemande, take thee, Autumn Hughes, to be my friend, lover, and my wife. I promise to protect you, provide for you, and love you for all the days of my life. As long as I have air in my lungs, you and the children we bring into this world shall never go without. It is from deep within that I welcome you to share the rest of my life with me, today, tomorrow, and always. Autumn, I love you, and this is my vow to you."

Autumn's heart fluttered at the sound of the words she had longed to hear since she'd told him her sentiments.

"Autumn, do you have something to say, or would you like to repeat?" the minister asked her.

Autumn swiped her tears away and whispered to her sister, who whispered to Karashae, who whispered to Chaianne, and then to the DJ, who starting playing "You" by Jesse Powell. Autumn began her vows. "For the longest time, the only ones who knew my heart were God, my sister, family, friends, and of course, me. Lately, I've had the privilege of sharing it with you. I didn't realize just how lonely I was until you entered my life and then had to leave.

These past seven weeks have been torture. I never want to experience that kind of pain again. Abaki, the fact that I've remained single for this long only further solidifies that God had a plan for me all along, and that plan included you. It seemed like when you entered my life, the heavens opened up. I promise to love you, cherish you, respect you, and uplift you. I promise to allow you to provide, protect, and possess. I am willing to allow you to be the head of our household, just as Christ is head of the church. I may not be perfect, but today, in front of family and friends, I vow to be your wife, and all that it entails. Abaki, this is my solemn vow to you."

The bridesmaids wiped their eyes, trying to contain the tears. This impromptu marriage ceremony proved to be one of the most heartfelt any one of them had ever witnessed.

"The rings please," the minister prompted Sebastian, who walked to the front. Although his boxes were empty, Karashae had him do it for good measure and practice, and her baby didn't disappoint.

Abaki reached into his inner coat pocket, pulled out the ring, and placed it on Autumn's ring finger. Karl had given Abaki's ban to Summer, so before Autumn had a chance to inquire, Summer had reached out and handed it to her. They both went through the spiel, and after fifteen short minutes, Autumn was Mrs. Abaki Lemande.

"By the power vested in me, it is my pleasure to

introduce Mr. and Mrs. Abaki Lemande!" the minister announced.

Everyone stood, clapped, whistled, and cheered.

Autumn wasn't worried about the formalities of the ceremony because Karashae had told them that they could treat the ceremony as an elopement and have the marriage license signed as soon as they got it. The DJ played All-4-One's "I Swear," a special request by Abaki, and the two of them shared their first dance. All those who got to witness Autumn's ring marveled at its exquisiteness.

"Damn, sis, Abaki spared no expense on this. This shit looks just as big as the ones those celebrities wear. How the hell he manage that?" Summer asked, unable to hide her astonishment.

When Abaki turned his attention back to Autumn, she asked him, "How rich are you?"

"Rich? Autumn, I would say wealthy is more like it. That has been the status of my family for generations. My father's great grandfather acquired some land, a gold mine, and it has been passed down ever since. Although this is the smallest the Lemande portion has ever been, it still generates vast profits. But we can talk about that later."

Autumn looked at Summer, who was standing with her mouth wide open. Autumn gaped at the beauty before her and realized that it was the same style ring that she had admired while ring shopping with A.J. to prepare for his proposal to Summer. When he came to congratulate her, she hugged him and asked if he had something to do with it. "Maybe," he replied and kissed her on the cheek.

They had the hall for another hour, and the DJ made sure everyone stayed on the dance floor until the party was over. When twelve midnight struck, the DJ slowed down the music, signaling that the party was coming to an end. "Okay, everybody, on behalf of the newly married couple and their families, thank you all for coming out. You ain't got to go home, but you got to get the hell outta here," he bellowed. The crowd laughed.

Autumn fared her guests well, thanked them all for coming, and when she made eye contact with her husband, he excused himself from those he was talking to and came to her.

"Are you ready?" he asked her.

"Yes," she replied, looking into his eyes with lust.

Even though they had just said "I do" Autumn couldn't ignore the fact that she was now Abaki's wife and she wanted nothing more than to feel him inside of her at that moment. It was raining really hard, so Abaki told Autumn to wait in the hallway while he ran to get his car. He pulled up right in front and got out to help her in.

While stopped at a red light, Autumn leaned over and kissed him deeply. "You definitely made this the best day of my life. Thanks for everything, husband."

Abaki smiled. "You are more than deserving, wife."

"Does that mean we can urh um?" Autumn asked suggestively.

Abaki didn't answer her. Instead, when the light turned green, he drove off, heading to a secluded area. He pulled into the parking lot of an abandoned warehouse, not too far from the banquet hall and put the car in park. At first, Autumn felt unsure, but a smile quickly spread across her face when she realized what he was doing. Her heart raced and her vaginal muscles contracted. Unbuckling her seatbelt, she eased onto Abaki's lap, straddling him gracefully. She planted sensual, wet kisses all over his face, neck, and baldhead. In between, she told him how much she loved him and how happy he made her. She thanked him for seeing in her what so many men had failed to see. She thanked him for being what so many men failed to be.

Abaki's member began to rise and he could feel his balls begging for relief. "Will the rain bother you?" he asked her.

She shook her head "no." After opening the car door, he stepped out with Autumn's legs wrapped around his waist. The rain hadn't let up; it was coming down just as hard as when they'd left the banquet hall. He carried her to the hood of the car and gently placed her on top. Autumn couldn't care less about her hair, her makeup, or her dress. The man she was going to spend the rest of her life with was about to take her adult virginity. Abaki eased the hem of her dress up her legs, under her butt and willed her to lie down. While holding her up by her thighs, he bent and placed his mouth on her love box. He planted sweet, soft kisses all over her flesh before using his tongue to spell "I love you" on her vagina.

When Autumn screamed that she was cumming, Abaki continued to lick her love button until she pushed his head away. She let her bottom slide to the edge of the hood and he helped her off. They switched positions so that he sat on the hood of the car. She unzipped his pants so she could access his dick. Taking him into her mouth, Autumn performed like only she could. When Abaki was on the brink of an orgasm, he pulled out of Autumn's mouth before allowing himself to cum. In a matter of seconds, he had her legs spread and her hands on top of the hood. He gently pushed down on her back to help her arch it. He squatted and licked her from the top of her pubic hairs to the crack of her ass, and just as a parade of moans left her lips, he entered her deeply.

"Ahhhh!" Autumn cried. Her heart fluttered and she closed her eyes. They both moaned in satisfaction. Had it not been for the heavy rainfall, Abaki would have seen the tears that were falling from Autumn's eyes. "Abaki, baby, that feels so good. I love you so much. Please don't leave me again. Please promise you'll never break my heart and you'll love me forever," she moaned.

Abaki leaned down and whispered softly in her ear, "I promise to never leave you again. I promise to never hurt you and to love you forever." His breath tickled the inside of Autumn's ear, turning her on even more. Abaki's strokes confirmed his words. Every movement seemed to make a pledge of its own, how her happiness meant everything to him and how he'd do whatever it took to keep a smile on her face to match the one in her heart. When Autumn announced that she was about to cum, he pulled out.

"Abaki, baby, why'd you stop?"

"I need to see your face. I need to look in your eyes while you're cumming."

He lifted her so that her legs were wrapped around his back. He held her tightly as he eased her back down around his member. Autumn used the hood, grill, and bumper of the car to secure her feet so she could have some leverage. Abaki held onto her as she rocked and rode him like a jockey. Autumn's eyes rolled into the back of her head. He held Autumn tightly as she rocked him into oblivion. The two of them announced that they were cumming together. For the longest time, they just held each other as their love juices became one with the elements.

After regaining composure, Abaki held Autumn in his arms as if letting her go would end his world. He squeezed her tightly, and at that moment, she was sure that their spirits had connected with their other halves. Autumn experienced feelings she had never felt. This was a love she knew was real. She wasn't some sex-crazed teen, driven by hormones anymore. Long gone was her young, naïve twenty-something-year-old self who was too vulnerable to a man's touch and meaningless words. She was a grown woman, who would no longer be hurt, disappointed, and misled by fraudulent contenders. She had transformed from a caterpillar into a beautiful, strong butterfly, who trusted in herself and her faith, and in turn, was rewarded with her ultimate heart's desire. Autumn Hughes had finally found a love worth waiting for.

Still holding onto her husband, Autumn looked up into the sky and whispered, "Thank you, God, Mommy, Daddy, and Grammy, for helping me secure the other half of my soul. Thank you! I've been awaiting a love like this!"

Ever After

As promised, Abaki blessed his wife with the wedding she'd always envisioned and made sure they had it on the day that was significant to her for more than one reason. Valentine's Day was Abaki's birthday and her parents' anniversary. The wedding took place at a lavish 3500-square-foot home on over three acres of land. Their guests marveled at the picturesque grounds. The lawn was neatly manicured, centered by a beautifully constructed fountain. A massive willow tree hovered nearby, providing a natural shade for the fifty guests that had gathered to share their big day. Abaki had hired an event planning company to install a dance floor and tent in the backyard. A custom-made aisle ran from the pool house to a newly renovated gazebo.

The two of them wanted to honor their deceased relatives, so the wedding combined a "Love is in the Air" feel with a "Heaven on Earth" concept, and Karashae had done an excellent job of coupling the two. After vows were exchanged—again—Autumn and Abaki joined inside the house for a quiet moment alone.

Abaki reached for Autumn's hand and pulled her close to his chest. "Did I fulfill my first major role as your husband?"

Autumn stood on the tips of her toes and pressed her lips against his before answering. "Abaki, you've been doing that since we said 'I do' the first time. And if you did nothing else for a very long time, that would be enough."

Abaki reached into his pants pocket and presented Autumn with a small square box. She opened it, and a set of keys lay inside. "Then would gifting you this house be too much?"

Autumn gasped, covered her mouth, and stepped back. "Baby, you didn't."

Abaki pulled her back in. "I did. And I hope you, my blafrican queen, will do a great job of making this castle our home."

Autumn wiped the tears from her eyes and reached underneath her dress. Abaki raised an eyebrow in suspicion, but remained silent as she pulled a little envelope from the safety of her garter belt and handed it to him. She watched intently as Abaki opened the envelope and removed the contents.

"And I will also do my very best in raising our little princes and/or princesses. The doctor saw double." Autumn waited a few seconds and then lowered her head and eyelids when Abaki didn't react the way she'd expected. He'd been telling her he wanted a family, and now that she had shown him proof that they were starting one, she didn't notice a reaction until she looked back up and saw a tear leave his right eye and trickle down his cheek. When she went to wipe it away, he softly grabbed ahold of her wrists and kissed her hand. He let his lips travel up her arm, to her neck, her face, settling on her lips. He picked her up and carried her to their two-story master bedroom, where he removed her wedding gown and made sweet love to his wife. He didn't bother to hide the stream of happy tears that steadily graced his face. Autumn had made Abaki the happiest man in the world, and in turn, he would make sure she was just as happy, because everyone deserved a happily ever after, especially his beautiful wife.